LAST SEEN
IN THE VALLEY

ELLE GRAY

PROLOGUE

THERE WAS A CAR ACROSS THE STREET. IT HAD BEEN THERE for over an hour, just sitting opposite the house. A dark blue Toyota Yaris. Silent. Still. Watching him.

He shifted in his seat, blinking rapidly. Had it been there the day before, or was his mind playing tricks on him?

His thumb was throbbing from where he had picked at it, the skin hanging off, dry and pointed beneath the nail. Glancing down, he noticed a bead of blood blooming over the skin.

The clock behind him ticked loudly as his gaze moved back to the car.

He couldn't see inside it. The windows were at the wrong angle, reflecting the sun and making them look tinted. They weren't tinted, he had checked.

Did I check?

Licking his lips, he repositioned himself for the fourth time, the creak of the chair as familiar as his heartbeat. Every muscle in his body ached, eyes itching, skin crawling as if tiny creatures were scuttling all over it, burrowing into his bloodstream.

It was almost five. She would be back soon. *Thank God.* It was easier when she was home; things started to make sense again.

The blood from his thumb had smeared over his forefinger, the brightness of it contrasting with the pale expanse of his skin.

He looked back out of the window, and a chill ran through him at the sight of a man standing opposite the front door of the house. Staring.

Was he there before?

After ninety-seven seconds, the man moved off, his stride lopsided and uneven on the baking sidewalk. His denim jacket was out of place—unnecessary. It was too hot to wear a jacket; perhaps he was using it to conceal what was underneath.

Two minutes past five.

She still wasn't home.

He watched Denim Man until he was out of sight, the car across the street still unmoving. His toes curled inside his shoes, teeth scraping over his lower lip as he fought back the urge to open the front door, go outside, and smash his fist through the windshield.

There was only so long someone could watch the house before they needed to piss. He had been able to hold off going to the bathroom for eighteen hours himself. *How much longer could they wait?*

An engine rumbled closer, like the thunder from a distant storm. Stretching out his neck, his heartbeat picked up at the sight of the familiar white Honda Civic that came into view. She must have left work right on time; that was good. Hopefully, she had checked her rearview mirror, as he had taught her, to make sure that no one was following.

Always change up your routine, never give them an excuse to get to you.

The car pulled up, the front end of the hood obstructing his view of the Yaris across the street. But Sheila was back now, so perhaps he didn't have to sit at the window all evening.

2

There was a line of ants marching along the cracked windowpane, the paint dry and puckering at the edges, tiny cracks skittering across the surface like little pathways they had built themselves. All a flurry of legs. Head, thorax, abdomen, head, thorax, abdomen.

So uniform, so similar. *How easy it must be to be an ant.*

Sheila was out of the car now, elegant and stunning in the hot sunshine. She was wearing a loose tank top, her blonde, shoulder-length hair stirred by the wind as she pulled out her bag. Standing by the car door, she became very still, the bag hanging by her knee.

Her back was turned to him, head bent forward, chest expanding and contracting on a long breath. He watched, uncertain. She looked overwhelmed. Maybe she had had a difficult day. There had been a lot of those lately.

Eventually, she turned, sharp red heels clicking up the path, tiny gravel stones skipping away from her as she fumbled with her bag, grabbing her keys.

I probably should have told her about the—

There was a violent crunch as the key was inserted in the door, and Sheila tried to enter the house and couldn't. All he heard was a quiet "Damn it," from the other side of the door and then, finally, he rose to his feet.

It was the first time he had been upright in over twelve hours, and he could feel the ache spreading through his spine, blood rushing to his head as he began unbolting the door.

Sheila didn't make a sound as he pulled back the locks. There were five in total, shiny and new, every screw he had embedded in the wood of the door feeling as if it secured his sanity as much as their safety.

The last lock released, and he pulled the door open, attempting a smile.

Sheila stared at him, unmoving, frozen in place for a long time.

"Have you slept?"

"A little," he said, nodding, and gesturing for her to come in. Her eyes ran over him, the brilliant blue of them that he loved so much, seemed starker and brighter in the dimness of the house.

"Why are all the lights out?"

"It's easier," he muttered, going back to his chair.

"And what the hell have you done to the door?"

"It's just an extra precaution."

"From what?" Her voice was sharp.

Slowly, his spine returned to its hunched position at the window, eyes level with the line of ants as they stomped past. He settled himself, resuming his vigil of the dark blue car.

"They're still out there, honey."

He felt, rather than saw, her shoulders slump, then jolted back in surprise as there was a loud thud as she dropped her bag on the ground. Before he could stop her, she jerked open the door and marched across the street.

A lance of fear sliced through him at the sight of her approaching the car. Sheila reached it and rapped on the window, one side then the other. As he watched, she flailed her arms wide, her brow furrowed, mouth set in a hard line.

Storming back into the house and slamming the door, she rounded on him, eyes sparking with fury.

Maybe I went too far this time. I should have told her about the bolts.

"I can't keep this up," she said, tears forming. "I can't do this. Not anymore. You need *help*, babe. Real, professional help. This isn't normal. You're in the same clothes as yesterday. You haven't shaved. Have you eaten?"

"Was there no one in the car?" he asked in confusion.

He must have missed them getting out—distracted by the ants. Maybe they'd moved when Sheila pulled up, knowing he'd be watching her.

"Of *course*, there's no one in there," she whispered, voice cracking. "No one is after you, sweetheart. Please. You have to stop this."

He shook his head. "You don't understand, Sheila. This is for our protection. I know you don't believe me, but—"

"What are you going to do? Sit at that window until you die? Because you haven't slept in thirty-six hours. This isn't natural. You look like *death*. Please. I just want you to sleep. Please."

Why are my hands shaking?

"They must have gotten out of the car when I wasn't watching," he said quietly, squinting through the murky glass.

Cool hands encircled his neck as he turned toward her, the beautiful face he knew so well, almost as well as his own, staring at him as if he were the most precious thing she had ever seen.

"You need rest."

Her hands ran over his shoulders. Tears were streaming down her face now. Why was she crying? She hadn't been home long enough to be crying.

Gently, the cool hands tugged him to his feet and led him through the archway into the next room. He found himself lowered onto a soft couch.

"Lean back," she said. "That's it."

The cushions enveloped him. They were so warm, so inviting. But he needed to return to his post. The denim jacket might return, or someone else could get into that car, and he wouldn't be at his lookout post. They might get in—they might hurt Sheila.

The shape of his wife disappeared, returning with a glass of water. She had her phone in her hand, her hands shaking just as much as his—she must be frightened. He should reassure her.

I can keep us safe.

Slowly, the darkness at the edge of his vision began to take over, the shape of Sheila fading into the shadows like a snowflake landing on black water.

Her eyes met his for just a moment, her lip trembling as she watched sleep drag him down into oblivion.

I can keep us safe.

When he woke up, he was alone. The house was dark and painfully quiet. Sitting up, he threw off the blanket that was over him, noting in a panic that it was almost 11 p.m. *I've been absent for hours—anything could have happened.*

He walked quickly through the house, searching every room, but something about the stillness around him suggested he was alone. Where had Sheila gone?

There was a note stuck to the refrigerator. A scrawled hand. She had gone to her sister's; she was sorry.

Frowning, he plucked the note from the magnet, scrunching it into his fingers as his teeth ground tightly together, the sound like a drill in his head.

"I can't keep you safe at your sister's, Sheila, what if they find you there?" he whispered as his eyes darted around.

Someone knocked at the door.

He spun round, stock still, muscles taut and ready to spring.

"Pizza delivery!"

He checked the time again. Could Sheila have ordered it? Possibly. But it was late, very late. Maybe she was coming back?

He shivered. Despite the heat of the day, the house felt cool. Sweat was dripping from his forehead, his whole body felt cold.

The knock sounded again, rat-tat-tat.

Shuffling to the door, his chest tightened at the sight of all the locks drawn back. He had forgotten to bolt them again after she came home. Foolish. Careless.

"Just leave it!" he shouted through the door.

"I got instructions here to make sure I hand it to you personally."

He swore.

The handle of the door was cold as he opened it a crack, peering outside at the young man on his doorstep, a black beard and wide smile on his face.

"Evening. Order for Sheila?"

"Just leave it."

"Like I said, man, she asked us to make sure we gave it to you by hand. Pretty nice tip. I don't wanna let her down."

Nails digging into his palm, he opened the door as wide as he could, just enough space for the box to move through the gap. The man didn't move, so he reached out and grabbed it. The edge of the cardboard slid beneath his nail, slicing through the skin as he yanked the box toward him.

"There you go then," the pizza guy said, chuckling. "You okay, man?"

"Just leave."

The man didn't move. The porch light above him was out, even though the bulb had been changed the week before. The man's eyes looked pitch black in the gloom.

"I'm fine."

"You don't look fine." The delivery man placed his hands in his pockets, his stance casual—wrong. "Maybe if you took better care of yourself, she wouldn't have left you." His voice was cold, the warm, friendly manner gone.

His fingers clenched around the box. "Who are you?" he whispered, suppressing the raging panic threatening to consume him.

"You should take better care of yourself. You don't look well. Sitting by that window all day and all night. It ain't gonna do any good, is it? You enjoy that pizza, though. It ain't like you'll have to share it with anyone now, is it? All alone." The dark eyes glinted. "We'll be seein' you very soon."

The pizza guy turned, the shiny black leather shoes on his feet entirely out of place with the red bomber jacket he wore. Gripping the handle of the door, he threw the pizza box after him, slices spiraling out at odd angles, skittering over the grass, staining the porch and the steps. Sheila wouldn't like it.

But Sheila was gone.

He slammed the door as all the bolts shot home one by one, the key turning, an array of security finally in place, but he knew that it would do him no good.

He sat back down in his chair, the shivering beginning to build inside him, his entire body trembling as he stared out at the empty street. The Yaris was gone, but it hardly mattered. They were watching him, just as he had always known they were, and he was running out of time.

And all the while, the ants kept marching.

CHAPTER ONE

S OMETHING WET AND SOFT PRESSED AGAINST ZOE'S cheek, and she jerked backward at the strange sensation, rolling over in bed with a low groan.

"Morning, buddy," she mumbled as Max jumped on her stomach, sharp claws scratching at her skin. She squinted at the clock. "Oh my God, it's 6 a.m. How'd you get in here?"

Max's only reply was to pant noisily in her ear, and then lie across her body, pinning her to the bed.

Zoe glanced at her bedroom door, which she had closed the night before and was now wide open.

"Have you figured out how to open doors, buddy? Because that's really worrying," she grumbled, yawning and scratching between his ears as he licked her chin.

Max, her German Shepherd puppy, was now almost seventeen weeks old. He was long, lean, and beginning to look like the adult he would one day become. His ears no longer had the adorable floppy quality that had captured her heart, always sticking up on alert, and she missed how endearing he had once looked.

Leo had told her that Max's coat would change as he grew, but she hadn't been prepared for how different his fur was becoming. He had once been pure black on his back, but now there was a collar of gold forming around his neck and little pale spots above his eyes that almost made him look like he had eyebrows.

She grinned as he huffed loudly, shimmying forward, and snapping playfully in the air with his jaws.

"You hungry, boy?" His ears pricked up. "You want some breakfast?"

He barked right in her ear and leaped off the bed in one fluid motion, skidding over the floor toward the kitchen. Zoe chuckled, pushing the covers off, but just as she swung her legs over the side of the bed, her phone lit up with a message.

She picked it up, a warm, fuzzy feeling fluttering through her body as she read Leo's text with a smile.

"We've been invited for breakfast, buddy! You don't have to deal with my cooking this morning," she shouted, and Max ran back in, his metal food bowl hanging from his mouth, cocking his head at her in excitement as if he understood every word.

She rose to her feet as he scrambled away again. Stretching, she listened to the quiet of the morning, the twitter of birds outside the only signs of the awakening morning.

Zoe had been in her new apartment for just over a month, and it was slowly beginning to feel like home. It was still strange to live somewhere that had so much space and her own bathroom.

In D.C., she had shared a bathroom at the end of the hall with three other women. It had only been workable because she was away so much. But in Sapphire she'd found her own little slice of luxury, and she couldn't imagine going back to that. Not only did she now have sunlight streaming in through the windows every morning, but also a beautiful view of the Blue Ridge Mountains right outside her front door.

She staggered through the tiny hallway from her bedroom and into the living room, grimacing at the mess she'd left the night before. Boxes and files were scattered everywhere in one corner, where she was attempting to organize her research into coherent stacks.

Zoe took pride in how thorough she was with any story, and up until recently, she had considered herself meticulously organized. But she had discovered, going back through her own work months later, that she had been mistaken about her efficiency. Everything was haphazardly shoved into folders, if it was filed at all. Some paperwork related to three different time periods, and there were things in the boxes—all of which should have related to her research on The Linman Group—that weren't even relevant to the story.

Her eyes moved over the mess on the floor, and she groaned unhappily when she saw a little puddle of yellow liquid on top of some of the papers she had laid out. Max trotted over to sit on her foot, and Zoe frowned down at him wearily.

"Sorry, buddy, did you need to go out?" she scratched under his chin. "That's my fault. I gotta start remembering to check on you before we go to bed."

She went to the kitchen, pulled out the rubber gloves from under the cabinet, and got to work clearing away the pool of urine. It had seeped in a wide arc across the floor, and Zoe was thankful, yet again, for the hardwood. It wasn't Max's first accident, but she hoped he would grow out of that phase soon.

She picked up the papers, laying them out in the sun beside the window to dry and pouring a little water on the Monstera plant Leo had given her on the way past.

Look at me being a grown-up and keeping a plant alive for over four weeks.

It was a glorious day outside, and the large glass windows gave her a perfect view of Sapphire Valley below her. After she'd given Max his breakfast, she stood for a moment looking down at the town.

It was June, and everything looked particularly pretty in the valley this time of year. There were red, blue, and white buntings hanging between the lights on Jefferson Street ahead of the 4th of

July, and bright red flowers spilling over the sides of the baskets on every lamppost.

The Panway River could be seen at intervals, winding its way around the town, sparkling in the morning sunshine.

Inhaling the faint scent of the mountain air, Zoe turned, checking the clock on the microwave, only to let out some choice words when she realized the time.

Walking past Max, who was enthusiastically eating a few pieces of kibble she had given him, she went to get changed, feeling a familiar buzz of excitement at the prospect of seeing Leo again.

Everything about their relationship was still brand new; she wasn't even sure if *relationship* was the right word, but they'd certainly been spending a lot of time together lately.

Zoe pulled on her jeans, her irritation spiking as she mulled over what to wear. There was a time she would throw on any old thing, not paying much attention to how she looked. With Leo, that had all changed.

Logically, she knew Leo couldn't care less what she was wearing. He lived on a ranch and only wore practical, hardy clothes when working. But Zoe always felt on display around him. He was so good-looking, she often wondered why he was interested in her at all.

Glancing in the mirror, she pulled at her hair—the soft, light-brown curls sitting at odd angles since she had gotten out of bed—and wondered if she should take a shower. Another text on her phone put that idea to rest when Leo asked if she'd set off yet. She grabbed a royal blue shirt, buttoning it as she pulled her bag from the chair at the end of the bed and went to get Max's leash.

Ten minutes later, she was in the car, heading to Leo's ranch. Although the sun was already warm, the humidity in the valley had risen considerably over the past week, and she had the AC on full as she stopped at a red light in town.

Sapphire was a lazy place first thing in the morning on a Saturday. Her eyes ran down the white spire of the church ahead of her as she watched Kyle, the pastor, scrubbing at some graffiti on the outer wall.

Several store owners were getting set up for the day, and there was a flurry of movement in her periphery as a delivery truck arrived at The Sapphire Café. As she idled at the lights, she saw Seth Bowen, the owner, step outside, nodding as he signed the form for the driver. Zoe swallowed guiltily as she pulled away before he could spot her.

Since breaking up with Seth a few weeks earlier after a couple of disaster dates, Zoe had been avoiding him. She'd been getting her lattes from Sam's Coffee House at the other end of town. She knew she'd eventually need to face Seth again, but that was going to be painfully awkward, and it felt easier to put it off for another day.

Driving around the far corner of the town square, she noticed Tony Waldron sitting in a lounge chair outside his hunting store, smoking a pipe. He looked like someone out of the history books. She waved as she passed him, and he raised one hand in greeting with a lopsided grin.

Max was already standing on his hind legs in the back seat as they neared their destination, slobbering against the window in anticipation. The ranch was one of his favorite places, and Leo had definitely become one of his favorite people—Zoe was fairly certain that Max preferred him to her.

As she drove up the drive, she noticed the silhouette of Gus Gonzalez in one of the fields behind the fence. Leo had met Gus as part of his volunteer work with the homeless community in Sapphire and was trying to give him a semblance of stability by bringing him to the ranch twice a week. Gus had been in trouble with the cops, and Leo was determined to make sure he didn't get mixed up with the wrong crowd again.

Gus was much smaller in stature than Leo, and was bent over, connecting some thick planks of wood to the base of a trough. The tank top he wore was dirty and littered with holes, and his hair was overly long and obscured his face from view. He glanced up at the sound of the car, watching her as she pulled up.

Leo emerged a few minutes later, his black T-shirt tightly wrapped to his taut frame, his jeans even tighter. Zoe ran her eyes over his long legs appreciatively as Max panted at the window, desperate to be let out.

"Maybe I should leave you in the car, buddy?" she said teasingly. "Remember how you used to be scared of Leo and wouldn't let him touch you at all?"

Max whined pitifully at her, and she laughed, getting out of the car as Leo approached her, grinning as he wiped his hands on the towel perpetually shoved in his back pocket.

"Don't often see you in t-shirts," she said.

Leo smirked at her. "Well, I *was* topless. I put it on special for you."

Zoe snorted. "I mean, don't feel forced on my account. Want me to let the tornado out of my car?"

Leo rubbed his hands together and crouched down in position. "Let me have it."

Zoe opened the rear door of her rental, and Max hurtled out at top speed into Leo's arms. Gone were the days when he was shy or scared of Leo; they were two peas in a pod now, and Max adored him.

Leo was soon lying in the dirt with the puppy jumping all over him as he laughed, trying to stop Max's teeth from scraping his face.

Zoe leaned against her car, watching them fondly, as Gus appeared at the end of the path and came through a gate behind Leo. He looked just as miserable and closed off as ever.

The tank top he wore looked like it was on its last legs, and Zoe wondered what he would say if she offered to buy him a new one—probably nothing. In the weeks she'd gotten to know him, Gus had said fewer than a dozen words in her presence.

"Hey, Gus," she said cheerfully, and Leo looked over at him from the ground, sitting up hurriedly and stopping the roughhousing as he rose to his feet.

Gus nodded to Zoe, his hair flopping over his eyes again as he fidgeted, staring at the ground.

"How was it?" Leo asked as Gus handed him the hammer he was holding.

"Nails broke."

Leo nodded. "That's alright, I'll come and give you a hand and bring some fresh timber from the barn."

Max trotted over to Gus and sniffed at him from a few feet away. He was still nervous around men, and Gus seemed unsure of the puppy, too. Slowly, Gus crouched down, and Max lowered himself onto his front legs and crawled toward him warily.

Leo and Zoe remained still as Gus extended a hand, and Max sniffed at it before huffing loudly and leaping away to chase a chicken pecking along the path.

"You wanna come in for some breakfast?" Leo asked Gus.

The kid rose to his feet, wiping his hands over his threadbare jeans, and shrugged.

"It's bacon rolls," Leo added. "Zoe's gonna sit on my knee and I'm gonna feed her."

Gus's face didn't change, but Zoe could now see a hint of amusement in his eyes. "Gross," he said with feeling. "I'll get somethin' later."

Leo waved him off. "I'll bring one out to you. You okay to feed the geese?"

Gus scowled. "Atsila hates me."

"Don't take it personal. She hates everybody."

Gus wandered away, kicking at a stone as he walked around the side of the house. Leo gave Zoe a tired look and nodded to the door as she followed him inside.

"He could have joined us," she said halfheartedly, secretly thrilled to have some alone time with Leo.

"I know, but he's been with us on so many mornin's already. I just wanted to talk to *you* today. Besides, I got a lot of work for him that's already taken twice as long as it should."

As they entered the house, Max bounded across the living room and catapulted into his bed with a happy growl, grabbing his toy and worrying it with his teeth. Max spent so much time at the ranch, it was like a second home.

"Is Gus still struggling?" she asked.

Leo sighed. "Yeah, he definitely doesn't have a head for ranch work. It's obvious he doesn't wanna be here."

"I'm not sure that's true," Zoe said softly. "I don't think he *likes* the jobs around this place, but I can tell he's grateful for all the time you're giving him. He doesn't get that anywhere else."

"Maybe. I don't know. He doesn't open up at all. Can't get a word out of him, and most days the only thing he gets excited about is my coffee."

"And your cooking, I bet. Speaking of which, I'm starving," she said as Leo turned to face her, his hands on his hips, dark skin glowing from the morning sunshine, and Zoe felt her breath hitch as the sight.

"Is that right?" he asked pointedly. "You orderin' me around now, Miss Fontaine?"

She chuckled as he leaned forward, gripping her wrist and pulling her to him, lining their bodies up as she felt heat rise to her cheeks.

"Um… yes?" she said with a grin.

"Uh-uh. I think I need some payment first," he said, leaning forward and capturing her lips in a long kiss that made Zoe's toes curl. As he pulled away, he held her suspended in his arms for a few seconds, his eyes assessing, before he turned back to the kitchen.

Zoe gathered herself, smoothing over her shirt before sitting on the bar stool on the other side of the counter.

It was her favorite place on the ranch. She loved watching Leo in the kitchen. He was a fantastic cook and had a back catalog of Cherokee recipes from his mother that included some of the best dishes she'd ever tasted.

He glanced at her with a soft smile as he got a bowl out of the cupboard.

"What?" she asked, frowning at him.

"You get this look about you sometimes," he said affectionately. "Like you're not sure why I'm kissin' you."

Zoe ran a finger over her collar uncomfortably, and he chuckled as he pulled a few eggs from the basket on the surface and cracked them into the bowl.

"I thought we were having bacon rolls?" she said hopefully.

"We are, but you said you were hungry, so I'm fixin' you some eggs. Your mom keeps tellin' me you're too thin anyways. And stop changing the subject."

Zoe fidgeted as he poured her a coffee and placed it in front of her, along with a neat little bowl of sugar cubes. She shrugged, nerves bubbling in her stomach.

"I guess I keep thinking I'm sixteen again."

Leo raised his eyebrows. "What?"

"Well, if I'd told sixteen-year-old Zoe that *Leo Rowden* would be interested in her, she would have died laughing."

Leo shook his head. "Well, that just shows you don't know squat at sixteen. I always noticed you in high school."

"You did not!" she said, laughing and throwing a sugar cube at him.

He dodged it effortlessly. "I did too. You used to wear glasses, and you looked all studious followin' Rick around, asking everybody on the football team for an interview."

"Yeah, and you were the only one who ever agreed."

"Hm, wonder why," he said pointedly, and Zoe shook her head.

"You don't have to pretend, Leo, it's okay." She had meant it to be a lighthearted joke, but it came out uncertain. "I was a geek back then, and you—"

"Hey," he said, pointing a spoon at her. "You don't know what I used to think, so stop puttin' words in my mouth. Besides, you're not sixteen anymore, and I'm *definitely* interested now. So you can pipe down."

She laughed as a piece of egg flicked off the spoon and onto the floor, followed by a clatter of claws as Max ran over to lap it up.

Zoe sighed, putting up her hands in defeat under Leo's steely gaze, and he nodded with satisfaction before turning back to the pan.

She watched him, sipping her coffee, but the doubt still lingered. Zoe Fontaine was unremarkable, messed up, and chaotic. Leo was clean lines, order, and good sense. Nothing about them seemed to fit, and it made her nervous.

She took the opportunity to take him in as he stirred the pan at the stove facing away from her, running her eyes down the line of his strong back and tight butt, still unable to fathom why he would look at her twice.

But maybe it didn't matter. He *had* looked at her, and that was what counted. Still, even through breakfast and their quiet day together on the ranch, Zoe never managed to dispel the feeling of unease inside her. It felt like all this was temporary, and it was only a matter of time before it came crashing down around her.

CHAPTER TWO

MONDAY MORNING HERALDED ANOTHER EARLY WAKEUP call, with Max licking her ear unhelpfully at 5 a.m. After a few attempts to get back to sleep, Zoe decided to go for a hike to clear her head.

The clean air of the Blue Ridge Mountains always made her feel better, and Max loved walking the trails. Each time Zoe began to get tired, his happy, scampering form kept her going.

The hazy sun trickled through the canopy as she reached the first peak, looking down on the valley below. The town of Whistle Falls was a familiar sight, the little uniform houses laid out like a Monopoly board nestled next door to Sapphire. Her eyes moved up the slope of the hill, to the pale shape of Linman Pharmaceuticals glinting in the sunlight.

She stared at the smooth, white building, the hair on her arms rising as her heart picked up speed. The grounds outside the laboratory appeared completely deserted—as usual. A small pipe on one wall let out soft plumes of white smoke, and the wispy clouds were the only discernible movement.

Max ambled over, flopping down on her feet as Zoe stood motionless, the wind ruffling through her hair, a feeling of anticipation and fear growing within her.

Linmans.

The name had brought her nothing but pain and trauma, and yet the tenacious part of her mind couldn't let it go. The files in her apartment, long left to gather dust, had become impossible to ignore.

Years of research and intensive investigation had sat in the dark for too long, and it was her job to bring them out into the light again.

I just never imagined it would be this hard, or that I could be so easily intimidated.

Zoe's jaw tightened, her teeth grinding together as she pushed her nails into the palm of her hand. She *knew* there was a story here. The question was whether she was brave enough to chase it.

And therein lay another problem. Rick Fisher.

Zoe suspected the editor of the paper where she worked was hiding something. A few weeks before, she'd been tipped off that Rick knew more than he was letting on about an organization called *The Sapphire Foundation*... linked to Linmans.

She was determined to talk to him about it and find out what he knew, but his recent erratic behavior had made it impossible to pin him down.

Rick was rarely in the office lately, had stopped replying to emails, and never answered his phone. He flitted in and out for minutes at a time, waving anybody off who wanted to speak with him. As a result, Zoe had been forced to take on more and more of his duties as editor.

When she asked what he was doing, he told her he was 'chasing a lead' and not to worry about him.

But I am worried. I can't afford for him to go off the rails.

Pulling out her phone, she checked the time. It was still too early to go into the office, but she had been so busy fighting everyone else's fires lately that a few extra hours wouldn't hurt. Tugging on Max's leash, they headed back down the valley to her car.

After a quick shower at her apartment and a protein bar, she stopped in at Sam's to grab a coffee and made her way to the office, two hours ahead of when she would normally arrive.

Unsurprisingly, it was deserted when she got in. Even the skinny IT guy, Bean, wasn't around, and he worked harder than everyone else put together.

She got Max settled in his bed beneath her desk and powered on her computer with a sigh.

Her inbox was already heaving with new emails, and she scanned through those she had yet to read, hoping that Rick might have gotten in touch. But there was nothing.

There were emails from three of the team, one with minutes from a town meeting they had covered. Another was a short article on market fluctuations over the weekend, with a few puff pieces for the local businesses. She smiled when she opened an attachment to find some beautiful photos from their local freelancer, Tom. He was regularly saving Zoe's bacon with the stunning images he produced.

She clicked through, noting a couple of obituaries for elderly residents and she smiled wryly.

That reminds me, I really should check on Gamma and see how she's getting on.

"You doin' my job, Fontaine?"

Zoe jerked violently back in her seat as she spun around to find Rick standing behind her desk. He looked pissed, his brow furrowed and dark circles beneath his eyes. His shirt was crooked, the buttons fastened incorrectly, and an empty coffee cup dangled from his fingers.

"Morning, boss," Zoe said. "Didn't know if you were in today."

"Well, I am. Why exactly are you approving layouts for the headlines?"

"Oh, I don't know," Zoe replied sarcastically. "Maybe they should send it to you for the fifth time so you can continue to ignore it. It's a *bi-weekly* paper, Rick, and you've been gone since last Monday. I've had to do everything."

Rick was already walking toward his desk, and her anger increased.

"Where have you been?" she asked, rising from her chair and following him.

"None of your damned business," he said.

"It *is* my business if you start blaming me for doing your job when you don't bother to try," she hissed.

"I had some things to take care of."

"Past tense?" she shot back. "So you're back now? Because I can't keep doing both of our jobs. I've got to get the library article written by Thursday, and I haven't had a chance to get down there because of all the balls you've dropped."

Rick rounded on her, his eyes flashing fire. "You want my job, is that it?"

Zoe threw up her hands. "Yeah, Rick, I secretly planned to make *you* go AWOL so I could become editor. Would you grow up?"

Rick opened his mouth and closed it again, sighed, and collapsed into his chair, looking exhausted. He pulled open the top drawer of his desk and drew out a packet of Skittles, ripping it open and shoving half of them into his mouth.

"Do you ever go to the dentist?" Zoe asked. "Because you must have a thousand cavities with the amount of sugar you eat."

Rick glowered at her, pouring the rest into his mouth, scrunching up the packet, and throwing it into the bin without looking. He leaned over his keyboard, eyes narrowing as he scrolled through his inbox without much interest.

"Did you copy me in on everything?" he asked.

"Of course I did, you moron. I'm not gunning for your job, I'm just trying to keep this paper running, such as it is."

Zoe pulled up a chair, watching him click through a couple of emails and giving them a cursory glance. She waited for a few more seconds but couldn't hold back her questions any longer.

"Are you going to tell me what's going on with you? You can't keep disappearing for days at a time," she hissed. "This paper is on its last legs as it is."

"Would you keep your voice down?"

"There's no one here!" She stomped her foot in frustration. To avoid throwing a fist.

"I told you I was following a lead," he snapped.

"Yeah. Nice and vague. So, are you going to tell me *what* this mysterious lead is that had you away from your desk for a week and a half?" she asked, beyond exasperated.

"It's private."

Zoe snorted. "Fine, if you won't talk to me about where you've been, can we at least discuss the Sapphire Foundation? I told you weeks ago that we needed to talk about it, and you've been putting it off ever since."

Rick's lips thinned. "And *I* told *you* that you needed to drop it, and you keep ignoring me. Read the room. I'm not interested in fueling your vendetta against Linmans."

Zoe stood up, slamming the chair back in place and making him jump.

"Look, either you want me on your side, or you don't, but stop playing stupid little games of cloak and dagger. Turn up when you're supposed to and answer your damn emails, or maybe I *will* take your job."

She turned, ready to storm back to her desk, when a cold, clammy hand gripped her wrist. Zoe spun around, startled, as Rick stood up, his eyes urgent and dark as he met her gaze.

"What are you doing?" she breathed.

"Christ, would you stop being so dramatic? Come with me," he whispered.

"What?"

"Zoe, for once in your life, will you stop asking questions and do as I say?"

With that, Rick turned away from his desk, walking to the door at the rear of the room that led to the archive storage. Zoe glanced behind her, but the office was still completely empty.

She felt profoundly alone as she watched Rick reach the door, one hand on the glass, the skin of his fingers leaving a pale handprint against it as he waited, nodding for her to follow him.

Alarm bells were ringing in the back of her skull, and she hesitated.

Don't be ridiculous, Zoe. This is Rick, not some madman. What could he possibly do to me here?

She shook away her absurd fears and glanced behind her one final time before slowly following him.

The archive room was large but cramped, tall shelves dominating the space, each one filled with hundreds of identical boxes stretching back into every corner of the room.

Zoe pushed through the door and stopped, frowning at the space before her. Rick was nowhere to be seen.

"Rick?" she said, her voice deadened and flat in the crowded room. "If this is a joke, it isn't funny."

A clicking sound from in between one of the shelves to her left made her turn, and she saw Rick gesturing to her from behind the stack.

Rolling her eyes, she walked over and put her hands in her jacket pockets, raising an eyebrow at him, deeply unimpressed.

"Now who's being dramatic? This is a little ridic—"

"Have you noticed anything strange lately?" Rick murmured, interrupting her, the same urgency in his gaze that set her teeth on edge.

"Strange how?" she asked.

"I don't know. People hanging around the building, coming to ask questions, that type of thing."

There was sweat on his brow and a greasy quality to his skin. Zoe felt a chill run over her skin.

"No. What are you talking about? It's just been me, Bean, and Angela for days. What's happened?"

Rick shook his head, making a scornful sound. "Nothing, I'm just…" He pushed his thumbs into his eyes so hard that it made Zoe wince. "Listen, I know things have been difficult the last few weeks. I'm gonna fix it. I have one last thing I need to do, and then I'll explain everything."

"Rick, you're freaking me out. Why couldn't you just tell me this in the off—?"

"While I'm gone, if anyone asks for me, tell them I'm out of town," he said gazing into the middle distance and chewing his lip.

Zoe shook her head. "Why? Where are you going?"

He nodded, the movement jerky, almost manic. "I can't say. But it'll all be explained, I promise. I'll call you tonight, and then I'll be back tomorrow."

"Tomorrow?"

"Mmm," he said, picking at his lip distractedly. She watched his nail slide under a chapped piece of skin, tearing it away until a tiny line of blood formed.

Zoe gripped his elbow. He pulled back, staring at her as if he had forgotten she was there.

"Rick, you're scaring me. Please tell me what's going on."

"Don't let anyone know I was here, alright? Just to be safe. I'll deal with everything else in the morning."

"At least tell me where you're going."

He made the same furtive movement. "It's best you don't know. It sounds bigger than it is, I promise. I think I'm just losing my marbles." He laughed nervously. "I always said paranoia was catching. I'm fine. Don't worry about me. I'll call you tonight, it'll be late."

"Call anytime. Text me if you need to. Are you sure I can't help?"

"No. No. You should go do your story about the library closure. We don't have long to get it drafted, and then I can review it in the morning."

Zoe had never believed anyone less in her life.

She stepped back hurriedly as Rick shook himself, the pallor of his skin even starker under the fluorescent bulbs above their heads. He gave her a slightly unhinged smile.

"I just need a few hours to confirm something, then I'll be back." He paused, giving her a long stare. "Listen, if you get a call from..." he stopped, frowning. "Never mind. Thanks, Zo."

He patted her awkwardly on the shoulder before leaving the room. She tracked him to the door, dread spreading beneath her skin as he walked out.

It wasn't the first time Zoe had witnessed that type of behavior. She had been very familiar with it when she'd been caring for her sister, Judy, during the black, endless despair of drug withdrawal.

CHAPTER THREE

W HEN ZOE WALKED BACK INTO THE BULLPEN, RICK was already gone. She stared at his empty desk, unsure how to process what she had just witnessed.

Rick wasn't well—that was obvious, and she didn't know whether she could take anything he said seriously. His behavior was completely unlike the man she knew. She felt helpless.

Returning to her desk, she stroked Max absently, listening to the silence of the building and trying to make sense of her spiraling thoughts.

The back door opened, and she spun around, hoping Rick had come back, but it was just Bean arriving for the day.

She nodded at him as he slunk inside, beanie pulled low over his eyes, reminding her of Gus.

Staring at her computer, she considered whether it would be wise to tell Bean, or any other staff, that Rick had been in the building. But he had specifically told her not to, and against her better judgment, she decided to give him the benefit of the doubt.

Maybe this will all blow over, and things will go back to normal. In a week, we might be laughing about all this…

She had to hope that could be the case—and in the meantime, Zoe had a job to do.

Flexing her fingers, she logged in and got to work, determined to make the most of the few hours she had before heading to the library.

It was good to be getting out into the field. For the last few weeks, it felt like she'd been stuck at a desk, reading endless complaints, urgent requests, and emails, and it would be nice to do some real reporting again.

Later that morning, Zoe finally headed to the Sapphire Valley Library. It was situated on the south side of town just after the bridge that crossed the Panway River.

The land where the library had been built was originally wide and barren, and the broken concrete underfoot had split, cracking in the heat of many summers.

Over the years, very little had been added to the area due to the woods surrounding it, and the plot of land stretched back for nearly half a mile, much of it overtaken by nature.

The two buildings that made up the library were in severe need of repair. The white slats on the front were crooked, with peeling paint running along the surface, and the shingles had a habit of dropping off the roof every time it rained.

But despite all of that, it was a respected institution and had been in the town for over seventy years.

Unfortunately, Dunridge Developments, an enormous real estate firm, had quickly seen the site's potential. With the increased population in the area and the need for more homes in the town, the piece of land where the library was situated was ripe for redevelopment.

Not only was it just off the main highway, but it had beautiful views of the Panway on almost every side as the river curved around and headed away toward Whistle Falls.

Zoe pulled up and headed toward the entrance. The sun glinted off a sign placed out front, stating proudly that the library was "FOUNDED IN 1950 AND STILL GOING STRONG".

Even to Zoe's eyes, it looked like a hollow statement. The building was listing to one side, the small metal steps leading up to the entrance were crooked and broken. Even the disabled access ramp was splitting along its length and had a large bulge in the middle from the relentless heat.

Two flower baskets hung from either side of the door, the red, white, and blue flowers brightening the general façade, but the whole thing smacked of a last-ditch attempt to prevent the inevitable.

She ascended the steps, looking at the bright, hand-lettered posters in the windows that read "WE STAND FIRM" and "SAVE THE LIBRARY". Zoe just hoped her article could make a difference. She couldn't imagine the daily visitors to the library were high—it was no longer in the best area for foot traffic, and the passing cars heading into town from the highway didn't stop… or even slow down.

As she walked inside, the picture didn't improve much.

Whereas most libraries would have a bank of computers front and center, the Sapphire Library just sported bare tables with flickering lamps at intervals along the center.

The carpet was a confusing mess of herringbone patterns, making Zoe dizzy. Even the ceiling lights were dim, casting a gray haze over the shelves. The walls were a lifeless shade of beige, sparse and dull. There was no color or *life* anywhere.

The door swung shut behind her, and a hawk-like face appeared behind the counter to her right, as the director, Evelyn Cooper, gave a cry of surprise as she came out to greet her.

"Hi Zoe, I wondered when you'd be stopping by!" she said happily, striding over, her long legs eating up the distance in seconds.

Evelyn Cooper was a tall woman with sharp, pointed features and skin that had a taut quality across her cheekbones making her look stern and unapproachable. However, Zoe soon learned that looks could be deceiving. Evelyn was effervescent, enthusiastic, and fiercely passionate.

Zoe was surprised when she discovered Evelyn was only forty-eight. She dressed in cardigans and long, unflattering dresses that flapped around her ankles at just the wrong height. The horn-rimmed glasses on a chain around her neck made her seem much older than she was. It was almost as if she was trying to look like a caricature of a librarian.

"Hi, Evelyn," she said, shaking her hand. "Is the meeting still happening today? I meant to call in advance."

"Yes, yes! And I see your interest has brought in other members of the Fontaine clan! I can't thank you enough for your dedication to our cause."

Zoe frowned as she followed her into the tight aisles between the shelves.

"Other members?" she asked, already knowing who would be waiting to greet her before she entered the space.

"Oh, look what the cat dragged in," came a familiar voice from her right as Zoe emerged at the other end.

"Hey Gamma," she said with a smile. Her grandmother, Lyla Reed, was seated beside a huge rack of DVDs at a beige plastic table. It was littered with papers and flyers, and as Zoe approached, Lyla spread her arms wide with a proud grin, showcasing it all with obvious delight.

"Hello Zoe," she said firmly, "we are staging a protest."

"I can see that," Zoe replied as she moved around to her grandmother's seat, and they exchanged a brief but fierce hug.

Lyla was looking better each time Zoe saw her. When she had arrived in Sapphire several weeks earlier, she'd been a shadow of her former self, but now there was 'meat on her bones,' as Zoe's mother would say, and her eyes were bright and alive with energy.

"What are you doing here?" Lyla asked. "Are you reporting on the library for the paper?"

"Yes," Zoe said, glancing uncertainly at the other person at the table. He was an elderly man and was giving Zoe a death stare. "I'm going to write the article for this Friday's issue."

"Oh, fantastic, did you hear that, Barry?" Lyla asked, raising her voice as she turned to the man.

Barry had to be in his nineties, small and hunched over, with a sour expression. His eyes were sunken, with one eyelid drooping down on the left, obscuring his vision. Red patches across his cheeks and nose suggested he liked a drink now and then, and he was chewing the inside of his cheek obsessively. His gaze didn't move from Zoe, and she shifted her weight uncomfortably.

"It won't make no difference," he said. "They won't listen. We got as much chance as a June bug in a hen house."

"Well, that just isn't true," Evelyn said, dropping her glasses on her chest and glaring at him. "If we fight we can win, I know it. These big organizations aren't used to grassroots campaigns. They expect us to lie down and let them walk all over us, and I just won't do it. We need this library to be here, educatin' people long after you and I are gone, Barry. Givin' up isn't gonna help, is it?"

Barry let out a chuckle that came out more like a wheeze. "Well, I'm gonna be gone sooner'n anybody else, so you better get crackin', woman!"

"And just what is it you think I'm doing?" Evelyn snapped back, gesturing to the endless sheets of paper in front of him.

Lyla caught Zoe's eye and rolled her eyes dramatically behind their backs. This seemed like an old argument, and Zoe would bet it happened three or four times a day. Barry grimaced, picking at a label on the box in front of him. He reminded Zoe of a child when his mother scolded him. Barry met her gaze, running his teeth over his lower lip.

"So, you're the famous granddaughter Lyla won't stop talkin' about," he said moodily.

"Uh, yeah, I guess that's me, unless she meant my sister," Zoe stated evenly.

"Oh, nonsense," Lyla said, shoving her playfully in the arm. "Zoe's the best reporter in West Virginia," she said proudly, making Zoe smile.

The sound of footsteps made her turn as a small woman bustled out between the shelves, carrying several books under her arms. Mrs. Bornstein. Her wiry brown hair was a chaotic mess, as usual, and Zoe gave her a one-armed hug as she passed, happy to see her old landlady. As Mrs. Bornstein reached the table, she prodded Lyla repeatedly until her grandmother shifted along to the next seat and Mrs. Bornstein sat down beside her.

Lyla and Mrs. Bornstein had only lived together for a short time, but it was a partnership made in heaven. Zoe had never seen Mrs. B smile so much.

"Alright," Evelyn said, clapping her hands together. "I think that's everyone. Barry, this is Zoe Fontaine from The Chronicle. Zoe, this is Barry Finnigan, he's worked at the library since it opened—"

"Not quite," Barry interjected.

"And he's going to be our main speaker at all our planned events."

"Uh..." Zoe said nervously. "How many events is that exactly?"

Her heart sank as all four of them exchanged excited looks. People in Sapphire were loyal to a fault, though they wouldn't want to be bashed around the head with a worthy cause every day of the week. If Evelyn organized too many protests, it would be a disaster.

"We've got posters that we're going to put all over town, and there's a meeting at the community center at the end of this week. I'm not holding it here because with the number of people I'm expecting to attend, we simply won't have the space."

She wasn't wrong. Shelves dominated every square inch of the library. Books bursting from all sides. It was impractically full, poorly organized, and old-fashioned—not a great combination for reminding the modern world they were still relevant.

"What's the status of the campaign so far?" Zoe asked carefully, glancing at Evelyn. "Has the planning commission sent through their recommendation yet?"

Evelyn shook her head. "It's still in review, although Penny, my friend at the city council, told me it should be any day now. The mayor is in our corner, which can only be a good thing. Did you know Dunridge is petitioning to reclassify the zone behind the library? That would mean that no one could park on this plot, even after they begin building!"

Barry growled. "That's how they get you, the little things we all took for granted. If people can't park, they won't come."

"It's even more essential that we get the word out about the meeting, we need as many people as possible to attend to show we mean business. Lyla, have you invited your friends from the home?"

Lyla nodded. "Such as they are. Tate is hoping they'll provide transportation."

"Great. Edith? Any more interest from the church crowd?"

"Oh yes, I've been talkin' to everybody I can about it," Mrs. Bornstein confirmed.

"Well done," Evelyn said happily, rubbing her hands together. Zoe forced a smile, as red flag after red flag rose in her mind. *They're getting the nursing home and the church crowd along? What about people who were born this century?*

"I have something else up my sleeve as well," Evelyn said, giving Barry a side-eye as she handed out flyers for them all to sort, "but I won't say more on that until it's finalized."

Zoe looked at her grandmother anxiously, noting the smug expression on her face, and was certain she was aware of what Evelyn was planning to do. She just hoped it wasn't anything too crazy.

"I'm not sortin' all this paper," Barry said irritably, crossing his arms over his chest. "Can't, what with my arthritis. It's bad enough that you keep leaving the boxes in my way when I'm trying to organize the kids' section for reading hour. Nearly broke my damn neck!"

"I'm not *asking* you to help with this, Barry, you told me twice you aren't going to," Evelyn said haughtily, as Mrs. B and Lyla pulled two stacks toward them and began to sort them into piles, keeping their eyes on the table.

Barry and Evelyn stared at each other, Evelyn's cheeks turning red with anger.

"Barry?" Zoe said quickly, his sharp eyes swiveling toward her. "Would you like me to interview you for the article? You can tell me about all your experiences and fill me in on its history."

Barry gave her a wide grin. "Well, now, that I can do."

CHAPTER FOUR

WHEN ZOE RETURNED TO THE OFFICE IN THE LATE afternoon, there was no sign of Rick. She checked her inbox, hoping he had at least reviewed his emails during his brief time in the office, but he hadn't replied to anything.

Chasers from two of their suppliers urgently requested payment for unpaid invoices, and a knot formed in her shoulders when she realized she had no idea where the digital copies would be stored. She fired off some placeholders, but everything else would have to wait until the next day.

Max was restless, and Zoe knew she would need to take him for a long walk if she didn't want another accident on her apartment floor come morning.

She shut down her computer and checked the time.

Ever since she'd seen Rick that morning, her frustration at his refusal to talk about the Sapphire Foundation had lingered, and slowly an idea had formed in her mind. She had decided that if Rick didn't want to give her the details, she would have to get her answers elsewhere.

It had been a member of the homeless community in Sapphire, a man named Mateo, who had first tipped her off about Rick's connection to The Sapphire Foundation.

Who better to expand on the facts than the source?

She grabbed Max's leash, waved to Angela and Bean, and headed out.

The homeless community usually hung around the Carmichael Bridge on the west side of town, and she decided it would be a good walk for her and Max, killing two birds with one stone. Before she was even out the door, Max was straining at the leash, eager for some exercise.

As she made her way down Jefferson Street, past the long slope up to the sheriff's department, Zoe's shoulders tensed at the sight of The Sapphire Café.

She knew she couldn't avoid Seth forever, and supposed now was as good a time as any.

Might as well get it over with.

Steeling herself, she headed up the hill, and Max's pace increased as he got excited by the possibility of a pup cup.

The café was fairly empty as she pushed through the door, and Seth, who was behind the counter, looked up.

His smile was a little off as he greeted her.

"Hey," she said as he came out from behind the counter to say hello to Max. "Is he okay in here? He's bigger than he used to be."

"Sure, we love dogs here. You want a pup cup for him?"

"Thanks."

He stood up, eyeing her warily for a few seconds. "Anything for you?"

"Uh, just a decaf latte."

Zoe fidgeted as he got it ready, looking around at the changes that Seth had implemented over the past few weeks.

The antlers above the counter had an array of blue, red, and white bunting hanging from them, and Seth had redecorated the tables so that the blue vases on each one had the same color flowers inside.

It looked patriotic and bright, and she wanted to tell him so, but couldn't get the words out.

Seth turned back, handing her Max's treat as he kept one hand on the milk jug, frothing it expertly without looking at it.

"Listen, I owe you an apology," Zoe said hesitantly. "I should have come in sooner, but I convinced myself it would be awkward, and then it got more awkward every time I thought about it."

Seth shrugged but didn't smile. "So much for staying *friends*, huh?"

Zoe swallowed. Ever since she had arrived in town Seth had been warm and welcoming, but it appeared those days were over.

After a painful minute of silence, he handed over her latte as she wrestled with Max to keep him from jumping up on the counter.

"I'm sorry," she said again. "I'll be sure to come in here more often."

Seth put his hands in his pockets, his jaw clenched. "I heard you and Leo are datin', now," he said, arching an eyebrow.

Zoe stiffened. "Uh… yeah."

Seth scoffed under his breath, shaking his head. "Congrats. I wondered why that double date was such a disaster."

"Oh no, nothing was happening then," she said hurriedly.

"Sure."

A young couple entered, and Seth half turned toward them to take their order.

"Okay," he said distractedly. "See you around, Fontaine."

She stared at him, wondering whether he might turn back to her when he was done serving them, but he turned his back, fussing with something at the register.

She left as quickly as she could.

Once she was out on the street again, Max jumped up, resting his paws against her thigh as she held his pup cup, his warm tongue licking all over her hand as he devoured it eagerly.

Zoe glanced back inside the café, watching Seth's easy smile through the window, guilt rising in her belly.

She kept forgetting how close-knit places like Sapphire were. In D.C., if she hadn't gone to the coffee house near her home, no one would notice for months, if at all. But here, it seemed her absence had been felt more keenly than she'd expected.

I should have told him about me and Leo. No wonder he's pissed.

Max took one final lick of the cup before dropping to the ground, and Zoe sipped her latte as they moved ahead, down the street.

About fifteen minutes later, she was nearing the bridge. It was an old brick monstrosity, most of which had crumbled to rubble. The main bulk of one arch remained, but that was all.

It looked like a monument to a more noble age, but it was covered with graffiti, and the neighborhood surrounding it had morphed into a haven for the less privileged in the area.

Her cell phone began to vibrate, and she rummaged in her bag, keeping an eye on the road ahead, watching a couple of shadows moving between the arches, hoping one of them was Mateo. She was still driving a rental, and she was dubious of linking her phone to the car's Bluetooth.

Finally, her fingers closed over her phone and pulled it out, risking a quick glance at Leo's handsome face looking back at her on the screen.

"Hey, Leo."

"Hey you," he said, making her smile. "I wondered if you were coming over tonight. We can do dinner and a movie."

Zoe's thoughts moved to the endless boxes waiting to be reviewed in her living room and she bit her lip. Leo knew nothing of this private project, and very little of what she had been investigating before she came to Sapphire. She wanted to keep it that way for as long as possible.

"Thank you, you know I would love to, but I have quite a bit of work to do tonight, and I think me and Max might grab a pizza and fall asleep on the couch."

Leo chuckled. "Is Rick still giving you grief?"

Zoe stared ahead, desperate to tell Leo what had happened that morning, but she hesitated, doubts forming in her mind.

35

Rick had been erratic, almost scared. Until she knew what was going on with him, the less Leo knew, the better.

"You have no idea," she said lightly. "He was there for about thirty minutes today and has run off again."

"Jesus, is that two weeks on the run now?" Leo asked. As he spoke, there was the sound of rapid barking through the phone.

"Are you neglecting your patients, Leo?" she asked, grateful for the change in topic.

"Never! That's just Sampson, he's a chihuahua, so I'm just putting on my body armor before I deal with him."

"Isn't that for Rottweilers?"

"The smaller the dog, the more psychotic they get. Trust me, I'm a vet," he said cheerfully, and she laughed. "Are you still at the office?"

"No, I'm taking Max for a walk." She paused. While on the phone, she'd parked the car, let Max out, and was now tugging the dog back as he tried to chase a pigeon. "I, uh, went to see Seth, by the way. I felt like I should. It's been a while since I've been to the café and I think he's kind of pissed at me."

There was a long pause. "Okay," Leo said slowly. "Do you think he has reason to be? I thought you parted on good terms?"

"I've kind of been avoiding him. And it seems he knows we're dating now. Guess that was inevitable, nothing stays private in Sapphire for long."

Leo blew out a breath. "Well, Seth Bowen sure knows how to hold a grudge; he's hated me for years."

"Yeah." She picked at the roughened edge of her phone case. "I wasn't going to mention it, because I thought it would be weird, but then I changed my mind."

Leo's voice softened. "You don't have to tell me every time you speak to the guy, Zo. This is a small town, you're gonna run into one another. Just don't jump his bones or I'll be having words."

Zoe laughed nervously, her anxiety rising when she considered everything she *hadn't* done with Leo yet.

"Where are you now?" he asked.

"I'm just dropping in on Mateo, I wanted to ask him something."

"Alone?" The tone of his voice made her hackles rise instantly.

"Yes, alone, I'm a big girl."

"I know that," he said stiffly. "But his crowd isn't always the friendliest. Watch out for broken glass with Max, too; he might cut his paws."

"Yeah," she said, irritated by the mollycoddling. "I'll do that. I can see Mateo now, so I'm gonna go talk to him. Good luck with the chihuahua."

"Thanks, I'll need it. See you later."

She hung up, putting her phone into her bag and blowing out a frustrated breath. Leo tended to treat her with kid gloves, and it wasn't the first time he'd suggested she couldn't handle something as simple as a house call without a *man* around.

He was one of the least misogynistic people alive, but that didn't seem to apply when it came to her safety.

"Don't get any glass in your paw, buddy, okay? Because I'll never hear the end of it."

Max looked up at her curiously, but when she scanned the ground, it was pretty clean. A couple of old mattresses had been dumped with some bed sheets, but no broken glass glinted in the late afternoon light.

She was about to walk to the bridge when a voice behind her sliced through the quiet around them.

"You here to see me?"

Max spun round, straining at the leash and barking viciously, growling at the back of his throat. It was the most aggression she had ever seen from him.

She pulled the dog to her side as she came face to face with Mateo, who had materialized behind her.

He was an imposing figure in a thick, black puffer jacket. His customary cart was absent, and he was standing very still, staring at her, a haunted look in his pitch-black gaze.

"Yeah," Zoe said, tugging at Max to try and make him calm down.

Mateo looked at the dog. Max had saliva dribbling from his mouth, his white teeth flashing into view each time he barked. Although he was standing behind Zoe's leg, he looked ferocious in that moment. Even Zoe was alarmed by it.

"Sorry," she muttered. "He never does this; I think you took him by surprise. Max, buddy, it's okay!"

"He's a smart pup. Sensible not to trust someone when you don't know them from Adam. Better to be on your guard." His dark eyes glinted menacingly, and Zoe stood up straighter, refusing to show how perturbed she was.

Mateo fixed his gaze on the dog, and slowly, Max calmed down. Something about it felt strange to Zoe, like there was a power in it she couldn't see. It was as if Mateo were having a silent conversation with her dog, which she wasn't privy to.

After a minute, Max was docile as a lamb, and Mateo nodded. He stepped around her, heading toward the bridge and reaching out an arm as if he was welcoming her into his home.

"There ain't many people here today. Not until Seth comes by. Think Lana's around, though. You met her before?"

"I don't think so," Zoe said, pulling a very reluctant Max along as she tried to calm her thundering heartbeat.

Maybe Leo had a point about coming here alone.

They moved beneath the overhang of the bridge, and Zoe noticed a shape huddled in the corner as she stepped into the shadows. She squinted at it, trying to determine if it was a person or a pile of junk.

It stirred, turning over to reveal a young woman, her head resting on the belly of a black Labrador asleep beneath her. She didn't open her eyes.

"What's up?" Mateo asked.

The base of the bridge was also surprisingly clean. A few pieces of trash had blown there, with Mateo's cart in the distance, but the fresh wind from the mountains made it feel more sanitary that it probably was.

Zoe turned to Mateo who was watching her with interest.

"Do you remember when you came to talk to me a few weeks back? You scared me half to death when you jumped out of an alleyway right in front of me."

Mateo smirked. "I got a habit of startlin' you."

"What did you mean when you said Rick Fisher 'found out' about the Sapphire Foundation?"

Mateo's eyes darkened, and his expression changed from open to closed off in a moment.

"You didn't speak to him?" he asked, sounding disappointed.

"Oh, I did. I've asked him about it a few times, but he refuses to tell me."

Mateo nodded. "Chicken shit, that's his problem. Didn't want to do nothin' before either, just like the other one."

"What other one?" Zoe asked, struggling to hold onto Max, who desperately wanted to go and meet the Labrador.

"Arnold Price," Mateo said solemnly. "The old editor of the paper. He came to see me, told me a load of bull about wanting to help, and then disappeared off the face of the earth."

"Max! Stop that," she hissed, pulling the dog to her side.

Zoe turned back to Mateo, who was leaning on his cart as if he didn't have a care in the world.

"Alright, so Arnold Price. What did he talk to you about?"

"He wanted to interview me, find out what I knew after the fire."

Zoe's pulse quickened. Her initial interest in the Foundation had stemmed from a fire that had destroyed the entire building several years earlier. At the time, it had been a state-of-the-art rehab center; burned to the ground practically overnight. Since then, it had been rebuilt as The Orchard Grove Nursing Home, but, despite her research, she had only been able to find sparse details on how the fire had started.

"Were you working there at the time?" she asked eagerly.

"I wasn't in the building when the blaze happened. Nobody was, or so they say."

Mateo smirked, readjusting his body against the cart.

"And did you do it? The interview?"

Another nod. "Sure. I didn't have nothin' to lose at the time. I was bitter, angry. And I had good reason to be. The Foundation let me go right after it happened, no explanation, no back pay. I lost my damned house because of Linmans."

Zoe stepped forward, the old excitement from her investigation beginning to spark to life again.

"So what did Arnold ask you?"

"A lot of things. He wanted to know how long I worked there, what I did, what I saw… I didn't tell him everythin', mind you. No point revealin' your whole hand, not when you got no guarantees of what comes next. And I was right in the end. He wrote it down, like you all do. Best friends for life until the story comes out and then you're a stranger again. All he wanted was his scoop."

"And did it?"

"What?"

"Come out? The story?" Zoe asked.

"Course not. He was fired before he could go to print."

"Arnold Price was *fired*?"

Mateo nodded. "Never saw him again. Couldn't pay my mortgage, lost my house. Ended up here after a long road downhill. Slope gets steeper when people don't believe what you're tellin' them."

Zoe cleared her throat. "I'm sorry Mateo, really. I didn't realize all of it stemmed from that point in your life. But I think you should know that Arnold Price killed himself, about two years after he left the paper."

Mateo's expression barely changed, but then he shrugged a shoulder, as if it were the most natural thing in the world.

"They must have really done a number on him," he said darkly, something in his voice sending a shiver right through her.

"And your story never went to print?"

Mateo shook his head. "The only person who can explain that one is your boss. I would suggest you stop hangin' around in the gutter with me and go ask him. *Make* him tell you, before you ain't got a chance to ask."

Mateo turned away, going over to a bundle of bags and sheets in the corner, and settled down to sleep.

Zoe felt guilty about it afterwards, but truthfully, she'd never been so pleased to get out of a place in her life.

CHAPTER FIVE

LEO FELT LIKE THERE WAS A HAMMER IN THE BACK OF HIS skull. He rubbed at his temples, trying to shut out the incessant pounding, but it was useless.

The noise was so bad in his office at the clinic that he hadn't been able to concentrate all day, and had only written up three reports, when he had fifteen in his backlog.

He sighed, rising from his chair and taking his coffee to the little kitchen between the reception and the observation room.

As soon as he set foot in the narrow space, Nancy appeared at the other end.

She had earplugs in her ears, a furious expression, and a t-shirt with six American flags overlapping in the center.

"I can't take any more of this," she said vehemently, "and it's only been three days!"

"I know," Leo sighed. "I'm sorry, Nancy, I'm going to speak to the site manager."

"Have you seen what they just brought in, what they're building?" she demanded, pulling the earplugs from her ears and glaring at him as if he had arranged everything personally. "Come outside and see."

Leo groaned as she stalked through the front doors and walked around the side of the clinic.

He placed his coffee cup down and followed her, an ache behind his eyes as he rounded the corner of the building.

The Skywolf Veterinary Clinic, which Leo owned, shared its land with a wide, empty lot at the rear of the building. Trees and thick foliage on one side dominated the space, but once they petered out, it was just a wide expanse of beige concrete, gravel, and rubble. It had been derelict for years and caused Leo few issues other than when the dust coated his truck in the parking lot.

But that had all changed about nine months before when some workmen put up a sign, erected some gates, and declared that *Linman Group Construction* was building apartments on the site. Ever since, Leo had been waiting for the day when something would happen, but it had remained empty for months.

Then, the previous Monday, Leo arrived at the clinic to bustling activity inside the fence line. From then on, trucks had been traveling to and from the site with men in suits and hard hats strutting around, pointing at things and pretending to look busy.

But the real problems began when the drill arrived.

Leo's little clinic was now plagued with noise from dawn until dusk. It was disturbing the animals they had in their care, their surgeons, their staff, and the patients.

He walked up behind Nancy, whose jeans had crystals all over them, sparkling in the sunlight.

"See?" she said, gesturing in front of her. "Look at that thing."

Leo held back a groan as he saw a drill twice the size of the first one being assembled inside the lot. They were on a level with the fence from the clinic, but the top of the rig was high enough that he could see it even at ground level.

"I can't work with that drilling every single day," Nancy said despairingly. "I just can't, Leo, we're going to have to find a solution, because nobody is gonna wanna leave their pets with us, if this keeps on."

"I'll speak to them, Nance, but what can we do? They're building right behind us, it's not like we can tell them not to dig the foundations."

"Oh, there are plenty of ways we could make it more manageable for all of us. For one, we could ask them to drill in the afternoons, that way I can book as many appointments as possible in the mornings. Or we could see if their schedule will stretch to the evenings or every other day."

Leo looked at her skeptically, not believing for a second that a huge corporation like The Linman Group would listen to a plea from a tiny clinic, but he nodded quickly as she turned to face him, her brow furrowing angrily.

"I'll get in touch and see if I can book in some time with them. They have to realize how disruptive it is," he said.

"Problem is we're out on our own here," Nancy muttered. "There ain't many houses in this part of town. A lot of its warehouses and the auto shop a few streets up. They live in noise all the time. They're not gonna care about all this."

Leo put his hands in his pockets, staring at the enormous drill with real concern.

How long do foundations take to construct, a few weeks? Months?

He had no idea. His worry grew as he looked back at his clinic, the business he'd built from the ground up, battling through endless obstacles to finally break even.

The past year had been dicey at best, and if profits continued to be as unpredictable as they had been he was going to be in real trouble. Cheaper, bigger chains were opening all over the county, and Leo had seen a sharp downturn in new patients lately.

"You know, I thought they might have forgotten about it," Nancy said, staring at the lot moodily. "I wondered if they'd bought the land and then it would just sit there for years untouched and quiet."

"Me too."

"I had a headache before I arrived this mornin.'"

"I know, Nance. I'll deal with it," he said curtly.

Leo could empathize; he had a headache of his own, but the problem with Nancy was that she was incredibly impatient. If something wasn't working, she would have a knee-jerk reaction to fix it—even if that made everything worse.

Leo suspected that the building work would last for weeks, and fear curled through his gut at the thought. If it continued, Nancy would leave—he was certain of it.

He couldn't run the clinic without her. Nancy Ashwood wasn't perfect. She hated technology, complained bitterly about everything, and could talk for thirty minutes without pausing for breath, but his clients loved her. If she left, he might have a mutiny on his hands.

Rubbing his fingers through his hair, he walked slowly back inside, pulling out his phone to see if there was any information on Linmans' website about the building works. Before he could do so, however, a Post-it was shoved in front of him.

"Nicole Miller, she's the site manager, I called and asked this morning. Google's not always good for that kind of thing. I found out she's got two dogs, too, so I'd play on that when you speak to her."

Leo took the Post-it, biting his tongue as he held back the urge to crumple it in her face.

Does she think I can't deal with this myself?

Nancy returned to her desk, the tension coming off her in waves.

He sighed, pushing down his anger as best he could. He needed Nancy on his side, or they wouldn't get any work done at all. Leo went over, racking his brain for something to say that would cheer her up.

"Thanks for this," he waved the Post-it, "I'm gonna email her today."

"*Call her,*" Nancy bit out. "Emailing people is useless, and you won't get a reply."

Leo shoved it in his pocket. "Are you goin' to the meeting about the library on Friday morning? I could give you a ride. We could get away from the noise for a couple of hours that way."

Nancy gave him a frosty stare at the change of subject, her lips thinning before she nodded.

"I reckon we could put a few of the flyers about the library up in the window here, too," he continued doggedly.

"I doubt anyone'll see 'em. No one's gonna want to come by with all this hoo-hah," she muttered.

Nancy's lip trembled a little when she said that, and Leo frowned, leaning against the desk and looking down at her quizzically.

"You alright, Nancy? I know the drilling is awful, but is there somethin' else goin' on?"

Nancy shrugged, swallowing heavily. "I'm fine." There were tears in her eyes.

"Nance, what is it?"

She sniffed, rubbing the back of her hand over her cheek. "Adrian's not been well. We're waitin' for some results, and I'm worried about him. All this ain't helping."

Suddenly, the tears she'd been holding back spilled down her cheeks, and Leo came round the desk in two long strides, putting an arm around her as she sobbed, leaning against him, covering her face with her hands.

"Oh, Nance, why didn't you say anything?"

She pulled back, sniffing violently as he handed her a tissue.

"Oh, because he doesn't want any fuss, and we don't know what's the matter with him. He's just not been right, all these problems with his gut. Lately, he hasn't been able to eat much without throwing it back up again."

"Do you need to be home with him? Because I can manage here," Leo insisted.

"No, no," she said firmly. "I'm better when I'm workin'. I'm sorry I lost my temper, this headache's runnin' me ragged."

"Listen, I'll make you some coffee. Come into my office and we can talk things through. If you need a change in hours or—"

"It's alright, Leo," she said, recovering quickly and putting up a hand. "I'm grateful, but I don't want to be a mess all day. I'll just get back to work. Coffee would be good, though. And yes, I'll be at the library meeting. These corporate assholes aren't gonna rip our community out from under us, too."

Leo's heart went out to her as she wiped her eyes and straightened in her chair, visibly pulling herself together as she gave him a tight smile. She turned back to her computer, slamming her palm into her mouse to wake her monitor.

Leo didn't know what to say.

Nancy's husband was a stalwart member of the Sapphire community. He worked at Linman Pharmaceuticals as a security guard, but had once been in the Navy, larger than life, bulky, and brash. He and Nancy didn't seem to fit together at all on paper, but whenever Leo saw them with each other, he could see the love they shared.

I sure hope the test results have good news.

He returned to the kitchen, making up two coffees instead of one, pulling the Post-it from his pocket, and saving the number to deal with later. As he did so, the battering sound of the drill started up again, and he closed his eyes in despair.

That evening, after work, Leo drove down Highway 48 toward Whistle Falls.

The summer's lingering sunshine was warm on his arm as he drove with the windows down and the radio on, a soft lightness to the evening that he loved.

June was a beautiful time of year and attracted a lot of tourists to the valley. Leo hated the quiet of the winter months, and the bustle of the summer was a welcome change. Now, with Zoe in the picture, everything felt real again in a way it hadn't for a long time. After the loss of Freya and having her ripped out of his life so suddenly after the crash, he hadn't expected to find happiness so soon.

He glanced at the passenger seat, missing Max's big eyes looking at him as he drove. Leo and Zoe had been caring for Max in a shared arrangement for a few weeks, and it had been perfect except for the times Max wasn't with him.

Leo had grown used to having the puppy in the car when Zoe was out in the evenings, or off chasing a story, but lately she'd been at The Chronicle doing admin more than she had been reporting. The times he'd had Max to himself in the truck had waned. He didn't begrudge Zoe taking Max to work with her to the office, but there was something nice about a companion on the road.

Leo's relaxed mood faded as he drove up the side street toward Sparrow Shelter. It was a subsidiary of Sparrow Meals, the food service where he volunteered once a month, and where, for the time being, Gus had been living.

Leo stopped in the single parking space out front and jogged across the road to the building. It was on the far edge of town, on Margaret Road—between a closed-down convenience store and a funeral home—and looked about as inviting as both.

Pushing through the double doors, he broke into a grin as he saw Paulie ahead of him. She was a beautiful soul who ran the kitchen for Sparrow Meals. She also acted as the unofficial manager of the shelter, spending a lot of her free time firefighting and wrangling those who wanted to cause trouble.

Paulie was the polar opposite of Anita Hererra, the *actual* manager of the shelter. Anita ran the place with an iron fist and didn't allow anyone a moment's rest if they stepped out of line. Gus had hated her on sight.

"Hey there, big man," Paulie said with her joyous little laugh. "You here to collect Gus?"

Leo nodded. "Yeah, he here?"

"Sure is. You gonna get him some more of that good home cookin'?" she said.

"I'm gonna try," he replied, leaning against the counter. "He talked much yet?"

"Nothin' except a few grunts. But that's teenagers for you."

"Any more news about where he came from, or his family?"

She shook her head sadly. "No. I don't reckon that boy has had anyone lookin' out for him for a long time. You're doin' a good thing, Leo."

He shrugged. "Doesn't feel like it's helpin' much."

"It will be. You just wait. Oh, speak of the devil, hey Gussie!" she said, and Leo turned, noting Gus rolling his eyes at the nickname, but there was a little smile on his face as he did it.

Gus had never cracked a smile in Leo's presence, and he felt an irrational stab of jealousy that Paulie had managed to elicit the reaction instead of him.

"Hey Gus," Leo said as the kid came level with him. Gus didn't speak, simply nodding his head in greeting.

Almost immediately, there was the tap of heels from the office down the hall, and Leo tensed as Anita rounded the corner. She was in her usual tight-fitting suit, with perfect hair and nails. Anita was an attractive woman, tall, and dark with a warm brown tone to her skin, but her eyes were cold.

"Will you be taking Mr. Gonzalez out this evening?" she asked briskly.

"Yeah, I'm taking him to the ranch, and I'll drop him off at ten—"

"Before nine-thirty, please."

Leo paused. "Uh, they said ten was the curfew."

"It was, until I caught him sneaking out last night."

Leo glanced at Gus as the teenager stepped forward, the boy's eyes filled with quiet rage. "I wasn't *sneakin' out*, I thought I heard somethin' outside my window."

Anita's impassive face didn't change as she marked something on her iPad.

"No one is permitted to leave their room after hours. No exceptions," she said icily, turning back to Leo. "Will Miss Fontaine be with you tonight, Dr. Rowden?"

Leo scratched his jaw, glancing at Gus. The kid looked three seconds from knocking Anita to the floor.

"Yeah, Zoe will be with us. I'll have him back by nine-thirty."

Anita ticked something else off on her list and walked away over the polished floor. Leo turned to Gus and raised his eyebrows. After an interminable pause, the kid finally spoke.

"I wasn't sneakin' out."

"Well then, what were you doing?" Leo asked.

Leo had meant it as an innocent enquiry but could tell from Gus's expression that it had been the wrong thing to say. The kid gave him a withering look before turning around and slamming through the doors toward Leo's truck, where he kicked the tire for good measure.

Leo turned to Paulie. "What did I say?"

She gave him a pitying look, sighing heavily. "Oh, Leo, he just wanted to know you were on his side."

She shook her head with a tired smile, gathering some files and heading toward the office. Leo went to his truck feeling more bewildered than ever.

I can't ask innocent questions now? What the hell could have been under his window, for God's sake?

The drive to the ranch was awkward, and Leo couldn't think what to say. He ended up rambling about Max for twenty minutes straight to try to get a conversation going, but Gus didn't say one solitary thing for the whole drive.

Leo was beginning to think he would never get through to him.

CHAPTER SIX

Z OE YAWNED AS SHE WENT THROUGH THE FRONT DOORS
of The Chronicle on Tuesday morning. She was
exhausted, having been with Leo until late the night
before.

Their evening had consisted of good food but lousy company
as Leo tried and failed to get Gus to open up. It was like getting
blood out of a stone.

Zoe was no psychologist, but the kid looked like he'd been
through a lot of trauma in his life. Gus was quiet in the extreme,
didn't want to talk about his past, and wouldn't engage with them
about anything. He sometimes became animated with Max, but
mainly just looked depressed and disinterested.

Leo had dropped him back at the shelter by nine-thirty, but when he returned, he looked so dejected that Zoe insisted on staying for the rest of the evening.

By the end of the night, she'd had too much wine to drive home, and what followed was an excruciating exchange where Leo invited her to share his bed, and she'd mumbled an excuse, eventually going to the guest room.

She felt like a failure, and it was only when she lay down in bed that night that she suddenly realized Rick hadn't called her like he had told her he would. Grabbing her phone, she tried his cell, but it went straight to voicemail.

After sending him a text, she'd gone to sleep with a weight on her chest.

When she woke up, there was still no response from Rick, and Zoe's anxiety only increased as she got ready for work. By the time she pulled into the parking lot at The Chronicle, she was dreading everything she needed to get done that day, hoping Rick hadn't called because he was already on his way back from wherever he had gone.

The next issue would be going out on Friday, and she had never done a print run alone before.

Surely, he won't leave me to do it by myself. I'm sure he'll be back any day now.

As she entered the building, Zoe hiked her bag up her shoulder, nodding to the receptionist as she pushed through the door, juggling Max's leash and her bag as best she could. She hadn't had a chance to stop off for coffee and hoped Bean's head didn't implode without its fourth espresso.

Stepping through the double doors to the familiar expanse of The Chronicle's main office, she stopped dead in her tracks.

It was full.

More people were standing in front of her than she had ever seen in the entire building, let alone the office.

Angela sat at the front of them all in her wheelchair, but the rest of the faces Zoe had only seen as photographs on the bulletin board by her desk. All of them had worked from home permanently until today.

There were two men, between forty and fifty years old, on the right of Angela. One she recognized as Anton Bielke, the marketing account manager. From what Zoe could tell, he did very little with his time except send fishing updates to the all-staff email.

Next to him was Daniel Swaine, the sports and staff writer combined. He was a great writer, but also a freelancer, and Zoe had never been able to contact him, no matter how many times she called. He was the kind of guy who got his copy in with a minute to spare and zero updates from conception to completion.

Lilith Robinson, the office manager, and the columnist, Miriam Mulllins, stood on either side of Angela like her bodyguards.

They were an eclectic bunch, most of whom Zoe had never met in person, and every single one of them looked furious.

Zoe stared around, her eyes darting to Bean, who was in his chair at his desk, his hands over his stomach, an expression of resignation on his face.

"Uh, morning!" Zoe said loudly as the door swung shut behind her with a heavy thud.

"Where the hell is Rick?" Anton barked without preamble, looking at Zoe as if she had stuffed him in her bag for safekeeping.

"Uh… I don't know. Has he been in yet today?"

Angela scoffed. "He hasn't been in the office for weeks, not for more than a few minutes at a time. What is going on? Are we all gettin' fired?"

Max was hiding behind Zoe's legs and whimpering. The atmosphere was beyond hostile, and she felt as if this was a planned intervention, arranged behind her back.

Anger simmered quietly beneath her skin, and she prayed that today would be the day Rick came back, knuckled down, and explained himself.

Why are they all looking at me like I know what's going on?

"Okay, first of all, 'hi' to those of you I haven't met face to face yet," she said evenly. "Second of all, I don't know a lot more than you do, but I want to find out what's going on, too. Let's go to the conference tables and chat this out, okay? Let me put Max in his bed."

"And why exactly is there a dog here?" Anton asked.

"Same reason he's been here the last few weeks, Anton. Rick allowed him to be," Zoe said, trying to keep her voice light, even as her irritation spiked.

There was general grumbling, but the crowd parted for her to get through, and she walked to her desk as Bean turned back to his computer, studiously ignoring them all.

I'm glad I didn't get him a coffee if he isn't gonna help with all this.

Squinting at the bulletin board at the end of the bank of desks, she took in the faded images of the staff, some of them taken over ten years before. Still, she could broadly confirm who everybody was, and other than Tom, the photographer, it looked like everyone else was in today.

This can't be a good sign.

She turned to find them all watching her, standing together behind her desk. Zoe felt like a mother hen leading her chicks around a yard.

"Anybody want to get themselves a coffee first?" she asked.

"I can make a bunch," Bean said from the back, and Zoe gave him a grateful smile.

I take back everything I just thought about you, Bean.

"I'll have a coffee, thanks," Angela called to him. She was the only one smiling, clearly trying to defuse the cloud of resentment hovering over the room. It didn't work, but Zoe was hardly a stranger to bad atmospheres and people being pissed 24/7.

In D.C., barely a day had gone by without some kind of bust-up in the newsroom. She had regularly stepped between her boss, Tripp Monroe, and one of the other reporters to prevent them from giving each other a black eye.

But today was different. Beneath the anger on the surface, she could see the worry and strain in every face.

Once upon a time, the Sapphire Valley Chronicle been a daily issue. But between the shifting digital landscape and various economic collapses, it slipped to twice a week, then weekly, and now every other week. Most of the staff worked two jobs to make ends meet, and even then, the pay was abysmal.

They're not angry with me. They're scared.

"Thanks, Bean," she said, leaning round the crowd to give him a thumbs up. "Everybody else, let's go and sit down, okay?"

They all trooped to the chairs and tables at the back of the office. Now that she came to look at it, even the furniture had an amateur quality about it. The chairs were smaller than average, with bright green legs and tarnished wooden seats. There were even carved images and names scratched into some of them.

Did Rick get these from an elementary school or something?

Zoe pulled out as many chairs as she could from where they had been stacked against the wall and settled everybody in a few minutes.

Bean appeared, carrying a tray of coffee, and there was a general rustling and murmuring as everybody helped themselves. Bean sat down opposite her, his eyes flicking around the group. He looked troubled by something and didn't meet her gaze.

"Okay," Zoe said firmly. "I'm Zoe Fontaine. I know you've probably read my work and seen my face in the paper by now, but that isn't the same as meeting in person. So, hello. It's nice to put faces to the names I regularly see in my inbox."

Anton scoffed loudly, and Miriam rolled her eyes.

"We know who you are," came a sharp voice from her right. "We want to know what's going on with Rick. You're his friend; he brought you in without consulting us and he pretty much relies on you for everything now. So where is he?"

Zoe turned to Lilith, who was sitting far back in her seat, watching Zoe with narrowed eyes. She had long bangs and thick, circular glasses with such a strong magnification they distorted the rest of her face. Buck teeth stuck out over her lower lip, and she wore enormous gold hoop earrings that clacked whenever she moved.

"Look, I don't know—"

"Save it," Lilith spat, cutting her off. "There's no way he just vanished without telling you where he would be. Unless this is a coup? Is that it? Was that the plan? Rick just hands the editor's job over to you on the quiet?"

Zoe was so taken aback by her tone that she found herself tongue-tied.

"He brought you in because you're his friend," Anton piped up. "This place hasn't hired anyone in years, and then he brings in some hotshot reporter from the city without a word? You even got the Stanfield story when Mim's been the senior writer here for over fifteen years. It's not right!"

Miriam winced, looking mortified as she glared at Anton. "Hey, don't bring me into this! Zoe almost got killed for that story, I wouldn't have wanted to take her place with some crazy cop in a cabin in the woods!"

"Hey, I'm on *your* side," Anton snapped at Miriam. "Don't backtrack now she's sittin' in front of you. I know we were all stumped as to why the hell he thought we could afford her. I've seen the accounts; we can't afford anything! This whole paper is goin' down the tubes."

Zoe cleared her throat, and everyone turned to face her.

"Look, I don't think it matters *why* I'm here, or what Rick intended when he hired me. He was helping me out, and I'm grateful for that. I don't take this place or this job for granted. I want this paper to succeed as much as you all do."

Anton waved vaguely in the air. "You could walk back into any job in D.C. and never think about this dump again. That's not the case for most of us. This is all I got. This and debts."

Everyone around the table was nodding.

At least now I know who organized this little intervention behind my back.

"Alright, Anton. You've made your point. And, not that it's any of your business, but I'm not planning to move back to D.C. any time soon. I just signed a six-month lease and got a puppy."

"Bully for you," Anton muttered.

"Rick hasn't been here, working, for over a week," Angela said. "He wouldn't let me talk to him last time I saw him and wasn't interested in anything I had to say. Does anyone know where he is or what he's doin'? Because we can't keep going as we are. Zoe can't do everything."

Daniel shifted awkwardly in his seat. "I haven't seen him in person for months. The last email I got from him was in May."

"I saw him two weeks ago," Lilith added. "He was drivin' through town. I waved… didn't even acknowledge me, and he looked terrible."

Zoe couldn't argue with that. Rick's appearance was never particularly refined, but lately he'd looked more disheveled than ever.

"He doesn't care about any of us," Anton retorted, "how do we get a paper out without an editor?"

There was a long silence, and then Angela wheeled her chair closer to the table, catching Zoe's eye.

"I heard he was seein' somebody."

Zoe raised her eyebrows. "Really? Who?"

"I don't know. It was about a month back, someone said they saw him with a lady in his car, but they couldn't see who she was."

"Okay, that might be something," Zoe hedged, determined to keep what Rick had told her secret for now. "Anybody else got any helpful information? This isn't just about getting Rick back, either. I want to make sure we get the final proofs to the printers on time for the Friday issue and if we need to prep for that now, then that's what we'll do."

None of them would meet her eye, but Anton and Lilith exchanged a meaningful look.

Lilith sighed. "You haven't been here that long, Zoe. Things have been bad for months. It wouldn't be the first issue where we missed the deadline. After Arnold left, Rick kept things running at first, and he seemed determined to make this paper something great. Then everything changed. He just stopped caring."

"Arnold Price. You mean the old editor?" Zoe asked.

That name just keeps cropping up lately.

Lilith nodded. "It hasn't been the same since he… left." That statement was met with a lot of nodding around the table.

"Okay," Zoe said with determination. "What we're here to do is get the paper to print, right? That's always been the goal; even without Rick, we have to get it done. Who's waiting on feedback from him?"

"You're takin' charge, are you?" Anton growled, leaning forward and glaring at her menacingly.

Zoe spread her arms out across the table. "Anton, if you want to do it, go for it. Miriam? Lilith? Angela? Anyone else, you're welcome to take charge instead. Believe me, I would much rather just get on with my *actual* job."

There was a long, awkward silence, and Bean scoffed, giving Anton a stink eye as the older man leaned back, looking more uncertain now.

"I'm waiting for confirmation from Rick on my story," Daniel said. "But I'm not sure he even read my last two articles, to be honest."

"Same here," Mirian said, "but then Rick's never cared about my baking column."

"Well, I care, and we're making this deadline," Zoe said firmly. "If you're happy for me to take a look and green light the stuff that's pending, send it to me. Anton, have we got any changes to the layout this week from new ad revenue?"

"No."

Zoe bit her tongue to stop herself from arguing as to why that was. Without proper direction, most of the staff had been coasting for months.

"Alright, everything submitted last week has already been reviewed, so I think we're just waiting for Tom's photographs from the community hall debate, and Daniel, you reported on the school's sports day, right?"

"Yeah, they got a star runner. I had an interview with him, too, but I thought it was too long."

"Send it through, and if we can add it in, we'll do that. Maybe we can make it a feature, a wholesome write-up should get people interested, and it'd be good to have some youth stories that don't involve drugs and alcohol."

Daniel instantly brightened, giving her a warm smile, and Zoe rubbed her forehead as she looked around at the rest of them.

"I know I'm not the editor, so I'm more than happy for all, or any of you, to weigh in on this. The main thing is we get the paper out on Friday and the final proofs to the printer by Thursday morning. So, if there are things you haven't done or you're waiting on, tell me. This is just temporary. In the meantime, if anyone hears from Rick, let me know right away. Just do what you do best and refer anything you're unsure of to me."

Zoe glanced at Daniel, who was by far the most competent journalist on the books.

"Daniel, if I run out of time, can you review some of it for me?"

"Sure, I charge by the hour," he said lightly, and there was a small titter of laughter around the table. It wasn't much, but it broke the tension. Zoe nodded, rising from her chair, and everyone went to their respective desks.

Zoe's fists clenched as she watched Anton grab his bag and leave the building. He had said his piece, staged a mutiny, and he clearly had no intention of hanging around to see the fallout.

What the hell does that guy do all day if the ads are on rotation? What work can he possibly be covering?

She turned to speak to Bean, but he'd already slunk away, and she frowned. There was a weird energy coming off him today.

As the rest of the staff dispersed, Zoe walked over to Rick's desk. The sight of it sent a ripple of concern through her. It looked different from the day before. He'd tidied it, and that never happened. In fact, all the junk, receipts, and papers that were normally strewn across it were gone.

He'd straightened up his keyboard and organized the Post-its on his monitor. He'd even wiped up the perpetual coffee ring on the bottom right-hand corner where he always put his drink.

Zoe swallowed, walking to the file cabinet, not bothering to look in the top drawer because it was only ever piled high with Skittles.

She opened the second and found his notebook with a lot of papers shoved inside. As she rummaged through, she found a receipt crumpled at the back from the local steak restaurant in Sapphire.

It was for two people, including steaks, chips, a bottle of wine, and one dessert.

Was he sharing that with his lady friend? If he has a girlfriend, could that explain where he is?

Her chest was fluttering with anxiety. He'd been acting really weird the day before and hadn't called her when he said he would.

No matter how unpredictable Rick had been in the past, he had *always* prioritized a print run. With a deadline on Friday, she would usually have heard from him by now.

This felt different. Worrying.

She pocketed the receipt, glancing through the rest of the contents. It felt deliberate, like Rick had sorted everything out for a reason.

She opened the top drawer, and a heavy weight plummeted into her stomach. It was empty. To anyone else, it might have seemed like a silly detail, but to her, it was the most telling of all.

Rick had completely cleared out his drawer of Skittles. They were always there, like paperclips or scotch tape. A staple part of his daily routine. The man basically lived on sugar.

If they weren't there, it meant he didn't think he would need them.

Did he know he wasn't coming back?

CHAPTER SEVEN

THE REST OF HER AFTERNOON WAS SPENT FIREFIGHTING, but she had to admit that having everyone in the office made a huge difference to the atmosphere of the place.

For once, she wasn't the only person sitting at her desk, her lonely typing filling the air.

Now, she could lean around and ask Miriam questions about the recipe she was publishing or how her column was coming along. In a world of working from home, she was beginning to remember what it was like to be in a 'busy' newsroom and thinking wistfully of the days at the Washington Express.

Have I made a mistake sticking it out here? My career would definitely be on a better path if I went back to the city.

But then, she wouldn't have her perfect little apartment, and her morning coffees. She wouldn't be able to drive five minutes to the mountains and enjoy a hike with Max in the early mornings. Not to mention, her relationship with Leo. She was barely keeping it together when she saw him every day; Zoe could imagine how anxious and insecure she would become if they tried to do things long distance.

She glanced around the office, watching people chatting together and listening to the murmur of voices. It felt good to be needed—and looked to for answers—for once, but whenever she glanced at Rick's empty chair, a wave of worry would sweep through her.

It had only been twenty-four hours since she had seen him, but something felt off.

Toward the end of the afternoon, she noticed Bean packing up for the day. He hadn't seemed like his usual self, and she rose, hoping to catch him before he left.

Just as she was about to call out to him, her cell phone began to vibrate. Convinced it was Rick, she pulled it excitedly from her pocket, only to groan as she saw her mom's name on the screen.

She closed her eyes. It was never a good sign when her mother called during work hours.

"Hey Mom," she said, answering on the second ring. "What's up?"

"Hello Zoe. Does there have to be something up for me to call my daughter?"

Zoe rolled her eyes. "No. Of course not."

There was a long, painful silence as Zoe waited for her to speak. "Did you need something? I'm at work."

"Come over for dinner tonight."

It was more of a command than an invitation. Zoe could already feel a headache forming at the back of her skull when she imagined the stilted, awkward conversation she would be subjected to.

"Tonight?"

"Yes. I've made lasagna. It's vegetarian."

"Will Phil be there?"

There was a short pause. "He does live in my house, Zoe, but I don't know what he's doing tonight. You really should stop this ridiculous feud with your brother. You're two grown adults."

Zoe's lip curled. "Yeah, it's definitely all my fault."

"That's not what I meant. Stop picking a fight. Come over at eight."

Her mom hung up, and Zoe had to suppress a groan. Bean was on his feet, placing his laptop in his messenger bag, and Zoe made a beeline for him, just as Anton appeared at her elbow.

"Where did you come from?" she blurted.

Anton gave her a dead-eyed stare. "I came back five minutes ago. I prefer working in the café down the road when I'm in the office."

Zoe arched an eyebrow at that ridiculous oxymoron. "What can I do for you?"

"I just spoke to Seth Bowen, and he wants to run a coffee morning to raise funds for the library. I wondered if we had space to include an ad for it in this week's edit?"

Zoe perked up at the thought of anything to help Evelyn's cause.

"Speak to Lilith, but I think we should. We can bump the weekly specials from the second page. It's nice that Seth wants to help."

Anton scoffed derisively. Cynicism seemed to be his baseline.

"Seth wanted to open a cafe in the library at one point. Did he tell you that?" he asked skeptically. "He just wants to expand his business and keep his eye in with Evelyn."

"Well, that may be true, but he doesn't have to pay for advertising to do that."

Anton shrugged. "Everybody is just out for themselves. Look at Rick. He couldn't give two pins about this place. He just does what he wants."

He turned around and sauntered back to his desk, taking a seat beside Angela. As he sat down, he leaned across, and they bowed their heads together like a couple of five-year-olds.

Zoe finally turned to speak to Bean, only to find he'd already gone, and she cursed under her breath. Walking swiftly to her computer, she shut it down, rubbing her hand gently over Max's back to wake him before running out of the office.

Bean had a little moped that he drove around town. It was a pile of crap that looked like it was seconds from falling apart but he had put a lot of love and attention into renovating it. Now, at least, it was a *gleaming* pile of crap, which was a mild improvement.

Zoe jogged over as he swung a leg over it and settled into the seat, the bright red helmet in his lap reflecting the sun as she reached him.

"Hey, I wanted to catch you before you left!" she said quickly, and Bean's face did something complicated, his hands jerking to the accelerator as if wanting to speed away and avoid the conversation.

"What's up?" he asked warily.

"Is everything alright? You're acting... shifty," she finished lamely, and Bean chuckled as he put on his sunglasses. They were mirrored, and it was odd not being able to see his eyes.

Bean sighed, staring ahead of him for a few seconds before pulling his hands away from the handles and into his lap.

"This whole thing is really weird. The fact that Miriam has come into the office means it's serious. I've worked here for two years, and I've only met her once." He shook his head. "Do you think Rick's comin' back?"

Zoe hesitated, looking at her own distorted image in the sunglasses.

"I don't know," she replied honestly. "I'm kind of worried about him."

Bean blew out a breath. "Me too. Rick's not exactly high-octane when it comes to the paper, but it's never been this bad. I emailed him about a phishing scam, as a test—he *always* responds to those—but it's like he's totally switched off."

Bean's Adam's apple bobbed, and Zoe cocked her head at him.

"What are you thinking?" she asked.

"I don't know. It feels like he might not be in the best place mentally. After Arnold, I just get worried. One of my friends started acting oddly like this, being erratic, going away for days at a time..."

"Was he okay?" Zoe asked hopefully.

"No." Bean's mouth turned down at the corners, and Zoe flexed her fingers, suppressing a shiver.

They both fell silent, the sun choosing that moment to go behind a cloud and covering the ground around them in shadow. Bean scratched at his stubble and took off his glasses again, his eyes filled with concern.

"Listen, I shouldn't be tellin' you this, he told me not to mention it to anyone. But Rick called me a couple of weeks ago— before he really went off the rails. He asked me to delete a load of files off the server."

Zoe stepped forward. "What files?" she asked eagerly.

"That's the thing. I feel like an idiot for not really paying attention. If Rick asks me to do something, I do it, you know? He's the boss. I barely looked at them. It was stuff he said wasn't needed anymore."

"From when?"

"Around 2015, I think. Maybe early 2016. He said he had the hard copies and didn't need the files anymore. That's weird, right? Most people prefer to keep the digital stuff."

"Yeah. It's weird. Thanks Bean. Is that what's been bothering you?"

He ruffled his fingers through his hair. "I just feel stupid. I was hungover, and I resented him calling me so early. I just did it. Only in the last couple of weeks did I realize I should have taken a beat and asked a few questions before blindly following what he said."

"What do you think the files were?"

"No idea, but he's never asked me to delete anything before. Not once."

Zoe nodded. "It's not your fault; you were doing your job."

Bean put his glasses back on as the cloud passed and the sun came out again. He nodded to her, turning on his moped with a sputtering start as he put his helmet on.

"Thanks, Zo."

"You might want to get that engine looked at," she said with a grin.

"Shut up, this thing runs like a dream."

He sped off, and Zoe coughed as a pall of black smoke followed him. Max looked crestfallen as he watched him go, and Zoe glanced back at the building.

All was not well with the paper; that much was obvious, and she needed to speak to Rick.

I have to find a way to get in touch with him somehow—the sooner the better.

Zoe drove to her mother's later that evening, with Max in the back. He was tired after a long walk and looked up at her miserably, just wanting to be home in his bed.

"I know you're exhausted, buddy, but you'll see your sister soon! After the initial barkfest, you always just curl up together and go to sleep, so you'll be warm and comfortable in no time."

Max gave her a slow blink, the little blonde eyebrows above his eyes making it look like he was frowning at her.

As she drove, a text came in from Leo wishing her luck, and she smiled. Zoe's relationship with her mother was sketchy at best, and volatile at worst, and she wasn't looking forward to their evening together.

It was odd that she'd invited Zoe for dinner. They hadn't spoken a lot over the past few weeks after the saga of her grandmother's care, and she rarely reached out like that.

She probably wants me to do something for her. God, I hope Phil isn't there.

After she parked her car, she walked up the familiar drive to the house. The lawn was immaculate, and Zoe could bet that, if she had measured it, it would be exactly the regulation length for the suburbs. Arlene Fontaine was nothing if not pedantic.

The door opened before she knocked, only increasing Zoe's agitation, but her mom gave her a smile and stepped back as Violet, her German Shepherd puppy that Zoe and Leo had rescued along with Max, bounded gamboling happily toward her brother as Max cowered away from her.

There was a sharp moment of tension as the two dogs sniffed each other warily, and then Max's tongue lolled out of his mouth, and they started to play together on the lawn as the leash was tugged out of Zoe's hand.

"We should arrange play dates for them," she said. "Max is the closest thing to a grandchild I've got."

Zoe watched the dogs, stoically ignoring her mother's comment as she walked into the house and Zoe followed, the dogs skidding past her on clattering paws.

The scent of lasagna drifted through the house, and Zoe hesitated in the doorway to the kitchen, noting two glasses of red wine on the surface.

"No Phil?" she asked.

"No, he's gone out for the night."

Because he didn't want to see me.

"Okay, well, how big is the lasagna?"

"Oh, you know, not too enormous."

The dish her mother drew out of the oven was big enough for twelve people, and Zoe wished she had brought Leo. He could usually eat enough for three people, and her mom tended to get offended if her guests didn't finish what she'd cooked.

"Smells good," Zoe murmured as they entered the dining room. It was old-fashioned, with a mahogany table and chairs that her mother had had since Zoe was little. They sat down, and Zoe sipped her wine. Her mother was drinking too, which was unusual. She tended to abstain from alcohol, but as Zoe ran her eye over her, there were puffy bags under her eyes that were new and a grayness to her skin.

"This looks good," Zoe said, as her mom gave her a watery smile.

"It's nice to have you over for dinner. Have you seen much of your grandmother lately?"

"Not a lot, no. I think she and Mrs. Bornstein are trying to change the world one day at a time. She's gotten in with Evelyn at the library, which should keep her busy."

Her mother made a snarling sound in the back of her throat and Zoe tensed, ready to defend Gamma from her mother's wrath.

"Evelyn Cooper has been battling cancer for five years, and now she's having to contend with this nonsense about knocking down the library. It's madness!"

Zoe nodded, relieved. "Leo told me the lot behind the clinic has fired up too, so he's dealing with drilling and heavy machinery all day long. Looks like the town is on the up and up."

Her mother sighed, tucking into her food, slicing up perfect little cubes of the lasagna and popping them into her mouth.

"I suppose we should be grateful that there are new properties for people to live in, but not when they're going to wipe the culture of this town away. Those houses will be big, beige boxes, that's all they ever are."

"I was thinking about that. Couldn't they just keep the library as it is, and have it as the first building in the development? Why knock it down—new people might use it and save them all this trouble."

"Oh, well, that's another thing. Evelyn can't talk about it openly because it would be the final nail in the coffin, but the whole library is practically sinking into the river. If it *is* saved, it will have to be moved, inevitably costing thousands to organize. New developers don't want to worry about relocating buildings from the 1950s. They'll just bulldoze it to save money."

"Is Evelyn's health still bad?"

She shook her head. "She's in remission, thank goodness, but this stress won't do her any good."

They continued their meal in silence, the dogs pattering in from the kitchen and flopping down together behind Zoe.

"How are things with Leo?" she asked, surprising her. Her mother even seemed genuinely interested.

"Good," Zoe hedged.

Somewhere in the world, there were mothers and daughters who naturally talked about relationships. They might even speak openly about their worries, insecurities, and fears. But that would never be Arlene and Zoe Fontaine. They just about managed civility on the surface, and that was it. Their relationship had improved over the past few months since Zoe returned to Sapphire, but it would never be openly loving or caring.

"I like Leo," Zoe's mother said suddenly. "He's very polite. You should always trust a man who has a way with animals."

"He's thinking about getting some llamas for the ranch. They're good at fending off coyotes, apparently."

"Oh! Well, that would be wonderful. How exotic. Does he still have that hooligan helping him?"

"If you mean Gus, then yes. He does."

"Why he wanted to take him on, I can't imagine. Once an addict, always an addict. That boy will rob him and run the minute his back is turned."

Zoe didn't reply. She wasn't going to change her mother's opinions on drugs or those who suffered from addiction. It hadn't worked with her own daughter, so Zoe certainly wouldn't waste her breath trying to convince her that Gus was a good kid.

She was fidgeting incessantly in her seat now, her eyes darting about the room whenever she looked up. Zoe was no fool; she knew she'd invited her there for a reason, and it was obvious her mother was dying to get to the point of her visit.

She waited for another few minutes, but when her mother didn't say anything more, Zoe decided to address it head-on.

"So what's this dinner in pursuit of? And don't say you just wanted to see me. I don't buy it."

Arlene's expression was pinched as she sipped her wine. Although she was drinking it, the level had gone down less than half an inch, whereas Zoe's glass was empty.

"It really wasn't about anything... I just..." She scowled, running her fingers over her neck and leaving pale red scratches over the skin. "Have you heard from Mr. Fisher?"

Zoe blinked at her. "*Mr. Fisher?* Do you mean Rick?"

"Mhm." Zoe blinked again as she watched her mother knocked back a mouthful of wine.

"Uh. Yeah. Actually, he's been kind of erratic lately, why do you ask?" she replied carefully.

Her mother's face fell. "Oh. I see."

"What is it?"

"No, nothing. I just wondered. I was supposed to speak with him recently, and he didn't call."

Zoe frowned. "What about?"

"Never you mind."

Zoe frowned at her. It wasn't so long ago that Rick had admitted he'd had a crush on her mom. The twenty-year age gap didn't seem to be a problem for him; in fact, he tended to favor dating older women from what she could tell.

Is Rick dating my mom?

"I'm afraid your guess is as good as mine." Zoe said quietly. "I'm actually planning to stop by his house. Have you been there?"

Her mother's eyes widened comically. "No, I haven't been *to his house.*"

Zoe watched, fascinated, as her mother blushed up to her hairline.

In principle, she had no issue with the two of them getting together. But if it *was* true, Arlene was a long way outside her comfort zone for the first time in her life. Her mom wasn't a woman who went against public opinion. She played it safe, crossed all the Ts, and dotted all the Is. If she and Rick *were* together and it got out, it would give the gossips fodder for weeks.

Zoe ran her eye over her mother's face, noticing the tired and pinched quality of her skin. In any other circumstances, she would have told her that she had spoken with Rick the day before, but she stayed silent.

"If I hear anything, I'll let you know. Did you have a message for him or anything?"

"No," her mother said sharply. "I … I just want to know that he's okay."

"Me too. I'll text you when I see him."

The tension bled slowly out of her mother's shoulders, and the charged air at the table lessened as she returned to her food.

"Thank you, Zoe, I'd appreciate it."

CHAPTER
EIGHT

Zoe didn't hear from Rick for the rest of the week, and as predicted, every task ahead of the print run fell to her. She was in the office until late on Wednesday night, wrangling with a panicked printer, and only just got the final proofs in ahead of the deadline.

What she really wanted to do on Friday morning was rest, but instead, she was headed to the community center on Redman Street. Today was the day of Evelyn's forum on the library's future, and there was no way Zoe could miss it.

Unfortunately, the center didn't allow dogs, so she had to leave Max at home. It was too dangerous him to have to sit in the back of a sweltering car.

She had set up a camera in the living room so that she could keep an eye on him while she was out, but it was one of the few times she had left him in the apartment alone. She was convinced he would chew through everything while she was gone. His mournful stare as she closed the door on him didn't help.

Despite her exhaustion, she was looking forward to the meeting, not because of what would be discussed, but because she knew Leo would be there. It was ridiculous, but it was true.

Her feelings for Leo were complicated. Her high school crush on him had never really faded, and now that they were dating, her emotions were in overdrive. She was falling for him—hard— which was why she was so terrified of things moving forward between them. On the way to the community center, she gave herself a firm talking to.

Do not get carried away.

Still, when she walked into the meeting and saw him standing at the coffee table, she grew a little weak in the knees. There really was no other man who looked better in a plaid shirt, in her opinion.

Leo was talking to a woman with long gray hair, glittering clips pinning it back behind her ears. Zoe assumed it was Paulie from Sparrow Meals. Leo talked about her a lot and admired her way of working a great deal. From his description of her, Zoe couldn't imagine it was anyone else.

Leo glanced over at the door as she entered, and the wide grin that spread over his face made her stomach flip.

Excusing himself, he came over to her—glancing behind him briefly—before putting an arm around her and kissing her quickly on the mouth, moaning quietly in the back of his throat as he did it.

"I missed that this week," he said, and laughed as Zoe turned bright red. "You totally have a crush on me," he said, still chuckling as she placed the backs of her hands over her cheeks—mortified.

"Shut up," she hissed.

He burst out laughing again and interlaced their fingers, tugging her over to Paulie, whose perpetual smile was firmly in place.

"Hey, love birds," she said, punching Zoe lightly on the arm. "You must be the famous 'Zoe.'"

Leo rolled his eyes. "I only mention her once every ten minutes, Paulie, you're exaggeratin.'"

Paulie smiled, catching Zoe's eye and nodding to something over Zoe's shoulder. "You got any idea who that is?" she asked, indicating a man in a dark suit who was already seated at the back of the room. "I figure a reporter might be in the know."

Zoe leaned around her to get a better look at him. Slick hair, slick suit. He was a carbon copy of Mr. Smith from The Matrix—very corporate with a stick up his ass.

"Dunridge probably sent a rep," Zoe said darkly. "I wouldn't put it past them to disrupt the meeting."

"I'll go sit on him if he tries; that'll shut him up."

Leo and Zoe laughed as they followed Paulie to some chairs a few rows back. Zoe had a knot in her chest at the sight of all the empty seats. About a hundred or so had been laid out in the room, but only half of them were full. Barry and Evelyn were in the front row talking together as Lyla and Mrs. B brought them a cup of coffee from the back.

Lyla glanced up as she spotted Zoe and gave an excited wave.

"Your Gamma sure loves politics," Leo said, his hand still loosely holding Zoe's. She had expected him to let go by now. The fact that he hadn't made something joyous unfurl inside her.

Calm down, Zo, keep it together.

They took their seats as Evelyn stood up and turned to the room. The crowd was still sparse at best, and Zoe watched Evelyn's shoulders slump as she took in the gaps in the rows, but the librarian rallied quickly.

"Mornin' everyone, thank you for coming," she said warmly, glancing at Barry who gave her a comforting nod. "I know a lot of you are busy livin' your lives, so the fact that you've come today means a great deal to me."

Her voice was shaking, and as she spoke, her fingers were rubbing together as she fought her nerves.

"I've been working at the library for over twenty years. Barry, for over fifty. We love it, and we believe that it's the beating heart of this community. We not only have people using it daily and relying on the space to get their work and research done, but we also have a huge contingent of young children who come for story time twice a month. We have readers from all over the county involved. It's the best time of day because all you can hear is the laughter of our young people ringin' through the building."

She took a deep breath, taking out some speech cards and putting on her horn-rimmed glasses.

"Dunridge Developments is planning to bulldoze the library next month to make way for new homes on our land. It's gonna be called 'Sapphire Glade' if you can believe it, but in order to create it they gotta knock us out of sight."

There was real anger in her eyes as she looked round at them all, and her voice began to shake.

"This library has stood in Sapphire since 1950. We know this community, we work with it, we plan outreach, we help organize nature trips to the river, and work with the Environmental Services to clear the Panway of waste and the trash that comes our way from Whistle Falls."

Zoe hid a smile as there was general grumbling from the room about their rival town.

"We've stuck it out, through thick and thin, and a lot of change. I know that many people don't think a local library is relevant anymore, but I don't agree. Real human connection is waning from this world. Every day we get more digital, less personal, and what our library gives is a chance for people to connect with one another. They can come to us, hold something in their hands, and talk about it with their community. That matters. Our book club has over seventy members now!"

Her eyes moved to the back of the room, and Zoe looked behind her. The guy in the suit was scrolling on his phone, bored and uninterested, but he looked up in alarm when Evelyn addressed him directly.

"To the man in the suit at the back of the room. I know you're from Dunridge, and you think that we'll either fall silent or back down. But we won't, sir. You come by any day of the week, and you'll see what this community does for each other. We've got a bake sale next Saturday to raise funds, and you're welcome to come and try the produce that real West Virginia folks can create."

She leaned back, giving him a long glare before addressing the rest of the room again.

"Seth Bowen is also organizing a coffee mornin' for us, which is going to be great. He's got a lot of new pastry recipes he wants to try out, and we all know how good his cookin' is."

There was a rumble of agreement as Leo's fingers tightened on Zoe's. Evelyn sighed, her expression turning sad.

"We have to fight for the library, because no one else will. I take care of it, I love it, and I'll keep working for it as long as I can. But we need all of you to support us and sign the petition at the front of this room. That will stop Dunridge in their tracks."

There was a smattering of applause, but Zoe could feel how tense Leo was beside her even as her own shoulders stiffened.

"They don't just got a *hard copy* petition, though, right?" Leo whispered. "That's not gonna do a thing."

"Maybe it's online, too?" she said hopefully.

"Still," he said. "They need *sponsors*, people who'll back the library, put their money where their mouth is. To someone like Mortimer Dunridge, a list of signatures is just red tape he can bulldoze through."

Zoe shifted in her seat as the elementary school principal, Kerry Jameson, rose from the second row and went to the front.

She was instantly more impressive than Evelyn Cooper by her appearance alone. Evelyn had looked visibly nervous, whereas Kerry was sure-footed and certain as soon as she was in front of the crowd.

She wore a pale pink suit that molded to her body perfectly, the white silk blouse beneath making her look classy and self-assured.

"I'd like to second Evelyn's statement and thank you all for coming," she said. "I cannot express in words what the library has done for my school over my tenure as principal. Evelyn and Barry are a bedrock of this community; they do more than just run the library.

"Over the years, I have seen the funding be stripped from them. Evelyn has saved for decades to finally keep it afloat, so that she could make the library the independent cornerstone that it is today.

It doesn't just entertain our children, our community, and support valuable conservation efforts; it represents something that matters more than anything else—our heritage.

"My school has pledged to support the library in any way we can, and we are helping to fund a bookmobile to bring their services to even more people around town. I'd urge you today to sign this petition, and if you scan the QR code at the bottom of the page, you'll find a link to the school's website where you can sign up for updates in our weekly newsletter."

"There we go. Thank God Kerry knows how to appeal to people who aren't in their eighties," Zoe muttered.

She glanced behind her again as there was the screech of a chair, and the suit stood up, his cell to his ear. He gave Evelyn and Kerry a pitying look before leaving the room.

I thought Linmans was bad, but Dunridge seems to be even worse.

Barry was next to speak, taking an age to rise from his chair, but once he started, he was engaging and passionate. He talked about the library's history and how it had evolved and adapted over the years. He was eloquent and sincere, and Zoe could feel the room warming up around her as he spoke.

She was surprised to see Lucas Watt, a local farmer, in the crowd. He and Zoe had almost come to blows a few months before, and he could be cantankerous and irritable, but he was one of the first to sign the petition when the speeches were over. Lucas and Barry shook hands as if they were old friends, and Lucas proceeded to stand at the front, glaring at the crowd, ensuring anyone who attended felt too intimidated to walk out without signing.

The meeting might not have been at capacity, but there were still a sizeable number of signatures by the end.

"I'm just gonna go say bye to Paulie, Zo, I'll be back in a sec," Leo said as he squeezed her hand and walked over to the side of the room.

Zoe signed her name at the base of the paper and scanned the QR code, which took her to one of the best-designed websites she'd ever seen. Kerry wasn't messing around with bringing their little school and the town into the twenty-first century.

"Zoe?"

She turned to find Evelyn standing behind her.

"Hi, great speech," she said, and Evelyn smiled, putting out a hand to move her away from the crowd around the table and to the edge of the room.

"I wondered if you knew of Rick Fisher's involvement in the library," Evelyn said.

"No, I didn't. Has he been working with you, too?"

"Oh, yes. Rick has been an advocate for our work for years. We have archives of The Chronicle going back decades because of his diligence. He has been supporting me and the library since he joined as editor and ensuring that some of the profits from the paper are put into keeping us open."

"That's great!" Zoe said sincerely. "I had no idea."

"I have to confess, the contributions have reduced over the years. I think Rick has been giving us funding from his own pocket, too."

A knot formed in Zoe's shoulders, Evelyn's words serving as yet another sign of how much trouble the paper was in.

"Is it true that he's missing?" Evelyn asked, lowering her voice, and Zoe glanced up sharply, Evelyn's wide eyes making it difficult to look away.

"Well, I don't think *missing*, is quite the right word. He's still working—following leads, that kind of thing," she said warily.

"If you hear anything, would you do me a favor and let Kerry know? She's been worried about him."

Zoe glanced back at the principal, who was speaking with Paulie and Leo on the other side of the room.

"Kerry was asking after Rick?"

"Mm," Evelyn said with a soft smile. "It's not my place to pry, but I believe they might be an item. Although, I don't think Kerry wants anyone to know."

Rick sure gets around.

"Yeah, I'll let her know. No problem. But he'll be back soon."

The words felt hollow, and as she turned to look at Kerry, a low-level panic began to bubble inside her.

If Rick *was* in a relationship with either her mother or Kerry, it was clear he wasn't just missing work but *being missed* by those around him. That suggested that he hadn't just failed to contact Zoe, but had stopped contacting his friends and family, too.

Zoe got out her cell and called his number for the fiftieth time, but it went straight to voicemail.

Bean's words of warning wouldn't stop bouncing around her skull, and she closed her eyes in despair.

Could I have missed something bigger going on? What made Arnold kill himself? Is Rick in trouble?

I'm a reporter. A damned good one. How did I let it get this far?

She was sick of everyone looking to her for answers when she didn't have them, and decided that after the meeting was over, she would go and find some for herself.

CHAPTER NINE

Z OE HEADED TO RICK'S HOUSE THAT EVENING, AFTER
dropping Max off at Leo's.

The Chronicle, having been abuzz with activity the day before, had been as dead as ever when she arrived there on Friday afternoon after the meeting. Bean was his usual self, four cups into his caffeine high by the time she arrived but still worried about Rick.

She spent the day calling Rick every hour, even sending him an emergency text to test if he'd get back to her.

A bit of digging into his information from Bean showed that Rick didn't have an emergency contact listed in their system, and Zoe remembered from their youth that his dad was a deadbeat, and he was estranged from his mother.

Does Rick even have any family to check on him?

As soon as she was done for the day, Zoe punched the address into her GPS, surprised when the route sent her out of town toward Whistle Falls. Rick lived further out than she'd imagined, and she was embarrassed that she hadn't already known that.

She had spent so much time being irritated with him over the past few weeks that it hadn't occurred to her that he might be struggling until now. She felt foolish for not having recognized the signs and set off as quickly as she could, hoping against all odds that he would be at home, and she could finally get some answers from him.

Rick's place was right in the middle between Sapphire Valley and Whistle Falls. It stuck out as the only house on a long country road that wound up a gentle slope into the mountains. There were thick trees on either side, and a wide turning just before the bend, which made it easy to miss.

A little sign on the drive read "Fisherman's Cottage," and Zoe wondered if it was a coincidence that Rick's last name was Fisher or if the house had been named after his family.

A jolt of shock ran through her as the drive emerged ahead. *I've been here before.*

When she and Rick had been running the high school newspaper together, Zoe had visited his house a couple of times to work on their articles together. It seemed all memory of it had been erased until that moment.

The house was much the same, although the drive up to it had been resurfaced recently. There had been gravel stone and more than a few potholes in her youth.

It was a two-story house with an ugly brick chimney along the near side wall and white wooden slats across the front, similar to the library.

The porch might have been homey with some color added to it, and the odd chair or two, but there was nothing. Zoe bit her lip—it looked abandoned. And she was beginning to fear the worst.

She got out of the car, noting no lights were on in the house, and walked up the stone path to the front door. Two handrails jutted out from the porch, flanking some cracked stone steps, but the dark grey wood beneath her feet looked recently swept.

"Rick?"

There was no reply when she knocked on the door, and Zoe waited, stepping back down onto the driveway to have a look at the upper windows of the house. The curtains were drawn, and nothing was moving. She felt sick.

"Rick?" she called again. The land around was silent, even the sounds of the woods behind were strangely absent.

Zoe strained her ears for the creak of a board inside the house, or the shuffle of feet as he moved around, but couldn't hear a thing.

Glancing behind her, she checked the road for anyone driving by, but it was far enough back that no one would notice her unless they stopped and came down the drive themselves.

Reaching into her bag, she got out the lock-picking set she had brought with her, making doubly sure there was no one in sight before moving to the door.

Many years before, when she had been a naive up-and-coming reporter, it had seemed inevitable to her young mind that she would be breaking into houses every day. So far, she had only ever done it with the owner's permission, and just once successfully.

Here goes nothing.

Bending down and squinting at the lock, she inserted the tension wrench at the bottom of the keyhole, leaving a bit of give against it. Then she added the raked pick, placing it into the top of the lock, beginning to move them up and down until the pick slid along the shear line. After a couple of failed attempts, she was able to pull the wrench to the right with a satisfying click.

Zoe made a mental note to put a bolt on the inside of her front door when she got home.

You just never know who will try and break into your house.

With one last look up the driveway she pushed the door open, poking her head around to see if there was any sign of movement.

A musty smell hit her nose as she peered through the gloom and stepped inside, closing the door behind her.

"Rick? It's Zoe," she called, but there was no answer.

The hallway was short, opening out almost immediately into a small space on the left, dominated by a large circular table.

Zoe let out a long breath as she looked over it. At least her suspicions that Rick had skipped town and taken all his possessions with him were finally assuaged.

The place was a chaotic mess.

It looked like a hoarder lived there, with boxes and old bags piled high on the tables and stacks of paper on every surface.

Zoe stared around her, wondering how the hell Rick lived like this. She moved forward into another short hallway that led to the kitchen. There were a few photographs on the walls, and a couple of Rick. Seeing his smiling face made Zoe's stomach turn over again.

The kitchen was small but well-proportioned and sensibly designed. Copper pans hung from the ceiling, and the black and white checkered floor, along with the duck egg cabinets, gave it an almost feminine feel. But the effect was ruined by the paper scattered over the floor and some of the surfaces.

She frowned. It almost felt as if Rick had been looking for something. Why was there so much paper in every room? Who searched like this?

Zoe took it all in, but as she read over some of the papers strewn around her feet, her confusion only increased. It appeared to be a collection of decades-old tax forms and newspaper articles. Several files were scattered over the floor, upended and thrown carelessly aside.

A small clock on the wall ticked loudly, making it seem even more silent in the house. Zoe shuddered, suddenly wanting to be out of there.

She checked the pantry, the back room where some laundry had been left to dry, and the living room. There was no sign of Rick.

Nervously, she went upstairs, the carpet muffling her footsteps. The house looked small from the outside, but it was much bigger than she had expected.

The bathroom was clear, the shower curtain pulled across the bath, billowing a little as she entered. It took her thirty seconds to build up the courage to pull it back with a violent jerk, convinced there was a man with a knife behind it.

But the bath was full of paper, like the rest of the house.

This almost feels deliberate. Who has a tub filled with paper?

The thought gave her pause as she walked along the landing, the odor of old food getting stronger as she reached the bedroom. There were some plates on the dresser. It looked like the remainder of spaghetti and meatballs.

Every surface was strewn with papers again. The only empty space was the bed, which looked recently slept in.

Maybe Rick really does live like this.

There was an alarm clock on the bedside table and a gray comforter on the bed, with throw pillows on the floor around the boxes.

As she stared at the room, feeling at a bit of a loss, something caught her eye on the carpet. It was a rainbow keychain, and it immediately caught her attention.

Zoe had been collecting similar keychains for years. Her own chain had now grown so long that whenever Leo drove her rental, he would complain that it was getting dangerous as the end of it flapped around his ankles.

She knelt down to pick it up and, as she did so, noticed a Post-it note under the bed.

The word "Zoe" had been written on it, and she grabbed it quickly, looking around for what it might have fallen from.

There were bags of papers and boxes all over the place. She sighed in frustration, realizing that it could have come from anywhere.

For lack of anything else to do, and with far too much in the house to contemplate going through it all, she grabbed the nearest box, placing it on the bed and removing the lid, finding it filled with files.

If nothing else, she could take them and look through them at home. Maybe Rick was trying to give her a hint at where he was—maybe this was a message just for her.

Did he know I'd break into his house? Or maybe I'm just desperate to find a clue in all this.

She picked up the box, staring around helplessly at the mess, wishing she had time to make more sense of it, but the urge to leave was growing by the minute. She wanted to get to Leo's, collect Max, and feel safe again.

Making her way along the landing, she listened for any other sounds, the box cumbersome in her hands.

Gingerly descending the stairs, Zoe paused at the bottom step, her breath hitching as she noticed something she had missed on her first sweep.

On the right-hand side of the hallway, beneath the low window near the kitchen, more papers had scattered from a stack on a low table. It looked as if they had once been neatly piled there, but had been disturbed and fluttered all over the floor.

What Zoe hadn't noticed was that the lock had been forced. Lowering the box to the floor, she walked over to the window and looked outside, but there was no sign of anyone in the yard.

The lock on the window had been ripped completely out of its socket; the splintered wood sticking up at odd angles against the glass.

Zoe looked down at the table and froze.

There was a partial footprint on the edge of it in the dust, as if someone had clambered through the window. She spun round, heart thudding.

Shit, were they still in the house?

There was no way of knowing when this lock had been broken. Perhaps Rick locked himself out and had to break it himself. But something told her that wasn't the case.

Breathing heavily, she decided it was time to leave. Snatching the box of files, Zoe walked quickly out of the house, grabbing a set of keys from a bowl, hoping that they were for the front door and she wouldn't need to break in next time.

Shoving through the door, she headed back to her car, but even as she did so, there was a movement to her left.

Stopping on the porch, she froze in place at the sight of a dark blue Toyota parked at the end of Rick's drive, blocking her exit. It hadn't been there when she had entered the house, and she felt sweat spring up in the small of her back at the sight of it.

All the lights in the car were off.

After what felt like an hour, but could only have been a few seconds, the car's headlights sprang to life and it reversed slowly and unhurriedly, maneuvering down the drive and back to the road before it sped away.

Zoe had never gotten in her car so quickly in her life. She floored it all the way to Leo's, checking her rearview the whole way.

CHAPTER TEN

ZOE GOT TO THE OFFICE EARLY ON MONDAY MORNING, having spent much of the weekend with Leo.

After leaving Rick's place, she immediately drove to the ranch, parking up the road a little way from the house to gather herself before going inside. The last thing she wanted was for Leo to worry about her, and turning up shaking like a leaf would only raise questions.

All the way there, she had been debating whether to speak to him about the events at Rick's house. Whatever was going on certainly needed more investigation. In the end, Zoe decided to keep it to herself. She didn't want Leo involved before she had all the facts. It felt too early to make a call; she would rather give him an informed view than the jumble of ideas swirling through her head.

After that, the weekend had been unremarkable, with much of her time spent at the ranch or in her apartment sorting through more of the boxes.

Rick had never been far from her thoughts, and Zoe prayed when she walked into the office that morning that he would be back at his desk again, laughing at her for all the worry he had caused.

But as the doors swung shut, she sighed miserably at the sight of his empty desk.

If he doesn't show up today, maybe I should tell someone what I saw at his house.

She didn't want to start tongues wagging and would hold off as long as possible before the town was abuzz with the rumor.

Nothing ever stayed private in Sapphire for long, and if Morgan Media, who ran the paper, found out about Rick's disappearance, all hell would break loose. It wasn't just his job at stake, but the jobs of everyone who worked at the paper.

For now, it was better kept buried, but whenever she thought back to that car on the road, her fingers started to shake.

Zoe had been followed before; she'd been threatened before, and what she had witnessed on Friday night made it all come flooding back.

Is Rick being threatened? Is that why he left?

"Zoe?" She jumped in her seat, brought back to reality by the figure of Bean standing beside her desk. "You okay? You've been staring into space for a really long time."

Zoe forced a laugh. "Sure, sorry. Did you need something?"

"I bought you a coffee for once. You're always buying them for me."

He placed it on the desk beside her. "Thanks, Bean. I appreciate it."

"You're here early."

"Yeah, I thought I'd check my email before I headed to the school, want to stop in on Kerry before—" she stopped.

Zoe had been considering visiting the sheriff's department after talking to Kerry. She wanted to make inquiries about the protocol for a missing person and how she might report it—but wasn't ready to share that with Bean just yet.

"Before…?" Bean asked. He was watching her now, his eyebrows raised.

"Before I have more arguments with Anton," Zoe muttered lamely, shrugging a shoulder. "But I'll be heading out soon."

"Why did you need to come in at all?"

"What?"

"The emails. Why didn't you just check them on your phone?"

Zoe paused. "Um… I didn't know I could set it up on my phone. Is that a thing? I thought we were living in the dark ages in this place."

"Hey!" Bean said, looking genuinely offended. "I've been overhauling the email system for weeks. Have you actually read any of the updates I've sent out?"

Zoe cleared her throat. "Uh… of course! I always read them…"

"Uh-huh. Jesus, you try to keep people informed," Bean grumbled. "Give me your phone."

Zoe pulled it from her pocket and handed it over.

"I'll download the app for you. Just make sure any files are saved on the internal servers. Rick was forever saving things to his desktop, and it drove me nuts."

"Rick *saved* things?"

"I know, right?" He handed it back. "Put your work login into Outlook and you'll be able to reply to emails *in the car* and stuff. It's so much better now we've upgraded from chalk and slate."

"Yeah, alright, so I didn't read your emails. I promise I will from now on."

Bean laughed. "Don't feel too bad, Anton doesn't even own a cell phone and Rick's got his password taped to the underside of his desk."

"Of course he does," she said, grabbing Max and her bag as she pocketed her phone. "Thanks, Bean, you've saved me a lot of time today! If anyone needs me, they can call my cell. "

"What am I, your P.A.?" he asked with a smirk, and Zoe blew him a kiss as she left the office.

The elementary school wasn't far from The Chronicle. It was a relatively small building set back from the road, and had been revolutionized under Kerry Jameson's leadership.

Zoe highly approved of the rainbow color scheme as she pulled into the parking space, relieved to see Kerry's car was already in the principal's reserved spot.

The fence had been renovated recently, and each post on the route into the school had been painted to look like a pencil. She smiled as she passed by—Kerry had a flair for style, that was for sure.

The main entryway to the school was unlocked, and she walked into the hall through the heavy doors. It had a high ceiling, breaking into a long hallway with classes off to the right and left.

There was a receptionist behind a glass screen sorting through paperwork, and Zoe hovered until she saw her, looking startled to find anyone in the school this early.

"Can I help you?"

"Sorry to disturb, but I was hoping to catch Kerry before the school day starts. My name's Zoe Fontaine."

"Is this for an article?" the receptionist asked, a little more enthusiastically.

Zoe shook her head. "Afraid not, it's a really quick personal thing, but I won't take up much of her time."

The receptionist waved distractedly. "Don't worry, she's my boss, I'm not hers. You can go on back. She's in Classroom 3A, her office is being renovated right now, just knock and she'll let you in."

Zoe made her way down the hallway, smart gold numbers on the doors on either side leading her to a room about halfway down. She knocked.

"Enter!" came Kerry's voice from inside, and Zoe went in.

Kerry was behind the teacher's desk at the front of the class, next to a stack of reports. She was in another stunning silk shirt, which hugged her figure in flattering curves.

Kerry glanced over as Zoe entered and immediately put down her pen, rising to her feet.

"Zoe!"

Considering they had met briefly weeks before, it was impressive that the principal remembered her name.

"Hi Kerry, I'm really sorry to bother you so early."

"Not at all, come on in. Sorry about the classroom format, I needed my office repainted after a pipe burst. Worst luck."

"No worries, I hope this won't take long."

Kerry came over, and they both lowered themselves awkwardly onto the little desks scattered all around the classroom.

"What can I do for you?"

"First off, I wanted to say I enjoyed your speech at the community center. I really hope they get enough people to back it with all the attention it's getting."

Kerry rolled her eyes. "Dunridge Developments. They couldn't give a damn about the importance of a local library to this community. That place is an institution."

"As is Evelyn," Zoe said, knowing she'd hit the right tone when Kerry beamed at her.

"She really is. Evelyn is a force of nature. Was that what you wanted to talk about? Support for the library?"

"Well, generally yes, because The Chronicle is running some ads for them, but not specifically. I actually came to ask you about Rick Fisher."

Kerry's left eye twitched, just for a moment, and her shoulders lifted slightly as she let out a breath.

"Oh yes? What about him?"

"This is a little awkward, but I wanted to ask whether you and he were... well, an item?"

Zoe expected her to laugh it off, but instead Kerry's expressive eyes grew sad.

"No. Nothing like that. I wondered about it for a bit. We spent some time together earlier this year, but I don't think he was interested in the end."

"Oh,," Zoe said uncomfortably, "I'm sorry. Evelyn told me—"

"Oh don't worry," Kerry interjected with a wry smile. "Evelyn is *convinced* we're together. I'm not sure why. I think she likes Rick and assumes we're the same age, but I must have fifteen years on him."

"I'm not sure Rick cares about that," Zoe said with a shrug.

"No, perhaps not." Kerry gave her a strange look as she curled her hair behind her ear. "But either way, he's a decent man and has wanted to involve the paper in the school for a while."

"Oh really? Was that why you were meeting up?"

"Yes, he took me to dinner, actually." She tugged awkwardly at her sleeve. "Mixed signals."

Zoe scoffed. "Totally."

"Anyway," Kerry said, laughing. "He was asking me about the students. He wanted to add a column to the paper for them to write. I thought it sounded hilarious, considering most of them can't pick up a pen yet, but he wanted me to run some interviews with them. You know—what the young people think about Sapphire Valley and what they want to do. He was going to speak to the principal at the high school, too."

Zoe leaned back on the desk, amazed. Rick had never mentioned any of this to her, and she hadn't heard him speaking about it to anyone else, either.

Guilt flared as she thought of everything Rick had been trying to do with the paper, with his support for the library, and trying to work with the school; it seemed he was far more active in the community than she had given him credit for.

Maybe he isn't as apathetic as he seems.

"Thanks, Kerry, that's really helpful. Did you agree to everything?"

"Not yet. We were going to meet up last Friday, actually, but he didn't show. I was surprised not to see him at the meeting, either. It isn't like him to stand me up." Kerry pursed her lips, her expression hardening.

Zoe schooled her features into a neutral mask. "I'm sure he was caught up in something. When I see him, I'll remind him he was supposed to meet you."

"Thanks, but it'll have to wait until next week now." Kerry's tone was brisk, and she looked a little irritated for the first time. "I'm fairly busy these days."

"I'll be sure to tell him. Thanks again."

As Zoe left the school parking lot, her vague idea about visiting the sheriff's department solidified in her mind as she headed in that direction. Rick wouldn't have missed a full week of work and a meeting with Kerry without a word to anyone. Her earlier paranoia seemed to be well-founded. Something was wrong.

And what the hell happened to his house?

It didn't make sense, and she would never forgive herself if something more serious were to happen. She could either sit on it and protect the paper, and Rick's job, or tell the cops and file a missing person's report, setting the wheels in motion to find him.

CHAPTER ELEVEN

Z OE PARKED HER CAR OUTSIDE THE SHERIFF'S
department, still in two minds as to whether walking
inside was a good idea.

Right now, all she had were her suspicions, but more red flags
were rising each day. Aside from his absence from work, what
worried her the most was that Rick had stopped contacting those
closest to him.

He hadn't been in touch with the myriad of women he was
seeing, including her mother. Those who knew him best were
concerned, and that was before she even considered the state of
his house.

The more she thought about it, the more confused she
became. Someone had broken in, and she suspected they had
been searching for something.

But why was Rick's house in such a state to begin with?

It was almost as if he had left the paperwork there as a deterrent, so it made whatever they were looking for harder to find. But who were 'they'? And what would they have been looking for?

Zoe sighed, checking her phone for the final time, hoping against hope that she might have received a text from him. She had tried two emergencies now, but nothing had come back.

Her last message just said, "I'm going to the police". If that didn't get a response, nothing would.

She got Max out of the back as he yawned widely and clattered onto the asphalt. He sniffed around the tires before peeing against one of them and barking at a pigeon.

As she looked around, she noticed a suspicious lack of other cars in the lot. None of the cop cars were parked in the vicinity, and that was unusual, even for their sleepy little town.

No one was in the office, not even the receptionist.

Walking into the bullpen, there were no deputies at their desks. Max sat at her feet, sniffing excitedly in the air, before walking over to a trash can and hauling out a burrito. It took her a minute to wrestle it off him, and when she stood back up, she held in a groan at the figure standing in an office doorway a few feet away.

Sheriff Kissinger had a coffee cup in hand and was eyeing her with his usual expression of derision and irritation. Zoe gripped Max's leash a little tighter but wasn't about to run away like a frightened little girl.

I'm not sixteen anymore. He can't intimidate me.

"Sheriff," she said, nodding her head at him.

"Fontaine."

They stared at each other in silence. The only movement came from a small fish tank behind one of the officers' desks, where the usual solitary goldfish had been joined by a black companion perpetually circling each other.

"Where is everyone?" Zoe asked.

The sheriff pushed himself off the doorframe, sipping his coffee and walking toward her. It was so quiet she could hear the squeak of the gun in his holster.

The tension in her shoulders quadrupled as he approached, his eyes never leaving her face.

"Thought you'd be down there, what with you bein' a reporter and all."

Zoe frowned. "Down where?"

"You mean you haven't heard?"

She scowled. "Obviously not."

"There's a protest down in the town today, sprung up like daisies overnight. I hadn't even heard about it. But then Evelyn Cooper always hated me, so she wouldn't have wanted my deputies gettin' word."

"A protest about the library?"

"Yep, causin' all sorts of problems," he rocked forward onto the balls of his feet, taking another sip of his coffee.

Zoe inhaled discreetly, trying to get a scent of what was in the cup. The sheriff hadn't had the best record of staying sober on the job in recent weeks.

"Is that where Walker is? I was hoping to talk to her," she said quietly.

"*Deputy* Walker is in charge of keepin' the peace, yeah."

"Why aren't *you* down there?" Zoe asked, and it came out more accusatory than she'd intended.

To her surprise, Kissinger didn't bark back his answer; he just shrugged a shoulder.

"I'm up for retirement soon, plus I only just got here from Abbotsville. Better to get Walker into the meat of a thing or she won't learn what it's like."

Zoe nodded. "Right. Sure."

Her voice was toneless. She had already spent more than enough time in his company and was desperate to escape. Zoe could sympathize with Evelyn Cooper; Kissinger was easy to dislike.

She turned away, pulling Max behind her, and had one hand on the door before the sheriff stepped forward, clearing his throat.

"Listen, Fontaine," he said, his voice softer than usual. "I wanted to… uh, thank you."

Zoe froze, spinning in place and meeting his gaze. "Come again?"

Kissinger scratched at his jaw; his cheeks faintly pink as he shrugged his shoulders again.

"Walker told me you agreed to keep things quiet about… my behavior a few weeks back."

Zoe bit her tongue, holding in the tirade she wanted to unleash. Kissinger hadn't just been drinking on the job; he'd driven drunk, arrested an innocent man who looked at him the wrong way, and almost flattened her when he'd collapsed a few feet from where they stood.

She wanted to throw it all back in his face and tell him exactly what she thought of his *behavior.* But his expression made her hesitate.

It isn't everyday Sheriff Kissinger apologizes to me, after all.

"I've stopped drinkin', if you care. And I won't touch another drop rest of my life." His eyes were earnest and dark. "I appreciate you coverin' for me. You didn't have to, and I know you been through a lot with how things have been lately."

Zoe's gut clenched as her eyes skittered across the office to where Deputy Stanfield had once sat. The man had been crazy, deranged, and if it hadn't been for Zoe's investigation, he would never have been brought to justice.

There were a thousand things she could have said, and she was tempted to say a lot of the more immature ones, but instead she nodded.

"I'm glad you stopped drinking. That's a good call."

Kissinger snorted. "Yeah, well, don't got much choice. Wife chewed me a new one for almost losin' my job, so it's just green smoothies and water from now on."

Zoe didn't smile, watching as Kissinger's eyes moved to Max and his throat convulsed on a swallow.

"Is that… Is that the dog you rescued from…" his voice trailed off.

"Yeah. He was one of two puppies Stanfield had been torturing in his cabin. I gave his sister to my mom."

Kissinger stared at Max, chewing the inside of his cheek, and slowly crouched to the floor, offering his hand. Max eyed him warily, not moving for a little while, and then slowly he stepped forward and allowed Kissinger to stroke him briefly between his ears.

The sheriff got to his feet again.

"Glad he's got a better life now."

Without another word, he turned and headed back to the office, and Zoe pushed through the doors behind her.

Maybe it wasn't an apology for all that had passed between them, but it was a start.

She left her car at the station and walked down to the protest. Now that Kissinger had told her about it, she could hear the faint sound of voices raised on the wind.

The library was on the edge of the town, but as she made her way down the hill, she could see a crowd of protesters standing right in the center of Jefferson Street.

Cars were backed up on all sides, and it looked like whoever had picked the site of the protest had chosen well—it was stopping traffic from all areas of the town.

Jesus, this must be giving Walker quite the headache.

Zoe had seen a couple of protests in the town when she was younger, but all of them had been about government bills that were passing, with protesters setting up camp outside the town hall.

This one wasn't as big, but it was definitely causing more tangible problems.

She approached the crossroads, just up from the main square of the town. Tony Waldron could be seen on the corner, staring at the crowd like they'd lost their minds, smoking his pipe and talking to some other townsfolk. He was wearing a fishing hat with several hooks adhering to it as if he were about to cast a line and fish one of the protesters out for his own amusement.

Looking at those assembled, she estimated there were about thirty people sitting in the road, holding signs and placards, with Evelyn Cooper the only person standing in the center.

Zoe glanced around, searching for Barry. Eventually, she saw him, sitting in a wheelchair, eating an ice cream. He grinned cheerfully at anybody who shouted at them as they went by, particularly the motorists. She hid a smile.

At ninety, I guess he doesn't care about much other than local causes and ice cream.

Moving further along the street, she took in the scene with interest.

Max ducked between her legs as Evelyn started shouting over a megaphone into the crowd, and Zoe stopped to stroke him. His whole body was shaking, never comfortable with too many people and loud noises.

Glancing around, she headed to the side, ascending the steps of the Sapphire Café so she was slightly raised above the rest of the crowd.

Most of those watching were passersby, and there were blaring horns on all sides from the cars that had wanted to drive through the town. The whole of Jefferson Street was shut down, and Evelyn looked on top of the world.

Every few seconds, she would shout "Save The Library" and hold up her sign, and all the people on the ground would chant it back at her.

"Pretty effective, wouldn't ya say?" came a voice behind her, and Zoe turned to find Seth leaning in the doorway of the café, watching them all with an amused expression.

"I guess," she said, smiling warmly as he presented Max with a pup cup, and the puppy jumped up to devour it. "How's business?" she asked.

"Pretty good, considerin'! Evelyn kind of gave me a heads up."

Zoe laughed. She was pleased that Seth was being a little friendlier today, and he stroked Max as the dog licked up the last of the treat.

"You reporting on all this?" he asked.

"Well, I wasn't planning to, seeing as I didn't know it was happening, but I think we should get some people down here."

"Don't reckon you need to, isn't that one of your people?"

Zoe followed the line of his arm as Seth pointed into the crowd. She grimaced as she saw Anton sitting *with* the protesters, his bag and notepad by his side as he chanted along with the rest of them.

"Oh, God, yes, it is. Looks like Anton's playing 'reporter' again." She passed Max's leash to Seth as she noticed her grandmother at the front of the group. "Is there any chance you can watch Max for a few minutes? I just noticed someone else I need to speak to."

Seth laughed, taking the leash. "Your Gamma is my best customer. Ever since you introduced her to Chai lattes, she comes in every day! Go easy on her."

Zoe rolled her eyes. "Of course she does."

As Max whined behind her, she walked down the steps and made her way through the crowd toward two women sitting on the ground. Lyla and Mrs. Bornstein were dressed in matching pink jackets, holding their signs and beaming at the crowds.

Zoe increased her pace as she noticed her mother stalking toward them on the other side of the ring, and they both reached her grandmother together. Her mother looked incensed.

"Mom!" Arlene shouted over the sound of Evelyn's chanting. "Would you get up and let these people through? You have shut down half the town! Three of my patients have been stuck in this jam for thirty minutes."

Her grandmother looked up at her daughter, completely unfazed.

"Well then, they can join the cause! If they don't need a hospital it can wait."

Arelene bent down and tried to tug Lyla onto her feet. Zoe bit her tongue to keep from laughing as Mrs. Bornstein linked their arms together, preventing her from doing so.

"Mom," Zoe said gently. "I'm not sure that'll help."

Arlene looked at Zoe irritably before leaning around and waving at someone in the distance.

"Officer? Can't you move these people?" she demanded, as if Lyla wasn't her own family.

Deputy Walker's bulky form appeared by Zoe's side. She had gotten to know her well, and they often had a pretty good rapport, though at that moment Walker looked more stressed than Zoe had ever seen her.

"Dr. Fontaine, would you step back, please?" Walker said. "We'll be moving them on shortly, and I wouldn't want you to get tangled up in everything."

Arlene's mouth fell open in shock as the officer practically barged her out of the way, coming to stand alongside Lyla and Mrs. Bornstein. The deputy watched the crowd as horns blared from every direction.

"Hey Zoe," Walker muttered over her shoulder, nodding at her.

"How's your morning going?" Zoe asked blithely, and Walker rubbed a hand across her forehead.

"Yeah. Swell."

"You can't move us!" Lyla protested. "We're not doing anything wrong!"

"Ma'am this is a public right of way," Deputy Walker said and there were several boos from the other protesters.

Zoe noticed Nancy Ashwood, Leo's receptionist, sitting amongst them. Nancy tipped her hat at Zoe—it looked like it had been made from an American flag.

"The library is a *public right of passage!*" Lyla snapped back at Walker. "Community's no good if you have nothing holding it together."

Walker sighed, her thumbs tucked into her belt as she surveyed the world around her, looking faintly lost.

"What are you going to do?" Zoe asked as she took in the bodies all over the road. Some of the protesters were beginning to lie down.

"I could hose 'em," Walker said pointedly, and Mrs. B gripped Lyla's arm all the tighter. "But I think it might be easiest to talk to Miss Cooper about all this."

"When did it start?" Zoe asked.

"About fifteen minutes ago. Came right out of the damn blue, I was having my bagel, feet up on my desk and a nice quiet mornin.'" She scratched her head beneath her cap, blowing out a long sigh. "That's off the record," she said, squinting at Zoe meaningfully.

"I'm just a bystander today, don't worry. Actually, I came down here to talk to you."

There was a particularly loud blare of a horn from a side street, and a middle-aged man dressed in a suit leaned out of his window and started screaming at Evelyn.

"Jesus, someone's gonna get run over," Walker muttered. "What did you want me for?"

"I wanted to talk to you about a missing person," she said, nervous at the reality of what that meant.

It'll be all over town before sundown.

Walker's gaze sharpened. "A missing person? Who?"

Before Zoe could answer, there was a scream from one of the protesters as a truck in the traffic lurched forward within an inch of a woman's back, almost hitting her, and suddenly the crowd was moving.

People rushed forward, the loyal townsfolk rising up to protect their fellows. There were shouts on all sides as deputies descended out of nowhere.

Zoe grabbed her mother and dragged her backward as three people almost knocked them down, running toward the cars. Horns blared, people screamed, and there were a lot of curse words thrown about.

Lyla and Mrs. B didn't move a muscle, nor did the rest of the protesters. The town formed a protective ring around them, and now the deputies were hemmed in, standing between those seated on the ground and a ring of people protecting them from the cars.

"It's kind of beautiful in a weird way," Zoe said softly, looking at the loyal community coming together as Evelyn stoically continued shouting into her megaphone.

Zoe noticed someone flitting around the edges of the crowd, crouching down and leaning around people at an odd angle. She smiled as she recognized Tom, the paper's freelance photographer, snapping pictures of it all.

This is going to make one hell of a good front page.

"You're filing a missing person's report?" Arlene asked, snapping Zoe out of her thoughts as she turned to her, eyes wide with concern.

Zoe sighed. "I'm not sure what else to do. I'm assuming you haven't heard from Rick?"

Arlene shook her head. "The last I heard, he was headed to Charleston."

"What? When?"

"He said he wouldn't be gone long. Had to go and find something out."

"Okay. Did he say where?"

"All I got was a photograph on the morning when he arrived, but I haven't heard anything from him since."

"What was the photograph of?"

"Pancakes."

Zoe stared at her. "Rick sent you a picture of pancakes?"

She watched her mother's cheeks flush. "He sent me a picture of the breakfast he was having when I asked him how he was doing."

Zoe stared at her incredulously. "Mom, is there something you want to tell me about you and Rick?"

Arlene sniffed. "No. Not at the moment," she said. "But I'm worried, Zoe. Really worried. I think something might have happened to him."

Zoe stared at the crowd as the noise volume tripled. Deputies were trying to get protesters on their feet, but no one was cooperating.

They both shuffled back as Walker barged through, hollering at one of the deputies to stop pulling at a woman's coat.

"Could you send me the photograph? I think maybe Walker has enough on her plate today without filing the report, and if we know where he was headed, maybe I can find him."

Arlene looked at her with soft gratitude flickering at the back of her eyes. "You're going to look for him?"

"He missed a print run. He never does that."

Arlene nodded. "I've been trying to remember who he said he was meeting, but I can't recall."

"If that changes, you tell me. I'll head out tomorrow morning. This has gone on long enough."

CHAPTER
TWELVE

AFTER SPEAKING WITH HER MOTHER, ZOE COLLECTED Max from Seth and made her way through the protesters to speak to Anton.

"Finally come to join the party, huh?" he asked, looking up at her. Max lay down on the ground, cowering between her legs, and Zoe knew she needed to get him out of there as quickly as possible.

"Anton, what are you doing here?" she asked. "Are you actually taking part in this?"

"I saw everyone assembling and thought I would take some notes."

"Uh-huh, and the fact that you're the *account manager* and not a journalist didn't occur to you?"

"You see any other journalists around?" he demanded.

"Have you called anybody?"

Anton stuck out his chin stubbornly. "No. I don't need anyone else. I'm here, I have eyes, I can take enough notes and write an article just like anybody else."

"But it isn't your *job*," Zoe said irritably, as Max began to whine loudly.

"I'm using my initiative," Anton snapped. "What are you doin', other than terrifyin' that poor animal?"

Max was shaking now, the shouting from the megaphone and the chants of the protesters making the whites of his eyes visible. Zoe picked him up, rubbing at his belly, and he went meek in her arms.

"I'm calling Daniel," she finished lamely as Anton scoffed, continuing to jot things down on his notepad.

"You do that, boss!" he muttered sarcastically, and Zoe hastily made her way out of the ring of people and away.

Tom was on the edge of the crowd, crouched on the ground, and getting a shot of Evelyn hanging from the streetlight. He was completely bald, all of his hair choosing to grow on his chin, with huge, beefy arms and legs. He looked like a Scottish highlander and lumberjack all rolled into one.

"Anton givin' you grief?" he asked, standing up as he checked the shot.

Zoe lowered Max to the ground carefully, but the dog scrambled up into her arms again and wouldn't let her put him on the ground.

"He wants to write the article about this," she said testily, aware she probably shouldn't rat on Anton, but too frustrated to care.

"Yeah. Don't let him do that. He tried last year once, and Rick had to rewrite the whole thing. Anton'll never let you see what he's writin'. And then when he submits it, it's just a load of political rants."

He checked the camera, flipped through the pictures, and showed her the final one. It was a brilliant capture, Evelyn shouting into the megaphone, arm raised as the crowd surged around her. It made it look like half the town had shown up for the protest.

"Awesome work," she said genuinely. "Thanks, Tom."

"Heard there was an intervention last week, sorry I wasn't there, I was at The Globe shootin' the mayoral campaign. Anything I need to know?"

"Just keep taking pictures and we'll keep printing them," Zoe said distractedly as Max tried to claw his way over her shoulder. "I need to get this mutt out of here, drop me the images, will you?"

"Course!"

She headed back toward the sheriff's department, Max shaking like a leaf the whole way.

Zoe attempted to get him into the back, but he wouldn't let her lower him to the seat, whimpering every time she tried. It was enough to break her heart.

"Okay, buddy, it's alright."

In the end, she walked over to Leo's clinic, carrying Max. He was still shivering violently by the time she reached it, and she had to carry him inside.

Nancy was at the protest, and the reception desk was unmanned as she entered, but as the door swung shut Leo appeared, his head poking around the door of his office to see who had arrived.

He smiled broadly when he saw her, and then his brow furrowed as she approached him around the back of the desk.

"What's happened?" he asked, as Zoe tried to hand Max to him and he yelped so loudly she winced.

"I don't know, I went down into town. Kissinger told me there was a protest going on, and I was just trying to make sure we had someone on the ground recording it all. Is Max okay? He was really scared. I shouldn't have kept him there so long."

Leo's face morphed into what Zoe liked to think of as his "vet frown."

"Come through to room five, I've got a patient in ten minutes, but Nancy should be back soon."

"Yeah, I doubt that. Last I saw, she was lying on the road, refusing to move, with a deputy trying to drag her onto her feet."

"Oh, great," Leo muttered under his breath and moved them into the clinic room. It was small and enclosed, and Zoe could feel Max beginning to relax as the door shut behind them.

"I'm sorry, buddy," she said, tears welling in her eyes.

His little body was curled in on itself, and as she tried to pull him away from her, he whimpered again, his breathing shallow and panicked. Zoe looked at Leo anxiously.

"Was it just the protest that set him off? Or somethin' else?" he asked, his fingers moving to Max's mouth and checking his gums.

He listened to his heart as Zoe stroked over Max's warm fur, guilt consuming her for putting him in that position.

"I didn't think about it. He's always scared whenever there are lots of people. I didn't realize it was getting worse until he wouldn't let me put him in the back of the car."

Zoe's breathing hitched as she held back a sob, panic flooding her that she might have made Max sick from not acting quickly enough.

Leo's arm instantly came around her shoulder and held them both tightly against him.

"Hey, hey! It's alright. Zoe, it's okay. He's scared, but he's not in shock. He just got spooked, like fireworks. What we're gonna do is get him warm and somewhere real quiet so he can come down from the adrenaline high, alright? It's okay. It's not your fault."

Zoe wiped at her eyes, kissing Max on the head. "I'm sorry, buddy," she whispered.

"Come on. Let's get him a blanket, you can hole up in my office for the rest of the afternoon, and then I'll take us all home. How does that sound?"

Zoe nodded as Max's breathing began to calm down. "Thanks, Leo."

"Let's get him checked out, and then I've got some treats for you, buddy, okay?" he smiled mischievously at Zoe, soothing the tension in her body. "I might even have a lollipop for you, too, if you behave yourself."

Leo had given Max a mild sedative to get him to sleep, and the dog spent the afternoon curled around Zoe's feet under Leo's desk.

She had never felt guilt like that and vowed not to take him to such an environment again. It was the first time Zoe had seen a dog close to complete shock, and the shivering had been so violent she'd hardly been able to keep hold of him.

She was still on edge when she sat at Leo's desk and opened her email on her phone, dreading what new disaster might face her in the office that day.

Thankfully, there was an email from Daniel letting her know he had arrived at the protest shortly after Zoe had left. He had already written up his article, and now she just had to deal with the politics of explaining to Anton that whatever he wrote wouldn't get to print.

Damn you, Rick, you owe me bigtime for having to deal with all this shit.

After locking up the clinic, Leo drove them back to his ranch as they decided that Zoe's rental could stay in the sheriff's parking lot for the time being.

When Leo discovered she planned to leave for Charleston the next day to look for Rick, he was even more insistent that she stay for supper.

Half an hour later, she was curled up on the couch with Max in her lap, scrolling through her phone while waiting for dinner to be cooked.

The smell of fish pie wafted through the room, and the sound of pattering rain on the roof calmed them both. Max sighed heavily as he settled further into her thigh.

She stroked along his nose, watching the puppy's eyes take in the room around him. The trust in them made her chest ache.

At the sound of his food bag opening, however, his ears pricked up, and he hopped off her lap as if everything was normal. Zoe could see the relief on Leo's face as he scampered over to his bowl.

"He's eating, that's a really good sign."

Zoe went to stand over Max, both she and Leo watching the puppy consume the food at breakneck speed.

"I sometimes wonder if I should be concerned that he doesn't seem to chew," she said, a little smile flirting at the corners of her mouth.

"You doin' okay?" he asked, pulling her against him and squeezing her shoulders as she nodded, leaning into his gentle warmth.

"Yeah, I guess it just brings it all back, where he came from and what he went through."

"What you *both* went through," Leo said darkly.

"I just feel stupid."

"No, you're not allowed to feel stupid. That's forbidden from here on out. It's like people. Stuff's triggerin'. You don't know it's gonna hit until it does. When I came back from Afghanistan, I didn't realize what my triggers were until I took out the trash one night, the lid fell off, and before I knew it, I was flat against the earth like a sniper was after me."

Zoe looked up at him, frowning. "I didn't know that."

"It's a lot better now, been years since I was out there, but it took me some time to realize what I needed to avoid. Couldn't go anywhere too loud for a long time. I get where Max is comin' from on that one. You have to experience things to understand them, and now we know—crowds aren't a good idea until he's a bit older."

She put her arms around his waist, pulling him against her more forcefully, and he chuckled, resting his chin on her head.

"You stayin' the night?" Zoe stiffened immediately, and Leo huffed a laugh. "You know, we don't *actually* have to do anything, right? We can just cuddle for the next fifty years."

Zoe snorted. "Fifty years, huh?"

"I plan on livin' a long life, I could use some company," he said casually, and Zoe gave a high sound of protest as his shoulders began to shake with laughter. She pulled back, gripping his collar and pulling him down into a kiss.

"You're an idiot," she said, with feeling.

But as Leo leaned back, their eyes connected, and the heat in them made Zoe's breath hitch. In the next second, he lowered his head and captured her lips again in a gentle kiss.

Zoe didn't pull back, caught in the moment, her lips parting as his tongue gently pushed against hers. Both of them froze in place, the intimacy of it taking them by surprise. Then Leo's hands came around her body, pulling her more forcefully against him.

He moaned, low and quiet in the back of his throat, and the sound set a fire inside her.

Suddenly, they were plastered against one another, Leo deepening the kiss, their hands moving all over their bodies as Leo lifted her, depositing her on the kitchen counter and stepping between her legs.

Zoe gasped as he gently bit her bottom lip, pulling her against his body more forcefully as the kiss became even more intense—

And then Gus opened the front door, stamping his feet loudly as he dripped rainwater all over the mat.

They both stopped moving as Leo pulled back from her with a wry smile, his pupils blown, the sexiest look she had ever seen on his face.

But the mood between them evaporated instantly as he let her go.

"Dinner!" Leo said, giving Zoe a knowing look as she hastily jumped off the counter, and they pretended that nothing was going on as Gus tramped into the room.

"Did you get the chickens away?" Leo asked.

"Yeah. Is it true they're cannibals?" Gus said as he crouched down to pull off his boots.

Leo lifted the fish pie out of the oven and placed it on the side, looking at him quizzically.

"Uh, well, if you mean do they sometimes eat their eggs, then yeah, it can happen. But not usually in a healthy flock. Why, you seen somethin'?"

Gus shrugged. "One of 'em was actin' weird, and she was under the hut peckin' at one of them eggs. I wondered about it."

"Hm, she might be injured. Sometimes they do that. Thanks for tellin' me, I'll have a look at her tomorrow."

Gus nodded with a half-shrug. It seemed to be his default position. His first answer to most questions was "huh" even if he had heard you, and his general response was a shrug or a shake of the head. As a result, he didn't come across as particularly intelligent, but Zoe suspected he was much cleverer than he appeared.

"You want some pie before I take you back?" Leo asked, and Gus's eyes lit up.

"What kind of pie?"

"Fish," Leo said, grinning.

"Yeah. That sounds good."

Zoe went to help get the plates and cutlery out and was surprised to find Leo smiling down at the pie happily.

"What?" she asked.

"Nothing, it's just Gus doesn't usually ask what kind of food I'm serving. Up until today, if I gave him rusty nails, he'd eat 'em. The fact that he's askin' about it, having a preference–that's like a normal kid."

She smiled, bumping her hip against him. "You're too hard on yourself, you know. You're helping him every day."

Leo blew out a breath. "I guess. A lot of the time, he just doesn't seem happy to be here."

Zoe glanced back at Gus, who was on the other side of the room, crouched down beside Max and tentatively scratching behind his ears.

"If you imagine how many things in his life must have been taken away from him, how nothing could have been permanent in the last few years, you can understand why he wouldn't want to get attached to anything—or anyone. I think it's just taking him some time to trust you."

Leo pulled her against him again, kissing the top of her head. "Thanks, Zo."

The dinner was quiet, as it generally was when Gus was present. Zoe and Leo talked shop for a while, Zoe bemoaning the endless tensions in the office while Leo complained about the noise from the lot, and the total lack of response he'd had from the site manager.

But Gus only seemed to start listening when Zoe began to talk about Charleston.

"I was wondering who Rick might have been going to see," she mused. "Mom doesn't know. But I was thinking, if it was a contact he needed to speak to—and he hasn't told anyone who it is—then it can't be something he wants to advertise. I thought I'd start downtown and see where I end up."

"And the only lead you have is a diner?" Leo asked.

"Well, Mom sent me the picture of the pancakes, and it said 'Smiley's Diner' on the plate, so I'll start there."

"That's on the west side."

Both of them looked up at Gus, who was staring at his plate.

"Oh yeah?" Zoe asked. "Is that a good area?"

Gus gave her a sympathetic look. "Uh. Not really."

Zoe remained quiet, raising a subtle finger at Leo to keep him from asking any follow-up questions. After a short pause, Gus finally made eye contact with her.

"Is your friend wantin' to hide?" he asked.

A chill crept over her skin. "I don't know, maybe. Is that what people do when they go to that part of town?"

She'd been to Charleston a few times as a teenager, usually to visit her grandmother. More recently, it had been to see her sister Judy in rehab. The west side wasn't a place she knew.

"I reckon I know that diner," Gus said thoughtfully. "A buddy of mine was livin' around there for a while."

Zoe hesitated, hoping she wasn't about to blow the conversation out of the water.

"Was your friend living on the streets?"

He nodded. "Yeah. The boulevard ain't so bad, though. It's just off the highway."

"That's where my GPS said it would be. Anything you can tell me about the area?"

Leo gave her a warning look, but Gus seemed willing to talk.

"West side's kinda different dependin' on where you go. But there are a lot of vacant buildin's nobody really cares about or checks on regularly. I know 'cause I lived in 'em."

Leo's fingers flexed around his knife, his jaw tightening.

"There's a lot of motels and hotels in that strip," Gus continued. "He could'a stayed near there, I would say. That's where I would go, if I didn't want nobody to know where I was."

Zoe was excited at finally having a lead, and she smiled at him gratefully.

"Thanks, Gus, that's really helpful."

"You sure you should be goin' up there alone?" Leo asked.

Zoe fought back the angry dismissal she wanted to launch at him and nodded.

"I'm just going to look around. I doubt I'll be able to find him without more information. But if anyone at the diner remembers him, it'll be a start."

CHAPTER THIRTEEN

SMILEY'S DINER WASN'T WHAT ZOE HAD EXPECTED.
From what Gus had told her, she had anticipated a run-down building filled with truckers, bad coffee, and grease. But instead, it was situated near a bridge of the Kanawha River, and the neighborhood was a pleasant surprise.

It had clean lines, smart buildings, and zero trash. There were some green spaces dotted about, too, and nothing sinister.

Zoe felt a surge of hope—*maybe Rick is just hiding here, and I'll find him and bring him home.*

She parked in a spot opposite a row of bars that were shut up for the day, with the diner along a side street down a narrow alley. She was hungry... no, she was starving.

Zoe had left Max with Leo, not wanting to make the dog even more jumpy by taking him on a long car ride.

She'd woken up in the guest room, with Max over her legs, wishing she had spent the night with Leo. It felt so comfortable and homey at the ranch that her anxiety spiked instantly; her brain imagining a future where she felt settled and happy for the first time, only for it to be ripped away from her.

With that thought in her head, she had leaped out of bed and headed out on the road.

Every move she made in their relationship felt like a misstep, and she was already berating herself for not waking Leo to say goodbye.

Zoe got out of the car, jogging across the road to the alley, and went along a whitewashed street. It was paved in an uneven patchwork of sandstone, littered with drain covers beneath her feet that looked as if they had been there since the 1920s.

It was still early, and when she reached the door, she could only see one other person seated at a table inside.

It certainly didn't look like somewhere she would have expected to find Rick. Other than his strange obsession with Skittles, Rick was quite a foodie and had always enjoyed a high-end dining experience. This place didn't look like it would cater to anything but a beige palette.

Zoe sat down, pulling out a menu and looking around with interest. The black and white checkered floor reminded her of Rick's kitchen, but there were scraggly remnants of tinsel hanging in crescents along the window. The decorations looked as if they were there all year round and were visibly caked in grease. Dark brown chairs flanked black tables, and the tiles beneath the service window were chipped and cracked as if someone had taken a hammer to them.

Who were you meeting here, Rick?

A fresh-faced waiter eventually appeared from the back, twisting his long, violently curly hair into some sort of order as he approached her. There was a spike through his ear and black eye liner around his eyes, but his smile was bright and welcoming.

He walked over with a spring in his step. Zoe watched him, caught off guard by the enthusiasm that seemed to exude from him.

"Morning!" he said, with a thick New England accent. "I'm Connor. What can I get for you today?"

"Oh, thank you, I'll have the pancakes, please," she said, handing him the menu. "And the biggest coffee you have."

She couldn't get a read on him. He had a sachet to his hips that might suggest he was gay, but she didn't want to assume anything.

How many people are just one thing these days? A little flirting couldn't hurt.

"Thanks so much." She flashed him a grin, and his eyes dipped down to the neckline of her shirt before he returned the smile and sauntered away.

Zoe pulled out her phone to look at the photo her mother had sent. It looked as if Rick had been seated at the far corner when he'd taken it. There was a long crack in the linoleum that was just visible in the picture, and by the play of light over his food, he seemed to be opposite the windows.

The pancakes didn't take long, and the same waiter returned to the table to deliver her food, as a few more customers trickled in. The diner was clearly well frequented by regulars—there were even photos of some of them on the walls.

The pancakes were fluffy and covered with far too much syrup for Zoe's tastes—*yep, I get why Rick would order these*—but her hunger won out as she looked over them.

"Thanks," she said as the waiter gave her some cutlery wrapped in a napkin. "I was wondering, could I ask you something?" she said.

He cocked a hip to one side, crossing his arms over his chest as he waved to an elderly woman who walked in.

"Sure! You want an autograph?" he asked and then winked at her.

"Are you famous?"

"Oh yeah. I'm about to hit the big time. I play in a band here on the first Saturday of the month. Come check us out."

He handed her a little laminated card with an illegible font all over it and a *lot* of glitter.

"I'll do that," she said, placing it beside her plate and forgetting the name of the band immediately. "I don't suppose you were working here last Tuesday, were you?" she asked.

He thought about it for a second before nodding. "I think so. Why, were you here? I think I'd have remembered you."

Zoe grinned. "No, not me. But a friend of mine came in. He kind of looks permanently hungover and doesn't have a great sense of style?"

"You just named every man who ever walks through those doors, honey."

Zoe ran a hand through her hair. "He would have been about my age, brown hair, might have had a suitcase with him?"

Connor shrugged. "Sorry, I don't know. There were a lot of people that day—there was this parade thing happening, so we had a million walk-ins. Do you need anything else?"

"Uh, no, that's alright. Thanks, though."

He wandered away, and Zoe deflated. Now she had a breakfast she didn't want and no further information on what Rick might have been doing there.

She cut into the pancakes morosely and tried not to grimace at the sickeningly sweet taste. It wasn't even ten o'clock, and she was going to have a sugar crash by eleven.

The coffee was strong, though, and she savored it as she sat back in her chair watching the customers come and go. It was busier now, with about five or six people around her. They were a strange mix of older couples and businessmen. It wasn't just the waiter she couldn't get a read on—the whole diner felt off, as if it was trying to be something it wasn't.

"You know, you're in luck," Connor said, stopping by her table again with a plate in each hand. "I usually have a super terrible memory; it runs in my family. But I do remember a guy like you mentioned, now I come to think about that day."

"Oh yeah?" she asked, trying not to sound too excited.

"So, I don't really remember *him*. Kind of fades into the background, huh?"

"Sounds like him."

"But I remember the woman he was with. She was really tall and had *amazing* red hair. Almost down to her ass, coppery, shimmery, I was *dying* over it."

"And they were meeting each other?"

"Yeah, not for long. Maybe fifteen minutes. He had the pancakes too, I only remember that because I've never had to give someone two extra helpings of syrup before."

He gave a little shudder and headed back to the kitchen.

Zoe stared ahead of her, pondering what Connor had told her. Rick had said he had "one last thing he needed to do".

How many girlfriends can one man have, for God's sake?

Picking up her phone, she scrolled to the picture her mother had sent her, trying to work out if there could have been someone else opposite him in the photo, but it was a cropped close-up and revealed nothing new.

Even though Zoe had no proof that her mother and Rick were seeing one another, it didn't sit well with her that he had been meeting another woman that day. Zoe disliked the idea that he had been unfaithful, in whatever capacity that might have been.

She drummed her fingers on the table, craving toast now that she had had her fill of pancakes.

Scrolling through her phone, she called Bean.

"Hey, boss, good timing!" he said as he picked up. "Everyone's fighting."

Zoe frowned. She could hear raised voices in the background. "Where are you?"

"At the office."

Zoe rested her forehead on her hand. "Jesus, seriously? Are people coming to blows?"

"No, but Anton is having fits that you're not letting him publish his article about the protest. Good call by the way, he's basically a fascist."

"Bean, I know where your desk is in relation to Anton's. Would you lower your voice?"

"Whatever. I hate the guy, and he was rude to you."

"Thank you for the support, but while I'm not there, please just ignore them all and call me if anyone actually gets knocked out."

"Why are *you* calling me?" he asked.

"I need you to help me with something," she said, wondering if this was yet another mistake.

"Is it to do with your wild goose chase?"

"You mean me being the only one trying to find out where our editor has gone?"

"Yeah, that," he said cheerfully.

"Yes."

"Oh, thank God. I am so bored, I may die. What can I do for you?"

Zoe sighed. "So, you know how you said Rick's password is taped to the underside of his desk?"

"I do remember something of that nature, yes."

"Okay, can you get into his computer for me?"

There was a long silence on the line, and then the background sounds changed, as if Bean were moving.

"I have been waiting for this day. This is my moment. I'm basically Tom Cruise."

"Bean, I just want you to go into his email and see if you can find any recent hotel booking confirmations. They'd be for somewhere in Charleston. Don't do anything else."

"I can't renew his porn subscriptions for him, then?"

"Gross, and no. Please don't read anything you're not supposed to," she said firmly.

There was some tapping through the phone, and then a male voice piped up in the near distance.

"I don't know, Anton," Bean said in his usual bored drawl. "... Because I need to check if his machine has a virus ... No, I haven't heard from her ..."

There was the sound of rapid typing and then Bean sighed.

"Sorry about that. Anton's on the war path. I'll keep him quiet for as long as I can. Good thing he doesn't have a cell, huh?" There was a final decisive click. "Okay, I'm in. Give me two seconds."

She waited, a knot of tension forming in her shoulders.

"No hotel bookings I can see, but he might have booked those on his phone like someone born in the twenty-first century."

"Funny. Anything else?"

Another long pause. Zoe was relieved to hear that the shouting seemed to have eased in the background.

"Has Anton calmed down?"

"Of course. He left in a huff. That man has the maturity of a seven-year-old. Basically, if something doesn't go his way, he storms off."

"That tracks," she said wearily. "Is anyone crying or throwing things?"

"Other than me? I didn't get my morning coffee from you this morning, so I'm about to kill someone."

"Please don't do that."

He sighed again, dramatically. "Alright, fine. You're no fun. Ah, here's something."

"What is it?"

"Hm, I'm not really sure. It's a video file, but I don't get why he would have it. It's weird. It can't be relevant to where he is."

"Okay, send it over. I'll take a look."

"Pinging it to you now."

"Thanks, Bean. What makes you say it's weird?"

Bean's voice lowered considerably. "It was sent anonymously; on the day he disappeared."

CHAPTER FOURTEEN

B EFORE THE FILE COULD COME THROUGH, ZOE HAD TO hang up the phone. The Wi-Fi in the diner ran at a glacial speed, and it took an age for the attachment to arrive.

Her palms were sweating. She rubbed them against her thighs, frowning at the dewy moisture that ran along her jeans.

Maybe I'm more worried about him than I thought.

Above a string of emails from Anton ranting about his article not being submitted, Bean's email finally popped up.

At first glance, it didn't look like anything out of the ordinary. The sender was listed as anonymous. She zoomed in to check the details, but it was one of those 'Apple Hide My Email' addresses, which looked like a cat had walked across the keyboard.

The email contained a single video file. No subject line and no message.

I hope Bean hasn't just sent me porn as a prank.

She double-clicked on the file, and a video loaded onto her phone screen after a few seconds. Just in case it was unsavory, she angled her body away from the rest of the room, watching the white circle spin in the center of the screen.

Finally, it loaded. It was a black and white image from CCTV. The video depicted a three-lane highway with no discernible signs on the edges of the road.

The camera was positioned high up, so that the whole highway was in view, but the picture seemed distorted. Zoe squinted at it, wiping her phone screen futilely to try and get a clearer picture, but it remained pixelated.

As she examined the picture more carefully, she noticed the sky was dark with clouds. There was a chance the distortion was created by rain, but it was hard to tell.

With clammy palms, she clicked the play button, hoping she wasn't about to witness a fatal crash or something equally unpleasant.

The video began to play; it was short, only about a minute in total. She watched as the image remained the same for ten seconds or so, and then a car approached, going fast toward the camera in the other direction.

The distortion became clearer as she watched its headlights stream by, and she realized the footage was filmed in the dead of night.

She kept watching as another car came into view. It was driving at a more sedate pace away from the camera, and as she zoomed in, it looked like a classic Chevy pickup truck.

Her brother briefly had one in college, and the shape was unmistakable. It had a white stripe down the side, but the color of the vehicle's body was impossible to discern in black and white.

The Chevy continued driving up the road, reached the turn, and then the video stopped. Zoe played it again, confused, watching it in full three times before she went back to the email.

There were no other clues in it, and no explanation as to what she had just seen.

Opening the video again, she watched more closely this time, trying to see something—anything—that she might have missed. But it was, as it appeared, a truck driving slowly along a highway.

On the top left, almost invisible due to the pale background, she noticed a year—2017—but there was no other timestamp.

That in itself was unusual; most camera footage included the date and time on it. It almost looked as if someone had added the year after the fact.

"What were you looking for, Rick?" she whispered, attempting to put herself into the mind of her boss.

Who would have sent this to him, and what did they hope he might see in it? Watching the truck move across the screen made her think of that silent car outside Rick's house.

What the hell is this all about?

Sitting back in her chair, she sighed, her neck aching from being hunched over her phone. As the waiter passed, she held out a hand and he stopped, looking down at her, his eyebrow raised.

"Did you need more coffee?" he asked.

"No. Thank you for your help with my friend. I don't suppose you remember if they left together, he and the redhead? Did he take her somewhere after?"

He shook his head emphatically. "No. They argued. Or I guess argued's the wrong word, but it got heated, and then she stormed out. He definitely didn't go after her. I figured they'd just had a fight."

"Thank you," Zoe said, staring at the tired tinsel as it buffeted the window. "Just the check, please."

When she left the diner, she looked up and down the wide, straight road that ran along the river and waited for inspiration to come.

For the eighth or ninth time that day, Zoe wished she had spent time getting to know Rick better. If she had understood him, perhaps he would have talked to her and prevented this from happening at all.

It certainly didn't make him easier to find when she had no idea where to start looking.

She glanced at the diner and up the little alleyway, which ended in a dead end about fifty yards ahead. Gus had told her that his friend used to sleep around there, but she couldn't picture it.

Gus must have been there a few years before, because the area around her now looked on the verge of gentrification. She had read that the west side had pretty high poverty rates, but like a lot of cities, you could turn a corner and suddenly be in an affluent area just after you'd been walking past blocks of low-income housing.

Heading to her car, she picked a direction and started driving, dialing Leo.

"Hey you," he said as he answered. "You get there okay?"

"I did. I just had the most disgusting breakfast of my life; I need to come to your house again so you can feed me."

"I'll cook you breakfast any time you like. I enjoyed waking up with you this morning."

There was a pregnant pause, and Zoe shifted nervously. "Sorry about that, I didn't want to wake you."

"You mean you were freaking out about staying the night in the guest room again?"

She glared at his name on the car screen as Leo waited for a response.

"I guess I was."

"You know all I want is to spend time with you, right?" he said.

"I know."

"Alright, this isn't a conversation for the phone, so tell me what you found out."

"It's been scintillating so far. I met an androgynous waiter who saw Rick, or a man who could have been Rick, meeting up with *another* woman. Rick sure gets around."

"He was on a date?"

"No, apparently, he argued with a redhead and then left the diner. But I'm pretty sure it was him, I just don't know who *she* was. Are you with Gus?"

"Actually, yeah. I thought I'd bring him to the clinic to see if he vibes with any of the animals."

"And?"

"Well, he's fixed a bug on my computer that's been giving me issues for months and just showed Nancy how to print labels from the printer. So he's her favorite person."

"Wow, he's good with technology. Maybe that's his calling."

"Well, it sure ain't chickens. Did you need him for something?"

"I was wondering if you could ask him where he would recommend I start looking. Anywhere that there are hotels or motels that he thinks someone might hang out."

"Are you going door to door? That'll take weeks."

Zoe ground her teeth at his superior tone. "Do you have a better idea?" she snapped, and there was another silence on the line. Her stomach clenched.

"No, I guess I don't. Hey Gus, Zoe for you."

Gus came on the phone, and they had a monosyllabic exchange about where she could start searching. There were several streets running parallel with the river where the less classy motels were situated, and Gus reckoned she might have some luck there, but he sounded skeptical.

Zoe knew it was a fool's errand, but what other options were there? She had no leads.

When she hung up, she felt a sense of hopelessness and misery. Gus hadn't returned the phone to Leo because he was 'with a patient', but Zoe thought Leo just might not have wanted to speak to her after she snapped at him.

In the end, it didn't matter what Gus had told her—she saw Rick's car parked outside a motel about fifteen minutes after the end of the phone call.

Horns blared behind her as she skidded off the intersection and bounced over the bumps and potholes in the road as she came into the lot beside the motel.

She jerked to a stop beside Rick's car, her heart pounding wildly as she launched herself out of her rental, somehow expecting him just to be sitting in the driver's seat waiting for her. But the car was empty.

Slamming her palm against the roof, she looked around the entrance to the hotel. It was a classic, boxy design—rundown looking—with a dusty, empty parking lot. It was strangely situated in the middle of a huge space, but with no other neighboring buildings.

And thank God, or I might not have seen it.

The hotel was a rectangular shape, with dark red brick on the bottom and peeling white paint on the upper level. A grimy awning threw shadows across the lot as she took in the vending and ice machines on the far wall and a few abandoned bikes without wheels at the corner.

Rick's car was parked outside room 221, and it looked as if the hotel had keycards for the doors, rather than keys.

Not gonna be picking those any time soon.

She walked slowly along the path beside the rooms. There were six on this side of the ground floor, probably six more on the other—twenty-four in total, and any one of them could be Rick's.

She hoped the receptionist was absent, lazy, or easy to bribe.

Heading to the far end of the little path beside the rooms, an open door on her left read 'Management'.

She poked her head around, looking at a soulless wooden desk, beige tiles with a 1970s design, and a glass block wall on either side that should have let in some light if the hotel had been designed with the staff in mind. Instead, it was dark, gloomy, and depressing.

The woman behind the desk was like a parody of someone out of the 1980s. She could give Nancy a run for her money for her clothing, and the extensions on her nails were as long as Zoe's fingers.

The second she looked up, Zoe knew she was going to be a problem.

"Morning!" she said brightly. "I'm Zoe, I was wondering if I could book a room?"

Heavily lined eyes looked her up and down. "We're full."

"Oh, really? I just assumed there was a room available from the vacant lot."

The receptionist sniggered. "Uh-huh. Well, the lot don't fill up because people take the bus into town. We get a lot of workers here. Construction. They book 'em out in bulk."

Zoe leaned against the desk. There was a sad-looking fern beside her in a pot, the leaves curling in on themselves, seconds from disintegrating all over the floor.

"So, there's nothing available?"

The receptionist flicked a page of her magazine over. "That's what I said."

"I'm pretty sure a friend of mine is staying here," Zoe continued, deciding that offense was the best defense. "That's his car out front."

"Well, that ain't nothin' to do with me. He paid. That's that."

Zoe glanced over the edge of the desk, noting the computer screen was blank, as was the notepad and guest book beside the woman's arm.

Why is she saying this place is full when I can see the keycards stacked behind her?

"We work together, and I was hoping to talk to him. Could you tell me which room Rick Fisher is staying in?"

"We don't have anybody here by that name."

"You know all the guests' names by heart?" Zoe asked dubiously, and the other woman glanced up at her with a look that could kill.

"We don't got nobody here by that name. We don't got no rooms. Try The Ivy down the road, they got plenty of vacancies."

Zoe hovered, uncertain what else to say and trying to think of a new line of questioning, but came up blank.

"Okay, well, thank you anyway," she said evenly and headed outside again.

The sun was hot on her shoulders as she stood in the doorway and walked back to her car, taking off her jacket and glad she hadn't dragged Max all this way. He'd be baking in the back seat all day with barely a chance to get any exercise.

She leaned against the hood of her car, looking up at the hotel and wondering how she was going to find Rick. At least it wasn't hundreds of rooms, but she didn't relish going door to door. A lot of people who chose motels like this did so for a reason—they didn't want to be disturbed.

"What were you doing in a dump like this?" she muttered.

Glancing up at the sun, she got back in her car and drove it around to the other side of the building into the shade where she could watch the office.

The receptionist would have to leave at some point, and when she did, Zoe could creep inside without her being any the wiser.

For the moment, she was content to wait.

CHAPTER FIFTEEN

ZOE HAD NEVER BEEN KNOWN FOR HER PATIENCE, AND after twenty minutes, she was already growing bored and irritated as she thought about the receptionist's rude attitude.

She decided to take matters into her own hands, Googling the hotel and dialing the number before she could overthink it.

Predictably, the receptionist picked up after the phone had rung several times.

"Oh hi," she said, affecting a high-pitched Texas drawl. "I'm sorry to trouble you, but I'm stayin' at one of the hotels down the street, and my husband just told me he can see smoke comin' from one of the upper floors. Is there someone lookin' at that?"

Zoe hung up a minute later and held back a smile as the receptionist ran out of her office, far faster than she would have expected her to be able to move.

Getting out of her car, Zoe pushed the door closed silently and ran into the office, hoping that the receptionist would go to the upper floor and wouldn't return too quickly.

Jumping up onto the counter, she supported her weight on her arms and pushed at the mouse, relieved when the monitor sprang to life, showing the booking system.

It was an archaic screen, probably from the late nineties, with a dark gray background and multicolored boxes representing which rooms were booked. There were thirty in total, and only five of them were red. The dates when they had been booked were displayed beneath the boxes. She squinted at the log, her heart leaping with excitement as she saw that only one of them had the previous Tuesday as the booking date.

Leaning further over the counter until her feet lifted off the floor, she grabbed at the box of keycards, lamenting the terrible security system, and sifted through them, finding one of the master keycards in under a minute.

Pocketing it, she hopped back onto the floor and headed back to her car.

Poking her head round the door she was just in time to see the receptionist descending the rear stairs. She sprinted along the wall and back to her car, concealing herself around the corner and waiting for the receptionist to return to her desk.

Once she was gone, Zoe moved around the rear of the building and up the stairs. Rick's room had been marked on the system as the second floor, and she kept her footsteps as light as possible as she ascended and walked along the balcony.

She knocked quietly, hoping that by some miracle, a rumpled-looking Rick might open it, and all of this would be over.

There was no response. She knocked again. Nothing.

Praying that the key card would work, she hovered it over the black box on the door. There was a faint click, and a green light flashed as it opened.

Inwardly giving herself a high five, she slipped inside, and flipped on the light switch.

Zoe stared around her in disbelief, a sick feeling growing in her stomach.

The room was ransacked.

This time, it couldn't be explained away by endless files or boxes covering every surface. Rick's belongings were sparse, but every drawer had been opened, the mattress tipped up—and his clothing was scattered over the floor.

A knot of tension began to throb between her shoulder blades as she stepped over the clothes and papers lying on the carpet. Refraining from touching anything, Zoe crouched down to try and read what was written on the documents.

Several of them were in Rick's handwriting, which was illegible at the best of times, but on top of that it seemed to be in some kind of code. It didn't look like English, and she couldn't decipher it.

She stood up, moving sideways and stepping over everything in her path, covering her hand with her jacket, as she pushed the bathroom door open. Rick's toothbrush was still in its holder, his shaving kit on the side. There were even tiny pieces of his beard scattered over the sink, as if he had just evaporated into thin air.

Swallowing around the bitter taste at the back of her throat, she turned, looking around the room to see if there was any clue of what he might have been working on. She moved through the wreckage, stepping over a printout of his hotel reservation—Rick was a stickler for keeping hard copies of everything.

A solitary wrapper from a packet of Skittles lay in the trash, and Zoe's breath hitched as she looked over the carpeted floor beside it and saw a dark brown stain.

She stopped moving immediately. It was blood.

Glancing around the floor, she saw drops of it everywhere. A large patch was concealed by a piece of paper, and she pushed it aside with her foot.

The blood stain beneath was stark against the carpet, but there were no stains on any of the papers above. That meant the blood had splattered over it before the room was searched.

"Shit."

Zoe pulled out her phone. Her fingers shaking so badly she almost dropped it.

This was beyond her pay grade—she had to call the cops.

Before the cops showed up, Zoe had no choice but to come clean to the receptionist about her inelegant break-in. Hiding the keycard, she made up a story about the door being ajar when she'd arrived.

But it was clear the other woman didn't buy it.

"Were you the one who gave me that bogus story about the fire? Because you could go to jail for that."

Zoe rolled her eyes, too worried about Rick to concern herself with all the laws she'd broken.

The two cops who eventually arrived were a middle-aged man and his younger partner. After a quick sweep of the room, the sight of the blood spurred them into action. They immediately cordoned off the area, telling Zoe to sit tight until the detective arrived.

Her attempts to explain who Rick was and what she was doing there fell on deaf ears. The receptionist asked to speak to one of the officers privately, and Zoe scowled at her, certain that more trouble would come from her deception before the day was out.

She waited on the ground floor, one officer flanking her, occasionally speaking into his radio. The sun was hot and unpleasant, and Zoe looked longingly at the ice machine, wishing she had something to drink.

Eventually, a car drew up and parked on the other side of Rick's. A detective got out, his badge hanging around his neck with a pristine white shirt contrasted against dark slacks. He looked up at the hotel, but she didn't see his face fully until he turned around.

He stopped when he saw her, one hand on the car door as Zoe's blood pounded in her ears.

"Nate," she breathed, as he pushed his door shut and came around the side of Rick's car. The years fell away in an instant.

It was the same stride, same crooked smile. Nathan Lombardi— someone she had never expected to see again.

He was tall, lithe, and slim, but with a smaller build than Leo, a thick head of dark brown hair flopping over his forehead.

"Holy shit. Zoe Fontaine," he said, removing his sunglasses. "Are you the one who called this in?"

"Yeah," she said, recovering herself, and for a second they just stood and stared at each other. "You made detective?" she asked, finally.

He opened his hands wide so she could see his badge. "I sure did. How've you been?"

"Uh… good."

"You still living in D.C.?" His voice hitched on the words, a faint accusation in the question. Zoe picked at her thumbnail, shaking her head.

"No."

He scoffed, running a hand through his hair as he sobered, glancing up at the hotel behind them.

"What's going on, then? I got a report that this was a break-in?"

The officer beside her cleared his throat. "The break-in was by *Miss Fontaine*, according to the receptionist."

Nathan smirked, glancing at Zoe with a knowing look before he turned to the officer. "Alright, brief me and we'll go up."

The two men bowed their heads together, the officer glancing back at Zoe as he spoke.

Eventually, Lombardi slapped him on the shoulder and came over to her, his eyes less friendly than they had been, but then he smiled, shaking his head.

"You picking locks again, Fontaine?"

Zoe bit her lip. "Not exactly. I was kind of desperate. I'm looking for someone, and I need to know what happened to him. I let myself into the room but didn't know what I was looking for until I saw the blood."

"You touch anything?"

"No," she replied carefully.

"That's my girl. Okay, well let's go and see what we got."

Lombardi's whole demeanor was different from the cops. He didn't have their lazy saunter to his gait, but a stride of sharp purpose.

In under a minute, he was standing in the center of Rick's hotel room, looking around at everything as Zoe stood outside watching him.

He whistled. "That the blood?"

"I think so."

"And who was it exactly who was staying here?"

"His name's Rick Fisher, an editor at the Sapphire Valley Chronicle."

The detective looked up sharply. "Sapphire Valley? Isn't that your hometown?"

"Yeah."

"And you're looking for him because ...?"

"He's missing."

Lombardi stepped back over the papers and stood over her, his dark green eyes assessing as he raised an eyebrow.

"Fontaine, are you telling me after swearing you'd never set foot in that town again, that you're actually *working* there now?"

Zoe fidgeted. "Things change."

He gave a high bark of laughter. "Jesus, Mary, and Joseph. Ain't that the truth. You pissed off the manager something proper, by the way. She's ready for me to arrest you for breaking in here."

Zoe didn't move, waiting to see if he was serious.

Lombardi sighed, shaking his head. "Look, I don't want the paperwork, but any other detective would bring you in."

"I *discovered* the crime scene. I know stealing the key was bad, but he's been missing for over a week, and I'm really worried."

"Is there a report filed?"

Zoe sighed. "No. I didn't want to get him in trouble with the higher-ups at the paper. I thought he might be holed up here— maybe lying low. Someone's clearly after him."

Lombardi put his hands on his hips, assessing the room again. "Could'a done it himself."

"Why would he do that?"

"Well ain't that the kicker," he said.

The detective locked eyes with her, and for a moment she was caught in his gaze, touched by the concern running through it. Then he looked back at the room, the connection snapping like a chord under strain.

"So, you followed him here. What do you think happened?" he said.

"His car's out front. This isn't like him. He wouldn't just up and leave without telling anyone. Why would his car and his toothbrush still be here?"

"Receptionist says she hasn't seen him since Thursday last week."

Zoe crossed her arms over her chest. "Isn't she supposed to check in with her guests? What about room service, wouldn't they have found all this?"

"Fontaine, you have been in the big city too long. They don't have room service in a place like this, not on the regular. Most of the rooms probably don't get cleaned at all."

Zoe gestured at the chaos all around them. "This isn't normal, Nate, something's happened to him."

"That's as may be, but we need to get forensics in on this and some information on his whereabouts. We got your details?"

"Yeah, the officer took everything down."

Lombardi pulled out his phone. "Tell you what, you take my number, and I'll give you a call. Not like we need to catch up on the last five years, is it?"

Zoe's mind screamed at her to tell him about Leo, but she stayed quiet, not knowing if it would be weird to bring it up.

She pulled out her phone.

"Call me," he said, and the authority in his voice reminded her of old times.

"Your number hasn't changed?" she asked.

"Nope. Same as ever, just like me."

She scrolled through her phone to his contact details and pressed call. Sure enough, his screen lit up almost immediately. Lombardi grinned, putting his phone into the inside pocket of his jacket and taking one last look at the room.

"This guy who was stayin' here," he said carefully. "He wasn't a boyfriend, was he?"

Zoe laughed. "No. Rick and I were just friends." Her shoulders slumped. "Less than that, actually. More like colleagues, really. But I want to know what's happened to him. If he doesn't come back soon the paper's gonna die on its ass."

Nathan nodded. "Keep your phone on, Fontaine, I'll let you know as soon as I hear anything."

"Thanks, Nate."

CHAPTER SIXTEEN

L EO INSPECTED THE FENCE LINE ONE LAST TIME. THE
temporary pen where his new llamas would be living was
almost finished. He and Gus had spent the best part of
the previous evening securing it all, and it was nearly ready.

The brand-new wrought iron fence was in place between
two tall wooden posts, high-tensile wire wrapped around every
square inch to ensure they were secure. He'd done it double the
height he normally would, uncertain whether they might try to
make a bid for freedom.

There's always a chance the goat'll teach 'em to escape.

But he hoped they'd stay put. Llamas were curious but tended
to remain in one spot. Leo was only getting two to begin with, to
see how they took to ranch life. He was excited about it, loving

that they'd act as his guard dogs overnight, but any new animal was a big responsibility, and he could only hope they would like it there.

His eyes moved over the ranch, the horses grazing in the distance against the gathering dusk. Geese waddled about along the path among the hens that pecked at the ground, and there was a hoot of an owl behind him in the trees.

Clicking his tongue at Max, who was lying at his feet, he checked the gate one final time before heading back inside. The puppy was still jumpy, nervous of him in a way he hadn't been for a long time, and it broke Leo's heart to see his trauma surfacing again.

Bending down, Leo stroked between his ears, and Max allowed it even though his body lowered instinctively to the ground at the contact.

"It's alright, buddy, it's dinner time soon, and then you can get some rest."

Since returning from the clinic, Leo had been walking around the ranch seeing to little tasks about the place. He'd collected Gus that evening and given him a couple of jobs to take care of, but nothing too strenuous.

As he headed back to the house, Leo hoped he might find Gus relaxing somewhere or even helping himself to something in the kitchen without being invited.

Gus didn't touch anything unless he was asked to. He didn't even take a seat unless Leo told him it was alright.

His heart sped up as his phone vibrated in his pocket, and he pulled it out to see Zoe's name on the screen. Grinning, he answered it.

"Hey you, I was just wonderin' how things were going."

"Hey!" There was the sound of a key turning in a lock through the phone. "How's my boy?"

"You mean me or the dog?"

"Max, obviously. I only call you for updates on him."

Leo chuckled, looking down at Max, who was gazing up at him curiously. "It's your mom," he said to him. "He's doin' okay.

We've been takin' care of some jobs and gettin' the pen ready for the new arrivals. I still don't know what I'm gonna call them."

Zoe laughed. "I can't believe you name all your animals. How about Maxine and Maximillian?"

"Yeah, because that wouldn't be confusing. Besides, they're both boys."

"Maxwell and Maximus then." Leo laughed, shaking his head. "How's the drilling?" she asked, and his smile faded.

"Awful. I think it's gotten so bad we might have to close. Or Nancy might murder me, whichever comes first."

"Oh God, is it really that bad?"

"I've been calling the site manager for days, but they're not interested in talking to me. I sent them emails, and Nancy keeps goin' on at me that I won't get anywhere with that, but what can I do?"

"Nancy was born in 1850, that's why. Want me to see if I can pressure them with an article in the paper about it?"

"Isn't that abuse of power?" he asked, but his heart soared that she would offer.

"Probably."

"How's the search going?"

"Not so bad. I found out where Rick was staying." There was a pause as another door closed through the phone. "I ended up calling the cops. At this point, I'm pretty sure he's missing."

"What prompted that?" he asked suspiciously.

"Nothing," Zoe said, sounding too casual to be real. "I just have a hunch."

"So you found something?"

"His car. But the detective needs a missing persons report filed before he can make it official. I need to call the sheriff tomorrow and see if he'll do it retroactively."

"Jesus, I'm sorry, Zo. I know how worried you were about him. Is the detective taking it seriously? They don't tend to care much about us small-town folks."

She cleared her throat. "Actually, I know this detective pretty well, weirdest coincidence. He's a good cop, and I think he'll help."

"You know him?" Leo asked, his gut clenching unpleasantly.

"Yeah... actually, well... he's kind of my ex."

Leo pushed a hand firmly against his forehead, praying for patience.

"Huh," he said as casually as he could.

Zoe snorted. "I'm not going to jump his bones, either."

"Good. I was kinda hopin' to mark your card on that one."

There was a long pause, as he knew there would be. He had never been with anyone as nervous as Zoe about intimacy. She seemed completely terrified to bring it up. It was like being a teenager again.

"I liked sleeping over at your house, but maybe we can build into it slowly and have a midnight feast."

Leo rolled his eyes, but a throb of heat passed through him that she wanted to stay more often.

"Well, I'm glad you liked staying here," he said firmly. "Tell me this… what's his name?"

"Nathan Lombardi."

"Tell this *Lombardi* you're spoken for."

"I don't think I need to, we're ancient history—but I'll be sure to let him know."

Leo's chest loosened. "You at your grandma's old place yet?"

"Just arrived. It smells terrible and needs a good airing, but it's nice to be back here."

"Send me some pictures."

"I will. It's getting late, do you need to be taking Gus back soon?"

"Yeah, I should probably go and find him, actually. Will you let me know how things go tomorrow?"

"Of course, sleep well."

He smiled. "Of course. I'll be dreaming of you."

"Shut up, you idiot." He chuckled as she hung up.

Leo continued into the house, with Max flanking his every step, and found Gus standing in the rear hallway, looking at Leo's military photos.

He slowed, not wanting to spook him, watching as the kid moved along the hallway, taking them all in one by one.

"It's about an hour till I take you back. You want anything to eat?"

Gus straightened up, looking guilty. "Sorry."

"It's okay, you can look at whatever you want."

"You were in the army?"

"Two tours," Leo replied.

Gus's eyes lit up. "Does that mean you know how to fight?"

Leo raised his eyebrows. "Well, I might be a bit rusty, but yeah, I know how to defend myself," he said carefully.

"What about teaching me to hit someone?"

Leo rolled his tongue over his cheek. "Did you have someone specific in mind? Because if you hit Anita, it's gonna cause problems."

Leo smiled as Gus laughed. He had never seen him laugh before, but his whole face lit up, the melancholy in his eyes fading away.

"No. Nobody specific, but I've wanted to know how to fight all my life. I only want to defend myself. I got into a lot of fights on the street."

The fact that he was even sharing that tiny piece of information made Leo happy, and he beckoned him over.

"Come out to the grass, I can teach you the basics. But go easy on me, I'm an old man compared to you."

"What are you, like, forty?"

Leo scoffed. "I'm not even thirty-five yet, you little shit."

They made their way out to the field behind Leo's house, and he set them up facing one another.

"Okay, first thing you gotta realize is most fights aren't choreographed like in the movies. People either know how to throw a punch, or they don't, and a lot of guys just improvise. But if you're wantin' to defend yourself, protect your face, arms up. Like this."

Leo raised his arms in front of him, his fists blocking his face, and Gus mirrored his stance.

"Good, main focus is on your opponent. So make sure you keep your eyes on him. He might be thinkin' about what he's gonna do to you, but you need to be anticipating it as best you can. That way you can see a punch comin' and block it or dodge it."

Gus nodded, and it was the first time Leo had seen him look so focused.

"Keep your feet apart, like this. Firm foundation, but not so firm you can't move when you need to. Use your body weight to make the attack stronger; pivoting on your feet can double the impact of your swing. Try to stay mobile. Once you're on the ground, your opponent has the advantage."

"Can't I just knee him in the crotch?" Gus asked with a grin.

"That's one way to do it," Leo said, "but I think we can manage a bit of finesse."

Leo moved Gus so that he was standing opposite him.

"Come at me, as fast as you can, and I'll block your attack."

Gus frowned at him. "What, like now?"

"Practical always beats theoretical in my opinion."

"I don't wanna hurt you."

"You won't, just come at me as best you can."

Seconds later, Gus was on the ground, and Leo was helping him up.

"Let's try that again."

Over the next thirty minutes, Leo showed him the basics of situational awareness, low kicks, and palm strikes.

"I know you'll want to be Superman and punch them right off the bat," Leo insisted. "But that can break bones, and it hurts like hell—trust me. Slapping someone with a cupped hand or jabbing your palm into their nose as hard as you can is just as effective."

Gus was a good listener and a quick study, and by the end of the lesson, they were both hot and sweating in the evening air, laughing as Gus tried to hit Leo and he blocked him every time.

"You're too good at it!" Gus protested.

"Well, I've been trained to fight. You just started today."

"I've been in fights," Gus said, flexing his shoulders.

"Did you win any?"

Gus's gaze darkened. "A few."

"Well, this way you're not gonna be trying to win, you're gonna try to get away. But you're good, you learn fast."

"My dad taught me," Gus muttered, looking down at the ground again, and Leo chose his words carefully, not wanting to derail the positive mood between them.

"When was that?"

"When I was fourteen."

"Your dad still around?" Leo asked.

Gus shook his head, relaxing and running a hand through his hair, staring at the wide country around them.

"Nah, he died. My mom met someone else. We did *not* get along. I'd have liked to take him out with a palm to the nose, I can tell you that."

"Is that why you ended up on the streets?"

Gus nodded. "I probably could have stayed with a friend in the beginning, but I didn't wanna put anyone out, you know? In the end, I made new friends on the street. It's the cold that gets you, though. I could have survived if it never rained. I don't like the shelter, but Kyle is nice. It's good to be warm again."

Leo flexed his hands, trying to keep his face as blank as possible. He hated that Gus had been through all that alone and was only at the shelter because Leo had intervened with the cops. He sighed, checking his watch.

"I should take you back."

"Can we do some more next time I'm here?" Gus asked.

"I'm not sure I should be encouraging violence in the youth, but yeah. As long as it's defensive, we can do some more training."

"Awesome!"

Leo smiled as they headed back to the house. He whistled to Max as Gus grabbed his bag and they made their way to his truck. They would be cutting it close for the nine-thirty curfew, which even Gus seemed eager to adhere to.

Leo felt a lightness in his chest after their evening together, as if some of Gus's walls had finally started to come down.

Gus sat with Max beside him in the passenger seat, one hand resting on the dog's back, and Max was happy enough to allow it.

Things were moving forward unexpectedly, and Leo was pleased to see the change in Gus. He was more relaxed, more open, even on the short ride over, than he ever had been before. But Leo's good mood only lasted until they drew up to the building.

He got out of the truck with Gus leading him inside but as soon as the doors opened, Max was on high alert. Leo looked down at him in surprise as the dog began sniffing frantically.

He soon found out why.

Just inside was a black Labrador sitting at the feet of a young woman. Both of them looked in a bad way. The woman's skin was pale and pockmarked, the dog's coat in need of a brush with some sores around his joints.

Max backed off as the other dog's stance changed from relaxed to defensive in seconds.

"Hey, Gus," the woman said enthusiastically, coming forward. One of her front teeth was missing.

"Lana! Hey!" Gus embraced her and then pulled back, glancing over at Leo. "You remember Leo, right?"

Leo nodded at her. "Hi, how ya doing?"

He'd met Lana and her dog before, when he had been visiting the homeless community to see what he could do to help their pets. Lana had been on the streets for a while, and when Gus arrived in town, Leo had noticed a rapport between them. He was pretty sure they did drugs together, and his insides shriveled up at the easiness between them.

This can't be a good sign.

"Are you coming to stay at the shelter?" Gus asked her, and the eagerness and excitement in his voice made Leo's chest ache. Lana shook her head, her hands twitching by her sides, skin pale and clammy-looking.

"No. I just came to see you," she looked over at Leo. "Wanted to check you were okay."

"They might have space for you!" Gus said. "I can ask Paulie—"

"No. It's alright. I just wanted to come say hi. I think the boss lady wants me gone, but she said I could wait until you got back. I should probably go. I'm glad you're okay."

She slid along the wall and past Leo, trotting out the door, Bailey following behind her, the bright orange stripe on the side of her jacket stark in the evening light as she jogged over the road.

Leo turned back to Gus, who was red in the face and looking decidedly guilty.

"She come by here a lot?" Leo asked.

"Nah. I haven't seen her for a couple of weeks."

Leo didn't believe him. Gus always got twitchy when he lied. Leo thought back to what Anita had said about the curfew. Gus

142

had been doing something at his window late at night—Leo would bet money that he had been talking to Lana through it. Suddenly, the curfew made a lot more sense.

Gus gave him a vague wave and went back to his room as Leo turned, hoping to find Lana and check on Bailey while she was within reach, but as he went back outside, there was no sign of her. The road was completely empty.

CHAPTER SEVENTEEN

ZOE'S GRANDMOTHER'S APARTMENT WAS STARTLINGLY small when you first entered the space, but the long hallway that led outward from the front door opened into an eclectic room that glittered and shone from every surface.

Lyla's taste was everywhere, from the stained-glass stickers on the window to the crystals hanging from the ceiling. Now that she was back, Zoe could see why it had struggled to sell. The place was way too cluttered to appeal to modern buyers. Zoe still didn't approve of her mother's selling the place, but that argument was a lost cause. And now that Gamma was living with Mrs. Bornstein, it was a foregone conclusion.

As she placed her bag on the kitchen surface, she missed Max's presence immediately. Zoe had never been good at managing silence, and his happy scampering feet and panting breaths had been a soundtrack to her life for several weeks.

The apartment felt barren, despite all of the things on display, and she wanted some company. Dragging her speaker from her bag, she linked it to her phone and set it to a calming playlist, closing her eyes as the soothing music filled the space.

Then, she pulled out the box of files she had brought from Rick's house and got to work. Opening it, she stared at the contents despairingly, at a loss as to what to do.

What are all these files even for?

It was making her more determined to figure it out by the minute.

She pulled out the first bundle and began laying them on the table. Many contained notes from several years earlier, a few receipts, and printouts of bookings and confirmations.

There were old newspaper articles, all of them with different dates, and as she scanned over them, there didn't appear to be a pattern. It was as if Rick had gathered anything he could find and tossed it in.

Maybe he didn't leave me a clue at all. Maybe this is just a coincidence.

But something niggled at the back of her mind that she couldn't shake, and it spurred her on to the bottom of the box and some kind of answer.

Finally, after fifteen minutes, she had everything stacked in piles beside her, but she was none the wiser about what any of it meant.

There were more handwritten notes from Rick, all in the same strange code. Zoe stared at one page for a full minute, trying to make some sense of it, before pulling out her phone to run it through Google Lens.

It came back with a mismatched group of words that had no bearing on anything. She slammed her phone down on the table and sighed heavily.

Right at the bottom of the box, adhering to the side like a leech, was the Post-it she had found under his bed. Pulling it out she stared at her own name, wondering if it meant anything at all or if she was just hoping that it would.

Her finger rubbed over the base of the Post-it, and she felt compressions beneath the pad, as if something had been written on it and made an indentation.

She held it up to the light and felt a surge of triumph when she saw a word beneath her name, only visible as indentations in the paper.

Rummaging in her bag, she pulled out a pencil, placing the Post-it on the stack of paper in front of her, and began to run the lead of the pencil lightly over the base of the Post-it.

Slowly, through the gray strokes of the graphite, some thin white lines began to form. Zoe's chest fluttered as she realized she was revealing a word. Suddenly, Rick's actions didn't feel so random.

After a minute, she leaned back, reading it over and over. It was written in capitals that looked like Rick's handwriting.

DEVORIK

Placing the Post-it to one side, she pulled out the papers written in Rick's code, sorting them into a separate stack, beginning to read through them, energized by this new piece of information.

As she read down the documents, she could see a pattern of sorts, where Rick had used 'real' words now and again, and then coded words where he hadn't wanted anyone to know what he was writing.

There were two written in bold at the base of the page that were legible and in English, which said "The Depot". Turning it sideways, she looked at the other scribbled notation in the margin. "Kevin Munice".

Zoe reread the name, a memory sparking in her mind as she realized she had seen it before.

A few weeks earlier, when investigating the Orchard Grove nursing home, she had stumbled across Kevin's name on an old article in The Chronicle. Scrambling for her bag, she pulled out her notebook, flipping to the right date, and scanning over her notes.

"Article written in The Chronicle around 2015, from perspective of sister. Kevin, her brother, went into the Sapphire Foundation and never came out. Arnold Price, author."

There was that name again. Arnold Price.

Kevin had been a rehab patient at The Sapphire Foundation. And now his name had cropped up out of the blue in the margin of Rick's papers. Zoe slumped into her chair.

Could it be a coincidence?

After all, these papers from Rick weren't recent; maybe they had been notes he'd made at the time. Arnold was once the editor; perhaps they had worked on the story together.

But then, why did Rick not want to tell me about it?

Zoe scoffed. Now, the reason seemed obvious—because he was afraid. Afraid whoever was after him would come for her, too.

She clenched her fists, running her fingers over Rick's handwriting, wishing it could somehow give her a clue as to what he had been working on.

Devorik.

Something told her the name was important, but it meant nothing to her. A quick Google search told her it was an Americanized Czech surname, shared by dozens of people on social media—but none of that gave her a hint as to where it had come from.

She yawned, feeling the exhaustion of the day begin to take its toll, and she knew the next day wouldn't be any easier.

Gathering the papers into a stack, she placed them back in the box. As she did so, a small white square slipped free, impaled on a dislodged paperclip.

She bent to pick it up.

It was a photograph of a young man. He couldn't have been more than twenty. Two letters were scrawled in the top right-hand corner of the picture, "KM", written just above the tips of his fiery red hair.

The next morning, Zoe went to visit Judy.

She'd not spoken to her sister for a few weeks and hadn't seen her in almost half a year. Now that Zoe was in Charleston, it didn't feel right to be on her doorstep and not pay Judy a visit. She was nervous as she pulled into the clinic, the familiar walls making her stomach churn as she remembered the day Judy had arrived.

Zoe was one of the few people in her family who still gave Judy the time of day. She had been paying for her younger sister's care for months out of her own pocket. But there were still days when the anger she felt was impossible to ignore. It had cost thousands to tackle her addiction, and Zoe never knew if she could believe a word that came out of her sister's mouth.

Judy had lied to everyone throughout her addiction, stolen her mother's jewelry, left town, and never looked back. Zoe had taken months to find her before she finally managed to get her into a rehab program.

So far, it was working, but who knew how long it would last?

Tugging at her sleeve, Zoe watched the staff moving inside the building through the windows. Everything looked so calm and peaceful from the outside, but inside were dozens of people just struggling to wake up and get through each day clean.

She got out of the car and went inside.

It was rare for any family member to be allowed back to a patient's room. At first, her visits were always supervised, and she rarely saw Judy alone. Now, in the later stages of recovery, they could meet in the gardens or communal rooms—always with staff nearby. Privacy was a thing of the past.

Zoe took a deep breath before heading into the large lounge area. A few people were scattered around watching TV and drinking tea at the tables dotted throughout the room.

She spotted Judy immediately, her silhouette so familiar it was like a second skin. Her younger sister had always resembled their mother, but was far more beautiful than everyone else in the family. Or she had been, before the drugs had taken their toll.

Zoe moved through the room as Judy turned around, their eyes connecting across the space.

Her long brown hair that had once been thick and glossy was thinner, cut short to a bob that hovered just below her chin. Her eyes were still the color of a stream in spring, pale green-blue that changed depending on the type of light that shone around them.

Zoe was happy to see that the sores that had lingered for weeks on her face had faded now, and her complexion was pale and neutral instead of dry and damaged.

Judy smiled. Her teeth were in better shape, too.

"Yo, Zo," she said as Zoe came to sit opposite her. The two armchairs were modern and comfortable. She had expected nursing home stiffness and depressing chintz everywhere, but instead, the interior of the clinic was light and pale with colorful rugs on the floor that brightened everything up. It looked like the room had had a revamp since she was there last.

"Hey, Judy."

They didn't hug, and Judy curled up into her chair again, a loose-fitting sweater hanging from her slim frame, her feet bare, but there were slippers tucked under the chair on the floor.

"You said you'd drop by, I didn't know if you meant it," Judy muttered.

"Well, I did," Zoe stated. "How are you today?"

Judy inclined her head. "Today's a good day."

Zoe nodded, looking up as a nurse walked past, eyeing them suspiciously until she moved on. A silence fell between them, awkward and stiff. Zoe fought back tears. The first few minutes were always the hardest. It didn't seem real that this was the little girl she had built forts with in their backyard.

"Gamma called me," Judy said quietly. "I know you were pissed about that, so I thought I'd get it out the way."

Zoe shrugged a shoulder. "It's good she's still in touch with you."

"Yeah, well, she doesn't exactly call on the regular, but we speak every other week. I can't have a phone, so that's the best she can do."

"She wouldn't know how to use her cell anyway."

"Gamma said she's paying for this place now?"

Zoe looked up sharply, angry that Lyla would have divulged that information.

"Yeah. She agreed to help me out while I get myself settled."

"And you're in Sapphire. For good?"

"For now."

Judy pulled her feet further beneath her, rubbing at her toes and picking at her nails as Zoe fought a grimace. She'd lost a few toenails; her feet looked gnarled and badly cut in places, even though the scars were all healing.

"What are you doing in Charleston?" Judy asked.

"I'm looking for someone. He went missing a week ago, and his last known location was here."

Judy gave a hollow laugh. "Why would anyone pick Charleston to get lost in?"

"I couldn't tell you."

There was another long silence. Zoe glanced around the room, tamping down the urge to get up and run. The walls were closing in, the sunlight outside mocking her as she watched the other patients shuffle about.

How did it come to this?

"Have you found him?" Judy asked.

"No. Not yet," she said slowly.

"Who is he?"

"He's the editor of the paper in Sapphire. You remember Rick Fisher from school?"

Judy narrowed her eyes, rocking her head back into the chair.

"Oh yeah, the little guy who used to hang around with you doing the newsletter?"

"That's him."

Judy's expression darkened. "He's missing?"

"Yeah."

"Bummer."

Zoe could have laughed at how uninterested she sounded. "I'm only here for a little while. His hotel room was covered in blood, so I'm pretty sure something bad has happened."

Judy uncurled, sitting forward in her seat, always having loved a gory story. Zoe felt guilty for using Rick's disappearance to animate her, but it worked.

"Really? Like a lot of blood?"

"Some."

"Maybe he was kidnapped," she said, as if really thinking about it.

"Maybe. He left me a Post-it, so I've got clues coming out of my ass."

"What'd it say?"

"My name."

"Far out."

Zoe scoffed, and Judy smiled. Finally, the tension between them broke, and Judy leaned back, looking more relaxed.

"I'm sorry you have to come here. It sucks."

"I'd rather this than behind a dumpster."

Judy's expression became cold. "You heard from Mom?"

"I see her quite a bit now. Always a joy. And no, she hasn't asked after you."

"Figures. What about *shit for brains*?"

"Phil also hasn't asked after you."

Judy rolled her eyes. "Why would he? Mr. Perfect doesn't need anyone else except himself in his life."

"Amen to that."

Zoe's phone started to vibrate, and Judy glanced at her bag. "You need to get that?"

"No, it's alright."

"It's almost lunchtime anyhow. But it was nice to see you."

Zoe stared at her, dismayed. "But I've only been here for five minutes!"

Judy's mouth twisted. "What are we gonna talk about, Zo? How well I'm doing? How I'm gonna be out of here any day now and go back to a happy life? I don't think so. Things are the same. Come back when they're better."

Zoe recoiled. Seeing Judy so dejected was like a slap in the face, but she couldn't argue with her logic. Her sister looked better, but she had already been in the clinic for nearly six months and had relapsed twice. It wasn't a case of *when* she would be out but *if*.

I wonder how long Gamma can afford to keep paying for this place.

"Alright, if that's what you want," she said woodenly.

As if on cue, there was a rattle of plates as a nurse pushing a trolley came into the room.

Zoe stood, a hollow feeling in her chest as she stared down at her sister. Judy was small, vulnerable, and fragile, and Zoe was desperate to hold her but knew it wouldn't be welcome.

"You ever heard of something called The Depot?" she asked impulsively.

Judy raised her eyebrows. "Sure, why?"

"I wondered if it might be drug-related."

Judy snorted. "I can see why you're asking me, then, but yeah, it is. It's an abandoned bus stop on the west side of town. It's a place you can go and get pretty much anything for the right price. Why, you branching out?"

"Funny," she muttered. "I think Rick might have been there; he had written it in his paperwork."

Judy stood up. Glancing behind her at the nurses and other patients assembling.

"I know better than anyone that you can handle yourself, Zo, but be careful. They'll see you coming a mile off. You don't look like a customer, so they'll assume you're a cop. You don't want to get on the wrong side of some of those people."

Zoe nodded, and they stared at one another for a long time. After a few seconds, Zoe lurched forward and embraced Judy. She expected to be shoved off, but instead Judy's thin arms came around her shoulders and squeezed her so hard she could barely breathe.

"See you soon," Judy whispered, heading to the tables behind her. She didn't look back as Zoe left the room—she never did.

CHAPTER EIGHTEEN

O N Thursday morning, Zoe woke up disoriented, not knowing where she was. She'd missed two calls from Leo, and the lack of her typical morning alarm—a wet nose against her cheek, courtesy of Max—meant she'd overslept.

Her breakfast consisted of a cereal bar and a pot of long-life milk from her grandmother's cupboard. Her plan to air out the apartment was nixed by her forgetting to set her alarm, and it was already ten o'clock by the time she raced out the door.

Her plan for the day was to go through Rick's belongings. Of course breaking into his room again was probably off the table, being a crime scene and all. Not that she wasn't open to doing so, but she would have to plan it more strategically so she didn't get caught.

Her theory was that the cops would have cordoned off the room but wouldn't necessarily have stationed anyone overnight to watch the crime scene. Neither the cops nor the receptionist had asked her to return the keycard, so it was still in her back pocket.

If she could find out more from the papers in Rick's room, then all the better. At least she had something to go on now.

As she reached the hotel, Rick's car was still in the lot, but there were several others, too. She wondered whether any of them belonged to cops, and decided to play it safe until she'd gotten a good idea of who was watching the place. Nate might have let her off with a warning about the B&E, but he wouldn't look kindly on her tampering with a crime scene.

Avoiding the receptionist and parking around the back, she went up the stairs, keeping an eye out for any lurking cops. As she rounded the corner, however, she saw that her plan had failed before it began. A patrol officer was standing right outside Rick's room, steaming coffee in hand, looking as if he were settling in for the day. Zoe had to duck quickly out of sight before he noticed her.

Damn it, why do city cops have to do their jobs properly?

In Sapphire, she would bet that Kissinger would simply cordon off the hotel and be done with it. She cursed inwardly, wishing that she had taken photographs before she had called the police.

What kind of a journalist am I?

She walked quickly down the stairs and back toward her car but stopped as she heard a raised voice coming from the other side of the lot.

On the edge of the sandy gravel between the hotel and the road, was a Range Rover with a personalized plate. The car was pristine, like it had just come out of a showroom, and beside it stood a huge man shouting into his phone.

Zoe stopped at the bottom of the stairs, watching him curiously.

"I don't care what time it is, Darryl, you're going to wake him up!" he shouted. He was wearing a beautiful suit. From the galas

Zoe had attended throughout her career, she could tell it was tailor-made. The guy screamed money from every pore.

He had rich brown skin and tight curls closely cropped against his head, his beard cut in straight lines against his jaw.

"Because I said so, this place is supposed to be condemned! I have waited months already for this deal to go through, I'm not letting it go to waste because of some bullshit investigation." He hung up, swore colorfully, and slammed his hand into the car.

Zoe crossed the lot toward him, noting that the guy had a driver in the front seat, waiting patiently for his boss to stop ranting and tell him where he needed to go.

"Can I help you?"

Electric brown eyes met hers, and she stopped in her tracks. The guy certainly knew how to command a space.

"I'm one of the guests here," she said loudly. "Did you just say this place was going to be condemned?"

He pocketed his phone and walked over, towering above her, deliberately using his height to his advantage. He looked at Zoe as if she were as insignificant as the dust floating in the air around them.

"You know, it's bad manners for little girls to eavesdrop on people's private conversations."

It was an obvious trap, and Zoe didn't step into it.

She smiled. "Is a conversation screamed into one end of a phone private? It's hardly my fault you can't use your indoor voice."

The guy put his hands in his pockets, looking her up and down. It was hard to discern his age, but he looked like he could be late thirties or early forties. Something told her he was a CEO. An air about him suggested he was used to getting his own way.

"Well, I do apologize, Miss…"

"Fontaine," she said, sticking out her hand, but he didn't take it.

"Ah, that figures. You're the one who got the police called in for some small-time investigation to waste all our time."

"That's me!" she said brightly. "And you are?"

"Not in the mood to be nice when you're delaying demolition of this place until they get a forensic team in. The detective seemed to think it could take weeks, so I imagine you'll hear from my lawyer."

"For reporting a crime?"

"I've sued for less."

Zoe held back a strong urge to roll her eyes. "I'll bet. Is another few weeks really going to set you back enough to make a dent? What are you building? A strip club?"

"Apartments, sweetheart. And they'll be outside your price range."

"Oh, boohoo, I'm just devastated. If you're gonna get pissed because a man is missing, that's your choice, but this investigation needs to happen."

"Exactly," he retorted. "He's *missing*, not dead. I don't see why they have to wait to clear things up. Snap a few pictures, bag up his shit and leave my guys to get to work."

"You're well informed," she murmured.

"I ask questions when things get in my way."

"And right now I'm in your way?"

"Physically and metaphorically," he growled.

"You didn't give me your name."

"No, I didn't. I'm Mortimer Dunridge, and if you haven't heard of me, that's *your* problem."

Zoe's mouth fell open in shock. So this was the guy who was bulldozing the library in Sapphire. Now that she had met him, his focus on such a tiny project made even less sense.

This hotel, she could understand. It was right on the river, next to a main road, and ripe for development in the state capital. Sapphire was small beer in comparison.

"You heard of Sapphire Valley?" she asked.

Dunridge arched a brow. "You know, I would have pegged you as a small-town nobody. I'm glad my instincts are still spot on."

Zoe glowered at him as he chuckled.

"Yeah, I've heard of Sapphire Valley," he continued. "It's becoming a real pain in my ass, actually, but then, I enjoy building on water." He stretched an arm toward the river. "Triples in price when you can see movement out your window. Wouldn't expect a small-town girl to understand."

"I lived in D.C. for ten years."

"Oh, I know, *Zoe* Fontaine. I've read your mediocre articles."

"Listen, *Mortimer*," she said, her patience snapping as she stepped toward him. "You have hundreds, maybe thousands, of projects in play. You don't need to screw up my only chance of finding my friend because you need to flatten this place in a few weeks."

"It's a lot less than that. Why do you think it was *empty*? Nobody was supposed to be booked in after last week. I'm going to make sure this investigation is quashed, and I'm going to destroy that building. I suggest that if you want to get your evidence, you do so in the next twenty-four hours. And then run back to your little valley. I'll look forward to meeting you again when I raze that library to the ground."

With a smirk, he turned on his heel and went back to his car. It squealed away, a cloud of dust thrown up into the air that deposited itself all over Zoe.

She stared after it, fuming silently, watching the gleaming Range Rover burst effortlessly onto the main highway and surge away.

At least she had confirmed one thing. Dunridge and Linmans were two of a kind.

CHAPTER NINETEEN

A S SHE STORMED BACK TO HER CAR, ZOE WAS SUDDENLY grateful she had followed her instincts not to try and bypass the officer in front of Rick's door.

Nathan Lombardi was just pulling up beside her, his casual grin in place as he removed his sunglasses. He looked like a rock star, not a detective.

Bumping the car door closed with his hip, his eyes dipped down over her body before returning to her face.

"Are you messin' with my crime scene again?" he asked, his eyes lingering on her face as she walked to her car.

"I was thinking about it, but you have an officer stopping me from breaking in today."

Lombardi snorted. "At least you're honest."

"I'm assuming you haven't found anything?" she said.

"Why do you assume that?"

"Because you didn't call me last night."

He raised an eyebrow. "Were you expecting me to?" he asked, a teasing note in his voice.

"About the *case*," she replied flatly, but a smile tugged at the corner of her mouth. Lombardi always had been charming as hell.

"You're right, we haven't found anything yet." He sobered, putting his hands in his pockets. "This friend of yours was pretty off-grid."

"What do you mean?"

"Well, some of it wasn't intentional, I'm sure. He doesn't seem to have any relatives we can get ahold of, but that's not so unusual. It's more his social presence, or lack thereof. I heard of people without online accounts, but I thought they were like Bigfoot or something."

She sighed. "Yeah, that sounds like Rick. I'm not sure if he was paranoid or just lazy."

"You think something sinister happened to him?"

Zoe raised her eyebrows. "Do you?"

Lombardi sauntered around to her side of the car, resting a hip against it as if he were on vacation.

"Doesn't look good so far, but then a lot of these cases don't. He's a grown man, can you think of any reason why he would have dumped his car here and left town, for example?"

Zoe stared out at the river, trying to put herself in Rick's headspace. The last time she had seen him, all she could remember was his clammy skin, the sweat adhering to his upper lip, and the panic in his voice.

"I don't know what was going on in his life, but he told me he had one last thing to take care of and then he would explain everything to me."

Lombardi's face was grim. The concern in his expression seemed surprisingly genuine for a man who likely heard about such cases all the time.

"Well, I'm gonna look into it, of course, but we don't have any leads yet. If there's anything else you can tell me, then now would be the time."

The Post-it and the file in her apartment leaped into the back of Zoe's mind, but she kept quiet. Until she knew more, anything she told Lombardi would be smoke and mirrors.

"Other than the fact that I think he might have been dating my mom, I have nothing else."

"Your mom?" he asked, his eyes crinkling. "Man, I never even got to meet her. You two back in touch?"

"I didn't really have much of a choice now I'm living within a few miles of her house."

He smirked. "I guess not. And the reason you left D.C. and moved to a little sleepy valley you always hated is... for peace and quiet, right?"

"Exactly," Zoe deadpanned.

Lombardi pushed off the car. "Because Zoe Fontaine *loves* the quiet."

She crossed her arms over her chest. "Maybe I've changed."

He fixed her with a long stare. "Maybe."

Zoe shifted her weight, discomforted by the familiarity in his look.

"I'm gonna get forensics on Fisher's car, too, and if I find anything, I'll let you know. His address is listed as Sapphire. He still there?"

"Yeah, he lives between Sapphire and Whistle Falls, in a little house on the way into the mountains."

Lombardi's gaze sharpened. It felt like he was looking through her and somehow knew that she had broken into Rick's house, too.

"How long are you in the city?" he said finally.

"I'm not sure, probably a few days."

He nodded. "Alright, as long as you don't get in my way, we'll get along fine." There was humor in his voice, but Zoe grimaced.

"I learned my lesson on that one," she replied, and pulled open the car door. Lombardi stepped forward, his big body almost brushing hers as he placed a hand on the top of the door.

"I've thought about you, you know," he blurted out, his lips thinning as if he hadn't meant to say that. "I'm sorry for how I was back then, I was a stupid kid."

"It's only been five years, Nate."

"Yeah, and I've changed, despite what I said. I know you weren't trying to sabotage my career, I just got pissed because that article made me look like an idiot."

"Well, you *were* kind of an idiot, as was your partner. I'm not going to apologize for doing my job."

He laughed. "Yeah, same old Fontaine." He stepped back. "I'll call you, okay?"

"You do that, thanks."

She got into the car and reversed away, heading out of the parking lot with her eyes in her rearview.

It was unexpected to be around Nathan again. She hadn't seen him since he left for Charleston on the day they broke up. He'd even made detective just like he'd said he would.

What was odd was that it didn't feel weird. Nathan and Zoe fit together effortlessly. He was irritable, volatile, and a bit of an asshole sometimes. Their relationship had been filled with vicious arguments and fights, and every other day, she'd wanted to leave.

And therein lay the trouble. With Leo, she didn't want to leave. She wanted to cling to him like a limpet and never let him go. Nate was familiar, easy, and safe. Their relationship had been a car crash waiting to happen, but not half so terrifying as what she and Leo could one day become.

Zoe arrived back at the apartment that evening with a headache and a lukewarm bag of Chinese food. Nothing about the rest of her day had been enjoyable.

Her feet were hurting; she'd gotten trapped in a loop on the one-way streets twice and wasted several hours looking for details on Kevin Munice without uncovering anything new.

She stomped up the stairs, missing Max and wishing she had chosen pizza. Oil was seeping through the brown paper bag in her hand, and she grimaced as she held it up in front of her.

Quite the nutritious meal I have ahead of me. I really need to learn to cook.

She reached the familiar dark green door to the apartment, pulling out her three-feet-long keychain and inserting the key in the lock.

But as soon as it swung open, her breath caught mid-step. Something was wrong. A light was on that she hadn't used yet, the unfamiliar orange lampshade casting strange patterns over the walls.

The apartment smelled odd, like something was cooking, but she hadn't bought any food other than the bag in her hand since she'd arrived there.

Her heart started thudding as a shadow moved at the end of the hallway, the bulk of it tall and long against the wall as if someone was about to come at her. She stepped back, ready to run, until she heard the clatter of claws scampering toward her and a high-pitched whine that made the panic in her chest evaporate immediately.

"Hey, buddy!" she cried, ecstatic to see Max hurtling toward her, his ears flapping madly as he bounded practically into her arms, licking her face as his tail wagged frantically.

"He ruined the whole surprise," said a deep voice from the end of the hallway, and she looked up, grinning from ear to ear as Leo emerged from the kitchen.

"Oh my God!" she said, finally managing to put Max down on the floor again. She headed up the hall and flung her arms around Leo before she could overthink it. He took her weight on his back foot laughing happily and kissed her before she pulled back.

"What are you two doing here?" she asked.

"Oh, well, Max was missin' you and he wouldn't stop goin' on at me to come see you. So, we took a trip together. It's Friday tomorrow and Fran's handling all my appointments, so I thought we could make a weekend of it. Lyla was happy to give me the key," he added with a wink.

"I'm so glad you came," she said, as Max leaped between them and Leo caught him, holding him in his arms as the puppy used the new vantage point to look around the house.

"I can see that," he said as his eyes fell on the bag in her hand. "What the hell are you eatin'?"

She brandished it. "Uh… sweet and sour chicken? I think that's what I ordered anyway."

As she was speaking, she walked into the kitchen and stopped in her tracks at the sight of the candles on the little table and two plates set up for a romantic dinner for two.

"Oh my God, are we on a date?" she asked teasingly.

"Damn straight!" Leo replied. "Can I take your coat, madam?"

"Why, thank you kindly," she said, handing him her leather jacket and taking a seat. Max rested his head on her lap as Leo poured her a glass of wine. "This is so nice, thank you."

"You're welcome. I figured you'd be exhausted and eatin' horrendous Chinese food, so I had to come up and cook for you."

"It's the only reason I keep you around."

"I'm startin' to think that's true. If it's the last thing I do, I'm teaching you to cook."

"Don't listen to him," she whispered to Max. "Sandwiches for every meal, right buddy?"

Leo shook his head in disbelief, heading to the stove where she saw two thick slabs of steak ready to cook.

"Potatoes are in the oven. You need anythin' else? Wanna put your feet up for a bit or should I just get cookin'?"

"Feed me," she said, and Leo got to work with a smile on his face.

By the time he placed her plate in front of her, Zoe's stomach was growling loudly, and half her wine was gone.

"So, how's your day been?" Leo asked, taking a seat.

"Annoying, until now. Right now it's perfect."

Leo poured himself a glass of wine. "You find anything out?"

She sighed. "Nothing. Nate thinks something might have happened to Rick. It isn't a great sign when the detective on the case reckons it's foul play."

"This is Nate, your ex?" Leo asked, his jaw clenching as he glared at her.

Zoe sipped her wine, hiding a smile. "Yes, but ex from five years ago."

"Is he good lookin'?"

"I only date gorgeous men."

Leo's lips quirked, but to Zoe's relief, he gave up on that line of questioning.

"Did they find anything in Rick's hotel room?"

"Don't know yet," she said, keeping any mention of the blood out of her story. "He said he'd call me when there's more information. But I found something in those files I took from Rick's house."

She grabbed her notebook from the counter and handed it to him. Leo frowned at it.

"What am I looking at? Your handwriting is illegible."

"It is not! Halfway down the page—The Depot? It's a drug hotspot, according to Judy. I'm gonna go there tomorrow and see if anyone remembers Rick or saw him. There might have been a reason he wanted to speak to someone there."

"You saw Judy?" Leo asked. "How is she?"

Zoe shrugged. "Same as usual. In hindsight, I probably shouldn't have asked her about it, but it was pretty useful speaking to an addict. She recognized the name immediately, but it doesn't show up online when you search for it. The Depot is clearly for people in the know."

Leo placed the notebook down carefully, his face tight. "I'm comin' with you."

Zoe huffed. "I don't need a bodyguard."

"No shit. I'm still coming. Who knows what kind of people will be there? If it's somewhere drug deals go down, it's not gonna be pleasant. No arguments."

"Alright, but we should leave Max in the car."

"Agreed." Leo swirled his wine, giving her a side eye. "You don't think..."

"What?"

"Rick wasn't into drugs, was he?"

Zoe looked up at him, recalling Rick's appearance when she had last seen him. He had shown all the signs of someone who could have been going through withdrawal—but there was also every chance he was just scared and agitated. Rick seemed too sensible to do drugs. He wasn't someone she would ever have pegged for that type of thing.

"I don't think so. I'm hoping he was following a lead."

"What lead?"

Zoe sliced her knife through her steak, biding her time. In an ideal world, she wouldn't share what she'd learned with Leo. The story was too unpredictable, and there were too many unknowns.

But as she looked up at him, his brown eyes deep and dark in the candlelight, the play of his thick muscles under his shirt was all the more visible.

Who am I kidding? Leo can handle himself better than me.

"You remember when I was looking into Orchard Grove nursing home and found out it used to be The Sapphire Foundation?"

"Sure, it was a rehab facility, right?"

"Yeah. Well, Kevin Munice, that's the guy Rick might have been looking into, was a kid who went missing there around 2015. He went into the clinic and never came out. His name keeps cropping up. When I asked Rick about The Foundation, he wouldn't talk to me. Told me to drop it, and that isn't like him. Or it didn't used to be—any hint of a cover-up and he'd have been up all night researching it. But now, he doesn't seem to want to know anything about it."

"What has Kevin Munice got to do with this Depot place?"

"No idea. But those are the two pieces of information I have. Also, Rick met up with a red-haired woman when he arrived here, and Kevin had red hair. So either Rick has three girlfriends, or she might be related to Munice."

Leo sat back in his chair. "Three?"

"Uh, I may have forgotten to mention that I think Rick is dating my mom," Zoe felt her cheeks heat.

Leo blinked at her. "Excuse me?"

"I know. Don't ask."

"Wow. Just… wow."

"Hey! Don't be ageist, that's what I'm gonna look like in twenty years."

Leo belly laughed at that as they returned to their food and fell into companionable silence. The meal was excellent, the steak cooked perfectly, and the chips sharp and salty.

Zoe wanted to savor it and enjoy their time together, but by the end of her second glass of wine, she was yawning continually.

"You should get to bed," he said, and Zoe glanced into the tiny living room, noticing he'd already made up a makeshift bed on the couch. The sight of it made her incredibly sad.

"You're not sleeping on the couch, Leo. We can share the bed like grown-ups."

His eyes lit up. "Really?"

"Yes, really. I just…"

He raised his hands in the air with infinite patience. "Cuddling only, I promise."

His smile was an unstoppable force after that, and it made a bubble of joy burst inside Zoe to see how eager he was just to be able to hold her.

His happiness quickly faded, however, when he saw the size of the bed.

"You cannot be serious. No human being is this short," he said, lying on it with his feet hanging fully off the end, almost halfway up his calf.

Zoe laughed and threw a pillow at him. "It's this or the couch," and she shrieked with delight as he pulled her down on top of him.

CHAPTER TWENTY

Z OE WOKE UP WITH A SMILE ON HER FACE. THERE WAS A
weight on her chest, where Max's head rested on her
sternum, and Leo's arm was curled around her stomach.
Turning gently so as not to wake him, she took in his profile,
stroking Max's head and feeling content with the world.

"Staring at people while they sleep is creepy," Leo said, his
eyes still closed.

"Stop being so cute, then."

He smiled, squeezing her tightly before rolling onto his back
and stretching. Max gave a little huff of excitement and bounded
off the bed, using Leo's stomach as a launchpad.

"Ow, damn it, Max, I got ribs!" The puppy hurtled through
the bedroom door as Zoe burst out laughing. Leo glared at her as
they reluctantly got out of bed.

The bedroom in Lyla's apartment was small and had different wallpaper on each wall. The knick-knacks around the room had no rhyme or reason to them, and there were endless pieces of sparkling crystal hanging from the ceiling.

Zoe was loving it, particularly when she got to watch Leo dress.

They didn't discuss their night together, and she was grateful for the silence as she ran her eye over his muscular back.

"Why is this place so cold?" Leo grumbled as he pulled on a shirt and socks.

"The heating hasn't been on for months," Zoe complained.

"Yeah, but it's June!"

Zoe couldn't wipe the smile off her face as he continued grumbling, shuffling down the hall to the kitchen. It was all so wonderfully domestic.

As she pulled on a royal blue shirt and black jeans for the day ahead, she listened to the gentle sounds of Leo moving about the place. It wasn't the first time she had considered what it would be like to live with him.

She had fallen in love with Leo's ranch almost immediately. Thinking about the wide stretch of land, the beautiful views, and the quiet, comfortable living space, made her chest ache.

"You want eggs?" came a call from the kitchen.

"We don't have eggs," she shouted back.

"*You* didn't buy them. But I got chickens workin' hard for you, woman."

Grinning, she headed into the kitchen to help Leo make breakfast.

The Depot was ten minutes away from her grandmother's apartment at a curve of the river, toward the outskirts of Charleston.

It was a strange mixture of old and new as they drove toward it. After a low bridge and some long stone steps sloping down to the water, the road turned sharply to the left. On the corner was a run-down old bus stop, heavily vandalized and sloping to one side. Zoe could only assume it represented the namesake of the place.

They drove through a squat row of houses and some well-tended sidewalks, toward a more barren patch of earth. A tattered American flag flapped forlornly in the breeze, the cars passing the only sound, but even they petered out after a few minutes.

Some geese were waddling along the footpath ahead of them, and Zoe's eyes was drawn to a dark blue tarpaulin flapping in the breeze at the far side.

An underpass in the distance seemed to house the bulk of the visible tents, and although the homeless population looked bigger than Sapphire Valley, it was still smaller than those she had seen in D.C.

"I'd park up in that space just ahead," Leo murmured then looked about the car's interior. "You still renting this thing?"

Zoe nodded. "Yeah. I haven't gotten around to getting a car yet. But it's insured if that's what you mean."

"I more meant we can keep an eye on Max while we find someone to talk to. I don't want him walking all over this place, not with the potential for needles and such underfoot."

"Agreed."

She pulled into a turnoff opposite some leafless trees against a dark brown slope. The bank beside the road looked man-made, as if this had once been a construction site, later abandoned to the community.

Graffiti covered the walls nearby, and an old community center could be seen on the lower part of the road. It was boarded up with weeds clinging to the steps and smothering the railings to the entrance. There was little to no movement in the smattering of tents ahead of them. Or it seemed that way until they got closer.

Leo had his medical bag, and Zoe could see one mongrel dog chewing on a bone on the edge of the space.

"So what's the plan?" he asked.

Zoe scanned the road, the gravel and dirt running in straight lines ahead of them. The shadow of the bridge was dominant and ominous, making everything beneath it look sinister, whereas the tents in the sunlight seemed almost friendly by comparison.

"Let's head toward the bridge and see if anyone talks to us."

"They're more likely to get spooked," he said warily.

"Hm, well, at least we can give it a try."

Leo glanced at her. "And all you got that led you to this place is a couple of words in a margin on Rick's notes?"

"I know, I know, but it's something, at least."

"Is it? Rick might just have written it down as a reference. What if it's where this Kevin Munice hung out, and Rick never actually came here?"

Zoe pushed her hands into her pocket, running over her key chain one ring at a time.

"It's all I've got, Leo, and if Rick was following a lead, then there's every chance he *did* come here."

"Alright," Leo said, his shoulders slumping as he headed out. "Let's go make some friends."

The first tent they came to didn't have any signs of life, but there was the strong scent of a cigarette on the wind. They followed it toward what might have once been a bright red tent on the edge of the group.

It seemed to Zoe that there was a hierarchy of sorts. Those tents that looked the oldest and had clearly been there for the longest time were in better spots than the others. They tended to be close to the bank, sheltered from the wind, which she could only imagine would mean the occupants were warmer.

As they were passing the bright red one that was now more of a soft ochre color, a woman emerged. She was in her sixties, blonde hair streaked with grey and wearing a red fleece that matched the tent, some beaded jewelry around her neck.

Her mouth was turned puckered, and when she turned to speak to the little Jack Russell that followed her from the tent, it was clear she had no teeth. The dog was elderly too, tottering on unsteady legs behind her as she pulled out a jar of peanut butter and opened it for him.

She nestled the jar in a little hole in the ground that seemed to be specifically designed for the purpose and perched herself on a black fold-out stool as she began rummaging in a dark green plastic bag.

Leo and Zoe approached her, but it took several seconds for her to notice them. As her eyes moved to Leo's boots, she glanced up briefly before returning to her task, unbothered by their presence.

"Morning," Zoe said as she stepped forward.

The woman peered up at them. "Mornin'," she said, giving Zoe the once-over. "You with the college project?"

Emboldened by her lack of hostility, Zoe took another step forward.

"No. I'm sorry to trouble you, I just wanted to ask you a couple of questions if it's alright?"

The woman leaned back, looking between the two of them, her eyes catching on Leo as they travelled up to his full height. "And who are you, Big Bad John?"

Leo tipped his hat to her and held up a bag. "I'm not here to ask you anythin', ma'am, that's her job," he said, nodding to Zoe. "But I'm a vet if your little guy needs anythin'?"

Zoe could have kissed him when the woman's eyes turned bright and excited as she glanced down at the dog.

"You hear that, Mavis?" she cooed. "You're gettin' your claws trimmed today after tellin' me for months they needed it." She looked back up at Leo. "I tried doin' it myself with my knife, but they ain't strong enough. I heard you can hurt 'em if you do it too close to the ..." She waved, searching for the right word.

"The quick," Leo said. "Yeah, that can be a problem when she's got dark nails too. You want me to deal with that for ya? I can check her out at the same time and just make sure she's healthy."

"If you want to, I ain't gonna stop you."

Leo took a single stride over to the dog and hunkered down beside her. She was still too interested in her peanut butter to pay him much attention, and he began to get some items out of his bag as Zoe crouched beside the woman.

"My name's Zoe," she said.

"I'm Martha, but everybody calls me Marty, like Back to the Future."

"Hi Marty, it's nice to meet you."

Zoe pulled out the photograph of Rick she'd brought and handed it to Marty.

"Have you seen this man around here at all?"

Marty looked at it up close, her eyes barely open as she tried to discern the picture.

"My eyesight ain't up to much," she said, handing it back. "Tell me what he looked like, and I can try and help you."

"He's small, slim, often looks exhausted, and pretty disheveled. He might have been asking about a guy named Kevin?"

Marty looked as if she really thought about it. "Name?"

"Rick Fisher."

"Nope. Sorry. Don't think so."

Every now and again, there was a sharp click as Leo cut the dog's nails. Mavis didn't seem troubled by it, her long pink tongue still lapping at the base of the jar with enthusiasm.

"Has *anyone* come around asking about a guy named Kevin?" Zoe pressed.

Marty's eyes grew sad. "People come by askin' for a lot of folks. But I don't recall anyone with that name. Kevin's my brother's name. I'd remember."

"Thanks, Marty, I appreciate it. We've got some food that we brought with us. Is there anything I can tempt you with?"

Marty grinned toothlessly. "I like anythin'."

Zoe opened the bag filled with the sandwiches and paninis they'd bought on the way over and handed her some.

"We got some food for this one, too," Leo said. "She's got fleas, but I'll give her some treatment for that."

"Oh, thank you," Marty said as the dog finally pulled her snout out of the jar.

"How long has she had this rash?" he asked. Leo's mouth was set in a thin line, his fingers scratching gently behind the dog's ears.

"Rash?" Marty asked. "I ain't seen one. Can't see nothin' these days."

Leo's shoulders slumped a little further as he pushed a hand into his bag, pulling a packet out. "Alright, well, these wipes have a bit of medicine in 'em. It should help with the itchin'. If you can, try to clean beneath her legs at night, that should help."

Marty took the wipes, eyeing them suspiciously, and Zoe gave her a few sachets of dog food for Mavis before they moved off.

There didn't seem to be many other people awake, and as the sun came out from behind a cloud, it highlighted the state of the ground all around the tents. It seemed as if there was a drainage issue by the river, and some of the ground was boggy and damp. It didn't look at all sanitary.

Zoe could feel Leo's mood darkening as they made their way through.

They managed to speak to a few people, many of whom were monosyllabic at best and didn't want to be bothered. Leo assisted with a couple more dogs, but many people ignored their attempts to talk, and no one had seen Rick.

It wasn't until they were nearing the bridge that Leo stopped, staring ahead of him and peering at something in the darkness.

"Zoe," he said, and his tone immediately made her look up.

Under the bridge was a red-haired woman, bent over, speaking to a man with a cap on his head and a long, shaggy beard. She had a clipboard under her arm and a rain slicker over her shoulders, the color of her hair plainly visible in the stream of sunlight at the edge of the bridge.

It was tied in a plait down one side of her shoulder, reminding Zoe of Katniss Everdeen, from *The Hunger Games*.

"Do you think that could be the woman Rick was meeting with?" Leo asked.

Zoe shook her head. "I have no idea. Seems crazy that she'd just turn up here."

"Unless The Depot is where he met her?"

They both turned back to look at the car. There was no sign of Max at the windows anymore, and Zoe could only hope that he'd settled down to sleep.

"You go talk to her, and I'll watch him. I don't want to leave him in this place," Leo said.

"No, good idea. I'll only be a few—damn it where'd she go?"

Zoe hadn't turned away for more than a few seconds, but in that time, the woman had vanished. There was a long road beneath the bridge with tents and trash on either side that stretched for half a mile, but she was nowhere to be seen.

"Did we hallucinate?" she asked, exasperated.

"No. She was there. Maybe she went into one of the tents?"

"Stay here, I'll go see if I can talk to her."

"Be careful."

Zoe glared at him, handing him the bag with the remainder of the food inside, and walked swiftly beneath the bridge.

The air was hot and stifling under the metal ceiling, and the sharp smell of urine was strong as she headed through the semi-darkness. Zoe could just make out hunched shapes on both sides, and as she passed a group of three men, she could hear them laughing together and sharing a tin of what looked like sardines between them.

Smoke hung in the air, and the smell of bacon drifted toward her, though she wasn't certain if she was imagining it.

She was almost out the other side of the bridge when she heard an engine start. Whipping around, she saw a black Ford Focus make its way up to the road's edge from behind the bridge and speed away toward the highway. As it passed, she recognized the red-haired woman behind the wheel, staring ahead, a look of determined concentration on her face.

Zoe watched her car fade into the distance, a deep sense of despair filling her. She'd missed the opportunity to talk to her one and only lead.

CHAPTER
TWENTY-ONE

T HEY SPENT ANOTHER HOUR IN THE HOMELESS
community, but Zoe's hopes were dashed again and again
as people turned away, either refusing to answer her
questions, or telling her they didn't recognize the photograph.

It was pleasant to be able to distribute some food, at least, and
Leo could administer medication to the animals on the site, but it
didn't feel as if they had done enough.

By the time they had been there an hour, the sun was high in
the sky, and they had to head back to the car to ensure Max didn't
overheat.

Zoe wasn't surprised that the morning's work had been a
dead end, but Leo's I-told-you-so face was grating on her by the
time they got back in the car.

Max bounded forward in his seat to greet them, and as she started the engine, the dog rested his head on the central console as Leo stroked between his ears, giving him some water.

"So what's the plan, now?" Leo asked.

Zoe glanced at him irritably. "You don't have to sound so smug."

"I'm not smug, I just asked what you wanted to do next."

"I know you thought speaking to them was pointless."

"Alright, I wasn't sure it would lead to anything, but there was a fifty-fifty chance it might." Zoe scowled as he chuckled softly. "Do you need lunch? You're gettin' hangry."

"Shut up," she muttered, making him laugh all the more.

They drove back toward the apartment, but Leo was right— she didn't have a plan. Zoe didn't know what her next move was, and it was making her antsy. The first few days had been about looking for Rick, finding his car, and learning that he had stayed at the hotel. Now, the trail had gone cold, and she was out of ideas.

"Can I ask you something?" Leo asked, his long legs stretching out into the footwell as she opened the windows to give Max some fresh air.

"Of course."

"It's about Judy," he said cautiously.

Zoe turned to him in surprise, signaling to take the slip road. "Oh. Uh. Sure."

"You don't have to tell me if you don't want to."

"No, that's okay. What do you want to know?"

Leo turned his body toward her, remaining quiet for a little time, as if mulling over his words. Finally, he sighed.

"When Judy wasn't well. Did she lie about using?"

Zoe drove silently for a minute or two, trying to find the best way to respond. Leo's voice was so hopeful, it killed her to tell him the truth.

"Yeah," she said eventually. "That was one of the hardest things about it. My sister and I were always honest with one another. But toward the end, all the trust was eroded. She stopped telling me when she was using, but I always knew."

"How?"

"Lots of reasons. She'd stop answering her phone and then call me at 3 a.m. like everything was normal. Or she'd tell me she was going to work but then wouldn't remember what days she had been there. I learned to recognize the signs. She was never secretive; Judy's an open book. But she'd start inventing these wild stories when she was using. It was as if I was speaking to a stranger. Sometimes it was easier to think of Judy as a separate person when she was on drugs—someone I barely knew—because that was how it felt."

Leo was quiet for a long time, the gentle breeze filling the car with the scents on the wind, the sound of traffic in the distance a soothing whine.

The city was waking up around them, and as they reached a busier street, it was good to see healthy, happy people shouting and laughing together again. Zoe felt like a hypocrite for feeling that way, but watching suffering was never easy.

"Is this about Gus?" she asked quietly.

Leo rubbed a hand against his thigh. "Yeah."

"Do you think he's using again?"

"I don't know. Maybe he never stopped. I saw him with a friend of his, this girl Lana. I know her from my work with Sparrow. I've treated her dog Bailey a few times—he's a black lab, sweet as anything. She's doin' her best, I know she is, but she's an addict. I don't want him around her—but it's not my call. I can't imagine they meet up and do anything else. What could they have in common?"

Zoe sighed. "All I'll say is they might have more in common than you think. You're doing an amazing thing with Gus, Leo, and I say this without any judgment at all, but remember that for him, you're always the good guy looking at the bad."

"What do you mean?"

Zoe bit her lip. "Lana won't judge him. She won't care who he was, what he does, or what he puts in his body—by choice or not. She won't have any expectations of him. You do. That's a *good* thing, but it can be exhausting. For people who are struggling, addiction is as much about who they're with as anything else. There's a community—it might not be a healthy one—but it's close-knit and fiercely loyal. They survive together, and that's a powerful thing."

There was another long silence, and Zoe swallowed.

"Sorry—maybe that's not what you needed to hear."

"Not at all, but I'm glad I asked. I see Gus through these rose-tinted lenses. I wanna believe that a few hours on the ranch during the week is gonna save him. But that's naïve. The way you describe it, it sounds like the army. This group of people who know each other better than anyone else. You go through unimaginable things together, and no one can make you feel safe, or understand you like your unit. Not when you're at war."

Zoe smiled, a little shiver passing beneath her skin. Taking one hand off the wheel, she took Leo's in hers, and he squeezed it tightly.

"Thanks, Zo. I'm sorry for everything you went through with Judy. I'm startin' to see this tiny snapshot of it, and I can't imagine watchin' a loved one go through it."

"Thanks. It's nice to talk about her, even when it's the bad stuff, if it helps someone else."

The dash lit up with a call from her cell, and she frowned at who was calling stabbing the screen quickly before it disconnected.

"Hey Angela," she said, answering through the car speaker. "I'm in the car with Leo. What's up?"

"Oh, hi, Zoe! I'm glad I got a hold of you. We were all wonderin' where you'd got to. Are you takin' a few days off?"

Zoe squeezed the steering wheel in frustration. "I'm in Charleston, remember? I mentioned to Bean I had a lead to follow."

"Oh, that's right," she sounded entirely uninterested. "It's just, were you aware Morgan Media sent a new editor in to replace Rick?"

Zoe and Leo exchanged a startled glance. "Excuse me?"

"He arrived yesterday. Been askin' where you are for the last hour. He wants to get everyone together. I don't think he's been too impressed that you've been gone so long. I wanted to call and tell you, because he's a bit of a dragon."

Zoe closed her eyes briefly as she blew out a breath. "Alright, thanks, Angela. Could you please tell him that I'm working on a story, and I haven't just disappeared?"

"But *Leo's* with you?"

Zoe ground her teeth. "Yes."

"Alright, yeah, I'll tell him. You comin' back?"

"I'll be back by this afternoon."

"Great!"

The line went dead, and Zoe slammed her palm into the wheel so hard the car swerved.

"Whoa, careful, you'll break your wrist."

"Someone goes missing for a week, and they *replace* him? What kind of heartless pigs are running that place?"

"Uh, Zoe, Rick's been AWOL for much longer than a week." Zoe flicked an angry glance at him but deflated when he raised his hands defensively. "Don't shoot the messenger, that's what *you* told me."

She kept driving, checking the time. "We'll have to leave in less than an hour if I need to make it back this afternoon. Damn it."

"I'll help you pack up the apartment, let me take Max so you can deal with this new editor on your own. Any idea who it could be?"

"None whatsoever, but if he's a 'dragon' he's already very different from Rick Fisher."

By the time they'd packed up her grandmother's apartment, checked everything was secure, and headed back to Sapphire, Zoe was in even more of a lather than she had been to begin with.

Despite Leo's placatory tactics and gentle suggestions that she keep an open mind until learning the full story, Zoe could feel a vein pulsing in her forehead as she got back into her rental.

The fact that her investigation had been cut short and their weekend together had been curtailed was just another factor in her bad mood.

It turned out to be a good thing they hadn't traveled back together, however, as about half an hour into the journey, Detective Lombardi called her.

"Hey, Nate," she said, as she sped up the highway, self-consciously glancing in the mirror for Leo's truck as if he would somehow know who she was speaking to.

"Hey, you."

The simple phrase made her gut clench. "Do you have some news for me?"

"Are you driving?"

"Yeah. I'm headed back to Sapphire."

"Wow. That really was a flyin' visit. You comin' back any time soon?"

Zoe couldn't help but smile. "Yeah, I should be. Not sure when though."

"Well, until you do, I wanted to update you on what we've found out."

"Fire away."

"We're still running tests on the blood spatter in the hotel room, but the report on the car came back clear. Looks like he just parked and left it. He has a glove compartment filled with parking fines, though. I don't reckon he ever paid 'em."

"I got one of those myself."

"Yeah," Lombardi quipped. "And there are probably still outstanding fines from D.C. in there. Your parking habits haven't improved then."

"Apparently not. Do they know where the blood could have come from?"

"Where do *you* think it came from?"

She glanced at the screen, blindsided by the question. "I don't know. I wondered if he might have cut himself shaving."

Lombardi's only response was a scathing laugh. Zoe shifted back in her seat, wishing she could speak to him in person. It felt like the worst time to be leaving the city, and now she wouldn't have a chance to catch up with the red-haired woman until she returned.

"Alright, thanks for the update. Was there anything else?"

"You said Fisher was dating your mom?"

"That's what I thought. She's being super cagey about it. He might have had a thing with the elementary school principal, too. Seems he got around."

"Hm. Think you'll be comin' back here soon? It'd be good to catch up for real. Go for a drink."

Tell him you're dating Leo.

"Yeah, that sounds good."

Zoe's foot compressed the accelerator as she wove her way through the cars ahead, annoyed with herself and unable to explain why she was so reluctant to admit she was with Leo.

"Text me when you're back, Fontaine. I'll give you a call if anything else comes up. Have a good time in the sticks."

"Pfft. Yeah. Thanks, I will."

By the time she drove into the Chronicle parking lot, she was in a dark mood. Her growing irritation at being forced to come back early, and Angela's accusatory tone about her being 'away with Leo' only added to her growing rage.

Slamming the car door, she headed inside, ready to bite the head off of whoever the company had sent. Morgan Media owned three of the papers in the county, and The Chronicle was the smallest of the bunch.

Zoe could just imagine how the executives would view Rick's absence. They wouldn't have the time or inclination to investigate what happened; they'd just place a bandage over it and be done.

Well, not on my watch.

She stormed past the receptionist, who was looking a lot more alert and professional than she generally did, and pushed through the office doors, spoiling for a fight.

Every eye in the room turned to face her.

A man leaning against Rick's desk slowly moved to a standing position, his eyebrows raised, flat cap firmly on his head, hands shoved into his pockets.

"Tripp!" Zoe exclaimed as the door swung shut behind her with a quiet hiss.

CHAPTER TWENTY-TWO

"**W**HAT THE HELL?" SHE DEMANDED.

"Hello Zoe," Tripp said with his usual even tone. He wasn't smiling, and neither was anyone else in the office. "Where have you been?"

Zoe frowned at him. "When did you get here?"

"Yesterday afternoon."

Tripp's eyebrows were still raised, and several faces were fixed in her direction around the office. Zoe fidgeted. "I've been working on a story."

"You didn't check your emails? I asked for everyone to come in today."

Zoe glanced at Bean, whose lip was caught in his teeth as he turned slowly back to his monitor and began typing furiously.

Traitor.

She felt about three feet tall. "I didn't see anything about that."

Tripp was an immovable statue, and it didn't help that Angela and Anton were staring at Zoe judgmentally as if she'd committed some heinous crime. The knot of tension returned, pushing against her shoulder blades uncomfortably.

"Let's take a walk," Tripp said, grabbing his jacket and coming forward.

"I just got back," she snapped, but he ignored her, opening the door and nodding for her to follow him.

Zoe huffed, glancing back at Daniel and Bean, who were watching her with apologetic expressions, and followed Tripp out of the building.

Once outside in the sunshine, Tripp turned, eyes running over her briefly.

"Does this town have a decent coffee shop?"

Zoe stared at him in disbelief. "We're just going for coffee, like you showing up here as the new editor is totally normal?"

"Yeah. I'm thirsty."

Zoe rolled her eyes, leading the way across the lot and down the hill toward The Sapphire Café.

"This place is idyllic," Tripp said, his hands still in his pockets as he stared ahead. "I can see why you would want to live here."

"Yeah, sure."

The façade dropped as he exhaled loudly. "No, you're right. I can't. Do they even have public transportation in this place, or does everyone travel by horse and buggy?"

"Lap it up, Tripp. You're the one who's come to work here."

He chuckled. "Somebody woke up on the wrong side of the bed this morning. I thought you'd be happy to see me."

"Oh, of course! It isn't like I've left you thirty messages in the past few weeks, none of which you've replied to."

"Maybe I just knew I would be seeing you soon."

"Spare me, you can't kid a kidder, Tripp, and stop looking so damned pleased with yourself."

He snorted as they made their way toward the café. It was busy, the blue metal tables out front filled with people enjoying their lunch and gossiping happily together. Zoe could see Seth inside, flitting about manically serving everyone, and the place had a warm energy to it.

"Wow, this is a nice place," Tripp muttered. "Not a Starbucks in sight."

As they entered the café, Zoe chewed her tongue, holding back the barrage of questions she wanted to ask him.

"What do you want? Grab the table in the window, and I'll bring it over."

"Ooh, are you buying? I *am* being spoiled today, considering you look like you want to kill me."

"What do you want to *drink*, Tripp?"

He rocked onto the balls of his feet as they stood in front of the counter, deliberately drawing it out. "I'll have a flat white, thanks."

"Fine."

Zoe ordered from Sophia, the young girl behind the counter, who wore braces and had a friendly smile. Seth waved as she waited to get her drinks, and after a minute, came over, cloth and cleaning spray in hand, looking at Tripp.

"Who's the guy?" he asked.

Zoe scowled. "He's my old boss from D.C."

"Seriously?"

"Yeah. Looks like the higher-ups have brought in a replacement for Rick before we even know where he is."

Seth frowned, glaring at Tripp. If there was one thing you could guarantee in a small town, it was that they didn't like outsiders strolling in and taking people's jobs.

"Huh. Well, can I spit in his coffee or somethin'?"

Zoe laughed. "Let me see what he's doing here first, and I'll report back."

"He's pretty young for a boss, ain't he?"

"Don't be fooled. He's been in the business a long time."

"What's his name?"

"Tripp Monroe. He used to be my editor at the Washington Express. I can't imagine why the hell he's shown up here. Makes no sense to me."

Seth put his hands on his hips. "And what is so wrong with my town?"

"Hey! I live here; I'm on your side. But for someone like Tripp—I mean, he used to write articles for one of the biggest papers on the East Coast."

"Like you, you mean?" Seth cut her off, looking skeptically back at Tripp. "Maybe he wanted a quiet life, like someone else I know."

Zoe grabbed the coffees that Sophia placed on the counter. "Maybe."

"Has there been any word from Rick?" Seth asked with concern.

"Nothing."

He shook his head on a heavy sigh. "Well, I sure hope he's okay."

"Thanks, Seth, I'll let you know if I hear anything."

"You want an almond croissant? On the house."

Zoe beamed at him. "Definitely."

The café had air conditioning, but with the sun's rays shining through the windows and the humid air in the valley, the interior wasn't all that comfortable.

For lack of a table outside, Zoe and Tripp were forced to sit by the window in the full heat of the sun, and Zoe was uncomfortable in seconds.

She placed Tripp's coffee in front of him, and he immediately took a huge bite out of the croissant, without ripping it in half or assuming they would share it.

"What are you doing here?" she demanded, settling back in her seat and fixing him with a long glare.

"Same as you. Working."

"You don't want to work in Sapphire Valley, Tripp. Try again."

Tripp adjusted his cap and shrugged his shoulders. "Alright, seeing as you know everything, why don't *you* tell me what I'm doing here?"

"I have no clue. But you don't have any right to take Rick's job. He's *missing*. What are they gonna do, pay you both until he comes back?"

Tripp took another bite of the croissant, and Zoe wrestled it out of his hand, taking half for herself with a warning glare. Tripp smirked at her.

"When Rick Fisher comes back, and Zach Loman thinks he'll be back soon, he's gonna be out of a job. Sorry Zo, but you can't just disappear and leave your staff scrambling to get an issue to press without somebody noticing."

"And when he comes back, he's fired?"

"Looks that way."

Zoe tensed. She had hoped that there would be some leeway for Rick, but that had clearly been wishful thinking.

"How did you hear about the job in the first place?" she demanded.

"Well, that's your fault."

Zoe chewed her croissant, sipping her coffee and waiting for him to elaborate.

Tripp was infuriatingly measured in everything he did. Somehow the man could juggle seven things at once in the rapid-fire environment of a city newsroom, then flip a switch and wait and wait and wait and *wait*. It had been an occupational hazard that when they worked together, decisions took twice as long as they should have because he thought about things for days, not hours.

The moment stretched, and Tripp sipped his coffee.

"Would you stop looking at me like that?" he murmured. "I thought this would be a grand reunion, but I feel as if I'm seconds away from getting punched in the face."

"You ghosted me, remember?"

"And what did we have to say to each other? I wanted you to come back to the Express, and you didn't. What more was there to discuss?"

"Nice. So when we don't work together, we don't get to talk anymore?"

Tripp slammed his cup down with a clatter as several customers glanced their way, and he crossed his arms over his chest.

"Do you want to know why I'm here or not?"

Zoe hesitated as Tripp's jaw clenched angrily. "Alright. What happened?"

"I was offered a severance package. Months ago. I didn't tell you because I knew it would worry you. But the Express hasn't had a good year. Like, a *really* bad year. I knew it was only a matter of time before I moved on or was forced to. I've always wanted real autonomy over a paper, to decide what we run and what matters. This is a perfect chance to do that."

Zoe nursed her coffee, sipping it carefully as she stared out the window. What he said made some sense but seeing him sitting in the Sapphire Café was still jarring. Tripp was a hard worker, a good editor, and had a sensible head on his shoulders, but he didn't fit small-town life at all.

But then, I didn't think I did either until I came here.

"And you didn't want to just find another job in D.C.?"

"I'm crossing fifty, Zo. If I'm lucky, I might retire in fifteen years, and I've been burned-out for the last decade. You were going on about how casual it is here, how relaxed your life became. I get that's because of your idiotic boss—"

"Hey! Rick isn't an idiot."

"Tell that to the board at Morgan. He's been running the paper into the ground for years."

Zoe fidgeted, scratching at a hardened coffee stain on the rim of her cup.

"I'm not one to badmouth anyone, but I'm a facts man, Zo," Tripp continued. "The Chronicle has tanked. *Tanked* under Fisher's leadership. It wasn't so bad until this year, but there was no way he could hide it forever. He's been sitting back and watching it slowly fall off a cliff with zero attempts to prevent it."

Zoe didn't reply, watching the cars passing, an unpleasant feeling creeping through her. It wasn't pleasant to have her worst fears confirmed. Rick had let the paper nosedive; she just didn't understand why.

"This job isn't permanent," Tripp continued. "I'm here on an interim basis until they can clear Rick's desk, but until then, I'm looking forward to the challenge. Small newsroom, local reporting, it'll be like when I graduated, but this time I get to decide what goes on the front page. I get to talk to people in the grocery store about what matters to them. No one in D.C. cared who I was or what articles we wrote. Here, they might if I'm lucky."

He shrugged. "Besides, when I was eighteen, I worked for a paper a bit like The Chronicle, and my boss was a psychopath. I'm looking forward to ranting about the government in all our staff meetings and driving everybody insane."

Zoe's lips twitched, despite herself, and Tripp smirked as she placed her cup down, waiting for the punchline.

"Alright. So, why are we sitting here?" she asked. "Aren't you planning to give me a dressing down for being absent for three days?"

"That depends. What story were you working on?"

"I was looking for Rick."

"That isn't a story."

"It is to me."

Tripp's expression soured, and he leaned forward in his chair.

"Zoe, you're one of the best reporters I've ever worked with. Whether you believe that or not. I've missed you every day in D.C. No other reporter was a patch on you. What do you think made me come *here* specifically? I wanted to understand what it is about this place that is so 'unleavable' for my top reporter."

"You couldn't find out about Sapphire Valley on Google?"

"I'm serious, Zo. I need you with me on this. And the reason we're sitting *here* is because I thought a neutral setting might be better for me to ask you to be the Assistant Editor than in the middle of the office."

Zoe hesitated. That carrot was a good one to dangle, and Tripp knew it. The work she had done while Rick had been away was tantamount to being an editor, but Tripp knew she didn't want that job.

Assistant editor, on the other hand, was a bump in pay without the tedium of being in charge.

"You're offering me this on your second day on the job?"

"When something needs doing, I handle it."

Zoe finished her coffee and the end of her croissant as Tripp waited. The look on his face was so familiar it sent her right back to her time in D.C. He knew she was going to agree, he was just waiting for her to confirm it—it was infuriating how well he knew her.

"Fine, but Anton is gonna blow a gasket."

"Anton Bielke is a walking pressure valve; his default position is ready to explode. Let me handle him. So, is that a yes?"

"You're out of your mind." Tripp gave her a slow grin as Zoe rolled her eyes. "Sure. I'm in."

CHAPTER TWENTY-THREE

T HE OVERHAUL OF THE SAPPHIRE VALLEY CHRONICLE began the following Monday. It started as a low roar, becoming a scream by the end of the day.

Zoe had forgotten how tenacious Tripp could be.

Entering the office early as always, she felt her heart leap excitedly at the sounds of a real newsroom. With the arrival of a new boss, the whole staff was in the office, and there was a buzzing atmosphere again.

Everyone was at their desks. Daniel, Angela, and Anton to her left, Bean in his little corner alone on the right. Miriam and Lilith sat on the far left, opposite Tripp's desk, where Rick had once sat.

Zoe stood in the doorway, staring at the room, feeling off balance.

Should I have implemented some of this?

Coming from the Washington Express had given her a unique insight into a busy newsroom. It had been obvious how quiet and unmotivated most of the staff were when she arrived, but it had suited her at the time, and she hadn't wanted to step on Rick's toes. Now, she felt like a failure for the excitement and interest Tripp had added to the place in only a day and a half.

Max sat down on her feet, panting loudly as they both looked around the room. Every person was busy with something. Normally, Angela would have YouTube open, Bean would be slumped in his chair, drinking his fourth cup of coffee, with all the other monitors dark and lifeless.

Instead, Anton was on the phone with a supplier, sounding like he'd just secured a new account, and Daniel was shouting loudly across the room at Lilith, asking if he could get her opinion on something.

As Zoe stood, dumbfounded, the door opened, and Tom entered behind her.

"Mornin' Zoe," he said with a broad smile. "Whoa. What's happenin'?"

"New boss," she said as he came level with her. "Did you get the email?"

Tom shook his head. "Don't ever read 'em, sorry. Am I fired?"

"If you are, call me over and I'll show him some of the shots you took at the protest last week. Don't worry, I'll vouch for you."

Tom looked like a deer in the headlights. "I didn't even know this many people worked here; I was just comin' in to see if Rick had showed up. They really replaced him?"

"They did."

"Well that sucks."

He pushed past her, walking over to a vacant desk and dumping everything beside it as Zoe made her way to hers.

Max slunk beneath the table, not used to so many people, and settled into his bed, looking around anxiously as she stroked his head.

After a half-hour of sifting through her emails, there was still no sign of Tripp.

It was clear he had given instructions to most of the staff because Anton was already acting as if he and Tripp were best friends, but Zoe hadn't *seen* him since she got in.

Leaning around her desk to ask Daniel where Tripp was, she noticed something moving ahead of her through the narrow window in the double doors at the back. She got up and headed toward the archive room.

Placing a hand against the door, a shiver ran down her spine at the memory of the last time she had been inside. Rick's strange demeanor, their stilted conversation, and his assurances that he would be back to explain everything.

Yeah, that worked out real well.

She walked in and stopped just inside the doorway, her chest tightening as she looked at the room. A large desk now sat in the center, dominating the space. The harsh overhead lighting was gone, replaced by soft sidelights lining the walls, making the lack of windows less obvious.

Every archive box and shelf had been removed, and Tripp stood beside the desk with a crate of his belongings in front of him. Bean was underneath it, dealing with some wiring.

"Hey Zoe, I was just coming to get you," Tripp said, waving her over. "Come on in."

"Where's the archive?" she asked, a slight tremor in her voice. The room seemed barren, cavernous—every sound echoing loudly off the walls.

The past thirty years of the paper was at my fingertips, and now it's gone, stripped down to nothing.

"I moved everything into storage. They need to be digitized as it is, but we can see to that later. Mr. Ferris here is going to help me with it."

There was a thud beneath the desk as Bean hit his head and came out from underneath, looking horrified.

"Uh, it's just Bean, Mr. Monroe."

Tripp lowered the document he was reading. "Bean?" he asked.

"Yes, sir."

"Isn't your first name Axel?"

Bean met Zoe's alarmed gaze. *Did I even know what his first name was?*

"I drink an unhealthy amount of coffee, so Zoe gave me the nickname."

"And… do you like it?" Tripp asked, direct as ever.

"Yes, sir."

"Alright then, Bean. Carry on."

Tripp waved Zoe over again. Glancing around for a chair, she realized that the only seat in the room was reserved for Tripp. As she approached, Bean scurried out as fast as he could, and Zoe came to stand in front of the desk.

"Are you enjoying your power trip… Tripp?"

He looked up. "If you're referring to the lack of chairs, it wasn't intentional; I just haven't brought any in here yet. Stand for a few minutes. It's good for the circulation."

"Oh, it's for the good of my *health*, sorry, you should have said."

"So—we have everyone in today, is that correct?" Tripp asked, ignoring her sassy tone.

"Looks like it, Tom just got here, and that should be everybody."

"Tom Schilson. Yes. I've seen his work. It's good. It would be a lot cheaper if he were permanent, though. Do you know if he'd go for that?"

"I have no idea."

Tripp paused, his lips pursing as he shuffled through some papers. "Okay, well, can you find out?"

"What am I? HR?"

Tripp sat down, steepling his fingers. "I haven't told anyone you're assistant editor yet, but I *can* change my mind with this attitude."

"Tripp, you've been here five minutes, and you've gutted the archive room, given yourself an office away from all of us 'grunts' and handed the newest journalist on your books the top job. That doesn't set the best impression. Excuse me for telling you that to your face, instead of behind your back."

"Are you gonna be like this all day?"

"Most likely."

"I've been reviewing the accounts," he said, sighing heavily.

"That explains *your* mood, then."

"Things are bad, Zoe. You realize we haven't had any new ad revenue in eighteen months? *Eighteen months.* And dozens of new businesses have opened their doors in Sapphire Valley in that time; it took me four minutes to find that out. I don't know what Anton's doing all day, but it sure as hell isn't his job."

Zoe ran a hand through her hair, feeling claustrophobic in the quiet space. The archive room was ninety percent white with metal strips all over the ceiling, and the lack of color was suffocating.

"It sounds like Anton's putting that right at the moment," she said. "He was on the phone when I came in and for the last twenty minutes has been bragging about all the tasks you've set up for him."

"Yeah, because if I didn't give him something to do, he'd do nothing. The man has as much initiative as a paperweight. And don't even get me started on Angela."

Zoe bit her tongue holding back the urge to defend her colleagues. The truth was a lot of them *didn't* work hard, and she couldn't protect them from reality.

"What do you want *me* to do today?" she asked eventually.

"I want you to organize a staff meeting. I have a call with Zach in a few minutes, and after that, I want to meet with everyone who works here for half an hour each. I need to find out their history with the paper and what they do from their own perspective. After that, I can start judging them on their workload and merit."

Zoe's insides shriveled at those words. Most of the jobs at the paper weren't full-time anymore; it was hard to justify with a bi-weekly issue, but Rick hadn't made any cuts in pay to her knowledge.

Shit. Tripp's going to fire everybody.

"And what changes are you planning to make first? Will you perhaps get a potted plant in here? This room is giving mental asylum vibes."

Tripp paused, his lips twitching as he narrowed his eyes at her. "You're enjoying this, aren't you?"

"I mean… I wouldn't say *enjoying* it, but it's nice seeing you flustered. I think it's the first time that's ever happened."

"I want this to be a success. And, like I said, I'm going to need your help."

"I'll arrange the staff meeting, I'll even book the meetings in your calendar, how about that?"

"Excellent, thank you."

"Tripp, you know this is a small town, right? You can't come in all guns blazing and change everything overnight. You need to take it slow."

"We don't have that luxury, Zoe," he murmured. "There isn't much time before Morgan Media shuts this operation down. It's got to start making a profit quickly, or this paper is history."

Zoe had known the paper wasn't doing well, but seeing Tripp's worry and hearing the words aloud was quite different.

Rick, when I get a hold of you, I am going to wring your neck.

"Alright, boss. Well, I will do whatever you need me to."

"I want to overhaul everything, new design, new website, the works. I'm suspending this week's issue so we can get back to brass tacks and then return stronger with a bumper edition in three weeks' time. We're going all-in to get this paper back on track."

Zoe closed her eyes. *There is going to be a mutiny before the day is out.*

"Okay then. Sounds ambitious, but I have no doubt you can pull it off. By the way, my dog is here."

Tripp stared at her. "What?"

"My dog, Max. I have a dog now. He's under my desk. Rick didn't mind him coming into the office with me. I hope I can keep doing that?"

For a horrible moment, she thought Tripp would refuse. His brows knitted together ominously, and he took a deep breath, but finally, he shrugged.

"If he causes any disruptions or problems, he'll need to stay home."

"Understood." She rose, looking around her, feeling bereft at all the history now missing from the room. "Uh, where did the archives go?"

Tripp was already picking up his phone. "Already told you. It's in storage."

Zoe nodded, leaving him to speak with the head of Morgan Media, but as she walked out the door, something unpleasant uncoiled inside her. It seemed extreme that all of the files had been moved, and over a weekend when no one was around.

Why has Tripp done this? What am I missing?

She pushed away the question. They'd worked together for years. Tripp was an old friend; she was just being paranoid.

CHAPTER
TWENTY-FOUR

L EO ARRIVED AT THE SPARROW SHELTER ON MONDAY afternoon to pick up Gus.

It was outreach day, and Leo turned off the engine, mentally running through everything he would need as he went out into the community. He loved this type of work—seeing familiar faces, helping those who needed it most, and doing some good.

He planned to check on the dogs living on the streets, deliver care packages to those who needed them, and do as much as he could in the time he was granted. It was something he was proud to do, and it always made him feel more positive about the world around him—that was why he was taking Gus along for the ride.

Leo went into the entrance hall of the shelter to wait, but his stomach dropped as he walked through the door and found Anita standing at the desk. His hope faded even further when it looked like she had been waiting to talk to him.

"Hi Anita," he muttered as she looked up from the iPad.

"Good afternoon, Dr. Rowden. I wanted to speak to you about what you're planning today."

Leo glanced behind him to see if Gus was already there, but no luck. "Oh, yeah? What would you like to know?" he asked, keeping his tone casual.

"What exactly is the nature of the trip you're taking Mr. Gonzalez on today?"

"I go out into the community once a month and care for some of the animals who live on the street. There aren't too many though, thankfully. I thought it would be helpful for Gus to see the good in our community. That people are willing to help."

Anita scoffed. "I see. And you think that taking a vulnerable child back onto the streets he just escaped is *helpful,* do you?"

Leo shifted his weight, holding back the sharp retort he wanted to aim her way.

"Gus has been through a lot, sure, but he's got a unique perspective on that life. Seeing how well he's doing, that he has sought help, could lead others to do the same."

"It is not Mr. Gonzalez's job to *help* people in the homeless community of Sapphire Valley. He is getting away from that world. I do not condone taking him back into the lion's den."

"I'll be with him the whole time, Miss Herrera."

"I don't think that is the point."

"And why not?" he asked, folding his arms over his chest.

For a split second, her eyes turned fearful as they ran over his body. Anita Herrera was just over five feet tall and very petite against Leo's two-hundred-pound frame. In the empty space around them, he could see why she might be intimidated by him. He backed off, trying to calm his rising temper.

She pulled her iPad in front of her chest, making a derisive noise at the back of her throat.

"Whatever happens on this excursion is on you, Dr. Rowden. He is signed out under your name."

"He's not a piece of furniture," Leo murmured, and turned around to find Gus standing behind him. The kid was giving Miss Herrera such a look of loathing that Leo had to push him out the door before they came to blows.

Once they were in the truck, Gus punched the dash and sank low in his seat.

"Why is she such a bitch all the time?"

Leo tugged off his jacket and chucked it into the back. "She's just lookin' out for you, Gus."

"No, she isn't. She's keepin' tabs on me. There's a difference."

"Maybe, but she's responsible for you while you're under her roof. Imagine that it was you and you had custody of someone else. Wouldn't you worry about where they were going and what they were doing?"

"She's worried about her *job*. She couldn't care less if any of us drop dead as long as she has the right form to fill out."

"Alright, well, I'm not gonna argue with you about it, but I want you to be polite to her, okay? There aren't many shelters like this one in the county, and if you can stay there until you're eighteen, you'll have a better start than if you're on the street."

"Yeah, no shit," Gus spat sullenly.

Leo set his jaw, pulled the truck to the side of the deserted road, and stopped. When he turned in his seat, Gus's eyes went wide.

"You don't talk to me like that, is that understood? I'm here to help you, that's all I've ever wanted to do. Maybe you don't want my help. You have every right to refuse it, but I'm a person just like you. You wouldn't want some little shit talking sass at you and I sure as hell don't."

Gus blinked at him. "Did you just call me a little shit?"

Leo sighed, guilt building inside him. "You were bein' rude."

There was a charged silence as Gus uncoiled from his position by the window. Leo was surprised to see a little smile flit across the kid's face.

"I've been wonderin' if you ever lose your temper," Gus muttered.

"That's not me losin' my temper, kid. When that happens, I start breakin' stuff."

Gus resettled himself in the seat, relaxing a little more with every minute that passed.

"I can imagine. You're crazy big."

Leo shook his head. "I wish the guys in the army could hear you say that. They'd double over laughin' about it. *They* were big. I don't have the muscle for all that hulkin' about."

"What was it you said you did again? An animal specialist or somethin'?" Gus asked as Leo moved the truck back onto the road.

"Yep. I looked after military animals—mostly overseas. I made sure they were healthy, treated injuries, kept them fit for duty, that type of thing."

"And that's why you became a vet?"

"Kind of. My father was big into animals, so I've looked after 'em all my life."

Gus scoffed. "Must be a big step down havin' me at the ranch. I don't know what the hell I'm doin.'"

Leo gave him a side-eye, but he was pleased to see Gus smiling. "Uh, well, you've been a big help."

"Hah! That's bullshit. I swear that goose chased me for half a mile when I tried to feed her."

"In her defense, Atsila has a streak of pure evil in her veins."

"That's you *defending* her? Anyway, it's all good. I like her. She don't put up with anythin'. I wish I could be more like that. Only thing she seems to get along with is that random chicken."

"Esmerelda."

"Yeah, her. Zoe told me you name all your animals. I don't know how you can remember their names."

"They're all like people to me; they deserve identities."

Gus chuckled. "I'll remember that."

They drew up near the Carmichael Bridge, and Leo went to the rear of his truck to get his medical bag. He'd decided not to bring Max with him, choosing to leave the dog for a few hours on the ranch shut up in one of the larger rooms. The puppy was getting better at being left, but Leo didn't like to do it for too long.

"Is that where you got Max from? The army?" Gus asked, as Leo checked his equipment, ensuring he had enough medication for the day.

He looked at Gus, uncertain whether to give him an honest response about Max's past.

"Uh, no," he said eventually.

"I heard you and Zoe sayin' he was a rescue."

Leo closed up his bag, pulling it off the truck, beginning to walk toward the bridge. Gus fell into step beside him.

"Max was a rescue from somewhere in town. One of the, uh … Someone was abusin' his animals, and we found Max and his sister Violet in a shed out back. That's the reason he's so nervous around people—a lot of animals that have been abused don't like to get too close to anyone."

"Someone was hurtin' dogs in Sapphire?"

"Yeah. And cats."

"Oh my God. That's horrible."

"Yeah, well, he got justice, don't worry."

"Is that what happens when you lose your temper?" Gus asked lightly.

Leo halted, turning toward him, a swooping feeling of unease filling him as he looked into Gus's wide blue eyes.

"No. That's not what I meant. I might hurt someone if I really have to, but if I lose my temper, I break furniture, not bones. No one has the right to take a life, Gus. That ain't for anyone to decide but God."

"So he's dead then? The guy who hurt the animals?"

Leo grimaced. "He's in a coma far as I know. Hope he never wakes up."

"Jesus. Well, I'm glad he ain't hurtin' animals any longer."

"Me too."

They kept going in silence, their footsteps over the uneven paving slabs the only sound. But after a few minutes, the hairs on Leo's neck stood up, and he stopped, holding out an arm to Gus as his gut told him something was wrong.

"What is it?" Gus asked.

"I'm not sure. Got a strange feelin'." He turned to him, and exhaled slowly. "Can you stay here? Don't move or go anywhere. Stay by the truck."

Gus nodded, looking wary. "Alright."

"Just give me a minute. I wanna check somethin'."

He moved away, bag in hand, unsure what his gut was telling him, but he'd walked into enough battlegrounds to know something wasn't right.

It was too quiet beneath the bridge. There were always people and shadows shuffling around the place, but today it was eerie and still.

The wind ruffled through the weeds pushing up between the sidewalk on either side of him, and as he approached, there was a sound on the wind that chilled his blood. It was a high-pitched moan, haunting, cold, and echoing all around him.

Leo didn't want to go toward the sound, because he knew instinctively that whatever he found would be bad. But something forced him to keep going.

Reaching the edge of the archway under the bridge, a shadow moved, and from the darkness ahead of him, a figure emerged.

Leo stopped, his eyes coming level with those of Mateo. The two men stared at each other, the anguish in Mateo's face plain to see. Leo closed his eyes, knowing before he stepped forward that something terrible had happened.

On the right, low to the ground, was a large cardboard box, crumpled in on itself and covered with a slimy substance seeping upward from a puddle on the ground. Beside it lay Bailey, Lana's black Labrador, his tail silent and still, the sound Leo had heard coming from his throat.

The dog was lying at an awkward angle, and as Leo stepped forward he could see two feet poking out beneath him.

Lana's lifeless body lay beneath the cardboard, hunched forward, her body doubled over. Leo flinched at the sight of her wide eyes, staring ahead of her, but seeing nothing. There was a needle sticking out of one arm, caught in the vein where a dark circle had formed beneath it.

Leo moved swiftly forward, pushing past Mateo, and placed two fingers against her throat.

She had no pulse.

Leo closed his eyes, pulling out his cell phone, just as he heard a footstep behind him and spun around.

Gus was half in shadow beneath the arch above, his face stricken in a mask of horror as he took in the scene before him.

His mouth opened and closed on silent words he was unable to speak, and as Leo reached for him, Gus turned and ran at full pelt out from under the bridge toward an arch on the other side of the street.

Leo swore, sprinting after him.

"Gus! Gus, stop! Please!"

The teenager was spry, fit, and smaller than Leo, and with only a few seconds' head start, he was ten feet ahead of him.

Leo put on a spurt of speed, running as fast as he could into the dark alley at the edge of the cul-de-sac toward the neat rows of suburban houses beyond. He followed Gus's silhouette all the way down the alley, only ten yards behind him, but when he emerged, Gus was gone. It was as if he had vanished into the wind itself.

Leo was met with the familiar suburban picture of parked cars beside neat yards all around him. There was no movement to show where Gus had gone, and a thousand hiding places where he could conceal himself.

"Gus!" Leo shouted as an elderly man came out on his porch to stare at him across the street. "Gus!"

"Shut up! My grandkids are nappin'!"

Leo caught his breath, panic rushing through every vein in his body.

How could I be so stupid? I should have made him wait in the truck. I should never have even brought him here!

Turning to face the alley, he could see the outline of the bridge in the distance. He couldn't leave Lana's body in the dirt for the rats and the birds to destroy. He had to call the cops, do the right thing. But all he wanted was to find Gus and apologize a thousand times over.

Gus had experienced so much trauma in his life already, and Leo had just exposed him to more.

CHAPTER
TWENTY-FIVE

AFTER A BUSY MORNING, ZOE LEFT THE OFFICE IN THE afternoon to visit Evelyn at the library. Having missed rumblings of the first protest, she wanted to be prepared for any future events.

It was strange to have a boss who was enthusiastic about her ideas and articles for once. Tripp wanted the next edition to focus on the library and the encroachment of big corporations into Sapphire Valley. For once, the paper had a theme. Everyone was working on it, and the office had a sense of cohesion it had never had before.

Tripp was eager to get an op-ed from Evelyn, and Zoe hoped the librarian would jump at the chance to write about everything that had happened.

On her way out of town, Zoe drove by Leo's clinic, giving it a little wave out of the window as she did so. Her smile quickly faded, however, at the sound of heavy drilling that exploded on all sides as she neared the lot behind.

Wincing, she took in the massive contraption above her, dust swirling in gigantic clouds around it as it twisted into the earth. A line of trucks was queuing to get into the site, and there were hollering workmen on all sides.

Zoe grimaced. She hadn't asked Leo how things were at the clinic, too preoccupied with finding Rick, but it looked hellish. The lot was chaotic; movement, sound, and vibrations spreading outward from it like a heavy blanket. The noise was deafening even inside her car.

Nancy is gonna quit, and Leo will lose his mind.

As she drove slowly by, scowling at the Linmans' billboards, she spotted a familiar Range Rover parked on the opposite side of the road, sitting in a turnout. The significance of the license plate, which read "1ANDDUN", wasn't lost on her now that she knew Mortimer Dunridge owned the car.

Pulling her rental over to the other side of the road, she parked ahead of them and got out.

The windows were tinted, but she knew the occupant would have seen her, and sure enough, after a few seconds, the rear door opened. Dunridge emerged, all smart lines with a beautiful tan suit and white shirt—the man knew how to dress.

"Hello, Miss Fontaine," he said, shutting the car door and leaning against it with a smirk. "Have you grown tired of the big city already? I'm not surprised."

"And I *am* surprised you don't have someone to open your doors for you," she sniped, walking over to the car. "Is your driver only paid to be behind the wheel or something?"

"Merv does what I say, and I like opening doors for myself; otherwise, I look like a little girl."

"You do enjoy baiting me with misogynistic crap, makes me wonder if it's genuine or not."

"Who can say? Maybe you're just reading into things."

"Oh, and gaslighting, too. Well done." She crossed her arms over her chest. "What are you doing here, anyway? Tired of screaming at the cops, so you came to check out the little backwater you want to buy?"

Dunridge raised one manicured eyebrow, but there was amusement in his eyes.

"I'm just checking out the competition," he said, glancing at the lot and leaning his broad back against the car. "Quite an impressive venture for a little place like this."

"*Linmans* is your competition?" Zoe asked incredulously.

He cocked his head on one side. "In a way. They like to keep me on my toes."

"This town is getting quite a bit of attention from big corporations lately. Why did you pick this place for your little project?"

Dunridge snorted. "It's not a *little* project, Miss Fontaine, and I'll have you know I used to live in Whistle Falls."

"And you gave me shit about being a 'small town nobody."

The eyebrow raised again. "I had no idea our little discussion had such an impression on you."

"Don't flatter yourself. Besides, you're no better than me. You got out just like I did."

Dunridge looked past her, his eye running over her rental critically before looking back at his gleaming Range Rover. "Hm, I wouldn't necessarily say we're the same."

Zoe ignored him, cocking her head to one side. "So, what *are* you doing here?"

"Just like I said, Fontaine, eyeing up the competition. I like to keep tabs on The Linman Group, see what they're doing, and try to ruin it. It's a little game we play."

Zoe's ears pricked up. Anyone who disliked Linmans instantly became more appealing in her eyes.

"Linmans are a bit bigger than your company, though, aren't they?" she said, just to needle him.

Dunridge scratched at his immaculate beard. "So far. Sure. But I have plans."

"And the plans involve destroying the community library."

He laughed. "I offered Evelyn Cooper a very generous package to move out of that place, and she turned it down. She's too stubborn for her own good. People don't go into that library for anything but moaning and mingling."

"And you think that doesn't matter?"

"It might, but it doesn't make it profitable. She may be a good librarian, but she's no businesswoman."

"If you care so much about the library, then why don't you help her improve it?"

"Because that's not my job, Miss Fontaine. I'm here to make money, not babysit a woman who ought to know better."

"Couldn't you pick somewhere else, then? Why there?"

"You're kidding, right? It's five minutes from the highway, ten minutes from Abbotsville, and right on the river. That location has been derelict for years, and it's a crime. It could be stunning—it *will* be when I'm finished with it. Evelyn Cooper had her chance, and she blew it."

Zoe didn't like the sound of that. Evelyn had been adamant that she had had no contact from Dunridge Developments. *Why did she lie?*

"You're not going to make many friends with this project. Don't you own a string of hotels around here? Watch what happens when she starts a boycott."

Dunridge pushed off the car, straightening his shirt cuffs. "Hm, let's see who wins out in the end, shall we, Zoe?"

"I'd be interested to see—*Mortimer*."

"Did you ever find your man in the hotel room?"

Zoe looked up at him, surprised by the note of concern that edged his voice. He almost looked like he really cared.

"No. Since you ask."

"Well, I'm sorry. Missing people sometimes don't want to be found. Remember that. I've looked for my fair share of friends who went off the radar, and sometimes it just means they wanted some peace."

"Thanks for the advice."

Dunridge opened the door, glancing back at the lot before he got into the car, and there was something in his eyes for a moment—dark and angry.

"I'll be seeing you, Miss Fontaine. I would suggest that you give Miss Cooper the same advice I did. She doesn't want to get on the wrong side of my bulldozers, and I have no qualms about taking her and the library down in one go. Besides, you look like a modern gal, what would you need a library for? Have you ever actually been inside?"

He slammed the door, and the Range Rover immediately began pulling away. Zoe watched it pull out into traffic, and before it disappeared, a new idea had popped into her head.

When Zoe entered the library, she expected to see Evelyn coming to greet her as usual. Instead, she saw her standing at one of the shelves on the other side of the room, giving Zoe a waspish glance from under her glasses.

Zoe waited, but the librarian didn't come over to her, so after a few seconds she made her way across to the shelves where she stood.

"Hi Evelyn," she stated warily, and Evelyn's only response was to place the book she had in her hand on the shelf and move along. "Is something wrong?"

The librarian looked at her over the top of her glasses.

"I thought, when you came here originally, that it was going to make a difference. That your article would start a movement." She slammed the books back onto the shelves in a pile. "Instead, I'm told there's a new editor at the paper, and there won't even be an edition this week? How are we supposed to get the word out about the library when our local paper isn't even supporting us?"

"Hear, hear!" came a voice nearby, and Barry walked around the edge of the shelves, cane in hand, glowering at Zoe.

"But my article *was* published!" she retorted.

"You wrote about the town meeting and put in your interview with me," Barry said, "but we wanted to get the protest in there. That was what would have gotten people talkin'."

Zoe ran a frustrated hand through her hair. "Listen, I agree with you. Tom's pictures from the protest are amazing. But the paper is suspended for the short term, and that's not my fault.

Rick's disappeared, and Morgan Media sent in a replacement for him. He's a good guy, but he wants to overhaul everything we're doing. In three weeks, we'll have an issue dedicated to your cause in full!"

"Three weeks? What good is that to me?" Evelyn muttered.

"It's something, Evelyn. And you haven't been entirely honest with me either, before we start pointing fingers."

Evelyn and Barry looked mutinous. "And what is that supposed to mean?" Evelyn snapped.

"I just met with Mortimer Dunridge, and he said he offered you a generous settlement for this place. I'm not saying you should have taken it, or even considered it, but you should have told me it happened. As far as I knew, there had been radio silence on his end this whole time."

Barry turned to Evelyn. "You met with Dunridge?" His voice was menacing.

Evelyn raised her hands defensively, her lips curling into a grimace. "It wasn't worth it, Barry. He offered me half what I expected for this place."

"But he made you an offer?"

"Yes, but it was never to preserve the library; he still wanted to flatten it. I wasn't interested in the money; I wanted to keep this service alive."

In an impressive transition from surprise to determination, Barry's eyes moved to Zoe, glaring at her defiantly. "You heard her."

His fierce loyalty was touching. "Look, the paper is behind your cause," Zoe said patiently. "It always has been, and with Tripp joining the team it's going to get better, not worse. But we just have to wait a little longer before the articles come out. He wants you to write an op-ed for us, Evelyn. Your views on it all. That has to help, right?"

"Much good that'll do if we wait three weeks."

Evelyn stepped back and lowered herself into a chair, removing her glasses and squeezing her thumb and forefinger over the bridge of her nose. She looked exhausted, with heavy circles beneath glassy eyes, her shoulders slumped dejectedly.

"Maybe it's no use. What good can come of this? He's going to arrive and destroy it all anyway. In three years, no one will even remember the library was ever here."

"No," Zoe said firmly. "That isn't going to happen, because we *are* going to fight them and we *are* going to succeed."

Evelyn leaned back in her chair, looking up at her hopelessly.

Zoe pulled out her phone, scrolling to the images Tom had sent her of the protest. She pulled up the final image of Evelyn hanging from the streetlight, shouting into a megaphone as protesters stormed through the street beneath her, their arms and legs a blur of movement. It was a raw, powerful image, and the angle made Evelyn look like a sergeant commanding her troops.

Evelyn looked at it as a smile spread slowly over her face. "I look like a revolutionary."

"Exactly," Zoe said. "We'll get this out there and have hundreds more supporters, I guarantee it. People just need to have this in the front of their minds. Dunridge can't fight a whole town. Not this one, anyway!"

Evelyn rose to her feet, brushing herself down and clasping her hands together.

"Alright then, you'll tell me when it's going to print? I'll buy four hundred copies and plaster the walls with that picture."

Zoe laughed. "Of course I will. But, speaking of the paper, I actually had another reason for coming here."

"Oh, yes?"

"You mentioned you had a lot of old copes of The Chronicle stored here. Physical ones? Our archives were... moved, and I wanted to check something."

Evelyn was already moving, beckoning her to follow as she walked through the narrow shelves to the back of the room.

"Absolutely! That was one of the things Rick was doing. He'd send me a copy every week for us to store here. Then it became every other week, but we keep it all archived. He always joked that he didn't trust digital storage in case there was a zombie apocalypse. I've been keeping back-dated copies of the paper since 2000."

Zoe followed her to the rear of the room. Evelyn gestured to eight archive boxes neatly labeled with the dates and "The Chronicle" stamped on each one.

"That's all there is?" Zoe asked.

"That's everything since 2000," Evelyn said defensively. "So over a thousand copies, give or take."

"And they all fit in eight boxes?"

"Yep!"

Zoe stared at them. Astonished.

All that work, twenty-five years of journalism, boils down to eight boxes of information.

"Thank you. Would you mind if I looked through one of them? I had an article I was hoping to find and would prefer not to go all the way to Abbotsville again."

Evelyn gave her a long stare.

"And I won't!" Zoe said hastily. "Ever again. Who needs a library in Abbotsville when I have hard copies here?"

"I don't know, Zoe. Certainly not us."

She smiled as Evelyn left her to it, and she dove into the box marked "2015-Present."

Drawing out her notebook, she flipped to the page where she had made her notes on the Kevin Munice article and searched through the paper for the correct date.

Her heart lifted as she saw the image of the rehab clinic emblazoned across the page again. It was reassuring to hold it in her hands instead of reading it on a screen like before. Rick might have been joking about the zombie apocalypse, but the fact that the archive room had been cleared overnight was still nagging at her. It didn't make sense that Tripp would need to do that so soon.

She read through the article and finally felt the tension in her chest dissipate a fraction. She hadn't imagined it—the article was written from the perspective of Julia Munice, Kevin's sister. The piece of information Zoe hadn't noticed when she'd read it originally was the sentence in the article that listed Julia's place of work. It was referenced as a charity in Charleston, rehousing the homeless and had probably been included to drum up support.

Bingo.

Zoe could only hope her hunch was right and that this was who Rick had met with in the diner—and the woman beneath the bridge. Maybe if she could track down Julia Munice and talk to her, she might prove to be the link that held this whole thing together.

Making a few notes on the pad and snapping a photograph of the article for good measure, she put everything back in the boxes.

As she did so, her phone vibrated, and she answered without checking the caller ID.

"Zo, can you get to the Carmichael Bridge?" Leo's panicked voice came through the call. "Gus has disappeared."

CHAPTER TWENTY-SIX

B Y THE TIME ZOE ARRIVED AT THE BRIDGE, IT WAS EARLY evening, and the sky was a startling blue against the black backdrop of the mountains. The flashing lights from the first responders made for a jarring contrast as she pulled to a stop, Leo walking hurriedly toward her, his whole body taut and stiff.

As Zoe got out of the car, a deputy walked by, talking on his phone.

"*Some junkie OD'd so I'm not gonna be home until late, I'm sorry...*"

She looked to Leo, who came forward, and they embraced quickly before he pulled away.

"It's my fault. I brought him here. It was such a stupid thing to do."

"Slow down, Leo, what's happened?"

"I brought Gus along with me, because I thought it would be good for him to see the outreach program—what this community can do when they help each other. But when we showed up, I knew something was wrong. It was just weirdly quiet, and when I went under the bridge, there was a body."

"Jesus. Who was it?"

"The woman I told you about, Gus's friend Lana. I told him to stay put but…" his voice trailed off, his eyes dark and miserable.

"Did he see the body?"

Leo's throat convulsed. "Yeah."

"Oh God, okay. It's alright, Leo, we'll find him. He can't have gone far."

He shook his head. "He went up that alleyway, and I ran after him, but then he disappeared. I couldn't just leave her lying there. It isn't like Mateo has a phone to call the cops, and I didn't know how long she'd been dead. I've had so many people askin' me questions, but I don't have any answers, and all I want to do is get out there and find Gus."

"Alright. We'll go. Who do you need to talk to now?"

"I have no idea. Kissinger's questioning Mateo, but you can imagine how well that's goin'. They're not getting much out of him. Jesus, Zoe, if anything happens to that kid it's on me. I told them I'd look after him."

Leo's emotions were hard to read. His voice betrayed the panic running through him, but everything else about him was calm and collected. It was a strange mixture of realities—like watching a statue crying. Zoe couldn't get a read on him.

"Let's go talk to the sheriff," she said quietly. "Come on."

As they approached the bridge, a black body bag on a gurney was wheeled into sight and loaded into an ambulance. Zoe kept her eyes focused on the shapes of Mateo and Kissinger beneath the archway. She felt cold.

Mateo was chewing his lip and giving Kissinger a death stare. Zoe saw the sheriff notice her and Leo, but he didn't turn around until he'd finished writing something on his notepad.

"Can I go?" Mateo's voice was hard. He and the sheriff had never gotten along, and their animosity was never more obvious than in that moment.

"Don't go too far," Kissinger murmured. Mateo shoved his cart away and disappeared into the trees beyond as Leo stepped forward, towering over Kissinger and looking every bit the soldier.

"I need to go, too. I gotta find Gus."

Kissinger nodded. "Look, you've been makin' sure that kid checks in with us every week like clockwork, and I'm grateful for that, but he's gotta report in or I have to tell the judge."

Zoe expected Leo to argue, but he simply nodded. "I know that, Sheriff, I'm going to find him, and he'll be there like he always is."

"But you don't know where he went?" Kissinger asked skeptically.

"He was scared," Leo growled.

"Did he know the woman who died?"

"Yes."

"Well, seems to me that he needs to get better company, then."

A vein was pulsing in Leo's forehead, and Kissinger backed up a step, pocketing his notebook.

"You're free to go. I might need to call you in a few days if anythin' new comes up. You sure you're okay takin' the deceased's dog?"

Zoe frowned, glancing at Leo in confusion.

"Yeah. It's fine, he's in my truck," he said over his shoulder, already marching back toward it, and Zoe had to jog to keep up.

"You have her dog?" she asked, amazed.

"Yeah. I couldn't leave him," he said, his tone tight and a little defensive. "Bailey's not in good shape, and the animal shelter will put him on a kill list soon as look at him."

"Oh… okay. Of course," she said gently. "That's a kind thing to do. Let me park my car at the clinic, and I'll come with you. I doubt there's any use in us splitting up if you want to drive around the town. Are there any places you know of that Gus would go?"

Leo shook his head and climbed back into his truck. Bailey's huge black eyes were visible for a moment in the passenger seat before Leo's body obscured him.

"I'll see you in a few minutes."

He slammed the door and skidded away, and Zoe ran to her rental to follow behind. It took a lot to really rattle Leo, yet that threshold seemed to have been crossed.

They drove around the streets for hours that night, stopping every now and again, calling Gus's name. Leo went into The Red Cardinal and a few other bars on the off chance that Gus might have been seen there, but there was no sign.

Every minute that passed, his panic grew, and it was horrible to watch. Privately, Zoe doubted they would find Gus until he wanted them to. A kid like that knew how to hide and keep his head down; he'd been doing it all his life. Wherever he had lived before the shelter, it was likely that that was where he was.

"Didn't he say he used to live in a flophouse?" Zoe asked eventually after almost a full hour of silence. Bailey, who was the gentlest dog in the world, was sleeping between them, his head resting on Zoe's thigh.

"Yeah, but after the shelter took him in, I didn't think to ask where it was." Leo groaned, slamming his hand against the wheel. "I didn't even *think* about the shelter. He's missed curfew. They won't let him back in now. And I've left Max alone all day without any company."

"Max'll be okay, Leo. Don't worry. You're gonna show up with a friend for him later so he'll be just fine." She scratched between Bailey's ears, chewing her lip, and Leo glanced over at her, frowning.

"What?"

"Do you think maybe you should go back to the ranch? I was wondering whether that would be the best place to wait. Gus knows that's where you are. Maybe he'll go there rather than the shelter. He's never liked that place, and you did say he and the administrator don't get along."

Her toes curled in her shoes, waiting for Leo to explode with anger at the thought of abandoning the search, but he just sighed, a distraught look on his face.

"I've been thinkin' the same thing. I don't reckon he's gonna be visible from the road even if he is hiding somewhere. But who's he got to go to but the people he hung around with before? He was in that gang of thugs, stealin' and lootin' to buy drugs. What's to stop him going back there?"

"If he does that, it's his choice."

"Not helpful!" Leo snapped.

"Well, in situations like this, it isn't always helpful to pretend everything's okay. Yeah, Gus might go back to what's familiar, that doesn't mean he won't come out again when he's processed what happened."

Her voice was loud in the quiet truck, and Leo's jaw was flexing continually as he turned it around and headed back to the clinic.

"We can stop by Skywolf and collect your car. Are you stayin' over?" he sounded less than enthused.

"I need to drive to Charleston early tomorrow, so I should probably be at my place."

"You're drivin' to Charleston *tomorrow*? While Gus is in the wind?"

"I didn't know that at the time, Leo. He won't be found until he wants to be found."

"Nice," he grunted. "What the hell's so important in Charleston?"

"I'm going to meet with the woman we saw, the one who Rick might have met up with. Her name's Julia Munice."

Leo didn't say anything as they drove up to the clinic. Zoe's stomach flipped when he stayed silent, waiting for her to get out.

"I guess Max is stayin' with me, then," he murmured.

"I can come and get him if—"

"I don't need you to come and get him, I'm confirming that's what's happening."

"Yes, if that's alright."

"Of course it's alright!" he snapped.

Zoe ground her teeth. "Fine. I have to be in the city tomorrow morning, but I'll come back and help you look after work, okay? I need to be in the office right now, Tripp's up in everyone's business about what they're working on, and I can't just drop everything like I used to."

"Fine."

"Leo."

"What?"

"He'll come back."

Zoe opened the door and climbed out. Leo didn't even wait for her to get to her car before he was reversing and heading back to the ranch.

Zoe wanted to blame him for his behavior and rail at him for shutting her out, but she'd been there before. She knew exactly what it was like to lose someone you cared about to the streets, and there was nothing either of them could do now but wait.

The offices of The Small Change, the organization where Julia Munice worked, were impressive. It reminded Zoe of The Salvation Army, with bright red accents all over the walls, and a small shield on their logo.

From her research, it seemed that the charity's primary function was outreach—to try and help homeless people move into safe accommodation in the city. They had several programs, including temporary shelters offering beds and showers to those in need.

The Small Change was a little fish against other larger organizations, but Zoe liked the vibe of the place. It had an impressive website and had recently caught the public's attention after an A-list star had promoted their work on Instagram and TikTok. Pictures and banners were everywhere from her visit to the offices, and according to their website, it had been a lucrative pairing, leading to multiple new collaborations with major companies.

She'd called Julia Munice that morning on the pretext of wanting to interview her for the paper. Zoe wasn't looking forward to revealing her real reason for their meeting, but at least she'd gotten some time with her.

As she signed in, the receptionist asked her to wait on the plush red sofa in the entryway of the building, and Zoe perched there patiently until she saw Julia approaching.

She was tall, slim, and extremely beautiful. Her long hair and pale, freckled skin were striking, making her look more like a model than a charity worker.

Zoe stood as she approached, one hand outstretched with a friendly smile.

"Zoe Fontaine?" Julia asked in a strong southern accent.

"That's me. Julia Munice?"

"Oh good, we've got the right people," Julia said, grinning. "Come on up. I'm sorry I only had such a short time to see you today, but I'm intrigued. I haven't met anyone from Sapphire Valley in years."

Zoe forced a smile, following her through the security gates and up the glass elevators to the third floor. The offices were plush and corporate, nothing like she would have expected from a charity.

Julia's office was small but tidy, and she closed the door behind them as Zoe took a seat and got out her notepad.

"So, like I said, I was intrigued by your call. How can I help?" Julia asked, taking a seat behind her desk.

Zoe glanced around the office, noting a family photo behind Julia's left shoulder, her eye drawn to Kevin's face as a young man, standing beside a much younger Julia.

"I know we don't have a lot of time, but I want to be honest with you, Miss Munice."

"Julia's fine."

"I actually came to ask you about something personal."

Julia frowned. "Personal to me, or to you?"

"Both, I'm afraid. I'm sorry to barge in and do this cold, but I'm looking for a friend of mine. Rick Fisher?"

The other woman didn't move for a moment, and then she licked her lips, her gaze hardening. "I see. So this isn't an interview?"

"No. I'm sorry," Zoe leaned forward. "This isn't how I normally operate. I wouldn't have come if it wasn't urgent. Rick is missing."

Julia stilled. "What?"

"He went missing a few weeks back, and I've been looking for him ever since. I had one lead, and that was you. It's taken me a while to put the pieces together, but am I right that you met with him recently?"

Julia blew out a breath, straightening a pen on her desk. "Yeah. He called me out of the blue—looks like that rubs off on the people who work for him, too."

"I know, I'm sorry, I appreciate you're busy, but any information you can give me would help."

"He's really missing?"

"Yes. Was there anything strange about his behavior when you saw him?"

"Hah!" Julia leaned back in her chair. "The whole meeting was strange. I hadn't spoken to him in years, and then he calls me up out of the blue. He refused to tell me what it was about over the phone, and then when we did meet up, he was jumpy as hell."

"What did he want to meet with you for, if you don't mind me asking?"

"No, I don't mind. To be truthful, the whole thing's been playin' on my mind a bit. I'm glad it's not just me it didn't make sense to. Do you know how I know Rick?"

"I assume it's to do with your brother?"

Julia nodded, her face devoid of emotion. "Yeah. Kevin went missing about ten years back. Rick wasn't involved then, it was mainly Arnold, the editor of the paper, who was investigating all of that. Kevin went into a rehab facility called the Sapphire Foundation, but he never came out again. The way the administration tells it, he overdosed and died, and then there was a fire the same night. But I never bought that. I always believed something had happened to him."

"Was there any evidence after the fire, any remains discovered?"

Julia scoffed. "Nothing. He up and vanished like he'd never been there. We had to have a funeral with an empty coffin, and every time I tried to find out what had happened, they'd shut me down. That was what first interested Arnold in the case—it wasn't the fire so much, it was that no one was telling me what had happened to my brother."

"And what did Rick want?"

"It was weird. He was spitting out all these questions about if anyone had been asking about Kevin, if I'd had any calls or emails about the case. I told him the same thing I'm telling you— nothing… except from him. He was the first person to mention Kevin's name to me in years. Until now."

Julia's hazel eyes met Zoe's, and she cleared her throat.

"You know that Arnold Price committed suicide, I take it?" Zoe asked.

"Yeah. Only because Rick took over the story afterwards, but that petered out real quick. He was calling me a lot to begin with, and then it all just stopped. I was too exhausted to chase it—wanted it dead and buried, you know?"

"And… do you think he's looking for Kevin? Is there any chance that your brother might be alive?"

Julia's eyes went wide, and then she laughed. "No. He's dead. Just like all the others."

There was a knock on the door, and a young woman with a laptop in her hand opened it.

"Sorry Julia, Larkwell just arrived for the meeting."

Julia's hands fluttered over the desk's surface, grabbing her iPad as she rose, nodding to Zoe.

"I'm sorry, I have to go, but that's everything I told Rick. Our meeting lasted for ten minutes, tops, and then I left. I'm really sorry he's missing. Take my number and call me if I can help more."

Zoe stood. "Did the two of you argue?" she blurted, as the other woman rounded the desk and came level with her. Julia glanced at her warily.

"I wasn't pleased that he'd pulled me out of work and was dragging up the past again. My brother is dead, he deserves his peace. Those assholes weren't interested in him when he was in their care, they're not gonna be interested ten years on and I told him so."

She walked to the door, and Zoe forced out one last question as Julia opened it.

"What did you mean—he's dead 'like all the others'?"

Julia's fingers curled more tightly on the handle of the door, and she shook her head, just once.

"He's dead, Miss Fontaine. I suggest you leave it at that."

Then she whisked out the door and was gone.

CHAPTER
TWENTY-SEVEN

ZOE DIDN'T HEAR FROM LEO ALL DAY, AND BY THE TIME she arrived back in Sapphire Valley, she had to head to the office.

"Where the hell have you been all morning?"

Tripp was standing by the door when she entered, like he'd been waiting for her, and several heads popped up as she walked to her desk.

"I was following a lead on a story. I told you that."

"What story—is that going to equate to an article?"

"Yes," she hazarded. "Why are you being so grumpy?"

"Bean, our only IT guy, was just telling me he 'doesn't do websites,'" Tripp muttered irritably as Bean slunk into the kitchenette to make himself a coffee.

"No. Well, that isn't his job."

"We can't revamp the paper without a decent website. Have you seen the one we have? It's not been updated since 1998."

"You're exaggerating."

"It doesn't *look* like it has anyway. Come into my office."

Zoe scowled at his back as she dumped her bag and followed him. "You know, you're not supposed to have an *office*. You could just sit with everyone else, like Rick did."

"Uh-huh, and that worked out real well," Tripp said, pushing through the door. There were now two chairs in front of his desk, and he sat behind it. "Where were you?" he said, indicating she should sit, too.

"Do I have to tell you my movements every second of the day?"

"You do when you're not in the office."

"You never cared in D.C."

"In D.C., you were following bank robbers. Here you might have fallen down a well. Not to mention the fact that I had *output* from you at the Express, Zo. You've barely written anything for weeks."

Zoe wanted to tell him that she hadn't had time while she'd been covering for Rick, but she didn't want to make things even worse for him.

"I've written about the library."

"Yeah, about that. We want to go hard on Dunridge on this. I want to eviscerate him."

She leaned forward, frowning at him. "What? Why?"

"Other than he's tearing down the community piece by piece?"

"Linmans are doing that far more than Dunridge is."

"Do you want to be run off the road again?" Tripp asked, his face a mask as he fixed her with a hard stare.

It was like Zoe had been gut-punched. Slowly, she recoiled from him, letting out a long breath.

"Excuse me?"

"The last time you followed your hunch about Linmans, someone tried to kill you, Zoe. I would think, having had that happen, that you might want to back off your vendetta against them."

"And *I* would think you'd know that scare tactics aren't going to stop me from doing my job."

"You had no evidence for what you were building, remember? I saw what you were pulling together, and it was sketchy at best—all assumptions and hearsay."

Zoe opened her mouth to violently protest that, but he raised a hand to stop her.

"The bottom line? Make a choice about where your loyalties lie. It wasn't at the Express, and it doesn't seem to be here, not judging by the way you're running around half-assing everything."

"I am not—"

"This isn't an argument, it's a statement of fact. I know you were chasing after Rick again this morning. I'm not stupid. Leave it up to the cops and do your job."

He flicked an irritated gaze her way and turned to his computer. Zoe took it as the dismissal it was and jumped to her feet, marching out of the office and quietly fuming as she collapsed into the chair at her desk.

Opening her inbox, she began to work through her emails, Tripp's words running through her head over and over.

The thing that got to her the most, that really got her back up, was that he was right.

She hadn't knuckled down to anything since she came to Sapphire Valley. She'd worked at the paper, doing the bare minimum because Rick never pulled her up on it. Her investigation into Linmans was sitting silently in files in her apartment, and she had taken no steps toward an answer. The only thing she'd committed to was Max, and half the time she left him with Leo because she was too busy to care for him.

She hadn't even committed to Leo properly.

Maybe Tripp has a point.

After working late that afternoon, Zoe headed back to her apartment, having spent most of the day dealing with several queries Tripp had sent her. It was the first time she had felt truly productive in a while, and it only reiterated his point.

Tripp's words had struck a chord, and she was determined to knuckle down and show him she was committed to the job.

There was a light drizzle of rain falling, and the humidity levels had been rising all day. She could feel the valley's heat increasing as she drove toward her apartment. The roads were fairly deserted, most of the traffic bunching around Jefferson Street, and she had the radio blaring and the windows down, wondering if she should brave going by the ranch to pick up Max.

She missed having him with her, but the lack of contact from Leo since their fight didn't fill her with much hope. Gus clearly hadn't resurfaced, and she wasn't sure Leo would even want to see her at the moment.

Making her way around a corner, Zoe watched a large bird of prey flap lazily upward from the side of the road. Her eyes caught on it for a few seconds only, before she looked back at the road and screamed, slamming on her brakes, at the figure standing in the way of her car just a few feet ahead.

Her veins flushed with adrenaline as she felt the car skid to a stop just ahead of Mateo's bulky form. Breathing heavily, she lowered the window as he wandered toward the driver's side.

"Are you insane? I could have killed you."

Mateo leaned down, the confusing scents around his body flooding into the car.

"I found Gus," he said shortly, and then turned back and wandered into the woods. Zoe stared after him, watching him disappear between the trees into the shadows.

"Great. Just great," she said aloud, glancing in her rearview at the deserted road and the total lack of witnesses.

She pulled over and got out, jogging after Mateo and walking under the dark canopy. The light rain didn't penetrate much in the woods, and she found Mateo waiting for her just inside, next to a wide tree trunk.

"He might run," he said warily. "He don't know you're comin.'"

"That's probably for the best. Is he alright?"

"He's fine. Been through worse."

Zoe didn't ask any further questions, and Mateo didn't elaborate. They walked in silence between the thick tree trunks and tiny saplings that were pushing their way up toward the light.

"How did he come to be here?" Zoe whispered as they approached a clearing.

"He smokes up here sometimes. Same as a lot of the kids. Wondered if he might be here."

"Did you come all the way out here to look for him?"

Mateo shrugged. "Leo done a lot of good for me. Wanted to help."

So the homeless guy in town is helping Leo more than I am. That's encouraging.

Mateo stopped, pointing ahead into a clearing. "Kid knows these woods. If he spooks he's gone."

"Thanks, Mateo," she said earnestly, catching his eye. "This wasn't scary at all, by the way," she said, with a rueful smile, and Mateo grinned.

"Ain't got no beef with you," he stated frankly, and wandered away.

Zoe waited until his footsteps had receded and then made her way toward the clearing. Something loosened in her chest when she saw Gus sitting on a log smoking a cigarette.

He was bent forward, hoodie up over his head, his arms resting against his knees.

Steeling herself for a chase, she stepped into the clearing. Gus looked up and rose instantly, his eyes darting all over the place until Zoe raised her hands.

"Please don't run, I'm in heels."

Gus hesitated, and that tiny pause allowed her to take a step toward him.

"I'm not going to force you to do anything you don't want to do, I just wanted to check you're alright."

Gus pulled the sleeve of his hoodie over his hand and wiped his nose, eyeing her suspiciously.

"Is Leo with you?"

"No, but he's worried sick."

Gus snorted. "Sure. More like raging mad."

"Are you alright?" she asked.

"I needed some space."

"I get that."

His hand ticked against his thigh, tapping it in a rhythm, and then he walked toward her, stubbing his cigarette out on a tree trunk.

"I tried to find the ranch last night, but couldn't remember which direction it was in."

Zoe sighed with relief. "Can I drive you? I know he'd love to see you."

"Don't think the shelter'll have me back after this. Ain't he gonna be pissed?"

"Don't worry about that for now. Let's just get you somewhere safe and warm."

They walked back through the foliage, Gus quiet and morose beside her, the stench of cigarettes and body odor surrounding him in a cloud. Once they reached her car Zoe turned the engine back on and the radio blared loudly, but she didn't turn it off, preferring the patter of a DJ to trying to make small talk with a teenager.

They drove in silence, Gus leaning heavily against the door. He looked exhausted, and Zoe would bet he hadn't slept since he'd run off.

Leo came out as they drove into the ranch, having recognized her car. He was accompanied by Max, who started barking with excitement and running in circles, but Leo didn't look pleased to see her. Zoe's insides coiled tight at the sight of his miserable expression, and she couldn't tell if he was angry with her or worried for Gus.

She pulled up, and it was only then that Leo saw who was in her passenger seat and lurched forward, running around the side and opening the door.

"Gus!" he shouted, pulling the poor kid from his seat and hauling him out. "Where you been?"

Leo made an abortive movement, as if he had wanted to hug him, but changed his mind. They stood, immobile, staring at each other, and Leo ran both hands through his hair, staring up at the sky in despair before looking over at Zoe.

"Where was he?"

"Mateo flagged me down. He found him in the woods."

Leo ran his eye over Gus, lingering on the state of his clothes, his expression grim. "Go inside," he stated firmly.

Gus didn't say a word, just wandered over to the door and into the ranch house. Zoe watched as Leo followed him, her irritation spiking when she didn't get so much as a thank you or an acknowledgement for bringing Gus back.

She followed them inside, closing the door behind them as Leo entered the kitchen. Max was docile now, standing beside Zoe's legs and not leaving her side, but quiet, sensing the atmosphere.

Gus stood in the center of the room, looking miserably down at Bailey as the dog came to greet him. Leo clattered about in the kitchen, moving mechanically, his shoulders stiff.

Men really are terrible at communicating.

Eventually, Leo approached Gus with one of his handleless cups of Yaupon tea. Gus took it, and they all went to sit on the couch.

"Where did you go?" Leo asked in a combative tone, as Gus sat up straighter.

"Away," he muttered.

"You didn't think to call me?"

"No."

"You didn't think I'd be worried about you?"

"No."

Zoe closed her eyes. Such a simple word, but it spoke volumes for what Gus had been through.

When was the last time anyone cared about this kid?

"Well, I *was* worried," Leo bit out. "Were you using again?"

Zoe winced as Gus stood up, throwing the cup of tea to the ground where it splattered everywhere. Max whined, running away to his bed and burying his nose under his blanket. Bailey, slumped at Gus's feet, looked between them balefully, as Gus glared at Leo, trying his best to appear domineering.

"What's it to you?"

Leo leaped to his feet, too. "Is that the solution, is it? You get upset, you get high?"

"Leo," Zoe said calmly.

"Upset?" Gus bellowed. "*Upset?* I just saw my only friend dead on the road, what do you think?"

Leo threw up his hands. "I told you to stay by the truck. You were never supposed to see that."

"Oh, so it's my fault?" Gus shouted.

Zoe stood up very slowly, putting a hand on Gus's arm. He flinched but didn't pull away.

"Leo, sit down," she said gently. "Both of you, just sit down, alright? This isn't helping."

Gus's chest was heaving, the rage in his eyes horrible to witness. Slowly, they all lowered themselves to the couch.

"Leo," Zoe said carefully, waiting until he looked at her. "I think there's something else you meant to say."

Leo stilled, closing his eyes as he collapsed forward, putting his head in his hands before finally looking at Gus.

"I'm sorry," he breathed. "I should *never* have taken you with me or allowed you to see something like that. It was unforgivable, and I'm furious with myself, not you. You didn't do anything wrong, Gus. I wouldn't have known how to react either if it had been me. I just… I was worried. I thought you might be dead. I'm sorry."

Zoe looked at Gus, who was staring at the puddle of tea on the floor and the cup that had miraculously stayed intact where it had landed. For a long time, Gus didn't move at all, and then, Bailey stood up and came and rested his chin against his knee.

Gus's shoulders started to shake.

Zoe felt tears build in her own eyes as the floodgates finally opened, and Gus started to sob. A few seconds later, Leo came to sit beside him, looping his arms around the kid and giving him a hug… maybe the first one he'd experienced in years.

CHAPTER
TWENTY-EIGHT

B Y THE TIME GUS AND LEO CAME UP FOR AIR, THE DRIZZLE
had turned to a downpour, and darkness was pressing
against the wide windows in Leo's living room.

Once Gus was recovered enough to speak, Leo rose and went
back into the kitchen to make them all another cup of tea.

They sat at the table, and an awkward silence settled between
them. Leo got up again and returned a few minutes later with a
plate of scones, placing them between him and Gus, who peered
at them suspiciously.

"What are those brown parts?"

"Golden raisins," Leo replied.

"And the red parts?"

"Candied cherries. An old family recipe."

Zoe took one, dunking it in her tea, which won her a frown from Leo. Gus noted his disapproval and copied the movement, making her smile.

They both bit into them at once and then groaned.

"Oh my God, is there anything you're *not* good at in the kitchen?" Zoe asked. "These are amazing."

They all dug in, and for a few minutes, the table was filled with happy munching. Zoe called Max over, who hopped up beside her on the chair and nestled his head in her lap, reassured by the quiet that had descended. Bailey ambled over after him and slumped down under the table with a long sigh.

"Thanks for bringin' Bailey here," Gus whispered.

"That's alright, I didn't want the shelter to take him," Leo said carefully, glancing at Zoe, as he scratched at the stubble over his chin. "Listen, Gus, you don't have to tell me where you were. But I just want to know that you were safe," he said finally.

Gus shrugged. "I had some friends I could stay with."

"Friends from your old gang?" Leo asked, and Gus stiffened.

"What Leo is trying to say is, we're glad you're safe," Zoe interrupted and got another frown for her trouble.

"I wasn't sure what to do," Gus muttered. "Lana was my only friend in Sapphire, like a *real* friend. She was trying to get clean. She *was* clean."

Zoe glanced at Leo, who didn't look like he believed him.

"I just wanted to be somewhere else, you know? Where I didn't have to keep reportin' to the cops, and answerin' people's questions, and meetin' curfews. That was the one good thing about livin' rough. I didn't have to explain anythin' to anyone."

"I get that," Leo said quietly. "Look, I haven't handled this in the best way, but I want you to stay with me for a while. There's no way Anita will ever let you out of her sight again after all this, and I understand why you wouldn't want to go back to the shelter. I want you to stay here and see if we can find you somethin' else to do other than terrify my chickens."

"You want me to live here?" Gus sounded bewildered.

"If you want to. But you have to swear to me you won't bring drugs here."

Gus ran a hand through his hair. "I don't do that anymore. I only took drugs because my friends were, and it didn't even help that much. I felt good while I was high, but then I'd come down and everythin' would be the same. I haven't taken anything since I went into the shelter, Leo, I swear."

Leo glanced at Zoe. She could see the hope in his eyes and his desperation to believe the kid. It wasn't her place to tell him Gus was lying; it would either come out in time, or he was really clean. Either way, Zoe knew that one way or another, this was a waiting game.

In the meantime, she had a plan for how Gus might get a little more out of life.

"Leo said you fixed something on his computer for him at the clinic?" Zoe asked.

Gus nodded. "Yeah. It wasn't really a *fix*. It's a basic anti-virus program that everyone else has had since the eighties. You should really get yourself a proper firewall as well, otherwise someone's going to compromise your data and you'll have no backup."

Leo cleared his throat. "Bunch of words there I didn't understand."

Gus snorted. "I can do it for you. There are a few that aren't too expensive, but you get what you pay for. How do you not have an anti-virus? Are you still listening to your music on iPods, too?"

"Alright, alright. I have a receptionist who prints out emails, come on, give me a break." Leo glanced at Zoe. "Why'd you ask about that anyway?"

"Well…" Zoe hesitated, mulling over the idea that had formed in her mind. "Tripp needs someone to, in his words, 'revolutionize' the Chronicle's website."

She sipped her tea, watching different emotions bloom over Gus's face.

"I don't know what that kind of stuff would entail, but if you're good with computers, and you want a bit of short-term work, I think it might be helpful for you to have some structure to your days that the shelter or the cops don't dictate—it'd be real work. And we have a monosyllabic twenty-something as our IT guy who subsists on coffee and croissants. I think you two would get along great."

Gus raised his eyebrows, looking at Leo. "And I could live here? Wouldn't you want rent?"

"You still have to look after the geese and chickens, that's rent enough."

Gus turned to Zoe. "You think they'd want to employ me? *I* wouldn't want to employ me."

Zoe chuckled. "I'd vouch for you. My new boss isn't going to cut any corners for you, though. He'll expect you to work hard, and if he isn't happy with you, he won't sugarcoat it. Trust me on that. But if it's something you think you can do—"

"I can do it. I used to create websites for my friend's bands all the time at school. I can do it. Are you serious? That's awesome!"

Zoe blinked. Sitting beside her was an animated, excitable young man instead of the morose, miserable teenager she had come to know. Leo looked just as surprised as she did, and Zoe gave him a small smile, hoping she hadn't made a huge mistake mixing her career with her personal life.

"And you've designed websites before?" Tripp stood with his arms folded the next day, glaring at Gus like he was a convicted criminal. Gus shifted his weight, nodding.

"Yeah."

"Okay, and is there one you can show me as evidence of this?"

"Uh… not really." Gus swallowed, looking at Zoe for guidance.

"Tripp, why don't *you* show him what you want and see if he can do it, rather than assuming he can't?"

Tripp gave Gus another thorough once-over before he pulled up a site on his phone and pushed it in front of the kid's face.

"This is *The Globe's* website; it's another paper that Morgan Media owns, but it's also our main competitor. The website is dogshit. Do something better than this and you're hired."

Gus plucked the phone out of Tripp's hand and scrolled through it, nodding as he clicked into the menus.

"I can do it. You're right, that website is dogshit," he said, handing back the phone." I can make yours better than that."

Tripp grinned. "You're hired for the time being. I'll give you a few days, and then we'll review. If you screw it up Zoe's fired, and so are you."

Gus paled as Tripp walked away, and Zoe patted him on the shoulder. "Don't worry, he's like that all the time; he doesn't mean it."

"He looked like he meant it."

"Come on, I'll show you where Bean sits."

"His name is Bean?"

"You'll understand after you've known him for half an hour," she said, as they walked over to his desk. "Bean? Can you set up another computer over here, please? Gus, this is Bean, Bean, Gus."

The two young men sized one another up and then nodded. That was all the interaction that passed between them.

"Why does he have to sit near me? I work alone," Bean said.

"You're not James Bond, and you'll both be doing..." Zoe searched for the right technical term. "Software stuff?" Bean snorted. "So if Gus has questions, you're the best person for him to sit beside. Stop being argumentative. Gus, if you need anything, you can come and speak to me. And I mean anything. I'd rather know if you do something wrong than find out in a few days' time when I get fired, okay?"

She left them to it as Bean dragged an old monitor out and started setting it up.

As she reached her desk, she checked her phone for the third time that morning. After the emotional reconciliation between Leo and Gus the night before, she'd suggested that she should go home to let Gus get settled in.

Zoe had expected Leo to protest and tell her he wanted her to stay, but he'd said nothing, and she hadn't heard from him all day. Squeezing her phone angrily, she threw it back down, totally clueless as to where they stood or what she should do about it.

Glancing back at Gus, she saw him and Bean standing silently beside one another, not making eye contact as they waited for the computer to boot up.

Maybe this is Bean's perfect companion.

Waiting for a few minutes until Gus was settled, rapidly clicking through multiple screens on his new monitor, Zoe turned to her own computer and got back to work. Now she'd been given permission to 'eviscerate' Dunridge in her article, she intended to do what she did best—research and destroy.

Thirty minutes later, she was getting thirsty and walked over to the kitchen, smiling when she overheard Bean telling Gus how helpful coffee was to keep your energy levels up. She wondered if Leo would count coffee as a drug and decided not to tell him about it.

As she stood waiting for the machine to heat up, she leaned against the counter and watched the office.

Miriam and Lilith were both on the phone, as was Anton, and even Angela was working on an article that had nothing to do with UFOs or aliens for once. Daniel and Tom were laughing, looking through images on Tom's iPad, and there was a general sense of excitement and happiness about the place.

It was like working in a real office, and Zoe had to admit it was a refreshing change. She felt buoyant and uplifted by it. Since Rick's disappearance, everything had been so mired in uncertainty that she'd forgotten how good it was to work somewhere that had an atmosphere.

Still, as her eyes drifted to Rick's desk, familiar anxiety rose within her. *Will he ever come back?*

"Hey, boss," Bean said, coming up behind her and swiping the pot off the coffee machine before she could get to it.

"Hey, I was waiting for that!"

"Snooze you lose," he said with a smirk, filling up her cup, too.

"How's Gus doing?" she asked and was anything but reassured by the grimace that crossed his features.

"You said he was 'good with computers,' not gunning for my job. He's like a ninja."

"Really?"

"Yeah. Whatever he did before, it was a lot more than websites. He's really good. I could do with his help with some of my work, if I'm honest. But he's already had Tripp come and stand over his shoulder five times in thirty minutes."

"Yeah, Tripp's not the most trusting person. Let me know if you think Gus is getting too deep, though, will you?"

"Too deep into what? The internet?"

"Good point."

Bean leaned against the counter beside her. "Did you have a chance to look at that footage I sent you?" he asked.

Zoe winced as she burned her tongue on the boiling coffee. "Shit, I completely forgot about that. Yeah. I watched it. Thank you for sending it through. What did you make of it?"

Bean shook his head. "No idea. I mean it's a car driving along a road, right? Not a lot to read into there."

"I wasn't sure why he would have had it in his inbox, though."

"Did you see the date? It looked like it had been added after the fact."

"I thought that too," she murmured. "That's weird, right?"

Bean shrugged, his eyes following Tripp as he came out of his office to chat with Daniel and Tom. Zoe watched as Tripp looked around the room, his eyes settling on them both. Bean stiffened.

"Listen, uh, I found something else on Rick's machine, but I think I should probably talk to you about it somewhere outside of the office."

"What? Why? What is it?"

"Later," Bean said and sidled away.

Zoe went to the refrigerator and pulled out the milk, dumping too much into the scalding cup before she went to ask him what the hell he meant by that. She had begun to think that they might never find Rick, and now it seemed that Bean had a lead he had been sitting on all this time.

Am I the only one who cares about finding him?

And just as that thought entered her head, Nathan Lombardi walked through the door.

CHAPTER TWENTY-NINE

ONCE AGAIN, LOMBARDI LOOKED LIKE A MOVIE STAR.
The badge around his neck was the only thing that suggested he was law enforcement. His outfit was mostly leather, from the motorcycle pants to the jacket over a dark blue shirt, and the mirrored shades and wide stance completed the look.

Angela's eyes almost bugged out of her head when she turned and saw him.

Lombardi removed his shades, looking around the room with interest, taking in the wooden partitions between the desks and the huge purple letters that read "The Sapphire Valley Chronicle" on the far wall.

Zoe could see the judgment in his eyes almost immediately—Nathan didn't do small towns for a reason.

A few seconds later, their eyes met, and Zoe walked over to him just as Tripp did the same.

"Can I help you?" Tripp asked.

"I'm Detective Lombardi with the Charleston Police Department. I'm here investigating the disappearance of Rick Fisher."

And there goes any hope I had that we could keep this quiet.

Tripp's brow furrowed as he glanced between them. "I see. I wasn't aware he had been reported missing. I'm Tripp Monroe, the new editor."

Nathan absorbed that information, his gaze lingering on Tripp. "Well, we have reason to believe his last known whereabouts were Sapphire Valley. When was he last seen in the office?"

"Around two weeks ago," Angela piped up, wheeling over to Lombardi with stars in her eyes. "That was the last time anybody heard from him."

Lombardi gave her a winning smile. "And you are?"

"Angela Stuart, one of the staff writers here at the paper."

"And two weeks ago, you saw Rick?"

Angela shook her head. "That was the last time he was in touch. I got an email from him that day, or maybe it was the Monday. But not since then. Is he really missing? Formally missing I mean?"

"We have reason to believe so, ma'am yes, that's why I'm here."

"And how do you two know each other?" Tripp asked, looking between Zoe and the detective suspiciously.

"Miss Fontaine was the one who reported the crime up in Charleston," Nathan said breezily as Zoe closed her eyes briefly in despair.

This is why I should tell people things before they blow up in my face.

"Oh, really?" Tripp asked, glaring at her. "And when was this?"

"Last week," Nathan turned to Zoe. "You didn't tell them?"

Zoe sighed. "I was hoping that Rick might show up, but evidently he isn't going to."

"You went to Charleston and found something on Rick, and you didn't tell us?" That was Anton's voice as he stormed over, looking incensed.

"Hey now," Lombardi said, immediately tensing as Anton came to stand beside Angela. "Miss Fontaine found where Mr. Fisher was staying and reported him missing; that's procedure. She doesn't have to tell anybody anything unless there's hard evidence, and there isn't. That's why I'm here."

Anton looked skeptical, but Zoe felt warmth spread through her chest at Nathan's defense of her.

"Listen," she said, looking to Anton and Angela. "I went up there to find him, and his hotel room was empty. I was worried, and I notified the local cops. I didn't want to take any chances in case something had happened to him. I hope he's alright, but we have no proof of that."

"So why is Tripp here? Does Morgan Media know he's missing?" Anton asked.

"No," Tripp said icily. "They thought he just up and vanished."

"Well now, in my book that's the same thing," Nathan said just as coldly, and Zoe had to hide a smile at Tripp's affronted expression. "Could I have a word with you, Mr. Monroe? It won't take long, I just have a few questions. I'll be back in a moment."

Tripp nodded toward his office, and he and Lombardi walked away, leaving Zoe standing beside Anton and Angela. The rest of the staff wandered over, several of them watching Lombardi with interest before turning to Zoe expectantly.

"Alright," she said finally. "I get that you're angry I didn't say anything, but I didn't want to create a panic when we don't actually know what happened to him. He could still walk through the door and be right as rain."

"But his hotel room was empty?" Anton asked, and this time he sounded genuinely worried.

"Yes, his car was there, but there was no sign of him. That's where I was last week, I was following a trail to find him, but it was a dead end. Then Tripp arrived, and I had other things on my mind. But I want to find Rick just as badly as the rest of you."

"What do you think happened?" Lilith asked.

"I don't know." Zoe's gut twisted as she remembered their final conversation, a conversation she hadn't disclosed to anyone, not even Lombardi. "Let's see what the detective has to say before we jump to any conclusions, alright?"

About fifteen minutes later, the detective emerged and Tripp called Zoe inside. She had expected a tirade and for Tripp to rage at her, but instead, he seemed fairly calm.

"I wasn't aware that there was blood in his hotel room. I get why you reported it, and I really do hope he's alright, but you should have told me."

"Noted. I wasn't sure what any of it meant. I was waiting to hear from the detective and things have been kind of crazy."

Tripp's eyes were bright with interest. "Didn't you *date* a Nathan Lombardi back in D.C?"

She rolled her eyes. "Jesus, your memory is annoying."

Tripp laughed. "Holy hell, the beat cop got a detective job."

"And so he should have, he's a good cop."

Tripp held out his hands as if conceding the point. "Alright, well, he's going to ask everyone questions about when they last saw Rick. Standard procedure, apparently, but it's gonna slow everything down when we had real momentum. I get that it's important, but it's shitty timing."

"I'll let Rick know it was inconvenient of him to go missing."

"Would you? Thanks. Anyway, I called you in here because Lombardi told me there's something brewing in the town again. Looks like another covert protest that he passed on his way up here. Go down there and see what you can find out—I imagine it's Cooper up to her tricks again."

Zoe rose. "You think it's about the library?"

"Why else would there be a crowd in Sapphire? This place only gets busy on market day."

"And when did you learn that, city boy?"

He raised an eyebrow. "Prove me wrong."

Zoe fell silent at Tripp's smirk. "Alright. Want me to take anyone with me?"

"No. Give me some of the Fontaine magic, please. Actually, take Tom and get some more snaps for the next issue."

As she pushed through the doors Lombardi was standing outside waiting for her.

"I think I might come down there with you," he said.

"Were you eavesdropping?"

"Yes. I'd like to get a feel for this town, after all, and it'd be nice to see what dragged you out of D.C."

"Aren't you supposed to be working?"

"I am. Fisher lived in Sapphire; I'm investigating Sapphire. Nothin' wrong with that. And everybody in this office seems pretty busy anyway."

He winked at her as he put his shades back on, and she returned to her desk, grateful that Leo had taken Bailey and Max to the clinic that morning. She grabbed her bag, called Tom to follow them, and headed out.

As they all walked down the hill together, Zoe had a strange feeling of déjà vu. There were the shouts of the protest from the main part of town, but this time she could see a crowd gathering on the main square.

"What are they all doing there?" she muttered, wishing she had some binoculars to be able to watch the crowd from a distance without getting involved.

"Didn't you see the sign?" Tom asked.

"What sign?"

"Dunridge put a billboard up in the main square advertising the new development. It's like they're asking for trouble."

"Maybe they are," Lombardi said. "Might want to see what the town's made of."

As they walked into the central square, about three dozen protesters were ahead of them, with Zoe's grandmother and Evelyn at the front of the crowd. Everyone had a placard above their heads, shouting in unison at the huge billboard that dominated the main square.

Zoe found herself agreeing with Nathan. The sign looked like an act of deliberate provocation rather than legitimate advertising.

As she scanned the square, the sun glinted off something to her left, and Zoe grimaced at the shiny Range Rover parked a little way away on the corner.

No doubt Dunridge is in there, drinking champagne and congratulating himself on riling everyone up.

The protesters were all gathering in a circle on the main square below the sign. It was flanked by stores and houses on all sides. There were faces visible in nearly every window around the square as people came out to watch.

Tom was snapping pictures, observing the movement of the crowd, with several store owners closing up their shops and joining in.

It was a different vibe from the first protest. This one felt charged with anger, as if things could escalate quickly, and Zoe watched apprehensively as two cop cars pulled up on opposite corners of the square.

Three or four deputies had walked down from the station and were already standing around the edges of the crowd, faces set in grim determination.

This could get ugly.

"Wow, losing a library. This is high-end stuff." Nathan muttered. "In Charleston, we get tiny protests about government corruption and civil rights."

Zoe ignored the jibe, distracted when she saw her grandmother in the crowd across the street.

Checking the road for passing cars, Zoe told Lombardi she'd be back and jogged over as Lyla waved cheerfully at her.

"Gamma, what are you doing?" Zoe said wearily. "I don't want you to get hurt."

"Oh, nonsense. Look at this thing," Lyla said, turning to the sign.

It read "Dunridge Delivers!" in huge letters and towered over everything in the square. Not only was it an eyesore, but it was completely unnecessary, and Zoe was beginning to lose all sympathy for the man.

Dunridge was asking for trouble, and Zoe watched as the deputies closed in around them. Walker was directing them from the road, standing beside her car and shouting for people to get back and keep off the street.

Lyla and the other protesters began chanting in response, their shrill voices making Zoe's ears ring. She backed off, turning around to head back to Nathan when her heart lurched at the sight that greeted her. Somehow, in the huge crowd that had gathered, her mother had found the detective and was standing beside him.

Zoe made her way through several bodies as people went to join the protest, pushing against several burly shoulders before she reached the sidewalk.

"Hi Mom," Zoe said, maneuvering herself between her mother and the detective.

"*Detective* Lombardi was just introducing himself to me," her mom said, the admiration in her eyes set Zoe's teeth on edge.

"Was he?" she asked, glaring at Nathan, who smirked back at her.

"I didn't know you dated a cop," her mom whispered.

"It was a long time ago."

"Someone said to me recently that it was 'only' five years," Lombardi murmured, and Zoe wanted the ground to swallow her up.

Luckily, she was quickly distracted from her humiliation when she noticed the Range Rover door opening and several men getting out.

Dunridge emerged, buttoning his jacket and flanked by two other men who could only have been his lawyers. The move was calculated and intentional and made him look like the dick that he was.

As he strode toward the protestors, Evelyn made the mistake of falling silent as she spotted him. The surprise in her face spoke volumes—she clearly hadn't anticipated that the CEO himself would turn up to confront her.

But Dunridge didn't give Evelyn Cooper a second glance; he simply turned to Deputy Walker and gave her a long, assessing stare.

"Clear these people out of the way, please, officer. I wish to speak to them myself."

"It's a peaceful protest, Mr. Dunridge," Walker stated. "They have every right to contest what you're doing."

"That's true, and you have every right to find a new position in this town once I'm through with this. Either you move these people and disperse this crowd, or you can kiss your chances of becoming sheriff goodbye."

"Stand up to him," Zoe murmured under her breath. "Come on, Walker, don't let this be your first call as acting sheriff."

Everybody on the square went still, watching to see what Walker would do. Slowly, the deputy raised an arm and beckoned her officers toward the crowd.

There were shouts and screams of outrage from several members of the townsfolk, and a few even tried to resist as the officers forcibly moved them out of the way.

Zoe sucked in a sharp breath as Deputy Simmons grabbed hold of her grandmother, far too viciously for her liking, and moved her out of Dunridge's way as he walked to stand beneath the sign.

Only as he reached the base of the thing did Zoe notice there was a built-in platform at the bottom of it that allowed him to step up and turn to face the crowd as if this had been a stunt all along.

"Unbelievable," she muttered.

Dunridge raised his hands. Whether by accident or design, the deputies were now all standing in a line holding the crowds back. It looked as if the police and Dunridge were in cahoots, and that was exactly what The Chronicle would print.

There goes my good relationship with Walker.

"Good morning, everyone," Dunridge said, his voice travelling easily across the now silent crowd. "It's good to finally spend some time in your little town. My name is Mortimer Dunridge, I'm the CEO of Dunridge Developments, and I am here to improve Sapphire Valley."

That statement was met with several boos from the more confident folk around them, the crowd murmuring angrily amongst themselves.

"Miss Cooper would have you believe that I am attempting to destroy the culture of this place. But I can assure you that is the furthest thing from my mind. I made Miss Cooper a generous offer to relocate the library *and* to preserve it, but she wasn't interested in entertaining such an idea."

Evelyn pushed against the deputies to try to reach him, her cheeks pink, fists clenched around the megaphone, but her slim frame was pushed back easily, and she stumbled against Barry, who almost toppled over.

"The Sapphire Glade will bring in hundreds of jobs, not just for construction but long-term opportunities." Dunridge continued. "It'll be a hub for new families to come to the area, raising house prices and boosting the local economy. I know you folks care about the Panway River and so do I. We'll work with local conservation groups to make it cleaner and safer for everyone, including building new drainage systems that are sorely needed. I didn't have to pick this town, but I did because I believe in it. If other organizations, such as The Linman Group, had taken it upon themselves to build this development, they would not have been half so diligent."

That was met with more booing, and Zoe noticed Lucas Watt and Nancy's husband, Adrian Ashwood, in the crowd shouting "lies" and in Adrian's case "bullshit" at the top of their lungs.

Dunridge was undeterred. He looked untouchable, flanked by his legal team, and Evelyn's cause had never looked so pointless or so bleak.

"I can see that this advertisement has angered many of you, and you want it removed. I am happy to do that. But the Sapphire Glade will be a boost for this town. It is a great project, and I believe you will come to see that in time. All the permits are approved, the zoning is in order, and we'll be breaking ground in a week's time. Miss Cooper, I suggest that if you wish to manage any further negotiations, you take it up with my lawyers. They'd be happy to accommodate you."

Tugging at his shirt cuff, he stepped down from the platform and walked away from the silent crowd and back to his car.

Slowly, all the placards lowered to the earth, and everyone looked to Evelyn for guidance, but she had none to give. Mortimer Dunridge had spoken, and it appeared that spelled the end of the Sapphire Valley Library.

CHAPTER THIRTY

"WELL, THAT WAS EXCITING," LOMBARDI STATED, watching Dunridge and his lawyers disappear up the road.

"Are you in town long, Detective?" Arlene asked, her hands fluttering on the bag strap at her shoulder.

"No, ma'am, not too long. I just had some things to review while I'm here."

"Oh, well, I'm sure if you need anyone to show you round, Zoe will be happy to help."

"*Mom!*"

Lombardi chuckled. "I appreciate that, I'll be sure to ask her." Lombardi removed his glasses, and her mom all but swooned in front of him. "So, Zoe tells me you and Mr. Fisher were in a relationship?"

Zoe's stomach dropped. *Why did I tell him that?*

Arlene opened her mouth to speak but was unable to make any noise other than an incoherent squeal. She stared at Lombardi, and all the friendliness in her expression evaporated.

"Did she?" she asked tightly. "Well, she is mistaken. Rick and I were just friends."

"You're sure about that?" Lombardi asked, his tone flat, aggressive even.

"Yes, Detective, quite sure. Now, if you'll excuse me, I have to get to work. Goodbye, Zoe."

Arlene walked primly away, her back ramrod straight as she disappeared around the side of one of the stores on the corner. And that was when Zoe saw Leo. Max and Bailey were at his feet on short leashes that Leo held loosely in his hands, but his eyes were pinned on Lombardi.

Oh hell.

"Did you have to poke my mom with that?" she snapped at Nathan.

"What?" Lombardi said, sounding completely unapologetic. "You're the one who said they were dating; it's hardly my fault you jumped to conclusions. Whoa, who's the cowboy?"

Leo was walking toward them; the leashes curled around his fist in a way that made Zoe's chest hurt. Unlike Nathan, Leo wasn't wearing shades and was laser-focused on the other man. Lombardi didn't move as he reached them, but Zoe could almost feel the air thicken as the two men sized one another up.

Max jumped up at Zoe, and the blessed distraction allowed her some time to gather her thoughts. When she looked back up again, Leo was watching her coolly, waiting to be introduced.

"Uh, Detective Lombardi, this is Leo Rowden, my..." She froze, all of the words that ever existed vanishing from her head.

What the hell do I call him? We've never had that conversation.

There was a long and excruciating pause as Leo waited for her to conclude her sentence, and then he stuck out his hand.

"I'm her boyfriend," Leo said firmly. "And you are?"

Zoe couldn't even enjoy the wave of excitement that rushed through her at those words, because it was overshadowed by the fury in Leo's eyes. He looked really pissed, and as Lombardi—the leather-covered cop—shook Leo's farm-roughened hand, Zoe wanted to sink into the earth and never emerge again.

"Boyfriend, huh? She didn't mention you to me," Lombardi said, his voice like silk. "It's nice to meet you, Mr. Rowden. Did you know Rick Fisher?"

Leo shook his head. "It's Doctor Rowden, actually. And no, I didn't know Rick well. Only in passing. Is that why you're here?"

"Sure is, wanted to see what this town had to offer. Last time I saw Zo, she was never comin' back here. And I mean—*never*."

Zoe winced, looking away, watching some of the protesters as they disappeared into the crowd.

"How long you two been datin'?" Nathan asked.

Leo looked at Zoe and raised his eyebrows expectantly. Blindsided and flustered, she meant to say "a few weeks," but instead what came out was—

"Not long."

Oh God.

Leo was all hard lines, his jaw clenched tightly, and Max wasn't helping. For the first time ever, the puppy seemed to have taken a shine to a stranger at first sight. He pawed at Lombardi's pants, and Zoe pulled him away, crouching down to keep hold of him.

"Sorry," she said, looking into their downturned faces.

"It's alright, I got a German Shepherd myself, he's probably after these." Nathan pulled out some treats in a plastic bag from the side pocket of his pants, and Max suddenly started whining. "Mind if I give him one?"

Lombardi addressed that question to Leo, who grunted. "It's Zoe's dog."

Zoe looked up at Leo, staring in disbelief. *My dog? Where did that come from?*

Lombardi turned to her, eyebrows reaching his hairline.

"*You* bought a dog? It's like you're a whole different person," he said, chuckling and throwing Max a treat, passing one to Bailey at the same time. Zoe stood up, and Leo thrust Max's leash at her.

"I gotta get back to the clinic. It was nice to meet you, Lombardi," he said, his gaze flicking to Zoe before he walked away, Bailey ambling beside him.

There was a long, awkward silence.

"Handsome guy," Lombardi said, pocketing the treats as Max strained to get to them.

"Yeah."

"You didn't mention him."

"No."

She felt the detective's eyes on her, and then he shrugged. "Alright, well, I'd better get back to your office and start speakin' to some people. Thanks for escorting me to this great event. Next there'll be a float passing by and I might just die of excitement."

Zoe didn't reply as he saluted her and walked back toward The Chronicle. Leo was out of sight by now, and Zoe felt faintly sick.

Zoe wanted to avoid Lombardi after that, and texted Tripp to say she was stopping by her apartment over lunch and would write up some of the article about the protest there.

Morose and disappointed in herself, she wandered back toward the road as the warm air whisked through her hair.

Why didn't I tell Lombardi about Leo? Maybe it was an act of self-sabotage.

It certainly wouldn't be the first time. Whenever Zoe had a boyfriend for any length of time, she would usually get an itch to end things—it had happened with Nathan, maybe subconsciously it had happened with Leo, too.

But she had never felt like this before—like her whole world might collapse when Leo was upset with her. It was infuriating.

Pushing through the front door of her apartment a few minutes later, she went to her computer and sat down to write, thinking of the best angle for the story.

She wanted to ensure that anyone in town who might have been living under a rock and missed the protests would hate Dunridge by the end of the week. The image of Deputy Simmons manhandling her grandmother flitted into her mind.

What is happening to this town?

Zoe sat in front of her computer watching the flashing cursor for several minutes, completely uninspired by what she had just seen. The misery on Evelyn Cooper's face had been awful to watch, and after Dunridge's very deliberate display of power, it looked even less like the library could be saved. What was the point of even writing the article? It wouldn't change anything.

She curled her fingers into fists and then released them, looking down at Max's endearing face as he chewed his toy. Everything felt like such a mess—Tripp wasn't impressed with her work, the people at the office were angry about Rick, and now Lombardi had made everything three times more complicated.

Her phone lit up beside her with a text from Leo, and she picked it up, a rush of nerves erupting in her chest at the four words illuminated on the screen.

We need to talk.

Zoe dropped her phone with a loud clatter and put her head in her hands.

Great, just great.

She stood and began to pace the room, running a hand through her hair repeatedly as she thought of all the ways she had made her life unnecessarily complicated.

"Why did I even come back here?" she asked Max, who put his head on one side as he watched her pacing. "Why didn't I stay in D.C., where my whole world was work? If you don't have any close relationships, no one can screw up your life!"

She groaned aloud. "Tripp's right, I half-ass everything. Rick's probably dead in a ditch by now, and I'm sitting here like an idiot writing about a library instead of getting out there to find him."

She stopped pacing, staring at the box that she had taken from Rick's apartment. The rainbow keychain was beside it, a spot of color against the drab floorboards.

Zoe stalked over to the box and threw open the lid, listening to the swish of cardboard as it slid down the wall.

Lowering herself to a cross-legged position, she began to pull all the files out until she reached the base of the box. Everything she had found from Rick's desk was there, and she was now more determined than ever to find something to support the case.

If she found Rick herself, Lombardi would leave, and suddenly that felt like the most important thing in the world.

Max's wet nose pushed at her cheek, and she stroked him, pulling him tightly against her.

"What did Leo mean, you're *my* dog, anyway? You're *our* dog." She kissed his head and began laying everything from the box out in front of her.

Max lay down beside her, his nose on her lap as she looked over everything.

She pulled out the receipt for the restaurant where Rick had taken Kerry, and found that it was fused against another one. Something sticky was adhering to the back, causing the papers to stick together, and she peeled it away, finding the remnants of a melted Skittle inside.

"Urgh, gross."

She peeled the receipts apart and read over the second one. It wasn't for a restaurant this time but for Waldron's Hunting store. Her interest rose when she noticed it was from the day after Rick had disappeared. He had only purchased one thing—a long length of rope.

Well, what the hell did he need that for?

Zoe dropped everything back into the box, grabbed Max, and headed out, determined to follow through on *one* thing in her life.

When she arrived, Tony Waldron's store was full of people. Many of the protesters were hardened locals, most of whom loved to hunt, so several had gravitated to the store after the protest broke up.

As she stepped inside with Max on a short leash next to her, several eyes turned toward her—all men. Steeling herself, she walked through the shop, trying to look like she belonged, but it was a lost cause. Every man there wore a hunting jacket, a plaid shirt, and a baseball cap. It was like looking at identical versions of Tony Waldron.

He was master of all he surveyed behind the counter, watching her with interest. Zoe was in heels, a leather jacket, and an expensive shirt from her favorite designer store in D.C.

I feel like a flamingo in a coal mine.

"Hey, Waldron," she said softly, approaching the counter.

"Hey, Zoe. Haven't seen you in here for a while. You need another key chain? I got a whole new set."

Zoe laughed. "Uh, not today, thanks," she said, pulling out the receipt. "I was wondering if I could ask you about this."

Waldron took it, putting on the glasses that were hanging around his neck by a thin chain.

"What about it?" he asked.

"Did you know that Rick Fisher is missing?" she asked.

Waldron's gray eyes snapped up to her as he handed back the receipt. "Missin'? No, I didn't. Sure is gettin' to be a habit at the Chronicle, ain't it?"

"What do you mean?"

"Editors in the Chronicle disappearin.'"

Zoe frowned at him, pocketing the receipt. Max jumped up, his front paws on the counter, and sniffed experimentally at Waldron before jumping down again.

"Arnold Price, you mean?"

Waldron shrugged, taking out his pipe and smacking it against the counter, as the compacted tobacco fell into the trash can by his feet.

"Shame about him," he said, but his tone was odd, too dry and light to be sincere.

"Well, Rick disappeared the day after he got that receipt. He bought a length of rope from you?"

"Sure did. No crime against that."

"Did he say what it was for?"

Waldron scoffed. "If I asked every man who came into my shop what they were usin' their purchases for, I'd lose customers real quick."

Cold shivered down Zoe's spine at his expression, and she nodded, disquieted by the intense look in his pale eyes.

"Alright, did he say anything to you? Was he acting strangely or anything?"

"Nah. Not any stranger than Fisher usually was. That man bought the darndest things. Always gettin' new fishin' tackle... but I never seen him catch a thing. Sat by the river for hours and didn't even take his line!"

"When was that?"

"Few weeks back. He was goin' on about the usual shit. I wasn't entertainin' it and I told him so."

Max flopped down over Zoe's feet with a huff of displeasure as a few customers left the store.

"Entertaining what?"

Waldron placed his pipe on the counter, mouth working as if weighing up his words, his hands set wide as he leaned toward her.

"You really don't know this stuff?"

"What stuff?"

"Hell, I thought you and Rick were friends. I thought he might have told you his beef with me."

Zoe's heart picked up speed. "No. He's never mentioned you."

"Huh. I'm almost insulted. Me and Rick go way back. Used to be pretty close before Price killed himself."

Waldron wasn't moving at all, his gaze fixed on Zoe, and it was getting unnerving.

"Why did you lose touch?"

"'Cause I sold Price a gun. Right before it happened, Rick never forgave me."

"Oh."

"Yeah. Price wasn't in a good way—what do people say nowadays—he weren't right in the head?"

"Uh, probably having mental health issues."

"That's it. But, like I said. A man asks me for a gun, I sell him a gun. Ain't my business what he's goin' through."

This country is broken.

"I get it. Is that what he used to kill himself?"

"No," Waldron said. "That's the thing, it was nothin' to do with it. But Rick reckons it contributed to his state of mind, or some shit like that. I never let him bully me about it—he could get pretty agitated."

"And he talked about it when he came to see you?"

"He did. Goin' on about how I shouldn't have done it, that maybe if I hadn't, things could have been different." Waldron sneered. "It's all the stuff I went through with the cops a hundred times. He was obsessin' over it again, but I'll admit Fisher didn't look all that well."

Waldron's gaze moved to the lines of cords, ropes, and hunting wire on the left of the counter. Zoe's mouth went dry at the sight.

"Thanks for your time, I appreciate it."

"You lookin' for him?" Waldron asked. "He don't like me much anymore, but I always respected Rick. Man's got a good heart. I hope he's alright."

Zoe glanced at the ropes, the long tangles suddenly ominous in the darkness of the store.

"Me too," she muttered, and made her way outside.

CHAPTER
THIRTY-ONE

AFTER LEAVING WALDRON'S, ZOE WENT BACK TO THE office, bracing herself for having to deal with Lombardi again, but instead, it was relatively quiet.

"Where's the detective?" Zoe asked Angela, who was sitting alone at her desk. Max trotted over and rubbed against her as Angela twisted her chair around and shrugged.

"He hasn't been back. I was kind of hoping he'd take me in the back and interview me, though, you know what I mean? I would commit more crimes if I could guarantee gettin' a detective like that on the case."

Zoe snorted. "To arrest you? I think that might not be the best start to a budding relationship."

"Sure, but what a way to go down," she replied with a wink. "Tripp was askin' for you to come in to see him when you got back, by the way."

Zoe rolled her eyes. "Great, more micromanagement," she muttered, and winced as Angela raised her eyebrows in surprise. "Sorry, Tripp and I have known each other a long time. I'm not saying he's a bad boss."

Angela shrugged. "I miss Rick. He never made me do anythin', but Tripp's sure got a plan for the paper. I've never seen things as busy as they've been recently. Can't be a bad thing for our jobs, huh?"

"Yeah. He doesn't mess around."

"Besides, I don't think it's micromanagement; he's got that new kid in there with him. Isn't he a friend of yours?"

Zoe was already moving before Angela had finished her sentence, getting Max settled in his bed as quickly as she could and heading for Tripp's office.

If he'd called Gus in to see him, that couldn't possibly be a good sign. The kid had only worked there for five minutes.

Zoe burst through the door, only to see Gus sitting calmly in front of Tripp's desk as they both turned toward her. Tripp had his computer monitor twisted around, and Gus was pointing at something on the screen.

"Oh, hey, Zoe, you're back! Take a seat," Tripp commanded, and Zoe went to sit beside Gus, giving him a confused look as she lowered herself into the chair.

"What's going on?" she said warily.

"What happened with the protest?" Tripp asked. "Tom said it got a little dicey."

"Dunridge did a speech and railroaded Evelyn Cooper by telling everyone how exciting the new development is going to be. I'm not sure anyone actually bought it, but it was obvious she wasn't expecting him to show up. It all kind of fizzled out after that."

Tripp barked out a dry laugh. "He's not shy, is he?"

"Dunridge is the CEO of a million-dollar company; they're rarely shy." Zoe glanced at Gus. "Is something wrong? Why is Gus in here?"

"I told you she'd think I'd screwed somethin' up," Gus muttered.

"That isn't what I said," Zoe replied, noting the smirk on Gus's face as she looked at Tripp. "*Did* he screw something up? Are we fired?"

Tripp laughed. "Nope. The opposite. Take a look at what he's produced in less than a day on the job."

He double-clicked the screen and opened a website that even the Washington Express would envy. The cluttered homepage of the Chronicle's old site was gone, replaced with clean lines, some beautiful photographs of Sapphire Valley, and easy navigation on the left-hand side.

Gus hadn't just redesigned the website; he'd changed the logo, making the hokey purple letters a sleek black, neatly formatted with a friendly font that Zoe could see would immediately appeal to their readership.

He'd included links at the top of every page asking for content from locals, encouraging people to reach out to the paper with their stories. The messy articles that oozed from every pore of the old website were no more, and in their place, striking images showed off the town's community and identity.

Zoe's mouth was hanging open, and she shut it hastily. "Wow, Gus, this is amazing."

"That's what I said," Tripp stated firmly. "This guy has the goods. I should have known you wouldn't recommend some hack, Zoe, but this is really encouraging stuff."

He turned to Gus. "I'd be willing to give you a contract to get this up to scratch. When do you turn eighteen?"

"December," Gus said, a little gloomily.

Tripp nodded. "That's alright, I can still get you signed up to work with us. This is impressive, I didn't realize how experienced you were."

Gus shrugged, and Zoe felt like shaking him. He couldn't have looked less enthused if he tried.

"I did some stuff for my friend Bobby. He has a band," Gus muttered.

"Well, I plan to pay you more than Bobby did. You wanna come work for me, or not?"

Gus shrugged again, and Tripp frowned at him. "That means yes," Zoe said quickly, trying to give Gus an encouraging smile. "Right?"

It was clear that the kid hadn't ever been offered a job before. Gus looked shocked to his core and picked nervously at the arm of the chair as his gaze flitted between Tripp and Zoe.

"Shouldn't you be hirin' someone with a GED?"

"Not unless they can do what you did in under eight hours, kid," Tripp said kindly, and Zoe felt a rush of affection at his tone of encouragement.

Gus looked to Zoe. "It's basic stuff—"

She held up a hand. "It's only basic when you know how to do it, Gus. Stop selling yourself short. You've done good work, and Tripp's rewarding you for it. I'll review everything so you know what you're signing up for. But I've worked for Tripp for a long time, he's a good guy, and he'll take care that you get a head start for once."

Although he still looked unsure of what was happening, Gus's frown lifted. He stared at Tripp, amazed, and Zoe finally witnessed the moment where someone other than Leo put any faith in Gus Gonzalez. The kid looked petrified but determined, his wide, expressive eyes growing bigger. Tripp raised his eyebrows, waiting for an answer.

Gus nodded, and Zoe made a little whoop of excitement, making him jump. She shoved Gus in the shoulder and was rewarded with a huff of laughter and a lopsided grin.

As Tripp began to talk through some of the basics of what he expected from his employees, overloading the poor kid with information he would likely forget, Zoe looked at the website on the screen.

Even on the surface, without diving into what he had done in too much detail, she could tell Gus had a knack for marketing. Local newspapers weren't like the Washington Express; they needed to have a sense of belonging, a place within a town and community. Gus had captured the essence of that on the homepage, incorporating local businesses prominently, encouraging reader engagement, and presenting their articles as professional, succinct, and well-organized.

Something about this new version of The Chronicle made it look like a paper that truly belonged to the town for the first time in years.

Watching Tripp talking to Gus, it felt like finally someone was giving him the chance he had always deserved. Zoe had watched Judy lose out on dozens of opportunities because of her history, and seeing Gus strike out on his own brought a tear to her eye.

Zoe had to drop Gus back at the ranch at the end of her workday, and despite Leo's ominous text hanging over her head like a sad balloon, she decided to ignore it and buy steaks instead.

No one can stay mad at a person if they bring them steaks and fries...

"Is all that just for us?" Gus asked as she deposited the grocery bags in the back of her rental.

"Uh, yeah. Did I buy too much?"

"That's enough food for thirteen. People who have money don't understand portion sizing."

Zoe laughed. "Well... I wanted to celebrate."

"All I did was build a website."

Zoe started the engine, trying not to let her frustration show on her face as she pointed the car in the direction of the ranch.

"I know you won't thank me for saying this, Gus, but you should be super proud of what you did today. You started a job and didn't get fired. In fact, you got *hired* for longer than I would have thought possible when I brought you in this morning. I thought it was gonna be a car crash."

He glanced at her, smoothing a hand down his thigh. "You're not like Leo."

"Why'd you say that?"

"You're more honest. He tells me I can do anything, but that isn't true. You thought I'd screw up today, and that's fair—I've screwed up *a lot*. I think it's better when people are honest. Don't tell me I can do whatever I put my mind to. That's bullshit."

Flicking on the turn signal, Zoe weighed her options. She wasn't sure how she felt about what Gus had said. There had been times in her life when she had told Judy she believed in her, even when she didn't. Zoe had lied to her sister over and over because of her own selfish hope that Judy would recover and be better.

Is it more hurtful to do that? Or should I have been completely honest?

"Listen, I'm not going to sugarcoat your life, Gus. I'm not even going to pretend I understand it because I don't. All I'm saying, based on what you did today? You should be proud."

Gus smiled, it was the rare little smile he gave when his first reaction wasn't a shrug, and she was starting to think it was the only genuine emotion she ever saw on his face.

"I guess. I can always screw up tomorrow, instead."

"That's the spirit."

The low metal fence on the entrance to the ranch came into view, and she slowed down, anxiety swirling through her chest as she imagined what Leo was going to say to her when she arrived.

"You're gonna hit that branch," Gus said suddenly as there was a clattering crunch from under the left wheel, and Zoe swore as she swerved out of the way of a piece of tree that had been placed on the edge of the entryway.

Max whined and put his head between their seats as Gus stroked him. Zoe swallowed, her nerves coming back in full force as she pulled up outside the ranch. They climbed out and Max bounded onto the driveway running around and peeing on his favorite fence post.

Gus muttered something about needing to head inside, and for a few minutes Zoe was left alone. She stood in the wide expanse of the drive, watching Max putter about, listening to the whinnying of the horses and the chickens clucking all around her.

God, I love it here.

Leo appeared around the edge of the house and stopped when he saw her, bending down to pet Max, who bounded up to him.

"Did you drop Gus off?" he asked. No greeting, no hello kiss.

"Yeah. I bought steaks for dinner, too. I thought I could cook."

Leo made a face. "Uh. Sure ... do you know how to cook steak?"

"Yes," she replied with more confidence than she felt.

"Alright, then."

"You said we needed to talk?" Zoe blurted, nerves gnawing at her stomach lining.

Leo closed his eyes, a gesture that only made her more apprehensive.

"Yeah, later," he said, turning around and heading inside without moving any closer to her. Zoe headed back to the car, Max trying to trip her up the whole way, and grabbed the bags out of the back seat.

If this is my last meal here, I'm going to make it a good one.

Thirty minutes later, she was ready to admit she had overestimated her cooking prowess. The looks on Leo and Gus's faces didn't help, and she was hot and sweating as she stared at the blackened steaks in the pan.

"Leo?" she said. "Help."

He was by her side in seconds.

His hands rested on her waist, and her breath hitched as he gently moved her to the side—not out of the way—but just to the left of the pan.

"I think you might have the heat too high," he said patiently. "Don't worry, though, you got another three steaks, we can cook those instead."

"Did I ruin them?"

"No," Leo said and glared at Gus as the kid snorted loudly. "You just, uh, you might want to put a little less oil in the pan. Also, I got a good skillet we can use for this instead. The fries are almost done, and the steaks shouldn't take more than five or six minutes."

"*Five minutes?*" she exclaimed. "I've been cooking them for thirty!"

"Yeah ... well, I didn't want to say anything 'cause you looked so focused."

"Oh my God, *you* do it," she said furiously, throwing the spoon in the pan and heading out of the kitchen, only to have him grab her wrist and tug her back.

"Hey, I'm not makin' this, you are, and the only problem is the heat. We can do it together."

Zoe looked up at his earnest expression, wishing she knew where they stood. "Alright."

With Leo's help, the steaks were cooked to perfection in no time, and while they were resting, Zoe made a salad, roping Gus in to help her, as Leo asked Gus questions about what he would be doing at the paper.

Once the fries were done and the steaks cooked, they sat at the table with Max and Bailey beneath their feet and Leo and Gus talked about the job, what Tripp had asked him to do, and his interest in website design.

It wasn't until the end of the meal that Zoe's nerves returned in earnest. Leo helped to clear the plates, and Gus did his usual end-of-evening mumble about needing to get some sleep. Leo watched him go but didn't meet Zoe's eye as they went back into the kitchen.

Zoe washed up as Leo went about making tea and her hands were trembling by the time they sat on the couch. Leo was opposite her, not beside her, and the gulf between them felt enormous and impassable.

"So, is this the part where we talk?" Zoe asked, as Leo sat staring into his tea, saying nothing. He swallowed, glancing up at her guiltily, and every insecurity and fear Zoe possessed exploded in her chest.

Well done, Zoe, you've managed to ruin the one good thing you had going for you. Nice job!

"Listen, Zo—"

There was a loud buzzing sound from Zoe's right as her phone began to vibrate angrily, almost pushing itself off the side table, as she stared at it.

"Do you need to get that?"

"No. It's just my mom, this is important."

Leo shook his head, rubbing a hand over his forehead. "Answer it."

Zoe grabbed her phone, flashing him an angry glare, and answered. "Hey mom, can I call you—"

263

"That detective is here." Her mother's voice was tight with worry. "He's making accusations, Zoe. About Rick and me. What the hell did you say to him?"

"Wait—Lombardi's there, now?"

"*Yes!*"

"Oh my God, look, I'll be there in a few minutes. Don't say anything, Mom. Not without a lawyer."

"Why would I need a lawyer?" Arlene hissed frantically. "Is this an interrogation?"

"Just stall him, it's a misunderstanding."

She hung up, rising to her feet, the dejected look on Leo's face making her mother's timing even more infuriating.

"Sorry. Something's happened with my mom, I need to—"

"That's fine. You head over there." Leo said, standing and going into the kitchen, his back stiff.

"Leo—can you just say what you were going to say and put me out of my misery, please?"

Leo spun on his heel, his eyes flashing fire. "Oh yeah, you'd love that, wouldn't you. Me do the dirty work and then it's all *my* damn fault."

Zoe stepped back at the venom in his words and stared in disbelief as he stalked out of the room, heading down the hallway and slamming the door of his bedroom behind him.

She stood in the center of the house, Max coming over and pushing his head between her legs as she considered going after Leo.

But what would be the use? I already know what he's going to say.

CHAPTER
THIRTY-TWO

A<small>S ZOE PARKED OUTSIDE HER MOTHER'S HOUSE,</small> Lombardi was at the end of the driveway straddling his bike and staring at her with a smirk on his face.

There was a time when the sight of him in his leathers would have sent her into a frenzy, but now his presence only filled her with shimmering, white-hot rage.

"Stay here, buddy," she said, as Max tried his best to leap through the narrow gap in the window and go greet the guy with the treats in his pocket.

Zoe got out of the car and walked over to him, deliberately slowing her pace so it took as long as possible.

"You came to question my mom?" she demanded.

Lombardi glanced at her mother's house. "Yeah, well, I thought it was about time we met, seein' as when we dated the two of you weren't speaking."

"I didn't realize when I told you about her relationship, we were on the clock."

"Uh-huh. You thought somethin' pertinent to the case wouldn't be relevant because you were makin' eyes at me?"

"I wasn't making eyes at you."

"No. Well, you got a cowboy to do that with now, huh?"

"Is there a problem here?"

Lombardi scoffed, shifting himself forward on the seat of the bike and removing his sunglasses.

"In most missing persons cases, they know who made 'em disappear. I'm coverin' my bases, Fontaine. And your mom had motive."

"Excuse me?"

"Fisher got around. You said it yourself. I went to meet the principal at the elementary school today, too. She wasn't exactly forthcoming, but she was nervous as hell when I showed up. He leads women on. Your mother included. Besides, there's over twenty years between them."

It was like talking to a stranger. Nathan's ease and the slight flirtation in his voice was gone, his stance aggressive and angry.

"Your mom has no alibi for the night he left, and she spends most days alone in the house. She said so herself. She could have come up to the hotel, found him with another woman, and gone ballistic."

"You're being ridiculous."

"Am I? Because from where I'm standing, I'm doin' my damn job."

Zoe crossed her arms, glancing at the house. Arlene was watching them from the bay window, the floppy ears of Violet at her side, as the dog barked at the man in their yard.

"My mom didn't have anything to do with this."

"Did she tell you she drove up to Charleston the morning after Fisher left?"

Zoe froze. "What?"

"Huh. So she *didn't* tell you. There's a receipt for gas in her car."

"And did you have a warrant to search it?"

Lombardi shrugged. "If people leave their vehicles unlocked—"

"It's a small town, Nate. People leave their *homes* unlocked."

"She couldn't explain why she was there," he said decisively, pulling his helmet on. "Unless she can come up with a decent reason for why she went to Charleston the morning he went missin' and came back the same day, then your mother has a problem."

"Why are you doing this?" she asked bitterly.

"Why am I doin' my *job*? Your mom knew Fisher, and she was in the same city where he went missing on the same day. There's blood on the floor of his hotel room. You do the math. Nine times out of ten, it's a lover's quarrel, and no one has heard from Fisher. Not even your mom. That seems odd if they're in a relationship, doesn't it?"

Zoe's stomach flipped as he cricked his neck.

"I came here wonderin' why the hell you ever came back to this town, and I gotta say, Fontaine, it's not makin' a lot of sense. Other than your dog and your cowboy, it seems to me you were willin' to give up D.C. for not a whole lot. Sure as shit shows that it wasn't me movin' to Charleston that broke us up."

Zoe stared at him, the wreck of her past decisions shining in his eyes.

"I didn't want to marry you, Nate," she murmured.

Lombardi scoffed again. "Yeah, no shit. I hope that cowboy has thick skin, for when you leave him like the rest of us. I guess I got my answer—you do what the hell you want, like always. I'll be in touch."

He sped away and Zoe watched him go, wishing their paths had never crossed. Pursing her lips, she squeezed her palm around her keys so tightly it almost punctured the skin.

Turning to grab Max out of the car, she headed up the drive to her mom's doorway, and it opened before she could knock.

"You know, I thought that young man was polite until he came into my house and started throwing accusations my way."

Violet sprang forward to sniff at Max, and the two dogs spent a little time getting reacquainted before Zoe followed her mother into the house.

"What did he say to you?" she asked as her mother perched on a bar stool. The back door was open, and Max and Violet bounded outside onto the rear lawn.

"What did *you* say to *him*?" Arlene snapped back.

"Are you telling me Rick is still just a friend? Because I would have hoped you'd give me more credit than that."

"Alright," Arlene sighed. "He was getting to be more than that. I liked him. But he was far too young for me. I reminded him of that every chance I got. There may be many men in their fifties willing to date girls in their twenties, but being a cougar is not something I ever envisioned for myself. It isn't something this town would accept in a hurry, either."

"You should care less about what people think and do what makes you happy," Zoe said flatly.

Her mother stilled, her eyes growing wide as she stared at Zoe. "Well…" Her mouth opened and closed for a few seconds, and then she cleared her throat. "I hadn't expected you to be in favor of such things."

Zoe sighed. "I wouldn't want to watch you frenching if that's what you mean. We haven't always seen eye to eye on things, I'll be the first to admit that, but I don't want you to be alone all your life."

Arlene's lips thinned, and she pushed the other cup of coffee toward her. Zoe sat down, watching the dogs roughhousing outside.

"Lombardi is certainly tenacious. When were the two of you together?"

"During the fallow years when you didn't speak to me," Zoe muttered.

She watched as her mom pulled her coffee toward her, spinning it in place. "You aren't interested in him any longer?"

"He's ancient history, Mom. He might be good-looking but he has the maturity of an eight-year-old boy. I just needed reminding of that."

"And Leo?"

"I'm working on it. He's pretty pissed at me at the moment. And don't pretend you weren't starry-eyed when you thought I'd dated a cop."

Her mother chuckled, sipping her coffee, grimacing and pulling the sugar toward her, dropping a perfect brown sugar cube into the liquid.

"I admit I thought Lombardi was very handsome, but Leo's grounded you in a way I hadn't expected."

"Excuse me?"

"I know Sapphire isn't where you wanted to be, and I know something brought you here that you don't want to talk about. But it wasn't until things with Leo began to get going that I saw my daughter finally look like she was ready to stop running."

Zoe stared at her mother, the familiar lines of her face starker somehow. For a moment, Zoe saw her own face reflected back at her but when her mother sighed, the image was lost.

"You know what I'm going to ask you, don't you?" Zoe said. "Why I was in Charleston the day after Rick went up there?"

"Exactly," Zoe stated, her fingers tightening around the cup. "It doesn't look great, Mom. Lombardi's a good cop, but once there's a motive that could link to a crime, any detective is gonna pounce on it."

Her mom fidgeted, and Zoe clutched her coffee harder than she'd intended. The heat permeated her skin, burning the pad of her thumb, and she hurriedly let go .

"I wasn't seeing Rick," Arlene finally murmured. "I don't want to talk about what I *was* doing just yet. It isn't the right time, but I didn't even know he was still there. He said he was going up to Charleston to follow a lead; he didn't mention staying the night. It wasn't as if we texted every day."

"You're really not going to tell me why you went up there? You never visit that city. Was it something to do with Gamma?"

Her mother's expressive eyes flicked up at her, and her lips thinned again.

She had a perfect manicure today, her nails dark red and shining as if they had only just been done. It was a stark contrast against the gray of the cup in her hand, and Zoe stared at the claw-like nails for some time, wondering if she really knew her mother at all.

"Zoe. I am asking you, as your mother, to please trust me. Rick's opened my eyes to a lot of things. I don't know whether it's a younger man's perspective, but he talked a lot about past regrets and making amends while there's still time. I think he lost someone, and it was plaguing him. That's why I was so worried when I spoke to you—I was concerned he might not have been in the best state of mind."

Zoe didn't move, her eyes fixed on her mother's face, the memory of the rope surfacing in her mind like driftwood.

"Past regrets… making amends…" she said slowly, her voice wavering. "Mom, did you go up there to see Judy?"

A breeze in the garden fluttered through the open door, bringing with it the scent of wild jasmine. The dogs skittered about on the lawn, falling over each other, and Zoe felt as if her heart had stopped in her chest.

Her mother put her elbows on the counter, pushing her fingers into her eyes and rubbing hard. She was wearing mascara, and when she pulled them away there were smudges of it around her eyelids.

"This is why I didn't want to tell you."

"Oh my God."

"Zoe. I know what you must be thinking. I tried to talk to you about it, but … Well, I know it would just start a fight. Besides, in the end, I couldn't go in. I tried. I drove all the way up there, determined to see how she was. I couldn't do it. I'm too angry. Too used to her lies. It's nice to have one of my daughters back in my life. It matters, and I've been thinking about Judy a lot."

Zoe shot up to her feet, her skin feeling like it was trying to go in every direction at once.

"You just showed up at the clinic? You do realize that could have made everything worse right, it might have sent her spiraling again—"

"I know. I *know*. Please sit down."

Zoe hovered, her palms sweating, heart hammering, as she tried to get her emotions under control.

For the longest time, she had prayed that her mother would be able to forgive her sister, that somehow, they'd find their way back to each other, to an equilibrium where they could coexist.

But that hope had turned to anger a long time ago.

Now, it seemed like the worst thing imaginable that her mother wanted to get back into Judy's life. After all the hurt and pain—all the times she had pushed away Zoe's concern, dismissed it out of hand. The *abandonment* Judy had felt from their mother's indifference.

Zoe didn't know how to feel.

"I've been reading a lot of forums online. Parents who've made the choice I did. To walk away. To stop trying. I told myself it was the only way to survive it. I still do some days..." Her voice was small. "But lately it's not enough anymore. I want to try; I just don't know where to begin."

Zoe knew she should be grateful. That in some twisted way, this was progress, that it signified a shift in her life, but all she felt was rage.

"Max!"

Her voice sounded strangled as she shouted his name, and her mother flinched. Max came cantering in from the yard, followed by Violet. Zoe clipped his leash to his collar and walked out of the house.

"Zoe." Her mother was following her. "Zoe, this is why I didn't want to tell you. It's all too early for you to know. But I didn't want you to think I knew where Rick was all this time, or that I could have hurt him!"

"Okay, Mom." Her voice didn't sound like her own.

"Zoe." The exasperation was back. Her mother had very little time for emotion, and anyone feeling too much in her presence quickly became the problem. "I didn't want to involve you."

Zoe turned around. "Why didn't you just explain to Lombardi that that was where you were?"

"I didn't want to tell the police that my daughter is an addict. What kind of mother would he think I am?"

Zoe wrenched open the door and closed it behind her cutting off her mother's spluttering explanations and walking back to her car. Tears that she had held at bay for a long time—perhaps years—started falling down her cheeks.

CHAPTER THIRTY-THREE

Z OE CIRCLED HER MOTHER'S NEIGHBORHOOD FOR SOME time, turning blindly down roads, unsure where she was headed.

Her mind was a jumble of disparate thoughts, none of which took hold as she skipped through different periods in her past.

One moment, she would be thinking of the day she left Sapphire, the relief she had felt not to have to deal with her mother any longer. She could hear the blazing fights in her head, the absence of her sister when she had needed her the most. The cavernous loneliness of that huge house as Zoe sat alone in her room, despairing.

Then she was standing over Judy's body, vomit across her sister's blouse, a bottle of pills scattered across the floor, panic screaming through every vein that her younger sister would die on her watch.

The only thing that brought her out of it in the end was Max. The wet point of his nose nudged repeatedly against her upper arm, eventually quieting her mind enough that she slowed down and pulled over.

Unclipping his harness, she allowed Max to scramble into the front seat, licking at her chin, his warm, steadying presence giving her mind a focus outside of her spiraling thoughts.

She wasn't used to thinking of her sister and her mother together in any capacity. The fact that her mom had decided to reach out because of *Rick*, of all people, made Zoe's hackles rise. Zoe had *begged* her countless times to allow Judy into their lives again, but her mother had been a stoic, unrelenting force.

How has Rick managed to get through to her when I couldn't?

Max bumped his nose against her chin again, and she gently lifted him from her lap and onto the passenger seat.

"Lie down, there's a good boy."

She restarted the engine and drove into town. The only thing she could think to do to distract herself from her imploding relationship and disintegrating family was to work.

I owe it to Rick to keep looking, if I find him and lift suspicion from my mom in the process, all the better.

From what both Waldron and her mom had told her, Rick hadn't been in a good state of mind. Her mom had talked about someone Rick had lost in his past, and Zoe could only imagine that it was Arnold Price.

Her initial research had told her frustratingly little about Arnold's death. Even the obituary she had uncovered had been vague—no cause of death mentioned, which was common in cases of suicide.

But someone would remember what happened. And unfortunately, Zoe knew exactly who. She didn't want to ask him, but it might help her fill in some pieces of the puzzle. She checked the time, wondering if he would even be at the department this late in the evening, but if Price was a link to what had happened to Rick, she had to try.

A few minutes later, as she pulled up to the sheriff's department and was relieved to see most of the cruisers were out front. When she entered the bullpen, it was only Simmons left at his desk.

The deputy looked up with a frown and raised an eyebrow as she lingered in the doorway. It wasn't a friendly look, but she didn't feel particularly warm toward him either after what he had done to her grandmother.

"Is Kissinger here?" she asked.

"Sheriff?" Simmons shouted immediately, without taking his eyes off her face. Kissinger appeared in the doorway to his office a few seconds later and blinked at Zoe before waving her over.

She pulled Max along beside her as the dog slunk forward, his belly practically to the floor, to Kissinger's cluttered office.

"Fontaine," he said, taking a seat and indicating she should do the same. "We gotta stop meeting like this."

Zoe pushed the door closed as Max went to crouch beneath the chair and took a seat opposite Kissinger.

"This about that upstart detective from Charleston?" the sheriff grumbled.

"Ah, you met Lombardi," she said with a wry smile.

"Sure did. What a douchebag. Thinks he's better than all of us, speakin' to me like some rookie. I could have knocked him on his ass."

Zoe inclined her head in agreement. The atmosphere between them was decidedly friendly compared to their past encounters, and she was loathe to trust it—Kissinger's moods could change on a dime.

"He said you two used to be an item," Kissinger stated solemnly.

Zoe chewed her lip irritably. "Yeah, well, that doesn't surprise me. It was five years ago."

"Never date a cop. Journalism 101," he said with a bleak expression.

"I'll make a note."

"So, if it's not the detective, what do I owe the pleasure?"

"Actually, this is a bit of a blast from the past, but I came to ask you about Arnold Price."

Zoe watched for any obvious reaction, but Kissinger's expression barely changed save for a twitch of his upper lip.

"Huh. Now there's a name I ain't heard in a while. What about him?"

"Could you tell me a little about how he died?" Zoe asked. "I've heard varying reports on it but can't seem to get anything conclusive. Were you around back then?"

Kissinger nodded. "Sure was. Wasn't sheriff, though. My first suicide. You don't forget a thing like that."

"It *was* suicide, then?" she asked carefully.

Kissinger leaned forward, and just for a second, his eyes flicked to the door and back to Zoe.

"Sure," he said, sounding less certain. "Why?"

"I'm trying to find out what happened to Rick. I'm wondering if the two things are connected."

Kissinger frowned as he shook his head. "Why would they be? I don't know why everybody's so concerned about Fisher, if I'm honest. Men up and leave for any number of reasons. Might have had bad debt, someone he didn't want to talk to no more. I said the same to the detective. I'm sure he'll turn up any day now."

"And if he doesn't?" Zoe asked, trying to keep her voice neutral.

"If he doesn't, I've filed the missing person's report, as requested. Lombardi was pretty insistent on that one—I'm guessin' 'cause he wants to dot the i's and cross the t's while he ignores it for the next two months."

Zoe sighed. "You really don't think it's odd? There was no warning."

"People go missin' sometimes. Maybe he got sick of the lousy writin' he was doin' and went to find his fortune. Who knows?"

She fidgeted, irritated by the sheriff's indifference. If it were a female editor who had gone missing, there would be a lot more scrutiny about the case. The fact that Rick was *male* meant people assumed he'd wandered off of his own accord.

"When did Arnold Price kill himself?" Zoe continued.

"Fall of 2017. He hadn't been in a good way for a while, though."

"How so?"

Kissinger blew out a breath that whistled through his teeth. "Thing is, he wasn't always popular. 'Specially with the articles he wrote. Used to write up a lot of stories during huntin' season about it bein' immoral and all that. You can imagine how people responded to that in this town. Eventually, they got so angry he had to stop publishing stuff like that, but he was always fightin' the good fight. Hated guns and anything to do with them."

"So?"

"Well, toward the end he started carryin'. So I knew he wasn't doin' so good. Had a license for the thing, but I was surprised he bought it. Was talkin' a lot about havin' to watch his back and such. I never really put much store by it, but he started bein' pretty erratic toward the end."

"How did he do it, in the end?"

"Drowned himself," Kissinger said matter-of-factly. "Found his car beside the river, abandoned. He'd already been gone a few days by that point. Parked it quite a way out. Nobody missed him."

"And the body?"

He shook his head. "We did try, but fall is when the river's at its peak. It was rapid and dangerous. No chance of divers gettin' down there. His family was informed, and they weren't surprised to hear it, either. But everyone knew that was where he ended up. Gun was in the glove compartment, so he didn't use it to end his life in the end."

Zoe twisted Max's leash between her fingers, picturing the edge of the river, wondering what would drive a man to walk into the water, knowing that he wasn't coming out again.

What did he need a gun for? Who was after him?

"Alright, well, thanks for letting me know." She rose, about to leave the room, when the sheriff stood and came to stand beside her.

"Listen, Fontaine," his voice was quiet and far softer than usual, eyes shifting toward the door and back. "Can I speak off the record?"

Zoe glanced up at him in surprise and then, after a second to think about it, gave him a slow nod.

"Look, I always wondered what was doggin' Price those last few weeks, what would have driven him to kill himself. Sheriff at the time called it a suicide right off the bat, before we had much of a chance to look deeper into the thing. Can't tell you why, but I had a gut feelin' he got it wrong. Somethin' seemed off. Right after it happened, some folks came to the department askin' about Price's death, and after that, the case got shut down real quick."

Zoe turned toward him. "Who were they?"

Kissinger shook his head. "Commissioner got involved. And before you ask—I never knew why. Editor of the paper, maybe they wanted it solved fast? Lord knows. Arnold was a good man, and he worked hard to keep that paper going. He didn't deserve to go out like that."

Zoe met his gaze, a lump forming in her throat at the sincerity in his eyes. It was rare for Kissinger to confide in her, especially about his job.

On impulse, she stuck out a hand. Kissinger stared at it in disbelief for a couple of seconds and then shook it, his eyebrows rising.

"Thanks, Sheriff," she said sincerely, and Kissinger nodded with a crooked little smile and went back to his office.

Zoe left the office with a new sense of purpose.

What if Arnold Price was murdered, and someone wanted to hush it up?

There was nothing to prove that the body had ever ended up in the river. What if it was buried somewhere in Sapphire, and the car was left there as a plant? What if Arnold had been on the wrong side of some bad people, and now Rick was too?

Zoe pulled out of the parking lot and headed for Rick's house.

Maybe there could be more clues to find at Fisherman's Cottage, and she wished she'd thought to go back before now. Maybe she'd just been looking in the wrong place.

CHAPTER
THIRTY-FOUR

B Y THE TIME SHE REACHED RICK'S HOUSE, THE SKY WAS
dark with rain clouds, and a storm was peeking over the
top of the mountains in the distance.

Zoe glanced at Max, who was settled in the back seat again.
She wasn't sure how he would react to thunder and lightning alone
and decided that taking him inside would be the better option.

As soon as she opened the car door, huge drops of rain started
to fall, and she pulled Max hurriedly out of the back. They were
soaked to the skin in seconds.

Glancing upward, the storm clouds were gathering—thick,
black, and dark above her head. It was the kind of sky that looked
as if it had settled in for the night, and even in the short run from
the car to the front door, Zoe was dripping water everywhere.

Leaping onto the porch, her shoes echoed loudly as Max scurried up behind, his tail between his legs. His coat was already drenched, and she wondered if Rick would mind him treading wet footprints all over the house. Then she remembered the state of the house in question and decided that Rick probably wouldn't care.

Fumbling around in her pocket, she pulled out her key chain, deciding that the best way to ensure she didn't lose the keys from Rick's house was to attach them to her own.

Her fingers scrabbled along the length of it, bright colored key rings flicking past until she came to the drab set she had grabbed from the bowl on her way out. A dark orange plastic tag was attached to them, and she could only hope the keys would fit the front door.

The porch roof was thin, and there was already water dripping down the posts on either side of her, puddles forming on the dusty surface.

Zoe inserted the first of three keys into the lock, not hopeful that she had the right set, and gave a relieved cry of surprise when it turned immediately. She shoved the door open just as a spectacular flash of lightning illuminated the house in stark white light. She tugged Max inside, pushing the door shut with her hip and listening to the thundering rain on the roof.

Max didn't seem any happier to be in the house than he had done in the car, and she looked at his miserable stare with a wan smile.

"I could have left you by yourself with thunder rolling over you, and you wouldn't have thanked me for that either."

Zoe shucked off her leather jacket, placing it over the back of a chair. The house was eerily quiet and dark, but she couldn't afford to turn on any lights without attracting attention. Though Rick had few neighbors who could see into the house, she didn't want to risk it.

Keeping Max close, she walked into the kitchen, looking around at the pale green cabinets and the papers all over the floor. It looked just the same as it had before.

Still, as she stood in the gloom and the silence of the house, a sense of unease began to form at the base of her spine. It didn't *look* like someone had been there, but it *felt* like they had. She had learned to trust her gut on that kind of thing, and it wasn't sending her any encouraging signals.

Listening for a full minute and hardly moving at all, she tuned in to the sounds of the house. There was a low whirring from the fridge, the humming of electricity in various appliances, and somewhere off in the distance, the quiet whir of traffic. Slowly, she let out a long breath. Max wasn't on alert, sniffing eagerly at the floor, and her shoulders relaxed as she watched him.

Still, the task before her seemed insurmountable.

Looking around at the files and boxes on all sides, she felt something akin to despair. Somewhere in this mess, there must be a clue. But where?

Rick must have known that if he disappeared, she would come looking for him. The question was, where would he have left something there for her to find? Zoe couldn't believe that he had buried it in a file stuffed full of old tax receipts.

Turning, she headed to the stairs, stopping at the base to listen again. Nothing. Max was wary now, though, glancing around and sniffing the air in a way that set her teeth on edge.

"You hear something, buddy?" she asked.

Max looked up at her, ears at attention as they always were, his eyes traveling up the stairs and along the landing. His nose twitched, the wet tip of it quivering as he sniffed the air. Then he relaxed, panting happily beside her.

Breathing a sigh of relief, Zoe made her way upstairs, checking each room for her own peace of mind, relieved to find there was no one else in the house.

Passing Rick's bedroom, she reached a room that could only have been his office. A little smile flitted over her face at the number of empty Skittles wrappers in the trash, and as she entered, her heart leaped at the sight of a computer in the corner.

Now, why didn't I come in here before? I could have saved myself a hell of a lot of time.

Max preceded her, sniffing everything in his path and taking a position beneath the desk just as he did at home. It was a familiar and reassuring action from him, and Zoe was grateful she had brought him with her.

Lowering herself into Rick's chair, she clicked a few buttons on the computer and was relieved to find that it wasn't powered off.

There was a four-digit code to get into it, and Zoe tried a few combinations without success until she put her brain in the world of Rick Fisher—the most predictable and lazy man on the planet. She typed in his birth year, and the computer sprang to life.

"Thank God," she said with satisfaction, and Max yawned expressively as she began to click through the files on the desktop.

The computer was old, running from a tower on the floor, humming loudly whenever she clicked on anything. The folders on the desktop were labeled meticulously, but nothing inside them suggested they had been left there for her to find.

If anything, her search of his computer made her more despondent. The folders contained a bunch of JPEGs and files that wouldn't even open when she clicked on them.

Several times, when she tried, a pop-up would appear saying that the machine wasn't connected to the internet. Most of what Rick saved seemed to be stored in the cloud, but for some reason, the Wi-Fi was off.

Zoe twisted around in her chair, looking helplessly at the floor, hoping against hope that the router might still be functioning, and that she could find it amidst the mess.

Then Max stiffened.

Slowly, he rose to his feet, every muscle taut, his ears twitching as if listening to a sound she couldn't hear.

His eyes were locked on the doorway, and Zoe froze as a low, rumbling growl sounded from the back of his throat.

"Buddy?" she whispered. "What is it?"

Zoe looked to the entrance of the room, fearful that someone would appear at any second and she would be trapped. Max was on high alert, his nose working, eyes fixed on a point ahead of him. For the first time, he looked like a real dog, his haunches tight and coiled to spring, his lip curling back to reveal sharp, white teeth.

"Max," she whispered again. "What is it, buddy?"

He didn't move for a moment and then took a slow pace forward. That step frightened her more than anything else could, because it confirmed to Zoe that he had heard something—that he had reason to move.

She stood up, keeping her hand against the back of the chair, trying to make as little sound as possible. And when she was upright, panic ripped through her.

Smoke.

There was smoke in the air, and suddenly the hazy quality of the gloom around her took on a new meaning.

Grabbing Max's leash, she ran from the room, her eyes suddenly stinging, as if her whole body had been on a delay and was only now reacting to its environment.

She braced herself against the doorway, her hand sliding against the smooth, white paint. As she looked to her left, Zoe let out a cry of despair at the faint glow of orange light coming from the base of the stairs.

Max was whimpering, but he kept close to her body, standing in front of her as if protecting her from this unknown assailant.

She picked him up, too worried to speak, and held him close to her body. Her agitation seemed to pass to him, and he fell silent, his soft paws resting against her forearm as she made her way to the top of the stairs.

Looking down, her breath hitched as she began to cough.

Below her, on the ground floor of the house that not half an hour before she had walked through without incident, flames now leaped from every surface.

How the hell did it spread so fast?

She had been picturing the source of the fire to be an appliance or something small that had caught alight. Zoe had imagined finding a fire blanket and dealing with the problem quickly. But there was no possibility she could put out this fire.

The flames were everywhere, leaping across the carpet, licking at the door frame and furniture around them. As she took a step down, the heat was already overwhelming, and she retreated quickly, her blood rushing in her ears almost loud enough to drown out the low, inexorable roar of the fire.

Glancing around frantically for another route downstairs, a cold shiver of terror ran through her body as she realized there was only one way out of the house.

Pulling Max close and gripping him as tightly as she could, she made her way slowly downstairs, listening to the horrible sound of the fire cracking and spitting from every direction as she held her breath.

How long can a puppy inhale smoke before he suffocates?

The heat built with every step as she descended toward the ground floor. Smoke, black and acrid, was rising too, smothering her for a few seconds before it rolled upward in great, billowing clouds.

Zoe coughed. The path to the front door was completely blocked off by flames. Max was silent, staring around at the house but mercifully not trying to wriggle free.

Even so, she clutched him all the tighter and backed up, her eyes falling on her jacket on the back of the chair where she had left it, slowly melting into the flames beneath. Her phone was in the pocket, and she groaned inwardly.

The papers all over the house had acted as the best type of kindling and the whole of the lower floor was lost to the flickering, vertical flames that sucked and built as she reached the top of the stairs.

Stumbling back, Zoe kept her arms around Max as she looked for a way to escape. Her eyes moved to the bedroom—could she climb onto the porch and jump down that way?

She ran inside and looked out the window hopefully, but flames were already licking the side of the house below her; the heat became unbearable even in the few seconds she stood there.

Running back into the hallway, she kept low, holding her breath for a long count of ten each time, attempting to stop her lungs from filling with smoke.

Break a window and get out.

Blinking back the stinging fumes, she ran to the office where the computer still whirred, its light filtering over the papers as if nothing catastrophic was happening beneath it.

Something crashed downstairs, an awful, creaking tumble that sounded like the kitchen cabinets collapsing. Zoe yelped as Max bolted from her arms, clattering over the boxes, scattering papers everywhere, and taking refuge in his hiding place under the desk.

"Max, no! Come here!" Zoe shrieked, shoving boxes aside as she tried to get to him, but that only made him back up all the more.

Zoe hesitated, her lungs screaming at her, panic ready to obliterate any other thought in her head as she stared at Max's terrified eyes. She had to get them out, and now her arms were free.

Running to the window, she gripped the metal lock with shaking fingers. It was an old-fashioned connection with a screw that she had to loosen before it would open. Her nails snapped and broke as she pulled wildly at it, desperate to escape. The smoke above her was growing darker, making it increasingly difficult to breathe.

Finally, the lock gave, and, coughing madly, she shoved the sash upward. As fresh, humid, oxygen-rich air rushed inside, there was a roar from the hallway, and flames burst forward, burning through the cheap carpet and consuming everything in their path.

Her way out was a slanting roof toward the back yard, slick with rain and steeper than she would have liked. It would have to do; they were out of time.

Launching herself back across the room, she reached for Max. The puppy was rigid, frozen in fear, his eyes wide as he panted, the smoke making him wretch.

Zoe's fingers stretched for him, scrabbling at his collar. He yelped as she yanked him hard toward her, gripping the leather of his collar with all her might and hauling him across books, papers, and boxes, careless of his fragile limbs, just needing to get him *out*.

Max whimpered and yelped again as she shoved him toward the window, the leash in her hands the only way she could keep hold of him as she pushed him out onto the ledge.

The dog fought her, claws clattering as he half sprang, half fell onto the roof. The tiles gave the soft pads of his paws no purchase, and there was a horrific few seconds, where the leash suspended him, his body hanging by the neck, sliding downward away from her.

Zoe was coughing violently, the heat of the flames behind her impossibly strong, as she lurched upward and pulled herself through the window. Her heels scrabbled against the wet surface, the rain still falling heavily all around as she kicked them off, watching them slide off the tiles and thud on the ground below, her bare feet barely able to find purchase as her toes curled painfully.

Max was a black wet mass of fur in the distance, a lump against the tiles. Keeping one knee hooked over the window ledge, she pulled at the leash, dragging Max's sodden body up to her, reaching frantically for his collar again before her fingers closed around the slippery, wet surface and hauled him into her arms.

One hand clenched on his fur, the other on the window frame, she lowered herself as slowly as she could onto the roof. In her mind, there was no possibility she wouldn't fall—the roof tiles were soaking wet, the rain coming down in sheets. She could hear the hiss of it hitting the fire below and knew it was only a matter of time before the roof was engulfed.

Closing her eyes, she tightened every muscle in her body, crouching on the sloped roof, and let go of the window.

Her feet kept a fragile hold on the tiles beneath, the shifting rain and Max's lopsided weight making it impossible to balance as she aimed for the gutter. It was made from metal, not plastic, and she could only hope it would bear her weight.

Zoe cried out as her foot suddenly lost its hold and her heel slid downward, beginning the inevitable, slow slide off the roof. Flailing madly, the fingers of her free hand clawed for purchase, rivulets of rain acting like a layer of oil as her fingers slid out from under her and she fell awkwardly back, crying out in shock as she slid to the edge of the roof.

Then, by some miracle, her foot connected with the gutter, caught and held.

The fire was still roaring behind her, the flames leaping outward, stretching long red fingers into the darkness of the sky. But in the chaos of it all, in that strange, suspended moment, she was granted a few seconds of stillness as her eyes adjusted to the darkness.

Staring down at the sodden earth, the orange glow created hazy, twisting shadows all around her as if the flames were dancing with one another, begging her to surrender to the rhythm.

Zoe gripped Max tightly, closing her eyes as she sent up a silent prayer that they would both survive the fall, and as the window behind her exploded outward, flames reaching for her with tendrils of bright heat, she jumped.

CHAPTER THIRTY-FIVE

L EO WASN'T SURE WHAT WOKE HIM. HE OPENED HIS EYES to the display on his alarm that read 2 a.m., and frowned, listening to any sounds from the ranch that were unfamiliar.

The animals tended to get antsy in a storm, and he could hear the rain thundering on the roof. Then he became aware of a sharp rapping at the front door, and Leo sat up, his heart hammering.

Leaping out of bed, he left his room to find Gus standing at the end of the hallway outside, blinking rapidly, frowning as Leo came level with him. Blue and red flashing lights could be seen through the door, and Leo glanced at the kid in query.

"Why are the cops here?" Gus whispered, looking small in the darkness around them.

"I don't know."

"I didn't do anything, Leo. I swear."

Leo put a hand gently on his shoulder. "It's okay. They might need a vet for something, go back to sleep."

Gus didn't move as Leo headed to the front door. He wasn't wearing a shirt and hugged his torso as he tiptoed through the chilly living room, his bare feet protesting at the cold slate floor beneath.

As he opened the door, Sheriff Kissinger was on the other side, and Leo raised his eyebrows at him. The sheriff was in his raincoat, but soaked through, rainwater dripping off his hat.

"Sheriff... is everything alright?" Leo asked, just before his heart stuttered in his chest at the sight of Max in the back seat of the sheriff's police car.

"Leo, you need to come with me, please. There's been an incident."

"Why is Max in your car?" Leo asked urgently.

"I wanted to make sure he got home alright, but he wasn't too happy about comin' anywhere near me, I can tell you."

Leo stepped out, careless of the heavy rain and the gravel beneath his feet. Kissinger followed close behind, opening the door to the cruiser as Max half fell out in his haste to escape it, leaping into Leo's arms gratefully, his body heavy from the rain.

Leo turned to the sheriff, throat tight. "Where's Zoe?"

"She was in an accident. I'll drive you."

"What?" Leo's knees felt like they might collapse. "What do you mean?"

"Are you alright to leave the dog with him?" Kissinger asked, nodding to Gus, who was standing in the doorway of the ranch. Bailey had ambled out beside him, and they were both staring out uncertainly.

"Yeah, give me one minute and I'll be back," Leo barked, walking as quickly as he could back to the house, so as not to panic Max. "Gus, you okay to watch the dogs? Zoe's been in some kind of accident."

"Yeah, course," Gus said with his usual monotone.

Leo thrust Max into the kid's arms without thinking, but the puppy was too frightened to protest much, curling in on himself against Gus's chest.

Leo ran back into his bedroom, grabbed whatever clothing he could find, and pulled it on, returning to the hallway in under ten seconds.

"I have my phone. Call me if you need anything, alright? The ranch chores can wait; just give Max some time. He can sleep in with you if you don't mind wet sheets; he looks spooked."

"Okay. I won't leave him. What can I do?"

"The most helpful thing you can do is watch the dogs. Take them for a walk on their leashes, don't let them out of your sight. I don't know when I'll be back."

"Is Zoe alright?"

Leo hesitated, one hand on the door, the shadowy figure of the sheriff in the distance making his chest ache. His head was already swimming with a thousand panicked thoughts, all of them terrible.

"I don't know. I'll text you soon as I do."

He slammed the door on their worried faces and ran to the sheriff's car.

When they arrived at the hospital, Leo sprinted inside, waving his thanks to Kissinger.

Following his instructions, he made his way toward the emergency department, passing the nurse's station as someone called out for him to sign in, but he kept moving, ignoring everything but his objective.

There was a line of beds in the main ward, and the sheriff had told him Zoe was on the end on the left. Leo made for the closed curtain, his heart thudding as he reached it, pushing it roughly aside in his haste and almost sobbing with relief when Zoe's gaze met his.

"Oh my God," he said, lurching forward and almost falling into the bed. "Are you okay?"

"Whoa," Zoe's arms came around him as he hugged her tightly.

Leo pulled back, searching her face. He could smell the smoke lingering in her hair, and some ash and soot were smeared across her forehead along with the remnants of mud and grit.

"The sheriff said there was a fire? What the hell happened?" Leo asked, pulling a chair up and sitting as close to the bed as he could manage without being in Zoe's lap.

Zoe's fingers entwined with his, and it was that simple action that allowed Leo's heart to slow down for the first time in over an hour. He stared at her, taking in the soft waves of her honey-brown hair, the sharp contours of her jaw. She was the most beautiful thing he had ever seen.

"I'm okay, a bit bruised, but they're not worried. I haven't gone home only because they said I wasn't allowed to go by myself."

Leo let out an involuntary snarl at that. "You're comin' home with me."

Zoe glanced at him uncertainly. It killed him to see it, and he decided in that moment they were going to hash out this thing between them, even if it was the worst timing on the planet.

"What happened?" he said finally.

Zoe brushed the back of her hand over her forehead. "I don't even know, really. I went over to Rick's place today. I wanted to see if I could find something that might help us find him. I've been getting so frustrated with the whole situation, I just wanted something tangible that I could use. I didn't even break in this time."

"This time?" Leo breathed.

"Uh… yeah. Anyway, it's not like I would burn the house down with me and Max still inside it, is it?"

"Max was with you?"

She nodded, tears building at the back of her eyes. "Is he okay?"

Leo's fingers tightened on her hand. "Well, he's not gonna enjoy the thorough examination I'll give him later, but Kissinger dropped him off. He seems alright. I'm more worried about you."

Zoe's brow furrowed and she caught her lower lip in her teeth—an expression that Leo knew well—she was figuring something out.

"I was in the house for less than thirty minutes, Leo. I was looking at his computer. I didn't find anything, and then Max kind of startled, like he'd heard something." Her wide green eyes moved to his. "The fire was everywhere. It spread so fast… too fast."

"How did you get out?"

"I had to open the back window and climb down the roof. I didn't have a lot of time to think. I should have tried to get out another way, but in the end, I had to hurl myself off the damn thing with Max in my arms. I landed pretty badly on my left ankle, but it's just a sprain, apparently, because of a laurel bush that broke my fall and scratched the shit out of my leg. It's a miracle I didn't break anything."

"Thank God."

Zoe was staring ahead of her, jaw working as she glanced at him furtively, then looked away.

"I know you're gonna think I'm crazy and paranoid again, but that house didn't burn down by itself, Leo."

"They usually don't."

"That's not what I meant."

"I know."

"Even if something in the house had sparked, like faulty wiring or an old appliance gone haywire, it took hold so fast. The whole place was ablaze in seconds. Don't get me wrong, fires *can* spread that fast, but when I looked downstairs, the whole living room and the kitchen had gone up. Two rooms set alight simultaneously? I don't think it could have happened naturally. Not like that."

"What are you saying?"

"I think Rick was onto something. Something big. That's why he's disappeared. If he ran, I think he had good reason to. When I went there before, there was someone watching his house."

Leo's spine went taut. "What? Why didn't you tell me?"

"Because I didn't want you to worry."

"Damn it, Zoe, it's my job to worry about you."

There was a long silence from the bed, and when Leo looked up at her, she was watching him with an unreadable expression.

"Is it?"

Leo glowered at her. "Damn straight it is."

"Is that what you wanted to 'talk' to me about?" she asked anger in her voice.

Leo scrubbed a hand over his face in frustration. "No. I got pissed because of that idiot detective and let my caveman tendencies get the better of me, okay? What I wanted to say was that he needs to back the hell off but you seem to have it in your head that I wanted to break up or something."

"Leo," Zoe sighed. "Have you ever sent a *we need to talk* text before?"

"What? No."

"Well, traditionally that's what they mean."

Leo rolled his eyes and Zoe laughed. Leo let go of her hand, leaning back in his chair and crossing his arms over his chest, glaring at her.

This was the side of Zoe he couldn't figure out. Sometimes things seemed perfect between them, beyond perfect. She was beautiful, funny, clever, tenacious—and then she would look at him like she didn't know why he was even holding her hand.

"Sorry," she said, sobering quickly, holding her ribs as she winced. "But I like the thought of you having caveman tendencies over me."

Leo frowned. "And why wouldn't I?"

She snorted. "Because I'm me. Boring old Zoe Fontaine. And you're *Leo Rowden*," she said, her fingers straightening the blanket over her legs. "It isn't like Lombardi could have ever been a threat to you."

"You mean the hot cop with the motorcycle? Sure."

Zoe speared him with a fierce stare. "I have zero interest in Nathan, Leo. Zero. In fact, having him back in my life just proved how much better it is with you."

Leo blinked at her, a low heat burning through him as a smile crept over his face. Zoe huffed irritably at his reaction.

"Oh yeah?"

Zoe tugged at her blankets, looking away. "Shut up."

"No," he said, leaning forward. "I think I need to hear this. You've been lauding your ex-lover all over me, introducing us like we were *friends* and lettin' him feed Max treats. I was picturin' the two of you riding off into the sunset with your matchin' dogs and matchin' bikes, expecting you to kick me out just as soon as look at me."

Zoe's shoulders began shaking with laughter at that image, and his perfect imitation of Lombardi's way of talking.

"Is that what I was doing?" she said, still smiling.

"Yes!" he replied.

"Well that's stupid," she said fervently. "I'm terrified of motorcycles."

Leo grabbed her hand, the smile on her face quickly fading as he leaned forward, waiting until her gaze met his before he continued.

"Zo, I swear I have never been as confused dating a person as I have been with you. Every time you're with me, it feels like you're waiting for the punch line. As if I'm gonna turn around and say 'thanks for the last few weeks, but I found someone better.'"

Zoe sighed, rubbing her eyes wearily and reminding Leo that this conversation should probably have waited until she'd gotten some sleep.

"I just…" Zoe exhaled, glancing at him before shaking her head. "I've had a crush on you forever, Leo. *Forever.* I used to think you were this unattainable jock in high school and then when I came back, I couldn't believe you would look at me twice. And if you did, why would you stick around? I'm a mess, and I keep getting myself into scrapes, and you keep having to come and save me. It's not exactly the quiet life I know you love."

Leo kissed the back of her hand.

"I've said it a thousand times, and you still haven't gotten it into your thick skull. I'm not goin' anywhere. Not now, not ever."

Zoe sighed. "People say that stuff but then don't mean it…"

"Well, I mean it. Although not right at this second." She looked up, startled. "Right now, I'm takin' you home. Everything else can wait until morning. Or the afternoon, or whenever you've had some rest."

"They're waiting on some bloodwork, and they want to check my oxygen levels after all the smoke," she said quietly. "You should go home and get some sleep, and I'll—"

"Zoe?"

"What?"

"Shut the hell up," he said, rising from his seat and leaning down to kiss her, long and hard to make his point. "I'll be here for as long as it takes, you idiot."

CHAPTER
THIRTY-SIX

B Y THE TIME THE NURSES HAD RUN ALL THEIR TESTS AND
Zoe was discharged, it was daylight outside. She felt like
her whole body had been hit by a truck, but had never
been happier to have Leo there to support her.

He dealt with everything, including going out to buy her
snacks when they both realized it was dawn outside and her
stomach was growling loud enough to wake the patient next door.

Leo ordered a taxi to take them home, and they sat in happy
silence, their hands held loosely together as they wound their way
back to the ranch.

The sun was up, and it was almost 9 a.m. when they finally
rolled up outside. Gus emerged with Max beside him, and Zoe

attempted to jump out of the car to greet the puppy happily, forgetting she had cracked a rib and couldn't walk on her ankle.

At her cry of pain, Leo was out and around the other side, helping her with a warning glare as Max pawed at her. The dog sniffed at her legs with interest, no doubt smelling the disinfectant of the hospital all over her as Zoe greeted him warmly.

"Are you okay, buddy?" she asked, as Gus tried to hold Max at bay. "Has he been okay with you?" she asked.

Gus nodded, hauling Max back toward him. "He's fine," he said, almost falling over. Max was becoming incredibly strong as he grew.

Leo lifted Max into his arms so Zoe could pet him more easily, and she smiled gratefully as the puppy licked enthusiastically at her face. Her body seemed to have broken the fall for him, and he seemed unharmed.

"Uh, Zoe?" Gus said suddenly, and she looked up at his tone. "Bean is here."

Zoe frowned as she glanced at Leo. "What? Why?"

"I told him he should leave, 'cause you're only just back from the hospital. But he came by to see you, he was just heading to work when you arrived."

Leo gave Zoe an unimpressed look as she leaned heavily against him.

"You are in no fit state to work. You need sleep. What does he want?"

"No, no, he wouldn't come here unless it was important," Zoe insisted.

Leo sighed. "Damn it, fine. But you are having some tea and sitting on the couch and if you look tired, I'm kicking him out."

Zoe beamed up at him as Leo rolled his eyes and they hobbled slowly into the house, trying to stop Max from tripping Zoe up as he enthusiastically greeted them all, tail wagging madly.

Bean was standing in the center of the living room, looking ready to bolt, his messenger bag over his shoulder, eyes bugging out of his head as he saw Zoe.

"Oh my God, Zoe, are you okay?" he asked, coming forward to help Leo get her seated on the couch.

"Yeah, yeah, I'm fine."

"No you are not," Leo said firmly. "Bean, is it?" he said, eyeing Bean suspiciously.

"Hi, you must be Leo."

"That's me. Look, can this wait? Zoe's had a hell of a night."

Zoe placed a hand gently on Leo's arm as she lowered herself into the chair.

"Leo?" He crouched down beside her, eyes full of concern. "Could you please check on Max? I'm really worried about all the smoke he must have inhaled."

Leo raised an eyebrow as Max barged into him, trying to get to Zoe. He laughed. "Alright, but I'm pretty sure he's fine. And I'm not leaving this room, don't think I don't know what you're up to. Max, come 'ere, bud."

As they went to Max's bed and Leo started examining the dog, she turned to Bean, lowering her voice.

"Is this about what you found on Rick's computer?"

Bean nodded solemnly. "Is it true Rick's house burned down while you were *inside it?*" Zoe frowned at him. "My dad's a firefighter, he was talking about it with my mom when he got home. I couldn't sleep after that."

Zoe nodded. "Is your dad okay?"

"Oh yeah. He's built like a brick shithouse. How did you get out?"

"Well, I had to jump off the roof, but I was lucky. Landed in what the doctors assure me was a soft laurel bush that broke my fall, but I'm not so sure it was that soft. Feels like a puma has used my legs as a chew toy."

"It's funny timing," Bean muttered. "I'm not one for conspiracy theories, maybe it just went up on its own, but the fact that Rick's missing and now this?"

Zoe was watching Leo, who had turned Max around for his examination and was observing them all, his expression grim.

Bean hitched his messenger bag up his shoulder. "Look, you must be exhausted. I'll speak to Tripp when I get in and explain that you're not able to—"

"I'm fine, show me what you found," she said firmly.

Gus and Bean exchanged an uncertain glance, but Zoe's tone brooked no argument, and Bean sighed, pulling Rick's laptop from his bag.

He settled down beside her—long legs crushed between the couch and the coffee table—and opened the laptop. Zoe glanced guiltily at Leo, who had finished his examination of Max, and the puppy was now cradled in his arms contentedly.

He rose, all six feet two of him, looking authoritative and stern against the bright backdrop of the window. Zoe let her eyes run over his body happily.

"Did they give you strong meds or somethin'?" Leo asked with an amused expression. "Stop makin' goo-goo eyes at me."

"Are you making me coffee? I'm injured."

Bean's head snapped up to look at Leo at the mention of coffee, and Zoe laughed as Leo rolled his eyes and strode reluctantly to the kitchen, muttering that he'd make a pot. Bean turned back to the computer, typing in Rick's password and angling it so Zoe could see.

"This is what I wanted to show you. But I needed Gus to help me with some of it. He's a way better hacker than I am."

Zoe looked at Gus in astonishment at the word 'hacker', and Gus's ears went bright red as he glared at Bean.

"What?" Bean whispered. "She was gonna find out sooner or later, anyway, man, it ain't like we did anything too illegal."

Zoe stiffened, glancing at Leo, but he didn't seem to have heard what Bean said. *Thank God.* She patted Gus's arm reassuringly.

"Thanks for helping," she murmured.

Gus relaxed as Bean opened a window to a cloud storage site. Zoe's excitement spiked as she remembered all the files on Rick's computer that wouldn't open without a cloud connection.

"When I was looking at his computer after I sent you that video footage, I noticed he spent a lot of time on this site," Bean explained. "His internet history from the two weeks before he went missing is pretty much just this website. I got pissed because I thought he was savin' stuff outside our servers again. I kept tellin' him not to do that, because it's not secure, but he always ignored me, so I went in and had a look. Just to check."

Bean glanced at Gus before he continued.

"I couldn't access it. I'm good with backend data stuff, but this wasn't a system I was used to. So I thought I'd ask Gus, seein' as he's a genius with computers."

For once Gus didn't refute that.

"Anyway, he couldn't access them either. There's a password to get in, and two-factor authentication. But he did manage to get to this dashboard somehow." Bean clicked the cursor, and a dashboard of folders appeared on the screen. Zoe noticed one of them was just marked with an 'L' but the rest didn't have recognizable names.

"It looks like Rick had been checking the access logs. I couldn't work out why he would do that, because I thought they were his personal files, and then we dug a little deeper."

Leo reappeared with a tray of cookies and a pot of coffee, and there was a short hiatus while Bean helped himself to a cup. Zoe wanted to knock the thing out of his hand to make him get to the point, and waited with increasing frustration as he selected which cookie he wanted.

"And?" she said finally, exasperated by the delay.

"And," Bean said patiently, "this storage site was accessed by someone else. The logs for the past few *years* are just Rick. He's clearly the only one with the password; that's why I thought it was a private account. But then, two weeks ago—bam—someone else signed into it. And get this, it's an IP address in Charleston."

Bean leaned back, looking proud of himself.

"They signed in the day before Rick left, and I remembered you said his car was found in Charleston? We ran the IP through a lookup tool, and it's from a house in the city!" Bean's eyes were shining with excitement now. "This cloud site is the only thing Rick was doing before he left. He combed these logs, and then he disappeared and drove to Charleston. What if this has something to do with him going out there? I guess there's a million reasons he might have done that, but it seems odd is all."

"But who would it be?" Leo asked.

"No idea," Bean replied. "But, as Zoe would say, it's a lead, isn't it? And we still haven't found him, and now someone has burned down his house. I think we owe it to Rick to go and see if it's linked."

"Definitely," Zoe said firmly. "How long would it take to drive?"

"No." Leo barked. "Absolutely not. You just got out of the hospital; you need rest, Zo. You're not goin' anywhere."

"I could drive you!" Bean said. "I finally got my license. Although I did fail my test like eight times."

"Jesus Christ," Leo slammed his coffee cup down on the tray. "Zoe, this is insane. You're not going out to Charleston a few hours after almost dying in a house fire. Have some sense!"

Zoe staggered to her feet, and Leo stepped forward to support her.

"Leo, I know you hate to see me like this, and I didn't enjoy being in the fire either, but this is important. What if we wait and something happens to Rick?"

"Zo, he's been gone for two weeks, somethin' could have already happened to him," Leo said slowly.

"I know. But I have to try. I owe it to him to find him, even if it's not the result I want."

Leo sighed, looking down at Gus and Bean.

"Alright. This is what we're gonna do. Gus and Bean, you go to work. Take Max and drop Bailey off at the clinic on your way. Tell Nancy I'm home with Zoe lookin' after her, and we'll head to Charleston in my truck. Bean and Gus, far as you know, we're at home, understood?"

"Cool," Gus said, standing up. "Now, who's James Bond?"

Leo snorted. "Just don't draw any attention to yourselves and don't let Max off his leash at all today, alright? If he's a problem, or you're worried about him, take him to my clinic and Fran'll look after him, but I don't want to leave her with two dogs when she has a shift full of patients to see today."

He turned to Zoe, and the authority in his eyes made her a little weak in the knees.

"You. You're takin' a shower, eatin' some food and you're comin' with me, not some kid who failed his test eight times."

"Hey! My mom says I can drive really well," Bean said, apparently oblivious to the irony in those words.

Zoe grinned, pulling Leo down into a long kiss as the boys made retching noises.

"Thank you," she whispered. "I prefer your truck to a *motorcycle* any day of the week."

"Keep talkin', Fontaine. I can just leave you here, you know."

CHAPTER THIRTY-SEVEN

T HE HOUSE IN CHARLESTON, WHEN THEY ARRIVED, WAS not what Zoe had expected. She had imagined an office building, perhaps even something linked to Linmans, but the reality was much more sinister.

It reminded her of the houses in every horror film she had seen. The metal chain link fence around the edge had holes through it that looked as if they had been made with wire cutters.

The grass on the verges was long and matted down in places with a thick oil-like substance that smelled of gasoline.

The front of the house was dilapidated, the windows on the front boarded up, as if squatters lived there. On the left-hand side, as you looked at it, there was a sunken balcony that looked as if it was about to crumble into the earth beneath.

The front door was black against the pale white of the wood, and the steps up to it had cracked in the heat, lying unevenly against some shattered plant pots, overtaken by weeds.

"You should stay in the car," Leo stated sternly.

"He speaks! I wasn't sure if you were going to talk to me, you've been silent for over an hour."

"We shouldn't be here, Zo. You're injured, and functioning on barely any sleep. This isn't a good idea."

"I need to find Rick."

"And you're following a crazy hunch from a kid who failed his driver's test eight times, in order to do that?"

"You're really stuck on that, huh?"

"Eight times is a ridiculous number to fail. It's a sign he shouldn't drive, is what it is."

"He may not know much about cars, but he gets computers. He's given me a tangible lead. I think that's got to be something we investigate."

"Well, then, let *me* go in there."

"And miss all the fun?" she asked, scandalized.

"You can barely walk."

"I can too," she said, hearing the petulance in her own voice. "Besides, you told me today that you're not going anywhere, so you need to stop being mad at me."

"Is that what I need to do?" he grumbled, but before she could clap back at him, he was getting out of the truck and coming around to her side. "Please be careful," he said with frustration as she jumped down on her good leg.

"I'm alright, Leo. Really. I don't know if we're going to find anything in there, but at least we might get closer to understanding what happened to Rick."

Leo frowned at her. "That's the first time I've heard you sound unsure this is going to end well."

She shrugged, her stomach flipping. "It's a horrible thing to think, but the more time passes the more I just can't believe Rick would disappear like this. He would have contacted someone by now... if he was able to."

"And there's another reason, on a list of several hundred, why we should go home and let the cops handle this," Leo replied darkly.

"And what grounds would they have to search this place? How would we even tell them we got the address?"

Leo squinted up at the building. "Could they just do it because it's creepy as hell?"

Zoe laughed. "Yeah, because that doesn't apply to half the houses in this state. Come on. Let's at least go see if anyone's home."

As they walked up the drive, the sky was ominous. Although the rain had eased off in Sapphire, it seemed that the storm that had raged overnight had been blown up toward Charleston, and there were heavy rain clouds over the house.

"That reminds me, I'm gonna need a new phone and a new jacket at the end of all this, mine got melted in the fire," Zoe grumbled, shivering as a cool breeze from the impending storm whipped through her shirt.

Leo swore under his breath, stalking back to his truck and returning a few seconds later with an oversized jacket that he threw at her. She caught it, raising her eyebrows at him as she fought a smile.

"You're not being very chivalrous, you know. I thought you were supposed to be my boyfriend." Leo's eyes softened as she pulled on the jacket.

"Of course I'm your boyfriend, which gives me the right to tell you when you're being an idiot."

They fell silent as they reached the steps to the porch. Tall grass brushed against Zoe's legs as she limped up the steps, glancing at the boarded-up windows to see if she could see anything inside.

There was no discernible sign of life, although scuffed footprints led up to the door and away again, and there was a piece of paper fluttering in the breeze at her feet. Leo gave her a warning glare as she tried to bend down to retrieve it and winced. He put a hand on her arm, leaned over to pick it up, and handed it to her.

It was a receipt for takeout, dated only three days before.

"Well, someone in here is ordering food anyway," Zoe whispered, glancing at Leo, who was very much in 'soldier mode'.

His shoulders were tensed, and he stood at his full height as he stepped forward and knocked on the door.

They waited, but there was no sound from inside.

"Maybe they're out," Leo was whispering, too.

"Out doing what? You're right, this place is creepy as hell."

"Would someone in a house like this even own a computer?" he asked.

Zoe glanced around and pointed behind her. "Look."

Some thick wires were protruding from the grass on the right of them at the front of the house. They wound their way across the small gravel path, engulfed by weeds, before lowering down into the basement of the house.

They exchanged a glance and then Leo knocked again. Still nothing.

Zoe pulled out her lock-picking kit and ignored Leo's furious glare as she stepped up to the door.

"Zoe, you are not serious."

"I am going to get into this house if it kills me."

"And it might. You don't know who this person is, or what they're doin'!" he hissed.

"There's no one home, Leo."

"There's no one *answerin'*. There's a difference."

"Just keep watch for me."

"You are unbelievable," he muttered, as Zoe pulled out the tension wrench and inserted it into the lock. It didn't take her long before it twisted beneath her fingers, and she turned the handle, surprised when it opened easily.

There was a sharp click from behind her and Zoe turned, astonished to see Leo with a gun in his hand, held at his hip, his eyes sharp and watchful as the door swung open.

"Leo, where the hell did you get a gun from?" she whispered.

"It's for our protection. You are the most infuriating woman alive. You don't know what we're walkin' into, and you will stay *behind* me, is that clear?"

Zoe stared at the gun, unaccustomed to seeing a firearm in Leo's hand. It made him look every bit the soldier, his whole body becoming one with the weapon, his stance, manner, and movement changing instantly with it held in his hand. She limped back, careful not to put too much weight on her ankle, and let Leo go into the house first.

Inside, it was dusty and run-down. There was very little furniture, and it really did look like the only occupants would be ghosts. Floorboards stretched back through a narrow hallway to a wide kitchen at the rear, and the layout reminded her a little of her mother's house.

The main living space was to the right, a huge and cavernous room with a high ceiling and an impressive chandelier, covered in dust and cobwebs.

Footsteps were scattered through the dust, but several had a fresh layer on top of them, and it was impossible to tell if anyone had been there recently.

The floor creaked beneath their feet, and once they were inside, Leo turned and closed the door quietly. As he did so, both of them took in the array of locks that had been fitted. There were six in total, heavy-duty bolts, well-oiled and shining as if used often.

Leo's gaze hardened when he saw that, and they looked at one another as if they were having the same thought.

Why were they drawn back? The occupants didn't want visitors, so why has it been left unsecured?

After that, Leo never left more than a foot of space between them as they moved through the house.

Zoe pointed silently to something ahead of them, and they walked into the living room. Beside the boarded-up window, there was an abandoned cup. Zoe placed her palm against it—still warm.

Leo's stance hadn't been relaxed, but suddenly he was on high alert, keeping his body in front of Zoe at all times, as she peered through the tiny gap in the board over the window.

"Someone was keeping watch," she whispered.

Leo nodded to the staircase that led downstairs, and they made their way over to it. The stairs led to the basement, and it was dark and silent as they peered into the gloom. Leo put a finger to his lips, and with a few careful steps, they began to make their way down the stairs.

Zoe's ankle was aching painfully by the time they reached the bottom, but her discomfort was banished from her mind when she looked around at the space they had found.

This was not like the upper floors. It was well used, with electrical wires and cables running in all directions. On the left-hand side was a pantry of some kind, stacked to the brim with tins and cans of any food you could imagine. At the back of the room, a large fridge whirred, and the floors around them were free of dust.

Leo raised his gun, aiming it around each corner as he came to it, and his calm discipline almost made Zoe more agitated as she listened for any sign of a threat.

Who the hell lived here? And why might they have accessed Rick's private files?

They moved steadily through the long corridor, both of them aiming for the back rooms without any discussion. For the first time since she had pursued the animal abusing crooked cop, Stanfield, through the depths of the woods, Zoe wanted a gun or something to defend herself. She was incredibly glad Leo was with her and marveled at how quietly such a big man could move.

The lights above their heads were lit with energy-saving bulbs, and they cast a dim, yellow light over his face and shoulders as he moved forward, making his skin look jaundiced and pale.

Suddenly, Leo raised a fist, and Zoe stopped, staring at him as he nodded toward a door ahead of them.

Zoe stiffened as she heard movement from inside it. The door was heavy-duty, as if leading into a vault at a bank with a huge lever on the outside.

They approached, both of them holding their breaths, and Zoe glanced at Leo. He took up position where the door would open, his gun held out, his eyes fixed on the lever.

Zoe took up position beside it and gripped the cold metal between her fingers and pulled as firmly as she could. The lever gave without issue, well-oiled and well-used, just as the bolt on the front door had been. She pushed the heavy bar upward, and the door swung open.

It was dark inside, and as Leo stepped in front of her, it took a moment for her eyes to adjust.

There was a man crouched in the corner of the room, remnants of plates and cans around his feet, the stench rank and overpowering. He was rail thin, his clothes hanging off him, a thick beard over his chin and jaw as he stared at them in disbelief.

"Rick!" Zoe cried, unable to believe what she was seeing. Rick lurched forward, hindered by the handcuff around his wrist, which was attached to the radiator beside him.

"Zoe, run!" he screamed, but it was too late.

Zoe felt herself shoved violently forward as Leo spun around, and they both stumbled back into the room, staring down the barrel of a shotgun pointed at Zoe's chest.

CHAPTER
THIRTY-EIGHT

Z OE RAISED HER HANDS INSTINCTIVELY EVEN AS LEO'S
gun remained high.

The man in front of her was small, well-built, and stocky. His eyes were an indiscernible color due to the bushy brows that hung over them and his thick beard that ended halfway down his chest.

"Put down the gun." His voice was gravelly, low, and menacing, his gaze moving to Leo. "Put it down or she gets a bullet in the chest."

Leo hesitated, glancing at Zoe, but after a couple of seconds lowered his gun to the floor.

"Kick it toward me."

The gun skidded in a languid arc over to the man's foot, but he made no attempt to pick it up. He merely stepped over it, the barrel of the shotgun still pointing at Zoe.

"Who are you people?" As he repositioned the gun, the catch clicked, and Zoe and Leo froze in place as it swung waywardly between them.

"Arnie," a voice whispered.

The man's attention moved to Rick, beady eyes alight and manic in the dim room. Rick's free hand was outstretched, his body knelt in the dirt and filth where he had been kept prisoner, yet his voice was gentle and calm.

"Arnie, put down the gun. These people are looking for me. I told you someone would come."

The shotgun swung back, this time pointed at Zoe's face, and Leo stepped a little closer to her, his expression murderous.

Zoe swallowed, glancing at Rick, whose eyes were fixed on the man, his gaze imploring.

"Please," Rick whispered. "They're not here for you. No one is here for you."

"You're Arnold Price," Zoe whispered as Rick sucked in a sharp breath and the man before her made a horrible sound, half chuckle, half snarl.

"Oh yes, they're not here for *me*. Too true, Rick, too true. Didn't I say you would lead them right to me? And here she is, knowing who I am within four seconds."

He was well spoken, no southern drawl in his voice, and when his eyes met hers, there was understanding and intelligence there. He looked crazy, but Zoe had a feeling he was anything but.

"We're here for Rick," she continued doggedly. "I didn't even know you were here. No one does. I followed a trail, that's it. We just wanted to find him. Please let him go, and we'll leave you alone."

Arnold scoffed. "It's already too late for that. They'll find me now; they'll have followed you here. If they didn't follow Rick, they'll follow you, and then all my work, all the time I've spent hiding, will be for nothing."

"We're not interested in you, sir," Leo murmured. "We just want to help Rick get home."

"Get home?" Arnold spat. "To that Sapphire cesspit? You think he'll be safe there? No one is. Nobody could be."

"Safe from who?" Zoe asked. She could hear her blood rushing in her ears. It was like being back in Rick's house with the flames beneath her, the crackle and smoke stinging her lungs, death only seconds away.

"What is this woman to you?" Arnold asked Rick, the end of the gun shaking now.

"She's one of the reporters, from the paper," Rick said clearly, his voice hoarse. "Arnold. Listen to me, this isn't about you. I told you someone would come for me. I warned you this would happen. Zoe's doing her job; she's been trying to find me, right Zo?"

Zoe nodded vehemently.

"And him? Who's this tall drink of water?" Arnold said, looking Leo up and down. "Looks like a cop."

"US Army," Leo stated, cool and unwavering. "I have no quarrel with you."

Arnold's eyes glazed over, turning back to Zoe, giving her a long assessing stare. She shifted her weight, uncomfortable with the thorough appraisal, then Arnold took a small step toward her.

"You're Zoe Fontaine."

Rick closed his eyes, lowering his hand as if defeated. Arnold leaned forward urgently, his mouth working, teeth scraping over his lip.

"You know who's after me. You must! Rick told me you've been looking into them. The Sapphire Foundation?" he shook his head, wild hair flying outward. "You gotta stop. A young thing like you? They'll eat you alive."

Zoe let out a shuddering breath. "You're talking about Linmans?"

"Who else?" Arnold said mockingly. "They ruined my life, they destroyed it, piece by piece, atom by atom, until there was nothing left. I lost my home, my wife, everything. They made it impossible for me to live in Sapphire. I had to get out. It took months. I couldn't think of how to do it, except to make them all think I was dead. But now they'll find me."

His eyes began darting all around the room, focusing on the corners, looking at things that weren't there. His shoulders tensed, the gun carving a quivering path through the rancid air as he glared into the shadows as if hands were about to reach out and drag him away.

The gun swung around, the barrel suddenly pointing at Rick, who scooted back into the corner, his hands raised—terrified. Ice flooded Zoe's chest as she watched the exchange, it didn't look like the first time it had happened.

"This is your fault!" Arnold screamed. "I've built a life here, it ain't much of one, but I was finally free! And you had to come and ruin it."

"I was looking for *you*," Rick insisted. "I care about you. You're my friend, you were my closest friend, Arnold, I just wanted to know you were safe."

Arnold stepped forward, and Zoe let out a cry of protest as his finger tightened on the trigger.

"I *was* safe, I was safe before you came. I made sure of it! Now look what you've brought here!"

"How did you get out of Sapphire?" Zoe asked, desperately trying to distract him. Arnold swung back toward her, the barrel lowering a little, his head on one side.

"I still had some friends left, people who wouldn't ever trust those heartless assholes. I begged, borrowed, and stole my way out of that town, and I'm never going back."

"No one's asking you to go back, sir," Leo said carefully. "We just want Rick."

"And what's he gonna do when he gets home, huh? Run over to the sheriff and tell him where to find me, that's what. I burned bridges before I left. I got scores to settle on every corner. I can't afford for anyone to know I'm alive. It'll get around and then it's all over."

"I won't tell him anything, Arnold, you know I won't," Rick insisted.

"I don't know squat!" Arnold bellowed. "I don't trust anybody, it's the only thing I'm sure of. You listen to me, Zoe Fontaine. You stay away from those people, you hear me? They know what they're doing. They'll bury you. They'll relish it. Don't ever give them the upper hand, and don't think you can beat them. I tried that and it almost ended my life. I haven't got much of one left, but at least I'm still breathing."

"What did you find out?" Zoe asked, unable to keep the question at bay.

"Zoe," Leo hissed in warning, but it was too late.

Arnold took aim at her again as Rick lunged toward him to try to stop him, the handcuff clattering loudly against the radiator.

"Why'd you want to know?" Arnold shrieked.

"She doesn't! Arnold, she doesn't know anything. This is ancient history. Linmans thinks you're dead, and it'll stay that way!" Rick was babbling now, his voice frantic.

"You never believed me, Rick!" Arnold choked out, his voice breaking on the words. "You always thought I was crazy, just like my wife, just like everybody else. They thought I was paranoid, delusional. But I knew. I always knew those people were out to get me right from the moment I printed that story about Munice. They were trying to discredit me, but that wasn't good enough. Oh no. They had to remove the problem completely."

The shotgun was weaving between Zoe and Leo now, every time it swayed toward Leo's big body, Zoe felt her gut lurch in terror even as Leo's muscles tightened, ready to spring. Arnold's gaze was becoming unhinged, sporadic; his feet shuffling in a staccato rhythm on the floor.

"Maybe I should take a leaf out of their book, huh?" he said, the gun finally coming to hover in front of Zoe, poised to fire. "I've been going about this the wrong way. I thought Rick had led them to me. I thought I had to keep him here, to stop them from finding him. But I was wrong. Of all the people back home, maybe he was the one person I could trust. But you. Zoe Fontaine. You've brought the wolves to my door. They might still find me, but not because of the two of you. They won't find you ever again."

Leo's hands clenched into fists, raw energy rolling from his body. Zoe knew instinctively that Arnold was going to fire. Rick was yanking frantically at his cuff now, trying to break free, and the forlorn clanking of the radiator might just be the last sound she ever heard.

"I can't go back," Arnold muttered, his eyes black. "I won't. Not for anyone or anything."

He raised the gun, arms bulging, finger curling around the trigger like a snake around its prey.

Zoe stared at the black circles of the barrel, her whole body paralyzed, bracing for the end—and then Leo stepped between her and the gun.

Zoe screamed.

Rick cried out in alarm, and as Leo lunged, the gun exploded with such force that it sent Arnold flying backwards through the doorway. Leo sprawled on top of him.

She froze, barely able to draw in a full breath, staring at Leo's body as it lay motionless, sprawled across Arnold. Then he lurched to life, hands seizing the gun barrel. The two of them wrestled against one another, rolling around the floor in a mass of limbs.

The bullet had gone wide, and Zoe looked up in disbelief at the jagged hole in the ceiling a foot from her head. Then, as Leo grunted and kicked out at Arnold, she came to her senses and ran to Rick, tugging at the cuffs.

"Where's the key?"

"He has it around his neck," Rick stuttered, his shoulders shaking as she tried to break the chain of the cuffs. "You should run while you still can."

"I'm not leaving you here."

She looked back as Leo hollered and Arnold swore loudly, their feet scuffing against the floor as Leo used his body to weigh him down, but Arnold was bulky and more muscular than Leo.

Zoe watched as Arnold tried to twist the gun upward and under Leo's chin. The barrel was inches from his face, ready to shatter his skull, and her mind went blank with fear.

Without conscious thought, she scrambled across the floor, dodging their flailing limbs, and grabbed Leo's gun.

The weight of it was foreign and unfamiliar in her hand, but she leaped to her feet, aiming it as close as she was able to Arnold's head.

"Let him go!" she shouted, just as Leo managed to rip the shotgun from the other man's grip and pushed himself back and upright, standing beside her, both guns aimed at Arnold's body.

The other man scrambled to his feet, breathing heavily; a much smaller and less impressive man without the weapon pointing at their chests. He stared between them, face pale, eyes wide with panic.

He was no coward. Arnold stood in front of two loaded weapons and stared them down as if he could dodge bullets.

"We just came for Rick," Zoe said again. "I don't care where you go, or what you do, but we're taking him back with us. I won't say a word to anyone about where you are. Neither will Leo, we both swear it to you."

Leo nodded as Arnold scoffed. "Much good your word is. The only person I trust is Rick and look what I've done to him. Won't be much forgiveness in that quarter anymore, either."

"I won't say anything, Arnie, you know I won't," Rick said softly.

Arnold's gaze settled on Rick, and there was such affection and understanding in it, Zoe was momentarily stunned.

Rick had always been an abstract figure to her. Someone she remembered from her youth, but a very different man from the one she'd known. In front of her now, in the charged air between their gazes, was real friendship, a bond she had never seen Rick have with anyone.

Arnold took one final look at them all, his shoulders slumping in defeat as he stared around at the home that had become his prison. After a long moment, his gnarled fingers reached up to his neck as he pulled a tiny key from beneath his clothes and threw it to the floor at Rick's feet.

"Get out, my friend," he murmured, voice strangled. "While you still can."

He backed away, his eyes darting between Zoe and Leo until he reached the base of the stairs, and then with a nimbleness that belied his big body, he sprinted up the steps and was gone.

CHAPTER THIRTY-NINE

A S ZOE EMERGED INTO DAYLIGHT, SHE WAS RELIEVED that the streets around the house were deserted. They must have looked quite a sight.

Leo still had his gun in his hand, keeping watch for Arnold. Rick looked like a drifter, with his scruffy beard, stained clothes, and matted, greasy hair. Zoe's ankle was hurting after launching herself across the room to grab Leo's gun, and they all stumbled out onto the front of the house like a motley band of misfits.

Rick took a deep breath and promptly collapsed onto the front steps, his strength giving out as he covered his eyes with the palms of his hands. Zoe sat beside him, one arm around his shoulders, hardly able to believe that they had not only found him, but that he was alive and relatively unharmed.

Leo stepped down beside them and went to keep watch on the road. Zoe was sure it was also to give them some privacy, and she was grateful to him for that. Rick's shoulders were shaking, with relief, grief, or sadness she couldn't tell.

After a long time, Rick wiped his eyes and sniffed, then sniffed his armpit and grimaced.

"Christ, I need a shower."

"Have you been in that room this whole time?" Zoe asked, feeling sick to her stomach that if she hadn't insisted on investigating his disappearance, he could have been left there forever with no hope of escape.

"Pretty much," Rick said pensively. "He would escort me to the bathroom once a day, but when I first arrived, I was sure he was going to kill me." He sighed. "That wasn't Arnold Price. He may go by that name, he might still look a little bit like my friend, but he's lost the essence of who he is."

"Why didn't he kill you?"

"I don't know. I'm not sure the Arnold I knew would have had the stomach to kill anyone, but he's volatile now, unstable. Who knows what will become of him."

"He said you didn't believe anyone was after him before."

"I didn't," Rick said, shaking his head. "You didn't see him in those final weeks before he disappeared. He was unintelligible. I was barely able to understand him. His wife Sheila was at her wit's end."

"But you thought he was paranoid?" Zoe asked.

Rick glanced at her, his jaw working as finally a small smile quirked at the edge of his mouth.

"I think *something* was happening. God knows I've had enough evidence of that. But who knows? I'm sorry you got dragged into this, Zo. When you talked about The Sapphire Foundation, I panicked. Everything to do with that place is bad news."

"I heard. I went to meet Julia Munice."

Rick laughed softly. "Wow. I should have figured you would be like a dog with a bone. Julia's one of the good guys, but I never did manage to help her find her brother."

"You think he died at The Sapphire Foundation?"

There was a long silence. Rick glanced up at the gloomy sky, his Adam's apple bobbing, eyes suddenly haunted. He looked to Leo, whose back was to them, before gripping Zoe's hand.

"Promise me you'll leave it alone, Zoe," he whispered urgently. "You have a good life; you're building something real. Don't throw it away just because of some sadistic company. You don't want to become like Arnold. He's right. Whoever was after him, destroyed him. They didn't need to kill him to make him crazy. You saw that for yourself."

"You want me to drop the investigation?" she asked, breath hitching.

"I can't make you do anything, but it isn't worth it. Nothing can be. He thought I was bugged, that I'd planted a chip in his brain in the night. The first day I arrived, he grabbed me, locked me up in that room, and made me strip naked to prove I wasn't wearing a wire. I really thought I was going to die, Zoe. That's what happens when you cross these people. They strip away everything you are."

"But that's another reason to stop them, isn't it?"

"Maybe. Why does it have to be you? You think once they're on your scent, it'll just be you that's in danger? Arnold's wife left him. They could destroy Leo, cripple his clinic, bury The Chronicle. You could lose everything and even things you didn't know you had. It isn't worth it."

Zoe looked up at the storm clouds gathering above their heads. The first light drops of rain were beginning to fall, pattering on the ground around them, and Rick didn't move, simply turning his face upward and sighing contentedly into the rain.

"How did you find me?" he asked at last.

"Bean. Well, Bean and a new tech guy we have at The Chronicle, actually. They searched your computer and found the records you'd been searching through. Is that how you found Arnold, too?"

Rick nodded. "No one else could access that system. No one. I knew as soon as I saw the login that he was alive. It might sound far-fetched, but I never believed he killed himself, even right after it happened. He might look crazy, but he wasn't a person who would take the easy way out. I think he proved that today."

As the rain grew heavier, Zoe licked her lips, not relishing what she was going to have to tell him.

"Listen, Rick, there's been some stuff going on while you've been away."

He turned to her, eyebrows raised. "Uh… is this about your mom? Because I kept trying to tell you, but it never seemed like the best time..."

Zoe scoffed. "No. Although, thanks for letting me find out from *her* instead of you. Actually, it's something else. Morgan Media replaced you pretty quickly. There's a new editor of the paper. He started about a week ago."

A small smile was playing over Rick's lips, and he gave a half-shrug. "Sorry, Zo, I know you think this is terrible news, but it's pretty much what I expected. I wasn't enjoying the job anymore anyway; there have been rumblings about replacing me for months. The head of the board hates me. Maybe he has good reason to, I wasn't exactly pulling out all the stops. What's the new guy like?"

Zoe thought of the empty archive room, the strange disquiet she felt in Tripp's presence, and the coincidence of his arrival right after Rick had left.

"He's good. He's doing well."

"Well, then, I'm glad."

"There's something else." When he turned, Zoe felt the courage drain out of her, but if she didn't tell him, no one would. "I went by your house to see if there were any clues that you might have left behind. You know what I'm like when there's a bit between my teeth. Anyway, while I was there… I'm not sure what happened, but a fire started on the ground floor. I don't know how. The whole place burned to the ground. I'm so sorry, Rick. I know how long that house has been in your family."

In stark contrast to his reaction about Tripp's arrival, Rick's face paled at her words, his jaw slack with shock, and real fear bloomed at the back of his eyes.

"Oh my God," he murmured. "Christ."

"I'm sorry. When we get back, I'm sure you can speak to the fire marshal, but I don't think it was an accident."

Rick shook his head. "I'm not going back to Sapphire, Zoe."

"What? Why?"

"What is there for me? It may come as a shock to you, but your mom isn't really that interested in a relationship with a failed editor, even if he is half her age. I got no house, no job, and the only person who seems to care that I was gone is you. I'd be better off elsewhere. I don't want them to follow me either."

"You sound like Arnold."

"Maybe he had a point. Zoe, why do you think I let that paper go to shit? Why do you think I lost all interest in what I was doing?"

His brown eyes sparked with a light she hadn't seen in a long time as he turned to her.

"I watched Arnold Price get steamrolled by that place. I watched him slowly fade away before my eyes, and all because he was doing his job. He was reporting on things that mattered in our community, not just Linmans, but real journalism. Issues with corruption, zoning laws, groundwater problems. Everything he could get his teeth into, he did it. And what did he get in return? Destruction and chaos."

Rick pulled himself to his feet, and Zoe followed hurriedly, searching his face as he looked up at the sky as the rain began to fall more heavily.

"Arnold paved the way for me to succeed him. He knew he was on the way out, and he set me up for life with that job. But when I tried to continue with his legacy, make sure we got the real stories out there, they started on me, too. And I didn't have Arnold's strength or resilience. He stuck it out, with threats, midnight phone calls, and people tailing him. When they started to treat me the same way, I only managed to bear it for a few weeks, tops. I don't know how he did it. I was terrified. A little guy against a big corporation like that? It's all pointless."

"I don't believe that, Rick. You've done everything you could."

"You're a lot braver than me. Hell, if you'd been the editor, I reckon they'd have crumbled by now. But I'm just me. I let the paper rumble on without much interest and allowed the articles to be about UFOs and local bake sales because those were safe. That's what they count on, Zo. That you'll pick the easy option. And I did. Arnold didn't. And look where it got him."

Zoe could feel the rain soaking into her clothes and running down her spine. Leo stood at the top of the path beside the gates, all of them getting soaked together. No one moved until Rick impulsively pulled Zoe into a hug, his arms clutching at her desperately.

"The password is 'Lethe07'," he hissed into her ear. "I know you too well to expect you to let this go. Just be careful, for Christ's sake."

He released her, leaning back as the rain hammered down around them. The air had turned cold, and his breath could be seen in clouds in the humidity that had built before the storm.

"Where are you going to go?" she asked.

"Somewhere with a shower. I'll contact you, but it might not be for a while."

"Are you gonna be okay?"

"Sure, Zo. I'm always okay."

"You know, I kind of called the cops in Charleston about you," she said, glancing at Leo, who was approaching them as the downpour continued, no doubt to force her to get in the car.

"You did?" Rick asked.

"Yeah. There's a detective on the case, his name's Lombardi, and he's accusing my mom of having something to do with your disappearance."

"Oh hell, bet Arlene loved that. Okay, leave it with me, I'll call him and tell him the case is closed. No cop in history was ever sorry to have less work to do. If he asks too many questions, I'll just make something up. I'm not selling Arnold out after all this time."

Zoe nodded. "Thanks. You promise you'll tell me where you end up?"

Rick looked back at her, rainwater dripping down his face as he nodded. "I promise, Zo. Watch your back. And thanks for coming for me."

"Always will. Can we give you a ride somewhere?"

"Is my car still at the motel?"

Zoe laughed. "Hopefully. It was a pretty shitty place."

"Well, if it's still intact, you can drop me off there."

They wandered back to Leo's truck through the rain and headed away from the house. Zoe looked back at it as they turned the corner at the end of the street, wondering whether Arnold Price would return once he knew they were gone.

She couldn't imagine what his life must have been like after he faked his death. Almost eight years of solitude and paranoia, all because he was trying to do the best job he could.

Lethe07. It felt like a lifeline and a curse.

CHAPTER FORTY

WHEN THEY ARRIVED BACK THAT NIGHT, ZOE WAS exhausted. Leo practically carried her over the threshold and into the living room, where Gus was waiting for them, alongside both of the dogs.

Gus was surprisingly helpful, making sure that Zoe had a blanket to lie beneath and a pillow under her feet. Leo gave him a brief rundown of the day's events, but Gus hadn't known Rick well. He was glad he was alive, in a way that any teenager was glad a stranger had been found, but otherwise didn't have a lot to say.

Zoe attempted to thank him for his help in finding the house, but Gus's ears turned red again, and he just mumbled something about going to his room.

Leo watched him go, smiling to himself.

"You're happy he called it 'his room' aren't you?" Zoe said fondly, and Leo nodded contentedly, before sitting down on the couch beside her and gently putting her legs over his thighs, stroking them softly.

"You okay?" he asked.

She thought about it, unsure how to answer. "I guess. I wanted him to come back. But then, that's because I miss him. I'm just so glad he's okay. It felt really weird leaving him beside his car in the middle of the city, though. Do you think we should have waited with him?"

"He wanted to go. I can't imagine what it was like being holed up in that room all that time. I would drive to the ocean and dive right in if I were him."

Zoe chuckled. "The ocean? From Charleston? That's a five-hour drive at least."

"It would be worth it—oomph," Leo grunted as Max jumped up beside them and collapsed over Zoe's stomach. She stroked his ears as he nuzzled against their bodies.

"Is this guy okay? He had a pretty traumatic day yesterday."

Leo scratched Max's rump, and the dog grumbled happily. "He's alright. He's been through worse, huh buddy?"

"We weren't impressed that you called him *my dog* with Lombardi by the way," Zoe said huffily. "I would like a retraction."

Leo snorted. "I'm sorry, but that guy was a douchebag." Zoe laid her head back on the arm of the couch and sighed, letting her eyes fall closed.

"Do you think Rick will call and get him off the case?" Leo asked.

"Well, technically, there is no case now. It's a missing person and the person is no longer missing… although…" she pretended to think about it. "Maybe I should call Nate and arrange a coffee date to let him know, instead."

"I will tie you to the couch if I have to," Leo growled, and Zoe chuckled happily.

The clock ticked as they lay together in silence for a little time, and then Zoe faked a yawn.

"You know, I'm pretty tired. I think I might get an early night."

Leo nodded, rising from his position and lifting Max off her lap as he helped her to her feet. She gave Leo a chaste kiss as she made her way to the guest room.

Leo followed, leaning against the doorframe, watching to see if she needed anything. Zoe hid a smile, grabbing her nightshirt from the bed and limping out of the room again and into Leo's.

She turned, noting his confused expression. "I thought you said you were tired," he said.

"Oh yeah, but not *that* tired," Zoe said. "I was thinking I'd prove to you how much I don't care about Nathan Lombardi, just to really push the point home."

Leo stepped forward, putting his arms around her, his eyes bright with interest. "Are you sure? You gotta be exhausted."

"Don't care. I think it's about time I showed you who's boss."

"Hah! Is that what's happening?"

"Sure is. But we'll have to be quiet, seeing as you have a house guest now."

Leo bent his head, landing a long kiss on her lips before pulling back. Zoe shrieked with laughter as he lifted her off her feet and carried her to the bed.

"I can work with that," he said cheerfully.

A few days later, Zoe was heading to the library. Today was the deadline that Dunridge had imposed before it would be demolished for good, and she had been hard at work since she arrived back in town, attempting to make sure he didn't get his way.

Today would be the day of reckoning, and Zoe was nervous as she parked her car in the empty space behind the library, hoping that her plans would somehow come to fruition at the eleventh hour.

Barry and Evelyn came out to meet her, both of them looking just as nervous as Zoe felt.

"What exactly is this about?" Evelyn asked. "You were very cryptic over the phone."

"I know, but I didn't want to reveal too much. Sometimes the element of surprise is best for both parties."

Evelyn's eyes moved over Zoe's shoulder as a familiar Range Rover arrived in the lot, parking up behind the library, as Dunridge got out. He was alone today, no longer flanked by a team of suited lawyers, and Zoe could only pray he would hear her out.

"What have you done?" Barry asked. "We don't want that lunatic setting foot in our library."

"I'm asking you to trust me, Barry. No one will make you do anything you don't want to do. Not on my watch."

Dunridge walked over to them, his long legs eating up the distance, and Zoe stuck out her hand.

"Hello Mortimer, what a pleasant surprise to see you here."

He raised an eyebrow as he shook her proffered palm. "Hm. Yes, I suppose it is. Miss Cooper, Mr. Finnigan."

Barry just grunted and turned around, marching back inside the library with as much dignity as his cane could afford him.

Zoe held out a hand for Dunridge to precede her, Evelyn watching her curiously.

"Trust me," Zoe said again, with more confidence than she felt. "It's going to be okay."

"How did you get him to come alone?" Evelyn whispered. "Usually, he has his cronies on either side of him."

"Well, I said that a less intimidating presence was more befitting the great institution he was a part of."

"Sapphire?" Evelyn asked.

"The library," Zoe replied with a grin.

Once inside, they all gathered around the main table in the center of the building. The shelves were close and oppressive as always, and the table was still littered with flyers from the protest. One of them, Dunridge picked up with interest, but then placed it back down with a frown.

Evelyn made a pot of coffee and brought it over, and eventually all four of them were seated around the table, three pairs of eyes turning to Zoe as she cleared her throat.

"Alright, so I'm sure you're all wondering why you're here," she said as Dunridge leaned back, one hand on the table and one crooked on his chair. He looked out of place in the drab, unpleasant lighting, and Zoe shifted in her seat awkwardly.

"I would like to make you all a proposition," she said gently.

"All of us?" Barry grunted.

"Yes, *all* of you."

"He's the one with the money," Barry growled. "Why isn't he makin' it?"

Dunridge doffed an invisible cap to him, as Barry's skin turned a dark shade of puce.

"Mr. Dunridge," Zoe said hastily. "You have stated quite plainly that the library brings in no profit and that you are happy to destroy it in favor of the Sapphire Glade development. That's right, yes?"

"Correct."

"Alright. You know, as well as anyone, that reputation in small towns goes a long way. If you are seen to bend on this, it isn't a cutthroat corporation you'll be working with, but a group of very happy residents. My proposal is simple: retain the library in the structures you already plan to build, then transfer its assets to a new location."

Evelyn pulled off her glasses and stared at Zoe. "*Lose* the building? But it's been here for decades."

"Precisely," Zoe replied. "I'd be the last person to say that any building should be torn down, but the foundation of this one is slowly sinking into the river. It's overcrowded, impractical, not well designed, and ill-equipped for your power needs. The bulbs in the overhead lights flicker constantly, and a significant portion of the building is lopsided. I don't want to lose a piece of this town's heritage either, Evelyn, but if we could retain the library as a compromise, retain your job, and keep the services running in a better, more modern setting, I think it would make a difference."

Evelyn's lips thinned, just as the light above them began to flicker on cue. The librarian raised her eyes to the ceiling, as did Barry, as they both exchanged a look.

Zoe turned back to Dunridge.

"My proposal to you is this. You will have to build a temporary showroom to sell the houses once they are built. Continue with that plan, but make it a permanent building instead, and transfer the library there. Once all the houses are sold, it can become the Sapphire Glade Library, named after your development, sponsored by you, and part of the community. Trust me, Mr. Dunridge, you'll get a lot further with the townsfolk this way than bulldozing it into the ground."

Dunridge looked at Evelyn. It was clear the librarian wasn't happy about losing the building, and Zoe could sympathize. She herself hated the modern monstrosities that were popping up all over the place, with clean lines and computers instead of cozy shelves and books.

However, the Sapphire Valley Library was rundown, struggling, and in need of extensive work to bring it up to code. If this could be a compromise and it could keep the library alive, it had to be better than nothing—she could only hope that Evelyn would agree.

"Miss Cooper," Dunridge said, leaning forward. "You have been a thorn in my side. A small thorn, but a thorn, nonetheless. I prefer an easy life, and I am going to build these developments one way or another. That said, Miss Fontaine has a point. This will help the community where I want people to buy my houses, and as long as we can modernize things a bit, and include some actual technology in this place, I think I could see myself agreeing."

Evelyn and Barry exchanged a long glance.

"I want the name retained," Evelyn said tightly. "The Sapphire Valley Library isn't just for the residents of the Sapphire Glade; it's for everyone."

Dunridge nodded. "Agreed."

"And I would like to manage removing everything from this building and retaining as much of the original interior as possible."

Dunridge glanced at the floor. "Agreed. But not the carpet. I can't look at that every day."

"Very well," Evelyn conceded. "And Barry keeps his job until he…" she trailed off.

"Until I die," Barry said helpfully.

Dunridge snorted. "Agreed."

Evelyn continued. "If we're going to turn the library into a successful business, I expect a share in the profits."

Dunridge's eyes were twinkling now. "I have no doubt it will be a roaring success under your leadership, Miss Cooper. But I have to use it to sell the houses first."

"Understood."

"Do we have an accord?

He stretched out his hand to her, and she shook it without any hesitation.

"We do, Mr. Dunridge."

Zoe leaned back in her chair with a loud sigh of relief as Barry put three sugars into his coffee and lifted his cup in a salute.

About half an hour later, Zoe walked out of the library, having left Barry and Evelyn in full planning mode for the upcoming changes.

As she stepped down the steps outside, the sunshine on her face was a warm balm, and it felt like a weight lifted from her shoulders as she breathed in the fresh air all around her.

"Well played, Fontaine," Dunridge said, coming up behind her. "I think you might have hit upon something that could work."

Zoe nodded, turning to him. "Of course I have. This is going to be better for everyone, trust me."

"I guess small-town women know what's best."

"I couldn't agree more," she said smugly, and shook the hand he offered her.

"I'll be seeing you again, I think," Dunridge said, his expression thoughtful.

"Oh, you can count on it," she murmured as he turned to his car and walked away.

Zoe headed toward her rental, listening to the Range Rover's engine fire up behind her and zoom away up the road. She turned back, watching it disappear, and just as she was about to get into her car and follow behind, something else caught her eye.

She stared at the road as another car approached on the opposite side, heading out of town. It was a Chevy pickup truck, with a white stripe down the side, just like the one she had seen in Rick's video.

Standing stock still, she watched it rumble by, and just as it drew level with her, a hand extended, a pipe waving at her as Tony Waldron's grinning face appeared at the window. Zoe raised a hand, waving back in disbelief.

"I still had some friends left, people who wouldn't ever trust those heartless assholes…"

Arnold's words repeated in her head as Tony and his truck slowly faded out of view.

Maybe she too had more friends in this town than she realized after all.

That night, Zoe sat in her apartment, with Max lying at her feet, and opened her laptop.

She still didn't know what she would find in the cloud storage site that Rick had given her access to, but she hoped it might contain the smoking gun she needed to go after Linmans again.

Clicking on the link Bean had sent her, she opened the homepage and typed in the password. Her fingers were trembling as the dashboard loaded, the spinning blue wheel in the center of the screen, making hope surge through her for the first time in months.

Then it loaded, but the page was blank.

Frowning, she refreshed it and felt dread creep slowly through her as each refresh came back with the same screen.

The storage site had been wiped clean. All the folders, all the documents and evidence, and years of Rick's research—gone.

After staring blankly at her laptop for several minutes, Zoe's shoulders slumped as she put her head in her hands. Yet another thread of her investigation extinguished.

Did Rick do this? Did he give me the password to tease me with it, and then rip it all away to protect me?

Rick knew the consequences of going after people like Linmans better than anyone. She had witnessed it herself in

Arnold Price, but Zoe never would have expected him to sabotage her like this.

Leaning back in her chair, she wiped a hand over her forehead as her phone lit up in front of her. Opening it, she found a message from Tripp.

Well done on the Dunridge Project. Good work today.

She stared at Tripp's name, missing the inherent trust she had had with Rick. If anyone had asked her three months back whether she trusted Tripp Monroe, her answer would have unequivocally been yes. But now she wasn't so sure.

Something was off about his sudden arrival, and she would need to be on her guard, hoping her suspicions were proven wrong.

Zoe stood, listening to the patter of Max's paws as he followed behind her to the edge of the room.

Dragging one of the boxes from the stack, she emptied everything out. It was time to stop half-assing this investigation. Linmans had almost killed her once; they'd ruined Arnold Price's and Julia Munice's lives, not to mention what might have happened at the Sapphire Foundation.

Zoe didn't want to put herself in danger again, or put Leo at risk either, and as Max's wet tongue licked her ear, she wondered if she had lost her mind. Her life felt as if it was finally stable, yet she was voluntarily blowing it up again, by choice.

Rick had warned her, Arnold had warned her, but Zoe had never been very good at stepping back from the brink when she was on the edge of something big.

She dragged out the next file, the name "Brett Conway" emblazoned across the top, and got to work.

AUTHOR'S NOTE

Thank you so much for reading LAST SEEN IN THE VALLEY and for continuing this journey with Zoe! We're just three adventures in, but already the twists are piling up, the secrets are getting darker, and Zoe's world is growing in ways I hope have kept you turning pages late into the night. It means the world to have you alongside for the ride, sharing in the mysteries, the suspense, and the heart of this series as it unfolds!

If you'd like to keep the momentum going, I'd love to invite you to join my MYSTERY LOVERS CLUB on Facebook. The group has been growing quickly with readers who love layered mysteries, and it's turning into a lively hub for sharing the adventures we're wrapped up in. I'm having so much fun connecting with fellow mystery lovers there, and if you're ready to dive deeper into the adventure, we'd love to have you join us!

I always aim to create the best reading experience possible for you, and if your time in Sapphire Valley already has you hooked, I'd truly love to hear about it. Reviews play such a big role in helping this new series find its footing, allowing other readers to discover Zoe and Leo's world while giving me a window into what you connected with most (and what you'd like to see more of in future books). Your feedback not only brightens my day but helps shape the stories to come. Even a few words make a big impact!

The next chapter in Zoe's journey, LIES IN THE VALLEY, sees her tangled in a case that hits closer to home than ever before. When the evidence points to her sister, Judy, Zoe will do everything in her power to uncover the truth. But Judy's long history of deception and carefully guarded secrets makes it nearly impossible to know who to trust. As the lies stack up and the danger grows, Zoe must navigate a deadly web where every choice carries consequences, and trusting the wrong person could cost more than she ever imagined.

I can't wait to share more of Sapphire Valley and these characters with you in the next book!

By the way, if you find any typos or want to reach out to me, feel free to email me at egray@ellegraybooks.com

Yours truly,
Elle Gray

CONNECT WITH ELLE GRAY

Loved the book? Don't miss out on future reads! Join my newsletter and receive updates on my latest releases, insider content, and exclusive promos. Plus, as a thank you for joining, you'll get a FREE copy of my book Deadly Pursuit!

Deadly Pursuit follows the story of Paxton Arrington, a police officer in Seattle who uncovers corruption within his own precinct. With his career and reputation on the line, he enlists the help of his FBI friend Blake Wilder to bring down the corrupt Strike Team. But the stakes are high, and Paxton must decide whether he's willing to risk everything to do the right thing.

Claiming your freebie is easy! Visit
https://dl.bookfunnel.com/513mluk159
and sign up with your email!

Want more ways to stay connected? Follow me on Facebook and Instagram or sign up for text notifications by texting "blake" to 844-552-1368. Thanks for your support and happy reading!

ALSO BY

ELLE GRAY

Blake Wilder FBI Mystery Thrillers

Book One - The 7 She Saw
Book Two - A Perfect Wife
Book Three - Her Perfect Crime
Book Four - The Chosen Girls
Book Five - The Secret She Kept
Book Six - The Lost Girls
Book Seven - The Lost Sister
Book Eight - The Missing Woman
Book Nine - Night at the Asylum
Book Ten - A Time to Die
Book Eleven - The House on the Hill
Book Twelve - The Missing Girls
Book Thirteen - No More Lies
Book Fourteen - The Unlucky Girl
Book Fifteen - The Heist
Book Sixteen - The Hit List
Book Seventeen - The Missing Daughter
Book Eighteen - The Silent Threat
Book Nineteen - A Code to Kill
Book Twenty - Watching Her
Book Twenty-One - The Inmate's Secret
Book Twenty-Two - A Motive to Kill
Book Twenty-Three - The Kept Girls
Book Twenty-Four - Prison Break
Book Twenty-Five - The Perfect Crime

Blake Wilder FBI Mystery Thrillers

Book Twenty-Six - *A Shot to Kill*
Book Twenty-Seven - *Double Cross*
Book Twenty-Eight - *The Silent Hunt*
Book Twenty-Nine - *The Hunter's Game*
Book Thirty - *No Ransom*

A Pax Arrington Mystery

Free Prequel - *Deadly Pursuit*
Book One - *I See You*
Book Two - *Her Last Call*
Book Three - *Woman In The Water*
Book Four- *A Wife's Secret*

Storyville FBI Mystery Thrillers

Book One - *The Chosen Girl*
Book Two - *The Murder in the Mist*
Book Three - *Whispers of the Dead*
Book Four - *Secrets of the Unseen*
Book Five - *The Way Back Home*

A Sweetwater Falls Mystery

Book One - *New Girl in the Falls*
Book Two - *Missing in the Falls*
Book Three - *The Girls in the Falls*
Book Four - *Memories of the Falls*
Book Five - *Shadows of the Falls*
Book Six - *The Lies in the Falls*
Book Seven - *Forbidden in the Falls*
Book Eight - *Silenced in the Falls*

A Sweetwater Falls Mystery
Book Nine - Summer in the Falls
Book Ten- The Legend of the Falls
Book Eleven- Whispers in the Falls
Book Twelve - Sins of the Falls
Book Thirteen - Shades of the Falls
Book Fourteen - Revenge in the Falls
Book Fifteen - Vanished in the Falls

A Chesapeake Valley Mystery Series
Book One - The Girl in Town
Book Two - The Lost Children
Book Three - The Secrets We Bury
Book Four - The Secret Cabin
Book Five - The Silent Enemy

A Sapphire Valley Mystery Series
Book One - The Girl in the Valley
Book Two - Scars in the Valley
Book Three - Last Seen in the Valley

ALSO BY
ELLE GRAY | K.S. GRAY

Olivia Knight FBI Mystery Thrillers
Book One - New Girl in Town
Book Two - The Murders on Beacon Hill
Book Three - The Woman Behind the Door
Book Four - Love, Lies, and Suicide
Book Five - Murder on the Astoria
Book Six - The Locked Box
Book Seven - The Good Daughter
Book Eight - The Perfect Getaway
Book Nine - Behind Closed Doors
Book Ten - Fatal Games
Book Eleven - Into the Night
Book Twelve - The Housewife
Book Thirteen - Whispers at the Reunion
Book Fourteen - Fatal Lies
Book Fifteen - The Runaway Girls
Book Sixteen - The Woman Next Door
Book Seventeen - The Grand Heist
Book Eighteen - The Fatal Getaway

A Serenity Springs Mystery Series
Book One - The Girl in the Springs
Book Two - The Maid of Honor
Book Three- The Girl in the Cabin
Book Four- Fatal Obsession
Book Five- The Secret Packages
Book Six - The Hunting Ground
Book Seven - One Last Secret

ALSO BY
ELLE GRAY | JAMES HOLT

The Florida Girl FBI Mystery Thrillers

Book One - *The Florida Girl*
Book Two - *Resort to Kill*
Book Three - *The Runaway*
Book Four - *The Ransom*
Book Five - *The Unknown Woman*

Made in the USA
Columbia, SC
14 January 2026

77955918R00186